MERCILESS SPY

82ND STREET VANDALS
BOOK SEVEN

HEATHER LONG

Merciless Spy/Heather Long – 1st ed.

ISBN: 978-1-956264-25-8

For Snow, the sweetest little psycho I've ever met.

SERIES SO FAR

FOREWORD

Dear Reader,

Welcome to book seven of the 82nd Street Vandals series. If you have not read the first six, stop. Do not pass Go. Grab book one: Savage Vandal, and start there.

Seriously.

This is a series that really must be read in order.

Okay, back to my welcome. Merciless Spy picks up a short while after where we left off in Dangerous Renegade. Need a snapshot? Pour yourself a drink, grab a seat, and let's get caught up.

Last time in the 82nd Street Vandals:

Emersyn and Rome were kidnapped by new players seeking leverage on Liam's mysterious king. While Brixton, the man they have contact with, explains that they will do what he wants, Rome plays the part of Liam to cover that they took the wrong twin. They also put a shock collar on Emersyn to keep "Liam" in line. In the meanwhile, the Vandals work to locate and get them back.

When Rome is forced to fight as "Liam" and his ring persona "Renegade," he does well until he's forced to throw a match and lose because there is a gun pressed to Emersyn's head. After Rome takes the beating without fighting back, Emersyn stabs the guy who put the gun on her.

While she isn't punished directly, at the next fight, she is handcuffed. Adam and Ezra join in the effort to retrieve them. Liam and Rome swap places in the locker room allowing Rome to slip out with the others. Adam takes the initiative to trade himself for Emersyn. The enemies of the king may prove their allies. He wants more information and he also wants Emersyn out of the middle of this.

Reunited with the Vandals, Emersyn and Rome are thrilled to be home. As always there are other troubles, but Freddie welcomes Em home with a first kiss. Though Jasper is still healing from his gunshot wounds, the guys throw a surprise birthday party for Emersyn at Lainey's prompting and the whole of the clubhouse undergoes renovations to repair it from the damage of the fire fight in Brutal Fighter, but also to arrange a new set of "living quarters" with the guys "rooms" tucked into a new suite with Emersyn's.

Rome and Emersyn also do some body painting with their work on decorating. Emersyn and Liam also hit the sheets after Rome smacks his brother upside the head to tell him it is okay to want her. Doc continues to work with Emersyn on her physical therapy and to earn forgiveness.

The guys even celebrate Christmas with a tree to help give Emersyn another new memory and one they enjoy too. Finally, Emersyn admits she wants a Vandals tattoo but isn't sure if she qualifies. Does she have to be a rat first? The guys assure her, particularly Milo, that she has always been a Vandal. Before they can celebrate that too much, Bodhi shows up with news about Mama Sharpe.

And… whew…that is where Dangerous Renegade ended

That's high-end view of everything that happened, but

there are a lot of pages so re-reads are not only welcomed, they are encouraged.

This, of course, is where Merciless Spy finds us and our Vandals only a couple of weeks after this revelation. The war is brewing and their journey is far from over.

The seismic shifts that have rocked their lives are not over. Not by a long shot. Please remember that this is a dark romance and there are definitely triggering moments with regard to abuse, assault, violence, and addiction. Take care of yourself.

And now, as always, the housekeeping notes:

For those of you who have never read a why choose, or reverse harem before, first let me thank you for picking this up and giving it a shot. Second, the heroine will not make a choice in this book or any other between the guys in her life. It may take her a while to reach that conclusion, but it's the journey that drives it. There are many ways to frame this kind of relationship, currently why choose fits it very well.

Also, this is the seventh book in a series. While there may be no specific happy endings at the end of each of these books, there will be one to the whole series, that I promise you. Some of these books will have cliffhangers, largely due to the size of the story, but the happy ending has to be earned.

Finally, I want to add one last note. Books are not written in a vacuum. Worlds are not created in silence. There were some deeply challenging moments as I worked on this book, and thanks to some of the most wonderfully supportive people and the best girl gang ever, I made it. We made it.

Happy reading.

xoxo

Heather

THE VANDALS

82nd Street Boys
   Jasper "Hawk" Horan
   Kellan "Kestrel" Traschel
   Rome "Hummingbird" Cleary
   Vaughn "Falcon" Westbrook
   Liam "Mockingbird" O'Connell
   Freddie "Unknown" Cleary
   Milo "Raptor" Hardigan
   Mickey "Doc" James aka Vandal
   Emersyn "Dove, Sparrow, Starling, Swan, Little Bit, Boo-Boo, Hellspawn, Ivy" Sharpe

Other Characters
   Elaine "Lainey" Benedict
   Adam Reed
   Ezra Graham
   Ms. Stephanie

CHAPTER 1

EMERSYN

The hum of the engine vibrated through me where I sprawled on the bed in the back of the cab. Jasper had insisted on a solid eight hours of sleep on our last break. While I was pretty sure he hadn't slept more than three hours, the other five had been very enthusiastic.

"Gonna pull off up here for coffee, Swan," he said in a husky, sex-drenched voice that sent shivers through me. "The restrooms are clean, and secure. We can also shower if you want."

Stretching a bare leg out and propping my foot against the passenger seat, I grinned. "We?"

His soft chuckle confirmed what I'd heard. "Yes, ma'am. If you're getting naked anywhere, I'll be right there. Security first."

Rolling onto my side, I propped my head up on my fist. "Well, never let it be said I'm not security-minded. I promised Kellan I would follow all the rules."

"All of them?" The level of suggestion in his tone just made me grin wider. "Remind me to thank Kellan when I get back."

"I'll thank him for both of us if you want..."

"Damn," he exhaled the word. "You know, I think we may be a little late getting back on this run."

I was still laughing as I sat up and looked around for where my clothes had landed. When Kellan first suggested that I go with Jasper on this run, I was a little concerned about the why. Since Bodhi's surprise appearance and the news about my mother, it had been one of the only things I could think about.

Saving Mom was already on the list, but no one was willing for me to go to the facility where she was being kept. Not even as her daughter. Especially not as her daughter. The only people behind her being committed had to be Dad or Uncle Bradley.

I could understand their concern, yet it didn't change the fact that I was worried about her. I've been worried about her for a while, and a little afraid. The questions of if she knew, what she knew, and when she knew it—they were all there.

But she was still my mom. She'd still wanted me and been on my side. Maybe it was foolish to hold onto that thought...

"Swan?"

I blinked the tears then swiped my hand over my face to erase the evidence that splashed to my cheeks. "I'm here." I cleared my throat. "Did you throw my clothes up there?"

He cut a glance toward me. "Behind you... and what's wrong?"

A wet laugh escaped me as I twisted and turned to find my clothes. He really had just tossed them up and over. "I was thinking about my mom. Then..." Shaking out my t-

2

shirt, I tugged it over my head. I had no idea where the bra was, but I could find it later.

I used a wipe to clean up a little before I pulled on my panties and finally wiggled into the jeans, then climbed down into the passenger seat.

"Then?" he prompted as he passed me water.

Uncapping the bottle, I stared out the window at the scattered traffic ahead. Despite all the shows I'd done and the scant number of hours on a tour bus, this was honestly my first time in an 18-Wheeler.

I liked it.

Thrusting a hand under my hair, I lifted it out of my shirt collar and leaned back, bare feet propped against the dashboard. "Then I wondered if I should be worrying. Bodhi brought us the information almost a week ago, and we haven't done anything yet."

With a sigh, I tilted my head back.

"And that sounded like a complaint." With all they did for me, how hard was a little patience?

"It was a complaint," Jasper said without irony or recrimination. "You're allowed to complain, Swan. It's not going to bother me or anyone else."

I cast a smile at him, and he brushed his fingers down my cheek. Too soon, my smile faded. "What if I'm wrong about her?" I didn't think I was. I didn't want to be wrong.

"Then you find out," Jasper told me, his voice never once wavering. "Parents don't have to be perfect for us to love them. They can be weak, and they can be frail. They can be mean sons of bitches too. Does it make us less for loving them?"

Twisting a little in the seat, I stared at him. "You are not the one I would pick for the philosopher."

His snort delighted me; it was so derisive. "I'm not a

philosopher. I'm a student of life, and I've got the scars to prove it."

Yes, he did have scars. The thought sobered me. Two of those scars were still healing and even though Doc had taken him off restrictions, he was still supposed to take it easy. Not that it slowed him down.

Before I could respond, he reached over to catch my hand. "Emersyn, you are allowed to love her. Now, the question of whether you can trust her is one we need to answer, but we *will* get her out for you and you can have the time to figure out what you need to figure out."

I squeezed his hand. "You guys do so much for me."

"Not enough," he said, the rumble in his voice deepening. "Not soon enough, either."

Cheek pressed to the seat, I studied the hard lines of his profile. A fierce expression had taken up residence there as he scowled through the windshield.

"Jasper," I murmured, and the corner of his mouth curved. "You don't have to comfort me."

Really? I raised my eyebrows. "You didn't have to save me either."

That got me a growl as he cut those stormy gray eyes at me. "That's not funny."

"Neither is you being upset about something you didn't know about, nor could have changed…" I sighed. This was not where I'd seen this conversation going while my body was still humming from his touch after our last break.

"It was our job to protect you," he argued. "We've always agreed to that being our task from the moment they adopted you, and we wanted to keep track of you. Be able to be there whenever you needed us. Not that…" It was his turn to trail off.

He'd released my hand and put both of his on the steering wheel, where the knuckles went white.

"No one saw what was happening," I told him as gently as I could. "No one was allowed to know, I learned that very young. The only people I ever told… they died."

He flexed his fingers on the steering wheel. This was not a conversation I'd had with him yet. The others knew, but they weren't revealing it until I was ready. While Jasper had been wounded, I'd been worried about telling him.

Wounded or not, I was actually scared to tell him. I didn't know what he would do. Of all of them, Jasper's temper had seemed the worst. He'd been almost volcanic when I first showed up.

Yet beneath all the glares, scowls, and harsh words was a powerful heart with a deep-set loyalty that threaded his core. His fury with Liam had been about perceived betrayal and his fight with Milo was over the loss of him, coupled with the idea that Milo didn't want me with any of them.

It put Jasper in a harsh place. Then the day Jasper asked me if the idea of them torturing Eric turned me on, and well, yeah—it definitely had. "I want to tell you something," I said slowly. "It's a story about me, my family, and why I'm worried…"

Opening the water bottle, I took a longer, deeper drink of it. I almost wished it was alcohol. Or a cigarette. Or… just about anything to steady my nerves.

"I'm listening," he offered and the rumble in his voice faded to something lower, earthier. "You can tell me anything, Swan."

"I know I can." That much had been clear. Even when they hated every word, they'd all been willing to listen and to hear me. Even when we fought. Maybe especially when we fought. "I like fighting with you," I told him, the thought taking form and seeing no reason to hold it hostage. He deserved to know all the things I liked about him.

About all of them.

He snorted a laugh and flicked a look toward me. "Good to know. I'll keep that in mind the next time you frustrate me."

That just made me chuckle, cracking some of the ice sliding into my bloodstream. Anytime I thought about my uncle, the chill was almost immediate. It was like something out of a horror movie. I half-expected to see my breath frosting in the air.

No matter how ridiculous the thought, I always worried he was just a step behind me. That he would *know* what I said or when I said it. That he would take another ally or friend from me.

"I'm serious," I said after a beat.

"That you like to fight with me?" The teasing note pulled a laugh from me.

"No... I mean yes, I do like fighting with you, although what I need to tell you now... it's not something I want to fight about. Can you listen to me without reacting? Or should we wait until we're somewhere for the night?"

Maybe I shouldn't have brought it up now. We were on a long haul and we weren't supposed to be breaking for another hour. Or maybe sooner. He'd brought up coffee and a shower.

"Emersyn." So much affection and feeling bound up in my name, holding me in place. "It's fine. Whatever it is, we'll handle it. If you need me to not lose my temper. I won't. But since this is tying you up in knots, I want you to tell me so I can fix it."

They all wanted to fix things for me. It wasn't that easy, but it also wasn't impossible. The Vandals made my life better, and they had been improving it from the day he walked into my dressing room and replaced the lock.

"Eric wasn't the first person to ever assault me," I said, ripping the Band-Aid off. "My relationship with him wasn't even an assault, to begin with...just a mistake made from the need to take control of my life."

A sigh whooshed out of me.

"Not just my life, but my body."

His knuckles whitened more. Dragging my gaze off his hands, I focused on the set of his jaw. He'd been growing his beard back in, much to my delight, but it wasn't quite as soft as it had been before.

At least not yet.

"I have a hard time talking about this," I admitted. "But I've been getting stronger. Part of that is all of you. You make me stronger." It was more than that. "You also make me want to be stronger."

That was part of it. I wanted to protect them too. As vibrant and powerful as they all were, they were also vulnerable. They all had their own demons, dark pasts, and trials. They also had a lot to lose from helping me.

Not once had it slowed them down.

Not from helping me escape Eric. From eliminating Eric. From protecting me from the bounty hunters who came looking. From the other gangs around their life. They didn't live a safe existence, although they took the additional threats posed by my presence in stride.

"I've been working on this, talking about it. I used to think if I said anything it would make it real. Not that keeping it a secret changed how much I hated it." I licked my lips, then picked at the corner on one of my nails. The bit of dry skin there held my attention. "The hardest part is that I knew what was happening was wrong and that I should have asked for help, but I didn't know how. All I knew was I needed to get away and then I thought I had..."

It was coming out all jumbled. It wasn't until Jasper pulled off the highway into a rest area and stopped the truck that I realized I was shaking. He twisted in the seat and captured my hands in his.

"Don't you have to tell them you're taking a break?"

"They can wait," he said firmly. He cut a glance at the side mirrors and then tightened his hands on mine. "Tell me what has you so terrified."

I wanted to apologize for even bringing it up. I'd been looking for the time to tell him and Liam. They were only the two, along with Milo, who didn't know. Their reactions worried me.

However, I'd already pulled at this scab and as with each of the earlier retellings, it came out easier. I told him about my uncle. I kept my gaze fixed on our hands as I explained what happened.

The tears took longer to come this time. So did the shame. It didn't matter how much this wasn't my fault, a part of me would always feel complicit. I kept what my uncle was doing to myself. I hadn't told my parents.

The very small handful of people I'd ever confessed it to had ended up dead. The doctor had been the last one I'd tried to tell. She'd been so kind and caring. She'd helped put me back together, then she was going to go to the authorities. A few days later she died in a car crash.

After that, I learned to say nothing. I could endure anything, and I doubled up my training. The more I stayed on the road, the more likely I was to stay away from him. It didn't always work...

"...but I didn't know what else to do until you guys took me."

Then, and only then, did I lift my gaze to meet Jasper's. The depth of emotion in the storm of his eyes staggered me. Fury lived there, only it was more than fury. There was a wild tangle of love and worry present.

"You were scared to tell me?"

"Terrified," I admitted. "I thought you would go after him."

"Oh, I'm definitely going after that piece of shit," Jasper said, his voice dipping softer as he held my gaze. "We're going to make him regret being born, but that's for later. Right now is about you."

The tears I'd been fighting spilled over as relief flooded me.

"Were you really that scared to tell me?" At my nod, he let out a huff of sound then dragged me out of the seat and over to his.

"Your side."

"Fuck my side, Swan. You need a hug and I need to hug you." He wrapped around me and I burrowed into him.

"I just don't want anything to happen to you," I admitted. "It was already too close when you were shot."

"We're going to be fine, Swan," he told me. "Trust us. We've got this."

CHAPTER 2

JASPER

The hot spray of water spilled over both of us as I hoisted Emersyn up in my arms. She wrapped her hand around my dick and angled, so she could slide right down onto me.

"Fuck," I groaned as I kept one arm around her and braced my other hand on the wall. The showers were kept pretty clean, and we had privacy, but I wasn't slamming her against any walls here.

"Pretty sure that's what we're doing," she teased, nipping my earlobe. Laughter bubbled up through the darkness swirling inside of me.

Her confession in the truck had gutted me. A wild cacophony of thoughts tumbled through my mind as she described her uncle and his abuse.

Dead man walking. I barricaded him into a dark corner of my mind. I wasn't going to focus on him while I had her hips rolling as she writhed on my dick. The strength in her as she lifted herself and then sank back down was dizzying.

The warm velvet fist of her cunt enveloped me with every thrust. As much as my hips trembled to take over, there was something intoxicating in her expression as she rocked against me.

She dug her nails into my shoulders and I glanced down, savoring the view of her taking every single inch as we moved together. There was a twinge on my side, but I ignored it. What was a little bit of pain when compared to the pleasure of fucking her.

With a light tug of her fingers in my hair, she pulled my head up and I followed willingly before slamming my mouth down onto hers. The soft cries vibrating in her throat seemed to translate right into my system. All I wanted was more.

Despite the desire, I forced stillness, letting her take the lead. The muscle control as she flexed around me edged me right toward ecstasy. I devoured her lips, though. The kiss was not something I could be remotely passive about.

It was half-killing me not to take over and drive us both to distraction, not that it would be a long trick. The hot water spilling over us just added to the sensation. Awareness of every inch of her flesh flush against mine held me riveted.

The slight weight of her as she gripped me and slammed me home. The pressure of her calves against my ass. The rub of her nipples on my chest. The scrape of her teeth against my lip. The thrust of her tongue daring me to tangle with hers.

Leashing my desire burned so fucking sweetly as her cries grew, then she dragged her head back and opened those sweet honey-brown eyes to stare up at me.

"Jasper..." The loving emphasis on my name stilled me

and I studied her. She trembled against me. Flexing my hand against her ass, I nipped a light kiss to her mouth.

"What do you need, Swan?" My voice came out hoarse, I had everything locked down from the need to pound into her to the need to kiss her until the only thing she could see, feel, taste, or hear was me. I wanted to erase all the dark thoughts, eliminate them as if they'd never happened.

Until the day I offered her the bloody sacrifice she deserved in the form of her mutilated uncle, I wanted to erase him. After that... well, after that he could be a bad memory, washed away.

Whatever she needed.

Whatever she wanted.

"Fuck me." The note of pleading clawed at me. "Please."

Yeah, she never had to beg me. "Hold onto me, Swan." At my command, she hoisted herself higher, tightening her grip, and I gave her ass a firm squeeze before I shifted my stance.

The angle was perfect as I tilted her forward while still bracing my free hand on the wall.

"Don't let go," I warned her.

"Never." The promise wrapped around me like an oath. Agreed. I would never let her go, either. The faint burn of my beard had turned her cheeks a ruddy, reddish shade. I loved seeing those signs on her. On her breasts. Her belly. Over her thighs.

Between them. The pulse of lust burst through the restraint I'd kept on myself and I slammed forward, driving myself deeper. She let out a low cry, her nails digging into me, yet her eyes were fixed on mine. The blown pupils begged for more and her lips were kiss-swollen and perfectly pink.

She was... perfection.

The leash gone, I rocked into her. Driven by the increasing sound of her moans, I aimed for that spot inside to drive her mad. For all her guarded expressions and care-worn wariness, Emersyn hid nothing of herself from me. She writhed, hips rotating with every thrust. The dance of fucking her was an addiction I never wanted to be cured.

The fierce clamp of her muscles was the only warning for her orgasm. Gritting my teeth, I rode through it, fighting to send her over again before I blew my own load.

The bite of her teeth into my shoulder as she screamed was everything I needed, and I let go. My spine went liquid as my release spilled out of me and then we were just clinging to one another. Fuck me, even my legs were trembling. The twinge in my side had become a real burn, except it was amazing.

Little kisses and lavishing touches from her tongue against my shoulder roused me and I lifted my head to find her nuzzling the bite mark she'd left imprinted in my flesh. The skin hadn't broken, but the details of her teeth were pretty clear.

"I think Kel is right," I teased her. "You are a raptor."

Pink suffused her face, just adding to her glow, and she let out a laugh. "I want to say I'm sorry…"

"Don't," I ordered. "I like being marked by you."

"You already wear my mark." She trailed her fingers over one of the vines of ivy twined in and around my tattoos. "You've worn it for a long time."

"Yes, but I like Emersyn's mark." Just like that, I nodded. "I want your mark on me, Ivy's and Emersyn's." We both glanced at my shoulder. "Choose what you want it to be, Swan, and I'll have Vaughn ink it as soon as we're back."

I should have done it sooner. Weird how oddly bare I suddenly felt without it. Her inner muscles still spasmed around me and we both let out huffing sounds as I finally slipped free. If I could stay hard and buried in her forever, I would.

Except the guys might get bitchy if I said there was no room at the inn.

Laughter burst out of me and I hugged her tight as she loosened her legs and then went to stand. Thankfully, I wasn't the only one shaking. She clung to me as much as I did to her.

"What's so funny?" The curiosity was adorable, so I told her. The fact her eyes widened and she burst into laughter made my own smile widen. Cupping her face in my hands, I tasted that humor and warmth on her lips.

"I love you," I told her. The words came so effortlessly for her. I hadn't ever said them to another person beyond my own mother and that had been before she died. However, Emersyn chased those shadows away, tore them apart, and reminded me what it was to love and be loved.

"I love you," she whispered. I treasured each syllable as they wrapped me up in their verbal hug. "I know I don't say it…"

"Shh." I pressed my finger against her lips. "You trust me. You talk to me. That's love."

Surprise flickered in her eyes.

"I trust you with me." I trusted her with everything. "I trust you with all of us."

Reaching for the shampoo, I poured some into my palm and began to work it into her hair.

"You told me something about you," I said slowly, gathering together my scattered emotions. How she turned me inside out and made me weak and powerful in equal measures stunned me. "Now I want to tell you about myself."

Her eyes were half-closed as I massaged her scalp. We didn't have a lot of time left. I'd booked a double, but I also hadn't rushed the sex. She traced her fingers up and down my sides, the lightness of her touch grounding me.

"You know I met Milo in foster care," I said. "Met you then too."

A laugh escaped her as I nudged her under the water and began to rinse her hair. I could wash her all day. The way she just let me maneuver her around and handle her. The spitfire who got in my face was still there, but now she was fighting *for* me now and not against me.

Not that I expected she wouldn't fight me if she thought she needed, too.

"Yes."

"Part of the reason I was in foster care," I said, gripping the blackout curtains I kept on this part of my past and dragging them open, "was because my father killed my mother."

Saying it hurt. Less than I expected, actually. Still, the pain was there, a bruise on my heart that had never quite healed.

"He was an abusive man," I said, then snorted a little. "He's still an abusive son of a bitch. I don't remember a time when I wasn't afraid of upsetting him, when I didn't try to get between them. When I think of them…I think of Mom as someone who was always bruised. She was so much smaller than him and he would slap her without a thought for the stupidest shit."

There were other hits. Other screams. Things I heard but didn't see. Sounds that haunted me.

With gentle hands, she cupped my face and I blinked down at her. "Come back to me," she was whispering and I bent my forehead to hers.

"Sorry… I don't talk about it." Didn't want to. Didn't want to think about them. Mom… "She was a beautiful woman and she was always kind to me."

It came out rougher than I intended.

"But she would never leave him. I remember asking her once, to run away…" The memory tiptoed out from the past and I sighed before reaching for the little bottle of conditioner. She'd brought her own things and I liked how this one smelled.

Working it through her hair, I combed my fingers through the strands. Her hair had gotten longer in the last year. I loved the way it felt when it spread over my skin or when I sank my hands into it.

"One night, I don't even know what started it. I never knew. He got mad. There was yelling. He started hitting her. Didn't stop." Sadness clawed at me. "I didn't realize she'd died, only that he'd stopped and she wasn't moving. I hid under the table…"

When she wrapped around me, it hit me that I was shaking and I held her tighter.

"I'm sorry," she whispered.

"Me too." I swallowed back the tears clogging my throat. "Me too, Swan. That was why…that was why when I recognized the fear in your eyes I couldn't leave you."

We were both silent for a moment and then she pulled back to meet my gaze. "Have I said thank you for kidnapping me yet?"

A smile tugged at my lips. "You might have mentioned it." It was the truth. When she'd come out into that courtyard and asked for a smoke, I'd seen the fear again. Then that son of a bitch followed her…

"I won't let anyone hurt you again," I swore. "None of us will. We're going to get you your pound of flesh. We're going to make them all regret the harm they did to you."

Her uncle.

Her father.

Her mother.

She didn't blame her parents, or maybe she didn't want to. But they were there and their job was to protect her. I could only hope her mother hadn't known…

If she did, though?

Yeah, nothing was saving her.

"Jasper... what happened to your father?"

"He's in jail," I told her. "Never getting out. He killed someone else when he was in there and it added to his sentence. I was kind of hoping at one point he would get parole."

The confession slipped out of me.

"Why?" No sooner did she ask the question than the confusion slipped away. "You wanted to kill him. You wanted your mother's pound of flesh."

Yes. No shame suffocated me when I nodded, and no judgment flickered in her eyes.

"If he ever does get out," she told me, tightening her grip on me. "I'll help."

"That, my fierce Swan, is why I love you so goddamn much."

She rose up on her tiptoes and kissed me even as the warning buzzer went off. We were going to have to get out of here, but fuck if I didn't feel cleaner than I had in years.

CHAPTER 3

LIAM

"They're late," I said, checking my watch for the fourth time. Impatience crept through me.

"They're on track," Kellan said as he walked out of the office. The warehouse, like the clubhouse, had undergone some refurbishment. The office actually looked like one. It also held updated logbooks, two desks, new walls, and a reinforced faux wall covering the fridge.

The fact the office looked homey had everything to do with dressing this place up for Hellspawn. She deserved to have warmth around her. I approved.

"I thought the schedule had them coming in late last night or early this morning." Irritation crept into my voice. There had been some cleanup needed and with new threats in the offing, sending her out with Jasper made her a roving target and harder to corner.

"It did," Kellan said, his expression bemused as he glanced past me to where the rats were busy off-loading one of the trucks that just came in this morning—*ahead* of schedule. "What's crawled up your ass and died? You aren't usually jumpy as fuck."

I disliked that description, no matter how fucking accurate. Cutting a look at Kellan, I just folded my arms. "I'm handling it."

"Right," he said, the tempered note in his voice warning me he wasn't thrilled with that response. "You know the rules, Liam. What are you handling?"

"A lot." It wasn't hyperbole. We had a lot in play at the moment, and in the king's last message, he hadn't been particularly happy with me. But he could just choke on it for now.

"Talk to me," Kellan said, but his attention wasn't on me abruptly, and I cut my gaze to where Freddie was entering, carrying grocery bags and followed by his "new" friend. Bodhi Cavendish.

Not my first choice for anyone's friend. Definitely not thrilled with his interest in Hellspawn or the fact he came all this way to tell her about her mother. I had feelers out there to see what I could find, but the Sharpes were playing it deadly quiet.

As far as I could tell, no one even knew where Emersyn was or that she'd escaped Pinetree. Even money said they didn't know her uncle had committed her. Then there was that piece of shit... Not only had he gone dark, he'd also fallen off the face of the earth.

No one knew where he was. Word had him in Dubai, Amsterdam, and more recently, Panama City. I doubted any of them were accurate. He'd gone into hiding. Tension threaded my back, along my spine and up to my neck until it dug in and squeezed my brain.

"What do you know about him?" Kellan asked, and I shook my head.

"He's a problem." That was putting it mildly. "Wild card. Positively unpredictable. He can go from zero to one-eighty without any warning. Rumors in school were he was into drugs, but I never saw any sign of it." It came across as more of an excuse than anything else.

"You don't like him." It wasn't a question.

I didn't need to reply. "It bothers me that Freddie called him."

"Freddie seems to trust him." There was a note of warning in Kellan's voice, but I'd already figured that part out.

"That could be a problem." I sighed, a sound Kellan echoed.

"Agreed." He glanced at me. "What are the other problems you're not sharing?"

"Nothing to—"

"Don't," he said, cutting me off with one word and a stern look. His expression went implacable, and I shook my head.

"Hey," Freddie said, and Kellan's expression relaxed as he turned to Freddie. "What's up? Boo-Boo back yet?"

"No," Kellan said smoothly as he glanced at Bodhi. "Mr. Cavendish. We weren't expecting you."

"Didn't warn you I was coming," the prick said with a smirk. "Besides, I was invited." He transferred that look to me. "O'Connell."

"Jackass."

"Hey," Freddie protested, shifting the bags from one hand to the other. "Bodhi's a friend."

"We know," Kellan said, shooting me a look, but I wasn't just going to roll over. Just because the guy did one favor didn't mean he would do another. Few people did anything for nothing.

A Cavendish *never* did a favor they didn't expect to have repaid in spades. They were more than willing to leverage everything. Not that I gave a shit. What he'd done for Emersyn, I would repay in blood if I had to. She wasn't owing him shit.

Nor was Freddie.

The smirk on Cavendish's face didn't remotely fade.

"I asked Bodhi over to play some pool while we're waiting for Boo-Boo."

I didn't scowl. Or glare. Tempting, but I kept it to myself. Whatever his play was, he needed to know I would be watching.

"Rome and Vaughn are working upstairs," Kellan said more readily than I would have. It wasn't an explicit order to keep him downstairs, but Freddie nodded. The new suite was not for public consumption.

"Sounds good." Freddie cut a look at me, but I shook my head once. If he wanted to ask me about Cavendish later, he could. But not right now. "Let us know when Boo-Boo is back?"

"Sure," Kellan told him, and Cavendish shot me another smirk. I flexed my hand, curling my fingers as each knuckle popped. I could remove that smirk. Keeping my expression neutral took effort, but I wouldn't give the prick the satisfaction.

"Hey, Freddie," I said as they were walking away. "Find me later, yeah?"

"Will do." Then Freddie grinned. "You gonna Big Brother me?"

"Maybe," I told him. "You never know."

He laughed, flipping me off with ease. Once they were both inside and out of earshot, I let my smile disappear.

"I really wish he wasn't spending time with him."

"I got that," Kellan replied. "But as I said, Freddie likes him."

"Yeah, and seems to trust him."

"Freddie doesn't trust just anyone," Kellan reminded me. "Not outside of us and even here—" He sighed.

"Yeah." There were times when Freddie didn't trust us enough to protect him. Didn't mean we wouldn't. Just that we needed to work harder to remind him we were here. "We'll just have to remind him."

"And keep an eye on Cavendish?" His dry tone held a trace of amusement.

"Definitely."

"Then we will. Now tell me what's happening with you." The order was evident in his tone. "And don't shine me on with some bullshit about you taking care of it. I told you, we're not doing that anymore."

I sighed. "It's nothing you can change right now, Kel."

"Then it's not going to kill you to tell me. We don't run alone. We aren't waging these fights alone. So tell me… or I'll tell Sparrow you're keeping secrets. I'm worried about you."

Pivoting, I met his gaze with a glare. "You wouldn't dare."

"Don't test me. She cares about you and won't let it go until she gets a damn answer. Which is good for all of us, even when it's annoying."

Fuck wasn't that the truth. I shook my head. "Leave her out of this one, at least for now." Not that she wasn't already aware of the issue. I'd just managed to keep her distracted from it for now.

"Then read me in."

"Blackmail should be beneath you." I folded my arms. I needed to do something before I started punching things.

"Sad for you that it isn't." His amusement softened the edge of those words.

Bastard. Then again, weren't we all? I rolled my head from side to side. "The king wants to meet her."

A gunshot probably wouldn't have shocked him more. Kellan cut a look at me.

"He's wanted to since we pulled her out of the fights with Rome." And it wasn't going to happen. "I'll deal with it."

"If you could have dealt with it," Kellan said in an even tone, "you already would have."

On the one hand, his faith was everything. On the other… "I'll handle it. I'm not taking her anywhere near that son of a bitch."

"Not arguing that… yet. Why does he want to meet her?"

Was he serious? "Does it matter?"

"Yes." He locked his gaze on me, and I shook my head. "Don't dismiss it out of hand."

"The answer is no."

"Liam…"

Fuck me. "Don't use that reasonable as-shit tone with me, Kel. Taking her to meet him is a non-starter." I'd rather put a bullet in my dick before I put her in front of that unpredictable son of a bitch. The last "meeting" I had with him, he wanted Adam assassinated.

"Are you done?" Kellan asked, and I rolled my head from side to side, cracking it as I locked my jaw. He said nothing more as he waited for me to come up with my answer.

Exhaling, I glanced at him. Based on his implacable expression, he wasn't impressed with my temper or the direction I was headed in.

"No," I told him. "I'm not. But you want to *discuss* this for some fucking reason." Fisting my temper, I fixed a look on him. "I'll listen, but I'm not taking her."

"Has he ever asked to meet with you personally before?"

Eyes closed, I tightened my grip on the anger spilling into my blood like a gaping wound that would not be staunched. "Kel, don't ask me to do this."

"I'm not asking you," he told me firmly. "Although you and Milo have been on this mission for years, and this is the first time your target has asked to meet with you in person."

"I don't trust him. I don't trust what will happen. And I sure as fuck am not willing to risk her."

"None of us are," he told me in that even tone that warned me to watch for the trap. "But if this is an opportunity we might not otherwise get, it's not our call to make."

Pivoting fully, I faced him and closed the gap. To his credit, Kellan didn't back down an inch from me. Fighting with my brothers was never my favorite thing. "She'll do it because she wants to *save* us."

"I know."

"How the fuck are you this calm?" I swore it was like chewing glass to get each word out. "You can't possibly want…"

"No, I don't want her in the middle of this. Don't be more of an ass than necessary." Even with his temper shining in his eyes, his tone was calm. "But we're also not making decisions *for* her. She's been controlled her whole life. We don't do that here."

I wanted to slug something.

"You've been teaching her to fight," Kellan reminded me. "I've been teaching her to shoot. To drive. Freddie has been showing her how to use a knife. Everything we do is to arm her and prepare her to protect herself."

"So, we just throw her to the lions. Right, No problem."

Kellan just shot me a look, and I swore, hands up as I turned away from him.

"I hate this, Kel."

Even when she'd just been Rome's girl, I didn't want anything or anyone touching her. Not that I'd ever really believed my own bullshit lies.

She already knew about the invitation. She'd been right there when he invited her.

"We talk to her," Kellan said as I stared across the warehouse. "We talk to everyone. This is not a plan that you or I can make, and then we inform everyone else."

"Milo will never go for it." At least I'd have him on my side in this.

"Milo didn't want her with any of us," Kellan reminded me. Dick.

"He didn't want her in this life," I corrected, not that Kel was wrong. Milo didn't want to see her as an adult. He wanted the baby sister he'd had to give up, but what he got was a daring, brilliant, and loving woman.

What *we* got.

"But it's *her choice*." Kellan wasn't wrong. No matter how much I wanted to argue and rail against him on this point, he wasn't wrong. I fucking hated it. "Not a fan of anything that could put her in harm's way, but she's one of us, Liam. Sparrow is not going to hide. She might—for a while—if we ask it of her. But if we put her in that cage and she lets us lock the door…"

We weren't any better than everyone else who had ever used her. Fuck.

"Doesn't mean I have to like it."

"No," Kellan said, gripping my shoulder as he shook his head. "We don't. We just have to respect her rights and her."

As if summoned by our conversation, the far doors began to roll up and the chains echoed through the warehouse as they retracted the door and guided it along the rails to open.

"She's back," I said without a second glance at my brother and strode across the warehouse, even as Jasper backed the truck right up and into the warehouse to be offloaded.

The sound of Kellan's laughter followed me, but I didn't care if I looked as eager as a teenager. I was. We'd sent her out with Jasper so we could clear the decks here and keep her a moving target.

That had been a *week* ago. A week shouldn't feel that long, but it had been an eternity. The fact the door to the club-house opened behind me served as a testament to the idea that I wasn't the only one eager to see our girl.

I didn't even wait for the truck to stop moving before climbing up the passenger door to open it. A smile lit my Hellspawn's face up as she turned to me. The scent of sex filled the cab, not that I could blame them. If I'd had her to myself for a week, I didn't think we'd have bothered with getting dressed.

Poor Jasper still had to drive.

I cupped her face and slammed my mouth down on hers while he chuckled. She opened to my kiss with a welcoming sigh that just helped to sand away all the bitter, painful edges left by the conversation with Kellan.

It was about damn time she was home.

Now to steal her before the others got any ideas.

CHAPTER 4

EMERSYN

The ease with which Jasper backed the massive 18-wheeler into the warehouse kept me in awe. I'd done a lot of driving forward, not backward yet. But it wasn't like he could turn around and look out the back window. No, he had to use the side mirrors as his only guide.

I held my breath even though I had complete faith in him. A part of me was still braced for the trailer to hit some part of the warehouse. He'd barely put the truck into park, when the door on my side of the cab opened.

Liam filled the opening and I barely got a single sound out before he wrapped me up in a kiss. Delight speared me as he swept his tongue across mine. Thankfully, I'd brushed my teeth after our breakfast stop. The sound of Jasper's laughter flooded me with a fresh surge of happiness.

The week away had been an adventure, but my ass was numb from the seat and the vibration of the truck. "I missed you," I whispered against Liam's lips when he allowed me a single breath before he kissed me again.

A whistle cut through the air, but a distant part of my mind recognized and acknowledged that Kellan was there. Excitement threaded through me as Liam half-lifted me out of the seat and then down as he stepped down.

The warm massage of his lips, along with the thrust of his tongue and the band of his arms holding me so damn firmly, were a welcome home I wanted to treasure forever. A low growl vibrated from his throat. I sank my fingers into his hair, and when he fisted mine, he finally lifted his head to press his forehead to mine.

"Vaughn, I will break your fingers," Liam said with such heat, and I tugged his hair to jerk his gaze back to me. "Figure of speech, Hellspawn."

"No, it wasn't," I told him in a ragged voice as I tried to catch my breath.

"Don't worry, Dove," Vaughn said, laughing softly. "I can handle Liam."

The grunt Liam offered up was not an agreement. The flash of humor amongst the heat in his eyes, though? That flooded me with warmth. "See," he teased in a rough voice. "He can handle me breaking his fingers."

"Share," Kellan said without an ounce of irony or teasing. Liam's sigh was heavy, put upon, and filled with just a hint of playfulness.

"Fine," he muttered, but the corner of his mouth kicking a little higher betrayed him. He nipped my lower lip. "You're going home with me tonight, Hellspawn."

Jasper's laughter drifted toward us. "Bets on Kel and the boys, Liam."

"I'll take that action," Liam said in a slow drawl as he slid me down his body to the ground. His grip was both playful and possessive. The temptation to grind against him was strong, but I already didn't want to let go despite being eager to see the others.

A week wasn't that long, but it seemed like an eternity. Liam squeezed my hips before he shifted, and then Kellan grinned at me as Vaughn scooped me up. Laughter spilled out of me as Vaughn wrapped around me.

His size had always been impressive, but there was security in gripping him as he practically shielded me with his whole body. Our teeth clacked once as I laughed into his kiss. Rather than be dissuaded, he rumbled a chuckle of his own.

"Dove is happy," he murmured against my lips. "Missed you like hell, but I'd let you go away for all the weeks if you come back like this."

Delight curled through me as I wrapped my arms around his neck. Over Vaughn's shoulder, I locked gazes with Kellan. The approval in his eyes as he glanced from me to Jasper then back again warmed me even further.

"I am happy," I confessed. "I'm back, and I missed you guys." But I didn't want them to think Jasper hadn't been great. "Jasper was amazing," I continued and he chuckled, his smile turning almost indulgent. Another kiss from Vaughn quieted me.

I sighed against his lips, then smiled as he pivoted to set me on my feet in front of Kellan. Lifting his arm as though an invitation, Kel raised his brows. I slid next to him, tucking myself under his arm as Jasper gave him a quick run-down on our trip.

"Sounds like it went well," Kellan said, glancing down at me. The warmth of Vaughn and Liam sticking close added to the feeling of being wrapped up in them.

"It did." Jasper's tone was firm. "We have a full load, too. So we need to break it up."

"Vaughn's got it," Kellan said, but for his part, Vaughn just groaned though his smile remained in place.

"I can help," I offered, but Kellan tightened his arm.

"Not today, Sparrow. Vaughn has this, and it's his turn."

Vaughn made a face, then flashed me a grin. "It is my turn, Dove. Go hang out with the guys. We'll figure out food when I'm done."

"She's going home with me," Liam said, arms folded. "I'll get her fed."

"We haven't decided on that yet," Kellan retorted.

"Not a 'we,' just a me." Liam's near-serene expression didn't remotely match the heat in his eyes. "I didn't get to see her for three days *before* you sent her away. Ergo, tonight is mine."

"Nice try," Jasper complimented him. "You're still not in charge. Swan will go…"

Biting my lip, I caught Vaughn's amused expression. Laughter filled his topaz eyes and he winked. "I think you forgot the rules… majority rules."

Smug didn't begin to describe his smile. Vaughn's silky voice wrapped me up in another embrace. I'd missed his deep croon almost as much as I'd missed him.

"You don't get a vote, Jas," Liam informed him. "You've had her all to yourself so that utterly cancels out any vote from you.

"They don't need my vote to get a majority. Even Rome will want her to stay here."

"Rome can come to my place too." Far from deterred, Liam's smirk grew as though he knew something they didn't.

"We'll discuss the care and keeping of Sparrow *later*," Kellan said, ending their debate. "For now, Vaughn, get the truck offloaded. Jasper, file your logs and tally up your invoices. Liam…"

"Take Hellspawn and go?" He didn't wait for Kel's answer, just held out his hand to me. "I'll get right on that."

Laughter fountained up through me. To be honest, the

discussion of me and where I would be going or staying in the third person—particularly when I was standing *right* there— should probably piss me off. Almost any other time, it would definitely irritate me.

But not right now, and not these guys.

I turned that over in my head a little. No, the discussion they were having didn't remotely bother me. Not on any level. The warmth in their verbal challenges and the playfulness in their gazes didn't make light of how absolutely serious they were.

Argument or not, they were having fun. It satisfied me on some deep, primitive level to see them teasing each other. Particularly Jasper. I wasn't sure how often the others got to see him like this.

I adored it.

Him.

Them.

Liam wanting me to go with him was certainly enticing. So was the idea of sleeping in my very own bed and being in the clubhouse with all the guys. Choosing would be a pain in the ass…

"Grab Sparrow's bag," Kellan said, laughing softly before he pressed a kiss to the side of my head. "Happy to be back?"

The low murmur of his question sank into my bones.

"So happy," I told him as he turned us to walk into the warehouse. We weren't hurrying. There was double the number of rats already working on off-loading the truck. "Are there…"

"Yes," Kellan answered as he guided me past them. "We've been taking care of some things and made a few changes. I'll bring you up to speed."

Kellan kept us on course for the clubhouse door and I glanced back to find Liam following. When our gazes locked, he winked. Fresh laughter swelled up inside of me. The interior of the warehouse was also busier, not just from the new crew there off-loading, populated with a bunch of fresh faces, but also with the sheer volume of stuff on pallets waiting to be loaded onto new trucks.

It was cleaner. Their cars were all lined up, side by side, facing the exit, with Liam's slotted neatly between Rome's and Vaughn's like he parked there all the time. As he should…

'Cause he belonged there.

"Why does it feel like I've been gone a lot longer than a week?" Even the air in the warehouse felt different. I stole a look at Kellan as we paused at the door and he entered the new code.

"Because you missed us, Hellspawn, clearly." Liam's simple answer made me snort.

The outer door opened and Liam followed us inside. His warmth at my back had me tilting my head up to grin at him.

"I really did miss you," I promised as Kellan opened the second door. Light, music, and the fresh scent of coffee spilled out to welcome us.

"Boo-Boo!" Freddie's shout carried, and I pulled from Kellan to meet Freddie's hug with one of my own. Kel's soft chuckle followed us, and I swore my cheeks were gonna hurt from all the smiling. Freddie gave me a squeeze then leaned his head back to look at me. "You look good. Hungry? We were just talking about making something."

"We?" I half-expected to see Rome, but Bodhi was a total surprise. "Hey, Bodhi."

"Hey, PPG," he said from where he stood by the new pool table. "Looking good. Ready to go find your mother…"

"Not yet," Kellan answered before I could answer. "We'll discuss that later."

Freddie slung an arm around my shoulders as we faced Kellan. "Maybe Boo-Boo wants to go," he suggested.

"I do," I said before this went anywhere. "But not until we have a plan." I met Kellan's gaze and he nodded slowly. "Not until we're ready."

"Cool," was Bodhi's only comment before he went back to lining up a shot. I liked Bodhi. He'd helped us before. His reaction to finding me in the doctor's office and how he'd gotten Freddie would forever endear the man to me. But I trusted my guys.

Kellan wanted to do more research, so we would wait and do more research.

"Go finish your game," Kellan suggested. "Sparrow, Liam, and I need to have a talk."

We did?

"Don't disappear?" Freddie asked me, and I pushed up on my toes to kiss his jaw.

"If I do go to Liam's, I'll tell you first."

"Good deal." He gave me another squeeze and then turned back to the table. We didn't linger in the living room or head to the kitchen. Instead, Kellan nudged me toward the stairs.

Liam followed, absent his earlier smile. If anything, his entire demeanor had taken on a grim tone. My stomach bottomed out as Kel opened the door to our new sitting room.

In addition to the oversized sofa, the end tables, and the massive television and armchairs, they'd added a regular coffeemaker in the corner. Liam dropped my bag in my room before he headed for it.

"What's wrong?" I asked Kellan as Liam seemed determined to stay on the move.

"We don't need to have this conversation now," Liam argued just as coffee began to spit and hiss.

"Actually," Kellan countered. "We do. It involves Sparrow, so we're discussing it with her."

"We don't need to…" Liam folded his arms, mutiny seeming to vibrate off of him.

"That still doesn't answer my question about whether something is wrong." The third-party discussion about where I was going or staying was fun. This was not.

"No," Liam said, even as Kellan stated, "Perhaps."

The pair glared at each other, and I swore more than anger flowed between them. Liam backed down first and shook his head.

"This is just gonna scare her."

"Maybe," Kellan said and I pivoted to face him. "But Sparrow's a lot tougher than she looks."

"I'm about to look pretty damn angry. What's wrong?"

The corner of his mouth kicked up into a smile that didn't touch his eyes. "The king apparently still wants to meet you. So we need to make some decisions about whether we're keeping Liam in place or pulling him totally."

Oh.

Shit.

CHAPTER 5

KELLAN

*L*iam's glare didn't dissuade me from reading Emersyn into this issue. As much as *I* didn't want her involved in all of this, we'd involved her. We'd involved her by bringing her in, by closing ranks around her, and by staking our claim.

We'd involved her further when she said she wanted to stay and we informed her she was, and had always been, a Vandal. Maybe this wasn't what Milo had in mind. No *maybe* about it. Milo thought the world she came from would be *better*, except wealthier and more elite didn't equal safer and better.

Clearly, it didn't. It never had. Look at the life Liam had been living amongst the so-called elite. Fuck them. I didn't really care what Milo wanted right now. Like I told Liam, we weren't making decisions for her without *involving* her. No one got to control her anymore.

No. One.

Her brow tightened as she studied me, then she glanced at Liam as she sat on the sofa slowly. "This is about the call on the night you guys got us from the fights."

One harsh exhale escaped Liam and he abandoned the coffee to go to crouch in front of her. "Hellspawn, you do not need to meet that man…"

"But—isn't that why you've been doing all of this?" It wasn't an unreasonable question. Liam had spent too many years doing this shit on his own. It was on all of us to remind him that he *wasn't* alone anymore. He should never have been in the first place.

Milo and I would never agree on the *why* behind the decision they'd begun when we were fucking *teenagers*. Leashing that irritation, I packed it away with the rest of my temper. This wasn't about my impatience with those decisions. I could only hope they made sense at the time.

Emotional blackmail was probably not the way to go, but Emersyn was a lodestone for all of us. My sparrow was every bit a fierce fighter; she'd had to be to survive. Piss her off, fight with her, or comfort her, I was fine with all of those.

"I'm doing this to protect the others," Liam said without casting a single look in my direction. "Protecting them includes protecting you. The last time the king demanded a meeting, he wanted me to shoot Adam."

I headed toward the coffeemaker to finish what he'd started. Let him work out his reasoning with Emersyn. At least she got more words than just "no."

"But you didn't shoot him," she pointed out.

"Hellspawn…"

"You didn't," she continued. "What happens to you if you don't take me with you to meet with him? Does he meet you? Does he have someone try to shoot you? Does *he* shoot you?"

Liam released an aggrieved sigh. "I don't want you to meet him."

stomach dropped as she stared at him until he nodded slowly, then she transferred that intense gaze to me.

"I hear you, Sparrow."

Her firm nod had my lips twitching, then she twisted in Liam's lap and focused on him again. If she hadn't already had his attention, that would do it. There was something utterly captivating about her ferocity. Maybe because she was so tiny. Or maybe because she seemed so fragile.

Fuck, maybe it was because we'd all kept her up on a pedestal for so long. Especially after seeing the bruises and the scars, and hearing the pain in her voice when she recounted her past. It made me want to keep a fortress around her. A fortress like we'd begun to build here, where every single one of us kept her safe.

When she pressed her forehead to Liam's and spoke in a softer tone, I turned back to the coffee to give them privacy. The fortress could never become a cage. If I did nothing else for her in this, I would damn well make sure the only one with the keys to bar those gates would be her.

Always her choice.

I gave them the time while the coffee finished. I poured three mugs before carrying them over to where the pair sat. Instead of sitting on the sofa with them, I settled on a chair and put the coffee mugs on the table.

"Thank you, Kellan," she said, shifting as though she was going to get off Liam's lap, but he just resettled her. She made a face at him, playful rebellion, but the fact she relaxed into him said she was right where she needed to be.

"Don't thank me for telling you that you may have to be in danger," I said. "Despite what Liam thinks, I'm not a fan of it."

"But you're not keeping it from me." The barest hint of a smile touched the corners of her mouth.

"No." I shook my head, even as I kept my gaze on her and

my expression placid. "No more secrets. Sometimes secrets protect, but more often than not, it's what we don't know that can hurt us."

She dipped her lashes before reaching for her mug. When she raised her eyes once again, she nodded. Liam and Jasper were the only two who didn't know as far as I was aware. It was time to change that.

"Agreed."

"Well, I'm still not a fan," Liam grumbled. "I'd rather you had no idea about the fucking king, the Royals, or any of the rest of it." Not because he wanted to lie to her but because he wanted to keep her safe.

"I could have been one," she said, glancing back at him and his expression darkened. "Adam and Ezra are… though Lainey isn't."

"Because they kept her out of it," Liam said. "She was leverage. Leverage the king probably used to keep them in line."

With that last word, he pinned me with a look.

"We'll protect her," I reminded him. "Sparrow's not a fool. She's not rushing off into anything, and she trusts us. We have to trust her."

"It's not about trust." He bit off each word, firing them as bullets.

"No," she said in a soft, almost teasing tone. "It's about thumping your chest and protecting your woman."

I damn near snorted coffee up my nose. Liam didn't fare much better, except that he hadn't been drinking coffee. She looked so smug as he gaped at her.

"You know what," he said after a beat, recovering far faster than I would have thought. "You're right. I am protecting my woman. *Our* woman. You're just going to have to live with that."

"I can do that," she replied. I lowered my coffee mug the

rest of the way. That was far too meek. Like—beyond cooperative. Liam's eyes narrowed. She took another long drink of her coffee before setting it aside and rising. "I need to go shower and change if I'm going back to your place."

Liam's shock showed in the fact he released her. Pausing next to me, she rested a hand on my shoulder. From this angle, Liam couldn't see her face.

"Are you sure it'll be okay with everyone if I don't stay here tonight?"

"Not at all, but they'll understand, Sparrow. Come back tomorrow?" Because while I wanted her to confide in Liam, and I wanted everyone on the same page, they weren't the only ones who'd missed her this week.

"I promise." Then she mock-whispered, "Even if I have to sneak out…"

"I heard that," Liam retorted, but he merely smiled at her when she grinned. Neither of us said a word as she vanished into her room. The moment she was out of sight, though, Liam focused on me. "What the fuck…? You're not telling me something."

I would neither confirm nor deny. It wasn't mine to tell him, though if Sparrow *couldn't* do it, I would if she needed the assistance.

Liam scowled, then rubbed a hand over his jaw. "Fine, you keep your secrets."

"Done bitching?"

He shook his head then leaned forward, elbows on his knees. "What do you think is going to happen if I take her to meet him?"

"No idea. You don't know, either. However, it's a discussion we all need to have. So we can better plan for it. We also need to press this issue with Freddie's friend about her mother…"

At that, Liam scoffed with a shake of his head. "Trusting Cavendish is a bad idea."

"We trust ourselves," I reminded him. "Freddie and Sparrow seem to trust him." Then before he could tackle that, I added, "And we'll make sure nothing happens to them. Now, tonight—you're going straight back to your place?"

"Why? Planning on following us?"

"One of us will," I reminded him. "In the city, we're not running alone. The road was different. She was not as easily trackable there."

Her uncle had gotten his hands on her once, that was not happening again. The fact he still had hands wasn't sitting well with me.

The guys might chafe over the restrictions, but not where Sparrow was concerned.

"Well, don't mind me if I don't invite you up, so you better bring a buddy."

I laughed at him. "I planned on it. If you decide to head out, I expect a heads-up."

Dislike filtered through his expression, but it was there and gone again. "Done."

"Don't choke on the cooperation, Liam."

He flipped me off and I chuckled. He could dislike it all he wanted, but he'd do it. We all would. Staying together was better. We used to know that.

"Kel…"

I raised my brows.

"If I can keep her out of it, I plan on it."

"I know," I said. "I don't disagree with keeping her out of it if we can…but not by lying to her."

Or by keeping secrets

"Fine, I'll just tell her she doesn't get to go."

"Good luck with that." I saluted him with my mug and he just scowled before he drained his coffee.

"I can be persuasive," he muttered. "Dick."

I shouldn't laugh at him. Not when I really didn't want her involved, either. But Liam had to accept, sooner or later, that the fierceness he'd seen in her from day one was what he was up against.

He'd get there.

Eventually.

Our girl was stubborn.

CHAPTER 6

EMERSYN

I took the time to braid my hair after the shower. The bag I'd brought with me didn't have much in the way of clean clothes leftover. Fortunately, I did have clothes here in any case. I grabbed one of Rome's hoodies to zip over my t-shirt. The leggings were warm enough and I stuffed my feet into boots.

As much as I wanted to spend time with Liam, I dreaded having to talk to him about everything. Telling Jasper had gone… well, it had gone well. Not that it was a word I wanted to associate with my uncle or my history. The quiet warning in Kellan's eyes told me I was running out of time.

I wanted to get my mother. Only getting her meant taking risks, and it also meant possibly opening us all up to exposure. With that in mind, I needed them all to know about my uncle. Liam was the only one besides Milo who didn't know.

A knock on the door pulled me around before Liam stuck

his head inside. "Damn," he rumbled with a hint of a smile. "You're already dressed."

The tease pulled a smile to my lips. "Disappointed?"

Snorting, he shook his head. "That's a trap." With a look around the room, he nodded to the bag. "Do you need it?"

"No, I still have stuff in Rome's room, right?"

"You're not gonna need clothes, Hellspawn." The heat licking those words warmed me to my core. "I just wanted to grab your stuff and head out before the other knuckleheads notice."

"You don't fool me," I told him as I grabbed my jacket. "You bitch about them, but you'd do anything for them."

"Absolutely," he agreed, sliding an arm around my waist and dragging me right to him once I was there. "And right now, I'm going to save their lives by getting out of here with you before they notice."

Laughter curled through me, but more than laughter, was also warmth and security. The muscles in his arm flexed as he tightened it around me, and they shifted in his chest when I spread my hands against him.

"I missed you," I told him. I'd missed them all so much, and if Kellan weren't right about him needing to know, I'd beg to stay here so we could all hang out tonight. "Maybe tomorrow we get all the guys together for pizza and beer and some pool?"

And I needed to dance. I needed the exercise. The time with Jasper had undoubtedly had some calisthenics. I'd definitely stretched, but it wasn't the same.

"We can do that," Liam said, cupping my chin before rolling his thumb along my lower lip. "Fuck."

"Right now?" The tease pulled a genuine laugh out of him. "I mean…"

"Don't tempt me, Hellspawn. Don't tempt me."

The invitation in his eyes to play thrilled me. "Or what?"

"Or I'll spank that gorgeous ass of yours until it's hot and pink. Then I'll fuck you until it feels good again." The way his mouth shaped each word, lingering on them almost like a caress, had my cunt clenching and my heart racing.

The thought of him spanking me should not be hot.

"Not hearing a deterrent there..." I ran my tongue over my lower lip, aware of his gaze tracking it. "I mean, I probably *should* hear one but..."

But he wouldn't hurt me. The trust swelling inside of me squeezed all my breath out. A laugh bubbled up, chasing that last bit of air and then I pressed a kiss to his throat and another to his jaw as I pushed up on my toes. I trusted these men. I trusted *Liam.*

"Good to know, Hellspawn," he said in a whispered groan before he caught my lips with his. The kiss robbed me of any air I'd managed to suck in, and I gave it up willingly. Kissing any of them was dizzying, and they all kissed so differently. Learning them, their kisses, and devouring the affection they showered on me gave me life.

A groan vibrated through me and I wasn't sure which of us released it. Finally, he dragged his head up even as I fisted his shirt.

"Time to go," he told me firmly, before clasping my hand. The wetness of his lips and the scorching heat in his eyes delighted me.

"You know my room has a bed," I offered helpfully as he all but dragged me out. Am I playing with fire? Absolutely.

"That's three." Liam all but growled the words.

Yep, that was a thrill. One I didn't intend to examine too closely. For now, I was delighted at the fact I could push him so far and he seemed to enjoy it every bit as much as I did.

Downstairs, Freddie looked up from his game and eyed us. "You're going?"

"Yes," I said, pulling from Liam's grip to give Freddie a

hug. He wrapped one arm around me and I swore I could *feel* him giving Liam the stink-eye. "It's important," I murmured to him. "He needs to know."

The stiffness in Freddie's posture eased, and he tucked his chin to my shoulder. When his hand found mine, I gripped it.

"You need me?" The offer wrapped me up in a much tighter hug.

"Always," I admitted, leaning back. "But I can do this."

Freddie studied me a minute then glanced behind me. Liam hadn't crowded into us. At Freddie's faint frown, I twisted to find Liam eyeing Bodhi, not that Bodhi seemed to be paying him much attention.

"You need me," Freddie said in a soft voice, "just call or text. I'll be there."

Turning back to him, I grinned, "Same goes for you. I'll be back tomorrow. Pizza, pool, and hanging out in the evening?"

"I can do that." He leaned in and brushed a kiss to my cheek. I let him finish before I pressed one to the corner of his mouth. It was all about degrees. He tightened his grip on my fingers even as I kept the contact light.

The swiftness of his brighter grin warmed me.

"Take care of Boo-Boo," he said to Liam. "I want her back in one piece and happy."

I laughed.

"You got it." Liam didn't take his gaze off Bodhi. "I expect the same from you, Freddie."

When I gave Freddie a questioning look, he shook his head. He didn't know what Liam's issue with Bodhi was. Then again, maybe it was just that Bodhi was a stranger to him. I wasn't that comfortable around him either, to be honest.

"See you later, Bodhi," I called.

"You got it, PPG. There gonna be beer for tomorrow night?"

"You're not invited," Liam said before I could answer, stepping right between us and cutting off my view. Right, argue about this later. "Family only."

The last two words stifled Freddie's argument, even if he squinted at Liam like he had questions. Later, I mouthed and Freddie nodded.

One more hand squeeze and it was my turn to tug Liam toward the door. In the antechamber, he paused to take my jacket and hold it up, only after I slid it on and he zipped it up did he open the door. The warehouse was even busier than when we went inside.

The number of rats was just...

"Did we get more people?" I asked, uncertain if it was even a topic to bring up here. Kellan said they'd made changes and he'd fill me in, but this was a *lot* of people. Liam eyed those who were offloading. The beeping from the loaders as they backed up, removing the pallets from the truck. There were even more already stacked in here and there were guys checking inventory sheets.

Liam shrugged. "Kel's hired kids from the neighborhood to keep them out of trouble. They aren't rats. They're employees."

Shock rippled through me. Wasn't that dangerous? Kel lifted his chin toward us and held up five fingers. Liam just snorted as he opened the passenger side door of the dark blue SUV.

Like his bike and sports car, the color was sleek and seemed almost primal. I needed a performance leotard in that shade. It would make for a great routine.

No sooner did that thought take purchase than my heart sank. Would I ever really get to perform again? The jacket and long-sleeved shirt hid the scars on my arms, but those scars were still there.

The physical therapy had helped. The exercises that Doc insisted I do, the cream he had me applying—it helped. I continued even if we didn't have formal sessions anymore. But it didn't take away the damage. Not all of it. No, my uncle and his goons had definitely done a number on me.

He probably didn't want me to ever have the excuse to leave him again…

"Hey," Liam's voice steered me back to the present and I snapped my gaze up to him. With one hand braced on the roof and the other on the door, he shielded me from the rest of the warehouse. "Where did you go?"

I shook my head. "Nowhere I need to be." Ever again. He studied me, his eyes narrowing, and I didn't have to imagine the questions or the suspicion. He wasn't hiding it.

"You can tell me anything, Hellspawn."

"Not right now?" I asked, more because we were in the warehouse, and I needed to get my head out of those memories so I could keep it together for the conversation we needed to have.

It was enough that I would have to tell him…

A muscle in his jaw ticked as he searched my gaze. All at once, he twisted and scanned the warehouse. There was no mistaking the murder his expression promised.

"It's no one here," I told him, pulling his focus back to me. The wild rage that seemed to hum under his skin was right there, plain to see. In the first couple of weeks I'd been here, that expression would probably have terrified me.

Now?

Now it just told me I was safe. Just like it had when he'd shown up at the fights. Like it had when he'd yanked me off the stage. Like it had when he'd moved in front of me at the club.

Like it had when he'd been yelling at me to not get on the damn plane…

That ventured a little too close to Uncle Bradley, so I shut that down.

"It's nothing here," I repeated. "I'll tell you—just not right now."

Time elongated as he studied me, then he blew out a long breath and nodded. "I'll be waiting for that story. Now, in you go, Hellspawn."

A whistle cut through the noise and I leaned to the side to see Vaughn and Kellan heading toward us.

I hadn't seen Mickey, but he was probably at the clinic. "Where is Rome?"

"He's fine," Liam said, his tone soothing even as he pulled out his phone and showed me a message.

ME:

Taking Hellspawn back to the apartment.

Rome responded with a middle finger.

I laughed. "He's gifted."

"Yeah, he is." The indulgence and affection wrapped around the exasperation. "He's also got a new project and won't tell anyone where it is."

Oh.

"So, if you get it out of him," Liam said and I grinned.

"Sorry, I keep the secrets you guys trust me with."

"Yeah, you do." He dropped a kiss on my lips just as Vaughn arrived and tapped him on the shoulder. "Too late, man, I'm stealing her."

"Borrowing," Vaughn told him as Liam backed off a step. "And Kel told me." He focused on me, and there was a question in those topaz eyes that boosted my confidence. Was I okay? Did I need him?

Yeah. I did. I needed him like I needed Freddie and Kel and Liam and Rome…like I needed Jasper and Mickey. I needed all of them, and every time that thought pinged through me, it was both terrifying and comforting. Because they were here and they weren't going anywhere.

They would and *had* fought for me.

I would damn well fight for them.

"I need tonight with Liam," I said as much to assure Vaughn as to apologize that I was taking off.

"Family night tomorrow," Liam said from the other side of the car. "Beer. Pool. Pizza. Our girl."

"We can do all of that," Vaughn said with a slow grin. There was no way he didn't mean to put the emphasis on the idea of all of them doing me, and holy crap… a shiver went right through me at the idea. I wasn't sure if that was fear or anticipation.

Maybe it was both.

I rose up on my tiptoes, but Vaughn didn't make me stretch. He just picked me up and then fused his mouth to mine. Wrapped up in all that strength, there was absolutely no room for terror.

The earlier darkness shuddered and fell away as Vaughn chased my tongue with his. I sighed into his mouth, sinking into him even as he cradled me. When I lifted my head, I dragged out his lower lip just a fraction and he grinned.

"I still want my new tattoo," I whispered.

"Whenever you want, wherever you want." He rubbed his hand against my back. "Now, get in the car before I change my mind and take you back inside and Liam gets butthurt."

Liam's scoff just made Vaughn grin and I laughed. "Tomorrow," I promised.

"I'll hold you to that." He winked, then set me on my feet. Glancing over the car at Liam, he said, "Look after her."

"With my life," Liam said it like a quip, but that wasn't how he meant it.

"And I'll look after him," I reminded them both because the idea of Liam dying for me wasn't romantic. It was heartbreaking.

I didn't want *any* of them to die for me.

"Yes," Liam said, his expression softening. "You already do."

"Don't you forget it." I squeezed Vaughn's arm, then slid into the car.

"One minute," Vaughn told him before he closed my door and I pulled my seatbelt on.

I waited until we were out of the warehouse, and they were following us to glance at Liam.

"How bad is it?"

CHAPTER 7

EMERSYN

*L*iam rested a hand on my thigh for the drive. At first, I thought it was just to calm my worry about the changes at the warehouse and the doubling up of our escort. Then it hit me, he just wanted to touch me, so I put my hand on his. Both the action and the thought settled me.

"Nothing bad happened while you were gone, Hellspawn," Liam said after a few minutes, his attention focused on the drive. Constantly checking everything, not letting his gaze rest in any one direction.

"It didn't feel like that." Verbalizing the apprehension from the increased activity almost felt like jumping at shadows. "I know why Kel and Vaughn are following us..."

"Yep, security." His even tone settled some of my jangling nerves. "No one is taking chances with your safety. Vaughn came so Kel had someone with him when he headed back.

We'll have someone with us tomorrow when I take you back —if I let you out of bed."

The sensual tease coiled around me. "And all the new people are because Kel is hiring?"

Liam sighed. "Yes, we—he isn't recruiting."

"You can say we," I scolded, rubbing the back of his hand gently. "You are part of the 'we'. You told me yourself that you never left them, even if that was how it had to look."

There was a touch of exasperation in his eyes when he glanced at me. "Thank you for remembering every little nuance of a conversation."

A grin stretched my lips. "Like you don't—and you're welcome." Seeing uncomfortable truths in each other had been our thing from the first moment he pointed out I was bleeding in the kitchen to when he followed me into the alley and I'd punched him for calling me princess.

Words were only words until they caused violently unpleasant associations. Everything circled back to my uncle…

His hand flexed on my thigh, reminding me not only of where I was but of who I was with.

"We're not recruiting, but we are shoring up the neighborhood. Coming at us through the people on the street? It may not be perfect, but it could work. Harder to bribe people who are already getting help, and it keeps more kids clean. Legitimate work with the Vandals feels badass, and they aren't looking to make their bones elsewhere."

"Did you make your bones?" Sometimes, the need to know everything about all of them consumed me. Making your bones sounded like something right out of a movie or a Netflix series, but it wasn't funny. If anything, I'd seen just how brutally serious this life was from my first few weeks with them.

Sliding a look at me, Liam shook his head. "Not a story you want to hear."

"Not all stories have to be pretty," I reminded him. Fuck knew the one I had to tell him wouldn't be. "You remember being in foster care with your brother, choosing to leave it, and building a life for yourself away from them—but you never truly left them."

A long sigh escaped him.

"You built a life that could support and help them. Took risks to protect them. Put your personal safety and your health on the line for them... I saw those fights, Liam. I've had you training me to fight. I thought I had some idea of your life, but I really didn't. Not until they took us."

Not until they put Rome in that ring and forced him to take that beating to prove a point.

"Hellspawn." Impatience crept through his tone as he cut another look at me before focusing on the road ahead of us. The exasperation softened the irritation in his voice.

Tracing my fingers against the back of his hand, I sighed. "I know you don't want to discuss it, but I want you to understand that I do see you and I have heard you. Every word you shared, every time you kept silent, and each time you've come for us—for me. I see you, Liam O'Connell."

When he turned his hand over and captured mine, I threaded my fingers with his.

"You're a lot more dangerous than you look, Hellspawn." The grumbled compliment made me laugh.

"Pretty sure you said that from day one."

That earned me a chuckle and eased some of the tension in his jaw. Exhaling, I squeezed his hand and stretched in the seat. I really did need to get to the studio. For a proper stretch, if nothing else.

Liam didn't pursue more conversation, so I settled for holding his hand and watching the stores and buildings flash by as we drove. The coffee shop on the corner, the dress shop on the other. A series of grocers, an antique store, and a bar that wasn't open yet. It had grown familiar, this city. I'd hardly spent time in most of those places, but they were familiar.

Familiar in a way few places had ever become. A year in Braxton Harbor, well, over a year now. A year with the Vandals. With my family. Less time with my brother, but we were getting to know each other more.

I hadn't seen Milo at the clubhouse, or Lainey. But she could have gone back again. I was the one who'd been gone for a week. I'd dig out my phone later and check in with her. Milo might very well be with Rome. When Liam turned into the parking garage for his building, anticipation and dread trailed their icy fingers up my spine.

When I shivered, he shot me a frown. "Should have told me you were cold."

"I'm fine," I told him. "Just someone walking over my grave." It was an old saying, and it spilled out of me almost reflexively.

His frown deepened into a scowl. "That's not funny."

"It's not supposed to be a joke," I told him, then stuck my tongue out at him. It was hard to fight the smile twitching the corners of my mouth as he glared. It wasn't until he needed to back into his spot that he released my hand.

Kellan and Vaughn pulled in front of us. Vaughn winked from the passenger seat, but Kellan met my gaze steadily.

"Mind if I go tell Kel bye?"

"Yes," Liam said in a droll tone, even if a wicked light danced in his eyes. "But go do it anyway."

Leaning over, I brushed a kiss to his jaw. Well, I'd intended to, but he captured my lips in a searing kiss that left me panting. "I'll be quick."

"Uh-huh," he teased. Our audience just watched with a

pair of amused grins, but it wasn't until I circled the car to the driver's side that I read the concern in Kel's eyes.

"I can do this," I assured him softly. Liam hadn't followed me, but I angled slightly to hide my mouth in case he had some secret skill like reading lips or something. So many hidden depths to these men.

"You call us if you need us, Dove," Vaughn said, but Kellan just covered my hand on the open window frame.

"We can be here when you tell him," he said, though if they were there and Liam took this badly, he wouldn't have any reason to stay. He'd just go and trust them to protect me.

"No, it's better alone. As much as I hate it, it—was better for Jasper too." Every time I told the story, it chipped away at more of Uncle Bradley's control. His web of lies and secrets wouldn't choke me anymore.

I dipped my head into the car and pressed a kiss to Kellan's lips. He held me in place for a couple of extra seconds. "Call us if you need us." It wasn't a request.

"I promise." Then I circled the car to give Vaughn a kiss goodbye too. "Tomorrow?"

"We'll take care of the plans." The smoothness of Vaughn's voice would never fail to comfort me. I could listen to him read the phone book.

Maybe I'd ask him to do that… just to check.

"Come on, Hellspawn. You can't miss them until they go."

I laughed as Vaughn flipped Liam off, but I blew them a kiss as I backed up. When Liam hooked an arm around me, I leaned into him and let him guide me inside.

The ride up in the elevator was quiet, and Liam checked his phone. I resisted the urge to peek at his screen. Not that there was much of an impulse, my stomach knotted all over again as I considered how to even broach the topic. He said nothing as he opened the door to his apartment. Once we were in, he locked the door and then leaned back against it to study me.

"My turn, Hellspawn," he said in a low voice. "How bad is it?"

Not glancing back, I curled my hands into my fists. Then forced my hands to relax as I scraped my teeth over my lower lip. I'd just told Kellan I could do this. Where had all that courage and bravado fled to?

"Maybe we make coffee first?" It was a deflection, but I didn't want to tell him. I never *wanted* to tell anyone. It would make him...

Warm hands settled on my shoulders, dislodging the weight of panic dragging me down. Closing my eyes, I fell back into him. Liam was not going to let me fall. For all his abrasive, bristling nature, he hadn't let me down.

Not even when I had given him no reason to come for me, he'd come anyway. Him. Rome. Freddie.

"Talk to me, Hellspawn," he said, his lips at my ear. "Tell me what's tying you up, because I can imagine a lot. None of which give me the target to erase the problem."

"I need to tell you something, and—I'm questioning every choice I've ever made." A coward's way out? Maybe. The very last thing I wanted to do was cause any of them pain.

When he would have turned me around, I shook my head. Instead of facing him, I rested against his chest as he wrapped his arms around me.

Closing my eyes, I took a deep breath and only after I let it out slowly did I begin to speak. "I know you stole me away to play and to fuck and to just have me to yourself. To be perfectly clear, I want all of that with you."

"But...?" he whispered the question in such a soft voice that it filled me with regret that we couldn't just fast-forward to that part.

"But there are some things you need to know. Answers to questions you've asked, and I've avoided answering."

Silence greeted my statement, but he squeezed me a little tighter and a little closer. Hooking my hand around his forearm, I leaned my head toward his shoulder and he rested his cheek against my hair.

He waited me out, letting me do this at my pace even as he offered me comfort. Tears pricked in my eyes. "I adore you," I whispered. "Even when you drive me nuts. Or maybe because you drive me mad. But…I adore you and how you love your brother and the Vandals. How you protect them, even how you antagonize them." A wet laugh escaped me. "I adore how you antagonize me."

"You didn't always," he murmured.

"No," I admitted. "I thought you were such a prick. Sometimes…I think you still are, but that's usually a choice you're making."

His soft huff of laughter was in no way a denial. "Sometimes you have to be cruel to be kind." It wasn't an apology, not that I was asking for one.

"You've been kinder to me than I deserved." Blowing out a breath, I forced the tears back. Flying took faith, and a leap. Liam wouldn't let me fall.

"You—we are a lot more alike sometimes than I want to admit." It was going to hurt to scrape through all the muck, to pull it all out. Yes, it got a little better each time. But Liam… he would have other questions, and maybe he, better than anyone else, would understand the trap I'd been adopted into.

The jaws of that steel cage that had closed around me long before I even understood what it all meant. The arenas where power was currency and everything could be bought and paid for, from silence to execution.

"The day you called me princess in that alley and I

punched you," I said, not quite gritting my teeth, even if merely giving voice to those hateful syllables ripped open a hellscape of nightmarish memories.

"You told me to never call you that," Liam said slowly, his lips near my ear. The warmth of his breath against my skin seemed to highlight just how chilled I'd grown. Tightening his arms around me, he let out a faint but unmistakable laugh. "You nearly broke my nose, so I took it pretty seriously."

"I'm not going to apologize." It was the same day Hellspawn had been born. That fragment I sorted out from the rest to hang onto.

"I don't want an apology," he chuckled. "It was fucking glorious. Pretty sure if I called you a name you didn't like right now, you could break my nose."

Grimacing, I shook my head. I never wanted to hurt him.

"I don't want to break your nose now," I said slowly, forcing my breathing to slow as I sought something else to look at, because I didn't want to imagine hurting him either.

"Not asking for an apology, Hellspawn. You never need to apologize to me. I literally just want to see you."

Liam made me crazy, but there was so much warmth in his voice and touch. Both lifted me and promised to carry me if I needed.

"How do you do that? How do you take something that should be dark and painful and filled with regrets and make it almost entertaining?"

He shrugged. "Better to laugh than cry. Better to inflict harm back on the ones who doled it out to you. I've made choices in my life, Hellspawn. Some I had no choice but to make, and others I just wanted. Somewhere along the way, I made peace with what I could control."

I knew this, I knew it from watching them. At the same time, I craved every morsel he shared.

"I wanted a better life for my brother. For the Vandals. Everything I've ever done, except for one choice, has always been about them."

Our gazes locked. Even when there was so much animosity between them, that was also clear.

"I told you that my parents would've welcomed Rome with open arms, and they wanted to. Mom—she tried more than once with him, but Rome didn't want this life, though. I did."

Rome had wanted Liam to have that. The love between them was so visceral it made me ache.

"This wasn't the life he wanted. He didn't want to leave the guys. He's never wanted much."

Except he'd wanted…

"Exactly," he said with a slow nod. "You are the one thing that he wanted and the one thing I refused to take. Didn't matter how much I wanted you, too."

"I'm very glad that we got through to you then." Thank you, Rome, for seeing it too. "I don't know if you've noticed, but I can be pretty stubborn too."

"No shit." Exasperation ballooned in those words and we both laughed. Oh, I'd needed that. Then he sobered. "Rip the Band-Aid off, Hellspawn. Tell me what you need me to know. You can tell me anything, abso-fucking-lutely anything."

"You know, I don't remember the group home or Milo—when I was a baby. I didn't know a life before the one I have." I spoke slowly, because while he said rip it off, I needed to ease my way into this. "Mom and Dad—they were my parents. They were always there. They cared about me. I mean, Mom cared. I think Dad did. I remember him caring."

It was weird. Dad and I didn't talk that much. Cards on birthdays. Always a present. Occasionally a call. Dinner when everyone was together. But did we have any real moments?

"Although the more I think about it, I don't know how much Dad was there. I feel like he was." Lately, I'd begun to question what I actually remembered about those relationships and what I'd manufactured to fill in the gaps.

"For as long as I can remember," I told him as I dug my fingers into his arm. "My uncle has always called me Princess. His princess. My darling sweet princess."

Every single appellation added to the sour taste in my mouth.

"I don't think he ever called me Emersyn. Not so I would remember it. I was his princess. The perfect princess. His—" I shuddered. I could do this. I needed to do this. Liam deserved to know.

I found his gaze fixed on me in the reflection from one of the photos on the wall. The glass wasn't perfectly clear, but clear enough for me to see the shadows of his eyes. Locking onto the view, onto him, I dug in for that courage.

"The first time that I really remember him praising me as his perfect princess was a day that he took me into his room so he could change my outfit into a frilly, lacy dress he'd gotten for me."

He'd taken his time changing me. With each layer he removed, he always petted and praised me. Then he repeated it when he dressed me up.

"Looking back, I understand that he was trying to groom me. He wanted to make me comfortable with his touch, to make it natural, even when I didn't want it. Maybe especially when I didn't. He always wanted to dress me up. There were always new things to wear, new outfits… nothing but the best for his princess."

Tears burned in my eyes, but I blinked them back. "When you called me princess in that alley, so soon after I'd just seen him, all I could hear was his voice and feel his touch, and I—"

"Lashed out," Liam said warily. "You didn't want to feel him anywhere near you, real or imagined."

"No," I exhaled that syllable and let out another shudder. "I hate how I feel when he calls me that. It reminds me of every single time he pushed his fingers into me, or pinched my nipples, or stroked my ass."

It was like lancing a pustulant wound, it all spilled out of me.

"He was content with petting and fingers... until I was ten, and then on my birthday, he replaced the petting with his mouth and his fingers with his dick." The description, distasteful as it was, came the closest to just the facts that I'd ever managed.

Liam stiffened, and I swore I could hear the rage crackling to life around him. If we were in some movie, the air would begin to burn and the wind would blow. Hell, we'd probably blow out the glass from all the windows.

"Why didn't you tell anyone?" The moment he asked the question, he stiffened again. The regret was there, visible in the unshadowed portions of his face. The reflection in the window gave me a path into his soul. "Because he had money and influence. Even if someone believed you...god-fucking-dammit."

Not having to explain that part helped more than Liam could ever understand. I'd seen the questions in others' eyes. Heard the dismissals uttered in contempt when the news reported stories of family molestation or rape.

"She must have liked it if she never said anything."

"He's such a nice guy. I have a hard time imagining him doing anything like that. Think she's just trying to get even?"

"Maybe she asked for it..."

"For a long time," I admitted. "I had no idea I could fight

him or say no. I ran away, trying to put distance between us. Only he always made me thank him for letting me tour and for…and for all the other gifts he gave me."

That burn of bile was back, though I didn't dare look away from Liam's gaze or the fire burning in his eyes. "When you called me princess, all I heard were all those things. It ripped me up…I *hated* it. I hate him. I never want to be that girl, trapped in her tower, where her uncle molests and rapes her whenever he feels like it. Worse, the tower isn't locked and bolted by real gates or doors but by money, influence, and power. By controlling the narrative and the very real knowledge that the only people I ever told…who tried to help me for real? Those people died."

How he always knew, I never understood.

"That would only lead to getting me punished."

"He's why you're so resistant to anal," Liam said slowly, the heartbreak right there in his voice.

"He punished me with it. He said someday I would like it. However, I never liked anything he did to me…even when he made me orgasm, it was always…" I shuddered, then swiped at the tears rolling down my face. "When you bought me all those clothes and wanted to dress me up, when you called me princess…it wasn't you I hated, Liam."

"Hellspawn," he said with a sigh.

"No, it was never you. It was the matrons at the balls, the mothers of the other society girls, and even the fucking nannies of the kids who could have been my friends if any of them were good enough." Disgust curled through me. "But none were. Not even Lainey. We met when we were five, at this really fancy boarding school. I was so happy to go there, to have a roommate, a real friend…then he changed it, so we weren't roommates.

"No, I was to be on my own. His *princess*," I spit out that last word, "never needed to share. Never needed or wanted for anything…and all anyone ever saw was my doting uncle. The man who indulged all my whims, wasn't I the lucky, lucky girl?"

I bit my lip, trying to halt the tears, but they clogged everything… my throat, my mouth, my nose, and burned where they escaped from my eyes.

"He was my personal jailer, and society handed him the key to burning my freedom and lauded him for my pain."

Every single time I'd cut myself open to scrape out the infection of my poisonous past, it bled a little more freely and came a little easier. Liam definitely didn't let me fall, his arms went to stone as I spread out all the dirty details from my earliest memories.

One more piece. One more piece. "He has been the architect of my whole life…and he always framed everything around me being his princess, his heir, his perfect Sharpe… and no one was good enough for me. That was why I went after Eric. I wanted to take something back…but eighteen months ago? Maybe a little longer…I found out I was pregnant.

"I panicked. Called Lainey…"

"She helped," Liam said in a dark voice.

"She didn't hesitate. Helped me hide it under another name. He still doesn't know. I didn't want him to ever know."

I kept talking, my throat as raw as my soul by the time we got to the weeks before they took me, to the days before Uncle Bradley put me in Pinetree.

His chest rumbled when I discussed the guards, the injuries…and he shifted his grip to my forearms where he could rub his thumbs against the scars.

Then… I was done.

"Now I'm here," I said. "I'm never going back to him."

"No, Hellspawn," Liam said in a rock-steady voice. "You're not. In fact, you never have to think about him again."

I wish that last part were true. "I still have to get my mother…"

"We will," he promised.

I sagged like someone had cut my strings, and I couldn't even keep my head up.

"I only have one question," Liam asked in a tone that betrayed nothing and at the same time, wrapped me up in the same strength his arms offered.

"That is?"

"Do you have a preference for how we get your pound of flesh? Or can I feed him to a woodchipper?" He might as well have been asking me whether I wanted whip cream on my coffee or not, and I couldn't help it.

I laughed.

I laughed and I laughed until tears were running down my cheeks.

Then I laughed some more.

When Liam turned me around, I went this time and wrapped my arms around his neck as he picked me up. Somewhere along the way, the laughter turned to sobs, but he didn't let me go.

And he never let me fall.

CHAPTER 8

LIAM

The apartment was quiet save for Hellspawn's soft, even breaths. When her laughter gave way to tears, I swore it sounded like something inside her had just collapsed and given way. Kellan's and Vaughn's watchfulness suddenly made a lot more sense. So did Freddie's.

They knew. If I had to bet, Rome knew too. So, was I the last to learn this dark, twisted, and ugly secret? Probably. Milo *definitely* didn't know because he hadn't lost his fucking mind.

Anger rolled through my system like I was doing shots of hard whiskey. It heated my blood about the same. On some level, I'd known it was bad. It had to be. Adam's pure loathing for her uncle. The fact the son of a bitch had her committed *after* his guards tortured her.

I'd *known* it was awful. Peering down, I studied her. Even in sleep, she held onto that ethereal quality that was at such odds with her earthy passions and fiery temperament. At the same time, there was no mistaking the tear stains on her face. Redness lined her eyes, leaving them puffy.

Carrying all that misery alone for most of her life? All of it? How the fuck had she *ever* learned to trust us? That fucker wielded his money and influence like weapons, chaining her up and punishing her while the rest of the world wanted to shake his hand.

I wanted to tear the son of a bitch apart. I'd wanted to kill him after he put her in that fucking hospital. Now, I wanted him to suffer. All I had to do was track him down, then disembowel him to start. Needed to inflict upon him every fucking injury he'd ever done to her, real or imagined.

The fact I could imagine a lot didn't help. *Goddammit, Hellspawn. Why didn't you tell me sooner? Before he went into hiding? We could be fileting him right now.*

That, however, was not about her. It was about my need to wreak havoc on him and every thought he'd ever had. I couldn't even be angry with her 'cause no sooner did that objection strike a match inside of me, ready to burn down the fucking world, then I put it out.

She didn't owe me anything. She'd pulled herself inside out to tell me, and told me everything I had to know. She'd told us all, at different times and in different ways…she'd tried to tell us.

Hating being called princess.

Not wanting anything to do with her family.

The fear—and it *had* been fear when she'd seen him at the hotel. Fuck me. I'd seen it and then—let it go. Let *her* distract me.

I stroked my fingers through her hair, carefully brushing the tendrils away from her face. She'd braided it before we left the clubhouse, but it was pulling out of the braid. It wrecked me how much suffering had been in her voice, especially when she'd tried to lay it out.

No, as much as I wanted to be on the way to gutting the asshole right now, I wouldn't leave her. Not because he didn't deserve it, but because she deserved to say how.

She deserved to make the calls on this. Didn't change my mind about wanting to do it, but then, the other guys were also waiting. That told me there was a plan.

A familiar alarm beeped on my phone, the pattern alerting me to who was opening the door when the locks disengaged.

I glanced over my shoulder and met the gaze of my other half. He glimpsed at me, then down, as if he could see her through the sofa. I nodded once. Closing the door quietly, Rome made his way into the room. Bracing his hands on the back of the couch, he looked down at her.

"She told you." It wasn't a question

"You already knew." Also not a question. He didn't have to answer. "When?" That one I would like an answer for.

"After we got back from Pinetree."

The first couple of nights when they were locked away in Rome's room. I sighed.

"It wasn't my secret."

"I know it wasn't—it isn't." I shook my head, then curled one of the wisps of hair around my finger. Adam hated her uncle. Really hated him.

Had he known?

No sooner had that idea occurred to me than I discarded it. Adam wanted to protect her from her family. Protect Lainey. Protect Emersyn. No—whatever he knew about Bradley Sharpe was bad, but this wasn't it.

Adam seemed to genuinely like my hellspawn. Liked her enough to ask her to marry him so he could shield her with his name. Not that I was ever going to let him do that. We'd give her our name, and shield her that way.

Or give her Milo's—

Fuck. My. Life.

Milo.

I scrubbed a hand over my face as I fought for stillness. I wouldn't disturb her for anything. It was still early afternoon, even if it felt like midnight.

"What do you need?"

I'd almost forgotten Rome was there.

"A time machine." I was only kidding a little.

"I'll make you coffee." He rested his hand on my shoulder and I glanced up at him. It didn't take much to read the understanding in his eyes. We would deal with this like we had everything else.

Together.

"Make one for her too."

I hesitated. The sound of the frother might wake her up. Maybe.

Should I say no to the coffee? On the one hand, I might want hard liquor more than coffee. No, I definitely preferred the idea of a shot of whiskey or four. That was more than enough reason to lean on the coffee.

I wanted a drink and I wanted to see her eyes. To see if the shadows had retreated. I wanted to reassure her—

I want her.

That was the final answer in every column. "Is it selfish to want to wake her up?" The question slipped out, a thief walking stealthily out from behind the cage where I should have locked it up instead.

"Yes," Rome answered without hesitation.

"Don't soften it for me or anything." The tease came far more easily. Rome squeezed my shoulder.

"I'm selfish with her too."

No, he wasn't. I looked back up to find him waiting. He'd wait until she woke on her own if I let him.

"Make the coffee," I said. "Please. I'm going to wake her up."

Because I truly did need to know she was okay.

"Okay."

Coolness replaced the space where Rome had stood. The sound of the grinder seemed far louder in the silence left in his wake. A grin pulled at my lips and I was still smiling when she shifted against me, and her eyes fluttered open.

I settled my own ragged feelings by continuing to stroke her hair. If I hadn't been watching her so closely, I might have missed the flutter of fear in her expression. Her pupils dilated, then she focused on me. All at once, her expression relaxed and a smile graced her lips.

"Hi," she whispered in a rough voice, left a little hoarse from her earlier crying. "You're still here."

"Did you honestly think I'd leave you?" Irritation crept through me that she'd been let down so fucking much in her life that loyalty surprised her.

"No…maybe…" She grimaced. "I just—I didn't mean to go to sleep, and I know you were angry. I was supposed to stay awake and…"

"Keep me from doing something crazy? Like hunt down the son of a bitch who needs to suffer?" I lifted my eyebrows. As gutted as I was over her life story, I wasn't remotely angry with her. "First, not upset with you at all. Angry about what has been done to you? Fuck yes, I'm pissed about that. But I am not furious with *you* at all. I'm in fucking awe of you." Abrasive and a little crude? Yeah, but this was my hellspawn and she needed that flat honesty.

"And second?"

"Hunting that motherfucker down would mean I had to leave you to do it, and I'm not leaving *you*. As for the rest, you get to make the call on the when, and the how."

Fresh astonishment flickered in her eyes, and then the

grinder in the kitchen went off again. A jerk of surprise went through her. While she sat up, she didn't leave the sofa or me but looked toward the kitchen.

"Rome's here," I said, running my knuckles down her arm. I felt, more than saw, the tension bleed out of her as she sagged.

Giving in to the urge to keep her close, I looped an arm around her and pulled her into my lap. "He's making coffee for us to make us feel better," I added a kiss to just behind her ear after I murmured the words. She pressed closer and then nuzzled her nose to my throat.

"He's taking care of us." It didn't shock her. My mirror had been focused on her from long before Jasper stole her away—

"Son of a bitch," I muttered. Curiosity flickered through her expression as she leaned back to look up at me. "I'm going to have to thank Jasper." It came out much more petulant than I could admit, but it was there.

Emersyn shot me a puzzled look, but then tracked her gaze higher. I smelled the coffee before Rome answered, "For kidnapping you. He owes Jasper for that."

He passed her coffee to her and when she shifted on my lap to lean up and brush a kiss to him in thanks, I got to enjoy the slow grind against my dick.

Yeah, the world needed burning down, and I had to thank Jasper. Both hard facts in my existence. I would have to be dead to not notice her or appreciate the pressure she exerted on my whole being just by existing.

Hands wrapped around her coffee, she smiled at me. "I told him thank you too."

The corners of her mouth twitched even as a grin dragged out of me. We stared at each other for a timeless moment, then I laughed.

Her soft laughter accompanied mine, and I cupped her

nape as we laughed together. Thankfully, tears didn't erupt from her, but I swore my eyes burned. Eventually, we caught our breath and I lifted my coffee to take a sip as she shifted her attention to Rome, who'd come to sit on the sofa with us.

"I don't need to thank Jasper," Rome told us bluntly. "I already did."

It set both of us off laughing again. I balanced her coffee when she reached over to kiss him, and it satisfied something pretty fucking primitive inside of me to see the pair of them together.

The day I came back to find them naked and in his bed, clearly having already fucked, I'd been both delighted for my brother and a little envious of him. I never wanted to take his place. Hell, I wasn't going to take anything at all.

Then he told me I was stupid and she reached for me as often as she did him. I could savor their closeness and be grateful for it. When she leaned back, her smile a little wilder and her eyes holding a hint of frenzy, I let go of her coffee so she could sip.

"Liam..."

"Hmm?" I focused on her. Honestly, I was pretty damn happy just sitting here with them right now. Happy was— happy was an odd emotion.

"I know this wasn't what you had in mind when you told me I was coming back here."

"Doesn't matter," I told her. "I don't care if we're fucking, fighting, or just being funny—time with you is worth it."

She opened her mouth then closed it again before she glanced at Rome.

"I don't want to fight," he told her. "Fucking is fine, though."

There he went being funny. She grinned, and it didn't take much to set her off giggling again. I didn't mind the fighting so much. She was hot as hell when she was angry.

"We're taking you on our date this weekend," I told her. "The three of us."

"The one we were—" she began, and Rome shot me a look. Really? Did I want to do that again?

"Yes," I answered both of them. "I do. I'll up the security, because precautions are good. The club reopens next week and I thought you might want to go, but this weekend is for the three of us. For what we had planned."

Teeth scraping over her lower lip, she glanced from me to Rome then back again. "Yes."

"Not even going to ask me what we have planned?" Her trust was a gift I refused to squander.

"Nope. I get to be with the both of you. I get to protect you while you protect me."

I trailed a finger down her forehead to her nose and then to her lips. "Are you protecting us from any other horror stories in your past? Because if you are, please don't. Just give us their names."

"And how much they need to hurt," Rome said, matching me beat-for-beat.

"You'd go after them for me, wouldn't you?"

"In a heartbeat," I swore to her. "Anyone and everyone who has ever hurt you. Just give us names, Hellspawn."

She gave the most delicate of shudders then glanced down at her coffee before looking up at me. The intensity in that gaze warned me before she said whatever had just occurred to her.

"Then let me help you with the king."

Yeah. That.

"Let me protect you, too."

"Us," Rome corrected and she flashed him a grin. Suck up.

"Us," she agreed with a nod and I sighed.

"*If* I can't find a reasonable alternative," I offered. "*Then* we'll discuss it." That was as far as I was willing to go.

"You have to discuss the alternative with us, so we know what's happening," she said after a long pause. "And we can weigh in."

"*Before* you move," Rome added and I glared at him, but he just met my heated glare with a bland look.

"Fine," I conceded. "Before I do anything, we'll discuss it, but I will devise a plan."

"Okay," she said, her tone a bit too playful to be meek, and I groaned. "Is this the part where you threaten to spank me again?"

I eyed her. "To be decided."

"Then I look forward to what you decide," she teased for real and Rome chuckled. Fine, let them laugh at me. Still… the fact I'd threatened her with a spanking before I understood the full weight of her history would bother me—except she was laughing.

Laughing. Living. Thriving.

Let them laugh. I took another long drink of my coffee. Tonight—tonight was just going to be about looking after her. Tomorrow, I'd put more people on looking for her uncle.

CHAPTER 9

KELLAN

*A*ttention split between the log on the computer screen and the book log from the most recent series of shipments, I took a sip of coffee.

"One hour," Freddie said as he sailed into the kitchen. "Bodhi and I are gonna pick up the pizza order shortly. Anything special you want?"

"Just one thing," I said, but even as I focused on him, Freddie stiffened a fraction. Pivoting, he faced me. "How are you doing?"

I hadn't missed how much time he was spending with *Bodhi*. Liam had made his feelings on the guy clear. Jasper seemed to be reacting with an uncharacteristic amount of caution and reserve. That told me more than anything he wasn't certain what to make of the man.

Doc and Milo didn't disguise their distrust but paired it with a certain measure of observation. They would let him hang himself. Vaughn and Rome were harder to read. They were far more neutral on the subject.

Despite our recent alliance with Liam's "friends" from school, I didn't fully trust Adam Reed or Ezra Graham. That said, I didn't mistrust them either. Not even Sparrow's friend Lainey had earned my complete trust. Skepticism was healthy.

Skepticism kept at least one of us back to see the whole field. To prepare in case a real threat came, all dressed up like a friend. Not at all unusual to us. Truth is, it was probably more common for us than should be comfortable.

Then again, go with what you know.

Bodhi—Bodhi hadn't earned my trust. He also hadn't earned my distrust. So, keeping him at arm's length while I observed protected my brothers and Sparrow.

Freddie hesitated, his hand on the door to the fridge. "What do you mean?" Maybe he understood just how long a pause it had been between my question and his answer, because he scowled.

Lifting the coffee cup, I took a drink and waited him out. Putting Freddie in a corner was about as effective as putting Emersyn in one. They had no reason to *not* come out swinging.

Someday… Someday they would heal enough, both of them. Then they would know that there were no corners where the Vandals were. Freddie was getting there, better than he had in years. Healing took a lot, and he was good for Sparrow and she for him.

"I want to say I'm great," Freddie admitted finally, his tone gruff, but the statement ended on a sigh as he popped open a can of soda before leaning back against the closed fridge. "I want to say everything is great. It's good. Better in some ways than it has been…"

He took a long drink from the can, his gaze a thousand

miles away. With a little shake of his head, he focused on me again.

"The problem is—I feel like the other shoe is going to drop. I don't know if that is paranoia or if something is really wrong. The last few months have had some serious downs but—also ups. You know?" He grimaced.

"Yes." I absolutely did.

"Now, her mom." Another long drink followed that very pregnant statement.

"Has she talked to you about her?" What little she'd said to me told me we were getting her out of that facility one way or another. What we did with her later would very much depend on how much she knew about what her brother-in-law had been doing with Emersyn.

"Not too much." Glancing down at his can, he seemed to chew on the words he didn't say. "A part of me says let her rot. She should have protected Boo-Boo, and she didn't."

I couldn't fault that logic.

"But Boo-Boo wants us to get her."

"So maybe she doesn't blame her." It wasn't a question. To be frank, it wasn't even speculation. We didn't know what the women knew or didn't.

"Boo-Boo doesn't have to blame her," Freddie said slowly, drawing out each word. "But I can. They *adopted* her because they *wanted* a kid, right? Why do that and then not protect her?"

"That's the ten-million-dollar question, Freddie." While we were all angry for her, furious that she'd suffered, and hated it—Freddie was going to feel this on a different level. It opened up old wounds, wounds I didn't think had been adequately cleaned out. "And it is one we will get answers to. We *will* protect her."

When he set the can of soda down abruptly and doubled over, I didn't jerk upwards or cross to him. Hands on his thighs, Freddie sucked in a deep breath, then another. I could almost hear him counting.

Cutting his gaze up, he fixed it on me. "I *hate* that it happened to her."

I hate that it happened to both of them.

"Never again." It didn't have to be a promise. It was fact. It would never happen to either of them again. I held his gaze, trusting him to read it in my expression. Freddie rarely opened that door to let me look after him. Jasper was just as likely to kick it down, so I could keep my distance, and take the long view.

"Do you believe me?" I asked finally.

He nodded as he straightened. "I do." Those two words were almost a whisper, but he didn't need to shout them. "Thank you." Another long breath and the dark clouds in his expression parted and a cocky grin tipped the corners of his mouth. "You're scary good at this shit, Kel."

"Gotta earn the paycheck," I retorted. A sound from the front indicated the door locks were disengaging had me checking my watch. "Go ahead and order the pizzas. Need cash?"

"I got it."

At my arched brows, he smirked.

"I got it. Bodhi and I have been betting on pool. He loses more than he wins."

Huh.

Halfway out the door with his soda in hand, Freddie flashed a wider grin. "Sometimes people feeling sorry for me is profitable."

"Get out of here," I said, laughing. He winked and took off with a wave.

"Boo-Boo," Freddie said with delight he didn't have to manufacture. She lifted the mood here with her presence alone. The murmur of conversations beyond told me that she'd returned with the twins.

Good, they hadn't called for an escort, so that meant they were both still with her. Milo hadn't said much when he got back after dropping Rome off. Nor had he said much about Lainey. His absences were growing more frequent and his focus more distant.

Glancing down at the books, I pulled out my phone. There was a lot we were juggling, but we all had resources. I sent a message to Doc. He was at the clinic, but I'd extended the invitation to join us this evening and he'd already said he would be here.

ME:

Think you can have your friends look into Bodhi?

DOC:

Problems?

ME:

Want to avoid any. Phillip Cavendish is the legal name.

DOC:

I'll take care of it. Need anything when I head that way?

I considered the question as the volume beyond climbed, and then Sparrow was in the doorway. Her eyes were a little red, hints of her crying apparent in the shininess of her nose.

ME:

Beer? If you have time. Don't be late.
Sparrow wants it to be a family affair.

I shut off the screen before he answered and slid the

phone away as I stood. She crossed right to me and I closed my arms around her.

"All good?" I asked, keeping my voice pitched low as I cradled her.

"Yes," she said at the end of a long sigh. Lifting her head, she glanced up at me. "I told him."

"There are no reports of wholesale slaughter, so I won't ask if it went well." The dry remark pulled a smile from her. Honestly, I hadn't expected anything less. One, he'd never leave her and two, Rome went over as well. His twin and Emersyn were the two people Liam cared about most on the planet. "How are *you*?"

"Better than I expected," she said, leaning back and smoothing her hands down my shirt. "It's never easy to say it, but…it's getting easier to get it out. Like it doesn't choke me anymore."

Her voice was a little rough. There was no mistaking the sound of tears or the shiver as she pressed closer. Tightening my arms around her, I said, "We can call tonight off and keep it quiet—"

"Don't you dare." A fierce light filled her eyes. "Please don't. I want tonight with all of you. Pizza. Pool. Maybe some alcohol…I just want to be with my family."

Tucking a finger under her chin, I held her gaze. "You can have anything you want. But if it gets tough at any point or if you need a break, just say so."

"I don't want to—"

"You're not going to upset anyone, Dove," Vaughn assured her from the doorway. I hadn't noticed his arrival and when I flicked my gaze to the hall, he shook his head. "It'll upset us more if you hurt yourself."

She bumped her forehead against my chest gently, almost like miming she was knocking her head. "I'm—I'm doing better than that. Really, I know I'm a little weepy right now, but Rome and Liam were great." She stole a look up at me and then over her shoulder at Vaughn. "They took good care of me and we watched movies and laughed some too."

Good.

"But?" Vaughn prompted.

"Bad dreams," she admitted. "It was hard to sleep. Harder than I thought it would be, and I was remembering bits and pieces of things that I'd forgotten."

"Do you need to talk about it?" I wouldn't push her. Not right now.

She chewed her lower lip as she pulled back so she could twist to see Vaughn and include him in the convo. But she didn't leave me. Instead she just leaned back against my chest and I rubbed my cheek against her hair.

"Not yet," she said. "I want to make better memories tonight. Milo is gonna be here, right?"

That made sense. She was worried about him. "No one will tell him." It wasn't a promise I made lightly or out of turn. None of us would tell Milo. *If* and *when* she was ready, we would support her. "It's not a decision you need to make now…"

"Or ever," Vaughn added. He didn't close the distance. Rather he kept a sharp eye on the hall, ensuring no one overheard.

She sighed. "I don't know how realistic that is. Especially when we're discussing getting my mother."

"Realistic or not, it will be your call." We wouldn't let anyone else make it for her. Vaughn nodded once.

Arms folded, he gave her a firm look. Their relationship had been the first one to truly bloom after we brought her here. In some ways, she'd trusted him before she'd trusted the rest of us, and to be fair, I'd needed to earn her trust back.

"What do you want?" The question was a good one. "I

know you said *better* memories. But what do you want? Today? Tomorrow? Next week?"

"I want our family," she answered without hesitation or pause. "I want all of us safe. I want—" She exhaled a long breath. "I want to strip every scar of fear he's left on me."

We'd been working on that.

"I want…I want all of you."

"So, nothing big then," Vaughn said slowly, the corner of his mouth curving up, and my sparrow let out a real laugh. "I mean, I thought you were going to give us a challenge."

"Getting my mom out might be a challenge."

"Maybe," I said. "Still, I've found that when we all work together, there's very little we can't accomplish."

Head tilting back, she looked up at me. "What do you guys want?"

"I have what I want right here," I told her. Milo was home. He was healing. Sparrow was with us. She was healing. Mickey and Liam were back where they belonged.

"For the most part," Vaughn agreed, and I frowned, but his slow smile said trust me.

"What part is missing?" she asked.

"The part where you ditch Kel and come over here for a hug."

Laughter spilled out of her and when she tapped my hands gently, I let her go and Vaughn scooped her up.

"Ass," I said, not remotely annoyed and he grinned.

With a glance at my watch and then the books, I made an executive decision. "Family night starts now…"

"Dove," Vaughn said in the most dramatic of voices. "You've done it. You've gotten Kel to relax."

I flipped him off but just stacked the books for finishing the next day and carried them up to my room. The twins were already at the pool table, and I paused to check on Liam.

"You good?"

He nodded. "We talking later?"

It was my turn to nod. "Family night first." Then I glanced back to where Vaughn kept Sparrow in the hall. "Everything else can wait a few hours…but then we plan."

"I'm in."

"Not a doubt in my mind."

Rome didn't say anything as he lined up his shot. He didn't have to. It was Emersyn.

We were all in.

CHAPTER 10

VAUGHN

"Be back with our girl by eight," Kellan informed me like I was gonna keep her out all night. Not that the idea hadn't occurred to me.

Leaning over me, Dove grinned at Kellan. "What happens if we're late? Do I get to spank Vaughn?"

"Hey," I said, then grinned. "You know…"

"Nope," Kellan said before I could even finish the thought. "Keep that thought to yourself."

I shot a look at Dove and her playful grin. The red rimming her eyes had faded, as had some of the shininess on her nose. Telling any of us her horror story wasn't easy.

Liam hadn't taken his gaze off her all night, only covering when she looked at him directly. Jasper had tracked the behavior, and so had Kel. It was hard to miss. The only one who might not have been aware *was* Dove. Even then, I didn't think she was oblivious.

Fuck.

Shaking the turbulence of those thoughts off, I jerked a thumb at Kel. "In or out, but Dove and I have a date."

He chuckled, then knocked on the roof before heading back to his car. Rome slid into the car with him, and I nodded. Kel had to go to the shop for a couple of hours so Rome would hang with him.

The faint roll of his eyes amused me, but it was Emersyn who laughed. "No one runs alone," she said with a grin, and I winked at her.

"Exactly. Kel needs to have his delicate ass protected too."

That earned me another giggle as the warehouse door rolled upwards and I accelerated out. A genuine one. She wasn't one who giggled often. I loved the sound of it.

"Something amusing you, Dove?"

"I'm imagining me spanking you," she admitted and a flush pinkened her face. Amusement and desire rippled through me. I enjoyed both too much to examine either reaction.

"Really?"

"Yeah," she said, covering her mouth with her hands and sneaking a look at me. "Not sure whether I should be embarrassed about admitting it."

"What are the other options?" Because now I was curious. Mainly because she didn't sound that uncomfortable about it.

"Entertained?" Was she telling me or asking?

I glanced at her, eyebrows raised.

"Turned on?"

Grinning, I focused on the drive. "Tell you what, I'll bare my ass for you later, and you can tell me what it feels like."

Pure laughter spilled out of her all over again and when she reached out a hand to cover mine on the gear shift, I opened my fingers so she could slot hers through.

"Vaughn?"

"Yes, Dove?" Amusement filled me when I caught Kel's expression in the rearview mirror. Whatever conversation he was having with Rome, Rome wasn't listening.

Rome was going to be Rome.

"Thank you."

That pulled all of my attention back to the car. "For what?"

"For you. Just… from the beginning, you've been in my corner and, yes, I know everyone was *now*, but then…"

"Well, I'm more in touch with my feelings than they are." The words rolled out readily. "I also like being your friend."

Her snort of laughter didn't hold a single note of derision. "Rome's in touch with his feelings."

"Rome has no filters," I corrected. "There's a difference. But I will concede that he is definitely in touch with his feelings."

"We're all a little fucked up in our own ways," she murmured.

Couldn't agree with that more if I tried. "All our broken bits make us unique. The chips, the dents, and the scars…"

She glanced down at her arms. "I hated these for a while."

"I get that. I hate anything that's happened to you without your consent." We danced around the subject sometimes, but other times? Other times she needed to hear the words. "How do you feel about them now?"

The shop wasn't that far from the warehouse, but Kel stayed with us until I pulled into a slip right in front of the shop. Usually, I parked in the back. But I had a rat working the street this week, keeping an eye on the vehicles.

"Wait for me?"

She nodded as I turned off the car and slid out of the driver's seat. Even with Kel parking right behind us with his hazards on, I still scanned the street before I circled around and opened her door.

With one hand in mine, she blew a kiss toward Rome and Kel. They both lifted their chins, and I chuckled as I waved before I scanned the street again.

There he was.

The rat glanced up from where he was playing his guitar, the case opened on the ground. I glanced at my car when he made eye contact, and he nodded. The area was a popular night spot for a lot of people with the upstairs bars. A street musician didn't get special notice.

With that dealt with, I got her off the street. Music thumped through the speakers. Lauren glanced over from where she stood behind the register.

She had the phone to her ear as she doodled something on the scratchpad. "If it's just a black ink tattoo smaller than two inches, you can usually just walk-in for that. If you want a particular artist, you'll have to—"

She rolled her eyes as she flashed a grin at us.

Nudging Dove down the hall, I snorted when Lauren drawled, "I'll be happy to explain it if you let me finish."

Customers were fun. Sometimes. When we got to my station, I unlocked the door and let her in. There hadn't been any customers waiting and I wasn't taking any right now. The only person I planned on inking today was the woman who came in with me, so I didn't leave the door open.

Once we were inside and I locked it, Dove settled in the chair and studied me.

"Need anything to drink before we get started?"

She shook her head. "No. I didn't answer your other question."

"I know," I told her as I started setting up. "You don't have to…"

"I want to, but…" She frowned and her gaze drifted to the art on the wall. I had a whole wall of photos. Some of my favorite pieces were up there. I flicked a look over the wall before returning to getting the ink loaded and the right size needles on the pen before I opened a drawer to pull out some papers.

Rome and I were still working on the design for her arms, but I had penciled a few sketches for her to look at. I turned up the music in my room, choosing a station that played some of her favorites.

That done, I refocused on her.

"I don't think I'll ever *like* them," she said finally, the sadness in her eyes pulling at me. "Mickey reminds me that scars are signs that I survived…" She looked back at her arms. "These are probably the most obvious scars, but… I have others."

Having seen them, I didn't need her to explain them.

She exhaled, scooting forward on the seat. "Every time I look at these though, I remember him. Before…"

Fuck, I hated watching her struggle for the words while wading through the memories and the feelings they elicited. As much as I wanted to wade into those memories and wage war for her, I couldn't. Covering one of her hands with mine, I gave it a light squeeze.

The corners of her mouth flickered upward. "I'm okay," she promised. "Just—it feels like I have to fight these memories to have my say. I don't *want* him to have this power anymore and for so long…"

"You couldn't tell anyone without endangering them." I knew that.

She blew out a breath. "I *hate* that he's still in my head."

"Poison…takes time to drain. More, you've let some of those wounds scar over." Before she could voice the objection flaring in her eyes, I added, "You had to let them scar

95

over to survive, Dove. The more you've shared, the more I see it. You had no choices before. Or am I wrong?"

I despised the pain clouding her eyes. It shredded me. She wasn't asking for comfort at the moment, however. She was asking for help.

We would give her anything she wanted, including taking apart the son of a bitch who locked her in the cage of her battered and bruised soul, leaving her to try and breathe because the only escape was through and risking others.

A risk she refused to take until Jasper took the whole issue out of her hands. He fucking stole her and I got to help.

My only regret was that son of a bitch Eric managed to inflict new physical wounds before we got her away. But he was dead, and we were here. May he burn in hell.

"I hate that he—that *Bradley* could do that to me. I never knew a life where he didn't control everything. I told myself performing in the troupe—it was my escape. It was, except…"

Every word pulled through gritted teeth dug at me. I wanted to make it easier for her. You know, fuck that, I wanted to fight the battle for her. I couldn't do that, unfortunately.

I could be here though. Back her play, give her support, and fuck up anyone who tried to take that power from her again.

We wouldn't be doing it. Kel had the right of that; let her come to us. Let her ask us for what she needed. Close the circle around her.

Vandals protected their own.

She was a Vandal every bit as much as we were and she'd bled way too much.

"You know," she continued finally, chin lifting and fire flashing in her eyes. My dove might be damaged, for we were all fucked up in our own ways, but she adapted and she thrived. Doves had an excellent knack for adapting to any environment. Caged, she'd found her rebellions and freedoms anyway. Free? She found them another.

The only difference was we were here for her now, when before, her only faithful ally hadn't known the full extent of it. I'd give Lainey some credit, that girl would rain fire down on the heads of anyone trying to put Dove back into a cage.

And we'd bring the fucking torches.

"I know?" I prompted when she'd gone quiet and her nose wrinkled as though she were irked with me for the nudge. Not that the warmth chasing the chill out of her eyes supported the idea.

"You know, the only place I was ever truly free was when I flew." The words were soft. "Before."

"You're right," I agreed. "I do know that."

A grin danced across her lips and she shed her jacket. "As free as I was when I flew, I didn't know how sweet freedom was until I didn't have to worry about him anymore."

Surprise struck a match in me. We hadn't dealt with him—yet.

"Yes," she told me, her gaze locking onto mine. "Telling Liam just—it unlocked something. I know you all want me to tell Milo—"

Correction, I pressed a finger to her lips. "No, I don't want that. Nor do any of us. Telling Milo will hurt both of you, and none of us would ever want to hurt either of you."

She kissed my finger and captured it. "Although he should hear it from me."

"Maybe," I said, not as confident on that point. Milo wouldn't take it well, period. He might not *believe* it from anyone else except her Lainey. Even then, I could see that causing issues.

"Maybe?"

"Dove, I will never tell you that you have to do something

that will hurt you. I think it will help… in the long run." I was feeling my way through this. "It may have escaped your notice, but we tend to communicate more with fists than words."

"No?" She lifted her eyebrows as though pretending surprise. "Really?"

"Hmm, you want to test that spanking theory, don't you?" The playful threat lit a spark in her eyes and I grinned. "As for the rest…the only thing I know for certain is that if and when Milo finds out, we want it to be from you. Because as much as it hurts, he doesn't deserve to be ambushed or have the information used like a weapon to inflict wounds on him."

That was what it boiled down to. No one got to hurt them—either of them—that way.

"I know."

Two words softly spoken carrying a wealth of meaning and trust. She pulled her shirt up and over, leaving her only in the bra where her curves were slowly beginning to fill in again.

I allowed myself a moment to just appreciate the way she had filled in. The hollows from her captivity were practically gone. The ripple of muscle was returning, but there was a swell to her hips that had been absent and a fullness to her slight breasts, giving them more weight.

They weren't quite a palmful yet, but fuck, I liked to play with them. Her nipples beaded beneath the fabric of the bra, straining as if they understood just how much I wanted to see those beautiful tits.

A red flush spread over her chest, and I stole a look to find her both grinning and blushing. The fact she could still blush delighted me. The faint dilation of her pupils betrayed how she was far more aroused than embarrassed.

My cock pulsed, the erection strained at my zipper, but I

made no moves to relieve it. Wanting and anticipation were a kind of pleasure in and of itself.

"If you want to take the bra off, don't let me stop you."

A laugh escaped her. The same kind of heady laughter she'd loosed when she challenged Milo to a game of pool the night before. It was the first time I'd seen her hit him with insults designed to pull him out of the funk he'd been wallowing in.

The funnier part was he'd been doing a good job of pretending he *wasn't* in a funk, even though we all knew him too well. I didn't think Dove had tracked that part of him yet. But she'd lured him right out with the way she played. A ruthless determination the siblings shared.

Did Milo even see how much like him our dove was? By the end of the evening, his laughter came more effortless, the shadows in his expression retreated, and wonder of all wonders didn't scowl or roll his eyes at us anymore.

Then, when she'd fallen asleep curled up next to Kel, all Milo had done was press a kiss to the top of her head before Kel scooped her off to bed.

Yeah, Dove rallied, but so was Raptor.

"Do you need it off me for the tattoo?"

"Nope," I told her. "That part would just be for me."

She chuckled as she appeared to consider it.

"Oh, and you need to tell me *where* you want your tat, Dove."

Catching her lip against her teeth, she studied me then reached behind her to unclasp the bra. It slid down her arms and bared those beautiful tits to my admiration. The nipples were definitely beaded and straining.

I was going to enjoy sucking them later. For now, I flicked up a look to find her eyes had lightened more and the smile on her lips deepened.

She stroked a finger along the curve of her breast, to the

spot over her sternum then down until her fingers rested right between her breasts—over her heart. "Here."

"That's gonna sting some."

"Life is pain," she told me. "So is love. Both are worth it."

Pen still balanced in my hand, I leaned forward to capture her chin with my free hand then kissed her. This wasn't an incredibly passionate kiss but more of a claiming one. Teeth and tongue, and she returned it in kind. When I slid my hand over the spot, she pressed her palm to the back of my hand.

The steady thrum of her heartbeat beneath my fingertips. Against her lips, I whispered, "Are you sure?"

"Yes," she said simply. "I love you."

That thrill flooded my whole system and I kissed the words right off her lips. The taste of them, sweet and tart, but so fucking amazing. She cupped my face and I don't know how long we stayed there, kissing as I traced my thumb in the pattern I would need to draw.

Finally, I pulled back to meet her heavy-lidded gaze. Her lips were swollen and glistening. I could probably get a few orgasms out of her before we started, but then we might never get to the tattoo.

She'd asked for the Vandals mark and I was going to fucking make sure she had it.

"That's going to take four to five orgasms at least for pain management later," I whispered. "Do you want those immediately following or after we get back to the clubhouse?"

Yeah, my cock throbbed at the idea and her smile grew. "Split the difference?"

"Three here? Three there?" I turned that idea over and nodded. "Done."

She shivered and her nipples peaked more. This was going to be the sweetest kind of torture. Turning the music up, I nudged her back in the chair so I could prep the area. I was going to freehand the tattoo.

I glanced down at the tat on her stomach and debated where I could add the rest of the birds. Food for thought…

"Vaughn?"

"Yes, Dove?"

"Do you want me to take my pants off too?"

Now that she mentioned it…

CHAPTER 11

EMERSYN

"Fuck," I exhaled as Vaughn curled his tongue around my clit to stroke it a moment before he teased it with his teeth. Pleasure unfurled like a hot desert wind blowing through me. Vaughn had nudged up the music in case I *screamed* even after he admonished me to be quiet.

I tried to twist away from his grip and grind against his mouth at the same fucking time as he thrust a third finger into me. The pressure from both his tongue and teeth, coupled with his fingers, split me apart and I came with a keening cry.

Vaughn lifted his head, a cocky grin in place. His lips and face were slick from where he'd been eating me out. His fingers curved inside me, sending another bolt of pleasure through me.

"I told you to be quiet," he teased. "Problem?" Even as he asked, he scissored his fingers and stroked that spot that had me shuddering.

Opening my mouth to answer, a soundless scream escaped because he sucked one of my nipples against his teeth. The competing sensations were pulling me apart. From the stroke of his fingers, the hum of sound as he lapped my nipple, to the burn of the tattoo settling into my soul. I loved their symbol, from the black daggers to the drips of blood.

I was a Vandal, and I was about to—

My hips bucked upwards and I damn near cried when he pulled his fingers away. Lifting his head, he watched me with teasing eyes as he licked his fingers.

Shudder after shudder raced through me and I stretched forward with trembling hands to open his jeans. "Eager, Dove?" The soft croon of his voice was all sex dipped in chocolate, heady and inviting.

"Yes," I said in a voice that still quavered. The hot weight of his cock filled my palm, and he gave a push against my hand before settling his hands on my hips. "You started it."

The last three words elicited a laugh from him that ended on a gasp when I rolled my thumb over his tip, teasing the piercing I loved so much. Even with every limb shaking, I ached for more.

Ached for *him*.

When he tugged me to him, I kept a hand on his cock and steadied the other on his shoulder. The music throbbed around us, but I didn't care that we were in the shop or that there were people around us.

They didn't matter.

The only thing that mattered was us. Being naked for the tattoo had started out as a game, one I was more than happy to lose—win? Win? Lose? You know, win/win worked for me.

Vaughn met my kiss with a fierce one of his own as he settled me on his lap. I didn't worry about any warming up.

Yes, he was thick and the stretch burned. But I was also soaked and it helped ease his passage even as his piercing teased me.

"Fuck," he swore in the middle of the kiss. The vehemence in the sentiment only made me chuckle as I managed to take all of him. It was still a bit of a stretch at this angle, but damn...

Head tilted back, I closed my eyes as I rocked up and then down again. The contraction of muscles gave me control; every downward thrust made the skin on my chest sting.

The sting added to the pleasure. The burn and the pull... just seemed to heighten how he felt inside of me. The pressure of his cock, the way it stretched me out while his piercing added to the impact—all of it was exquisite. He was exquisite.

"Vaughn," I exhaled his name like a prayer. Maybe it was. He flexed his hands on my hips and this time, he lifted me as he stood and then my back was against the wall. He surged into me, the rock of his hips giving no quarter.

Every strike of his cock lit me up. While I might be naked, he was still mostly dressed. His t-shirt stroked my nipples with every grind of our bodies. When he fisted my hair, I sank into his kiss.

I wasn't sure which of us was trying to devour the other, but it was a damn contest. Even as our tongues dueled, I gripped the sides of his face to keep him there as he ground into me. He flattened one hand to the wall as he balanced my hip with the other.

Breathing wasn't supposed to be optional, but I'd no sooner manage to gasp air around his kiss than he'd push it out of me with a thrust. The dizzying effect left spots dancing before my eyes as I clasped him closer with my thighs.

It seemed almost too soon for another orgasm to crash

over me, and then I was screaming into his mouth as he swallowed the sound. The piston of his hips was unrelenting, driving me higher and higher until I think I blacked out.

Or maybe I just came because then liquid fire bloomed inside of me as his release flooded into me. Heat flushed me, my skin seemed too tight, and his shirt seemed to stick to me in places.

Somewhere along the way, Vaughn had pulled my braid out. It was really hard to care about that when air seemed to be a precious commodity. A knock on the door penetrated the sensual haze and he lifted his head to glare at it.

"What?" The rumble of a growl in his sexy croon sent another shudder through me. The spasm around his dick didn't go unnoticed apparently because he gave me a slow grin.

"You taking clients today at all?" I didn't know the girl, but I thought she was the one from up front. I swear, I'd met her at least twice, and I never remembered her name. It was kind of terrible. With Vaughn's semi-hard cock still buried inside me, I didn't really have it in me to give too much of a shit right now.

"Nobody new," Vaughn answered.

"Got it." She didn't knock again or say anything more.

He glanced at me. "Good?"

"Oh," I answered with a laugh that stretched out the syllable and almost pushed him out of me. "Better than good. How does my tattoo look?"

The grin flirting with his lips grew as he dipped his glance to my chest. "Gorgeous, but I should probably stop playing and make sure we've got it all nice and treated before we return to the clubhouse."

He almost sounded forlorn and I couldn't suppress my own chuckle. "I love it, and you."

"That is the important part," he agreed before giving me a

light kiss. Pressing his lips to my ear, he whispered, "I love you."

The words sent another delightful shiver through me. I floated, both from the orgasms and the declaration. I barely felt him adding the ointment or the light bit of plastic to the tattoo.

"I want to get more…"

"Hmm?" He'd switched out for cool wipes to help clean me up. It was almost too much between my legs, but he seemed to be enjoying it as he worked the damp wipe over me.

"More tattoos."

"What do you want?"

I lifted my leg at his urging and let it rest on his shoulder as he took his time cleaning and studying me. I didn't think it needed that much "inspection," but I also didn't have it in me to hurry him along.

"No idea yet. I like some of yours…"

That snared his attention.

"I was thinking of getting one for each of you… like you have the ivy and the vandals."

"You have a hawk and a falcon," he murmured, running his fingers over my stomach and I grinned. "We can add the guys, though we may need to work on somewhere else."

"Yeah?"

"Balance," he suggested. "And I'm a little selfish about holding the place I have right here."

He pressed a kiss to his bird on my abdomen.

"But we'll work on it… do you want birds or some talisman for each of us?"

I turned that idea over in my head. Mouth open for a moment, I frowned before snapping it closed again. "I probably don't have enough skin for everything."

His soft chuckle teased me as he began to hand me my

clothes. "Dove, we can make anything happen, but if you plan on inking every part of your skin, we'll need to take a different course about how we plan them."

That probably wouldn't work, either. "I don't know that I want everything inked." I glanced at my arms. The scars I wanted to cover, but the outside of them? What about the rest of my legs?

Standing, I tried to ignore the trembling in my limbs. Yeah, I wasn't steady yet and Vaughn's grin grew slightly smug.

It was delightful.

"Can I tell you something?" Because the more I thought about the tattoos, the more I realized there were other considerations I needed to have.

"You can tell me anything."

I pulled on the panties slowly and rather than put the bra on over the new tattoo, I just pulled the t-shirt on without it. The jacket would hide my nipples and if it didn't? Well, look at my company. Who could blame me for being turned-on?

"Not sure how many tattoos I want to add to my arms and legs where others can see if I decide to continue performing." The words seemed to grow almost fainter as I gave them a voice. Or maybe it was me who got quieter with each one.

It was the first time I really said it aloud.

Vaughn held out my leggings as I tested the syllables. "Okay."

The simple acceptance startled me and I hesitated when I gripped the leggings. Despite the pure sensory overload, Vaughn was the only thing I saw and felt.

"Just—okay?"

"Did you want me to say something else?" The question was almost a throwback to one of our earliest conversations, and I wanted to smile, but at the same time...

"No," I said slowly. "I just...I hadn't really thought about going on tour again or if I would want to. Then, we're sitting here talking about tattoos, and all of a sudden..."

"You're thinking about touring." It wasn't a question but a carefully phrased comment confirming what I said.

"Yes," I said, testing the way it sounded. "Maybe...maybe I could do my own show? Not one that required a whole company." Did I want to do that?

"Is that what you want to do?" It was like he echoed my thoughts.

"Maybe?" Taking the leggings, I spent a moment pulling them on before I tugged on the socks and stuffed my feet back into the boots. The whole time, Vaughn waited me out. "I think I might, but...it would mean going on the road."

Before, touring was freedom and an escape. I didn't want to be home. But now?

I didn't want to leave any of them.

He held out a hand to me and when I glided my palm over his, he pulled me to him. With care, he cupped my cheek and locked his gaze on mine. "If it's important to you, then we figure it out. Some of us have more freedom to travel than others, so we'll make sure someone or someones goes with you."

Surprise fountained within me, and maybe it shouldn't have. "But what if—I mean, Kellan has the shop and Jasper drives. You work here."

"So?" He lifted his shoulders. "Doc has the clinic. Freddie and Rome are pretty flexible, and Liam would probably just finance your tours."

That made me blink.

"Either way, Dove—you fly, we fly with you. Maybe not all of us, but we can also come out and see you when you're closer and visit."

That was both crazy and— "I'd miss you guys."

"We'd miss you," he said without an ounce of melodrama. "But think about all the reunion sex. There are positives to everything."

I couldn't help it, I laughed. "Now you sound like Freddie."

"My man Freddie has some solid ideas."

That he did.

"The point is, if you want to tour, if you want to do it again then we *will* figure it out. Together."

I loved the sound of that. "It doesn't sound bad?"

"Do you want to escape us, Dove? Is that what it's about?"

"No," I said without hesitation. "Not at all. Just…" I hadn't been back up in the silks since I came back and at the same time, I wanted back up there. I wanted…to fly.

"Then it doesn't sound bad at all. It sounds like you want to pursue a dream, and you're telling me—ergo us—so that we get to be a part of it."

That sounded even better.

"Now," he continued. "I believe I owe you at least three more orgasms, but we need to head back to the clubhouse for those."

"Have I told you that I love you?"

He grinned. "You did, but I'm never going to get tired of hearing it."

I didn't think I'd ever get tired of saying it, either. After a soft kiss, he finished straightening up then helped me into a jacket before he fired off a text. Probably letting the others know we were on our way.

Warmth suffused me. I loved how they looked after me and each other. We were going home, where we could make plans and have orgasms.

If there was a little more bounce in my step, well, that was all Vaughn too.

I couldn't wait to show them all my tattoo. The fact I could *feel* it on my skin just made it all the better. They said I was one of them. I *was* one of them.

Now I had the mark to prove it.

CHAPTER 12

FREDDIE

The dart flew from my hand as I let it go and landed on the triple ring.

"Thirty-nine," Bodhi said, before he blew a bubble with the gum he'd been chewing. I'd told him he could have a beer, but the guy didn't drink alcohol when it was just the two of us. He didn't, and I quoted, like getting fucked-up on his own and he liked me not fucked-up.

That was pretty fucked, right?

I gave him a shrug and then backed up to let him take the next throw. Darts was a game I just liked. I could play it by myself or with others. I enjoyed hitting what I aimed at. He studied the dartboard while he rolled his head from side to side.

Honestly, I hadn't expected Bodhi to show up and stay. I wasn't complaining. I wanted to offer him a room, but Kel only allowed it *after* we put Boo-Boo on the road. I got it. They wanted to vet him. They planted him in a room down

113

the hall, one that used to be mine. No one stayed in Boo-Boo's suite except for us.

Hanging with Bodhi meant we were in the common room, not the suite room. Considering her butt print was on the wall, I was okay with that. No one needed to see it who wasn't us. It bugged me a little, yet she found it delightful.

Still, I wasn't going to let anyone else see it. She deserved her privacy. While Bodhi *seemed* focused on the board, the hairs on the back of my neck stood up. He was watching me too.

He didn't say anything before letting the dart fly and it landed square inside the inner ring on a five. Thirty-nine to five? I cut him a look but he returned it blandly. Taking his place, I picked out where I wanted the dart to land and flung it with ease. Third inner circle on the fifteen this time.

"Eighty-four." The epically dry tone pulled a smile out of me.

"To five," I offered up. "Gonna actually play now?"

Not looking at the board, Bodhi threw his dart. It landed on the bullseye. "Fifty-five," he corrected with a smirk, and I shook my head.

Holding his gaze, I threw my third dart and it landed on the third line, this time on the twenty. That was another sweet sixty points to my score making it one hundred and forty-four.

His third dart joined mine, the two trembling side by side. "One hundred and fifteen to one forty-four." Yep, smirk still in place.

"Tell me about Pilgrim Hills," I suggested as I crossed to the board and retrieved our darts.

He blew another bubble and shrugged. "High-end facility, very secure. Designed to not only keep people in but keep them docile and out of sight. If you tour it, it just seems like a luxurious facility."

"But?" You could argue Pinetree had been the same. The front-facing rooms and brochures all showed a serene campus with comfortable rooms, good food, and caring staff. You didn't have to go that deep to penetrate the facade of drugs, neglect, and abuse though.

A tremor rioted through my system at the thought of their medications. Some of those had been downright sweet in how efficiently they'd numbed everything. The memory, combined with my own nerves jangling, added to the feel of tremors. Sweat dotted my upper lip as I turned away to grab water.

Beer sounded way better.

You know what sounded better than...

"Me first?" Bodhi asked, giving me something else to focus on. I downed three gulps of water before turning back to find him studying the board, not me.

Yeah, I didn't buy that he wasn't noticing me either. On the other hand, Bodhi didn't say a word, so I left it alone. "Yeah, I won that round, so now you begin the next."

"Cool." He threw the dart with ease. "As for Pilgrim Hills, it's like every other facility designed to keep wealthier problems out of the way. There's what the public sees and there's what happens behind closed doors."

"What happens behind closed doors?" Boo-Boo's voice looped over me like a lasso and hauled me around. She must have come down from upstairs. I hadn't even realized she was back. Maybe she'd been napping?

Was I losing track?

Shit.

Before I could ask however, I found myself staring at her bare feet and then her bare legs. It took me a sec to recognize the hint of bruises around her shins and toes. Then I focused on the dance shorts and the t-shirt.

She'd been in her studio.

That made me feel a little better.

"Hey, PPG," Bodhi said while I continued to fumble around for words. I'd never had trouble talking to Boo-Boo before. Why now? "Behind closed doors? They're pretty much like the dicks at Pinetree. Drug 'em, light 'em up, leave them to drool."

The stricken look on Boo-Boo's face slapped all the discomfort right out of me. "That doesn't mean they're doing it to your mother, Boo-Boo."

"Doesn't mean they aren't, either," Bodhi added and I swung around to stare at him. He shrugged. "You be Mr. Positivity, and I'll deal with facts. Pilgrim Hills is fancier, more exclusive, and requires access to more than just a black card to get in. So maybe they dress it up when they fuck you over."

He seemed to be considering it.

"I can find out. Kind of curious myself."

Running a palm over my face, I scowled before I looked back at Boo-Boo. The worried look on her face had shifted a fraction with her frown. "Bodhi, I thought you'd already been there."

Wait, he had said something about being there. That was how he met Mama Sharpe. Right?

"I didn't hang out long," he said, picking up his soda. "Planned to stay longer, but it was boring. Also, dude, your turn."

Ignoring Bodhi for a sec, I focused on Boo-Boo. "Want to hang out with us? We're playing darts."

"Well, I'm playing," Bodhi added. "Freddie is talking to you."

"You were talking to her, too," I reminded him.

"Cause it would be rude to ignore her." His smirk suggested he was winding me up so I flipped him off.

"C'mon, Boo-Boo. Let's make you smile. You ever play darts?"

"Not really." She ventured closer, arms folded. I could see the top of the Vandals tattoo peeking out over the fabric of her tank, where it dipped in a u-shape. It had only been a couple of days, but it seemed like she'd always had it. I loved that it was on her. We all did. "Show me?"

Despite the question, she was chewing on her lower lip. I wanted to ditch the game and just give her a hug. Maybe go upstairs and try to coax her into a movie or something to distract her. We couldn't go yet. Not and leave Bodhi "unsupervised."

Kel and Liam were both working on verifying everything Bodhi told us. They had the details. Until they had all the angles, we weren't risking exposure for Boo-Boo. Not with her uncle out there. A part of me had to wonder if this was a trap to lure Boo-Boo in.

Then again, the news hadn't featured anything about Pinetree or the fire. Of course, it wouldn't…

When she bumped me with her hip, I flashed her a grin even though her gaze was more fixed on me now. "I'm okay," I told her before she could ask. "Let's play."

I cut a glance toward the dartboard then back to her before I flung the next dart and it landed on the triple inner circle on the twenty again, to add another sixty to my score.

"You're a ringer," Bodhi said, even though his dart hit the line right next to mine.

"So are you." When I sent the dart to hit, it trembled right on that edge, but it was another sixty points. Bodhi let out a laugh and I glanced over to find him collecting the darts this time.

"Tell you what, PPG. Why don't you play me 'cause your boyfriend is gonna roast me."

Boyfriend.

The description kind of made my stomach flip-flop. Boo-Boo's pinky stroked mine, and I hooked mine around hers without glancing down. "If she doesn't know how to play, you have to spot her five hundred points."

"Sure, you want me to spot you five hundred, PPG?"

"Does it matter who wins?" The glance she cut between us suggested it shouldn't however I just shrugged.

"He wants to change it up because I'm kicking his ass, and he can spot you the points." It was reasonable, and Bodhi agreed. I ignored the agitation scraping under my skin as Bodhi extended the darts toward her.

He was just giving her darts—not drugs or weapons or whatever my brain wanted to conjure. Bouncing from the balls of her feet to her toes and then back to her heels, she studied the darts and then the board.

"Do you think getting my mother out of Pilgrim Hills will need a distraction like getting us out of Pinetree?"

A flash of her sightless eyes in that chair as she gazed unseeing out the window shivered over my skin, leaving a trail of ice in its wake.

"Depends," Bodhi said. "Am I going first, or are you going first?"

No fucking way was she going into that place first or otherwise.

"You," she answered easily before I could object. "Assuming you mean darts."

Oh. Darts.

My mouth was dry, and the sweat dotting my skin had my shirt clinging to me. Did we have the heat turned up in here? I drained my water while Bodhi took his shot. A perfect bullseye.

All twenty-five points.

Pivoting, he eyed Boo-Boo. "You know how to throw?"

"I'll help her," I said before he could touch her. I liked

Bodhi, I really did. Except Boo-Boo didn't need to have anyone touching her she didn't want.

Ever. Again.

Pressing up against her back, I tried to keep some space between us as she held up her wrist and glanced at me. "I can help," I offered. Maybe I should have said that first.

I was all over the place, yet her smile quieted some of the jangling in my system. "I'd like that," she said. "Only you don't have to."

"I don't mind at all." Of course, I didn't mind. I *wanted* to help her. Cupping my hand over hers, I framed her fingers on the dart. "You hold the barrel like this. Then you focus on *where* you want the dart to land. You need to use enough force to get it there but not so much that you bounce it off the board."

She laughed, her arm relaxing as I helped her line up the shot. At this angle, it was impossible to miss the scar on her arm. All at once, I wanted to scrap the game and just go find her uncle. If I carved enough out of him, he'd be nothing **but** scars.

"Freddie?" The soft question pulled me to the present, and I sighed.

"Sorry, Boo-Boo." After pressing a kiss to her shoulder, I went back to my lesson. Once she was lined up, I checked her angle and her stance. This close, the scent of her shampoo and lotion tickled my nose. The hints of citrus and vanilla underscored the sweat. All of it was *clean*.

She was clean. Her sweat was work and art while mine was sour and broken…

"Like this?"

I shook my head a little. I needed to focus. "Yeah. You just need to know where you want the dart to land and let your body follow your eyes…"

"Like picking my spot when I spin?"

"I guess." I didn't know as much about that as I did darts. "Most of the time, if we can focus on where we want to be and keep our eyes on that prize, the rest of us will follow."

Only it didn't seem to work that way for me. She gave a little shiver, her arm dropping a little but I didn't even have to correct her before she lined it up again and then tossed it. The dart flew. It didn't hit the center or even the triple, but it did land solidly between the triple and the double ring—right on the twenty.

"Yes!" She gave a little cheer , turning to me with the barest of hesitations. Oh, she wanted a hug. I could do that. The softness of Boo-Boo pressing up against me was everything and too much all at once.

"Thank you," she whispered against my ear with such feeling, I floundered. All I'd done was show her how to make a shot. That wasn't a big deal. Her scent filled my nostrils, but the sour, bitter notes of my own stink overpowered it. It had to be suffocating for her.

Then she pressed a kiss to my cheek.

"Shit," I swore as I let her go and backed up abruptly. I didn't push her away, but I might as well have. "I have to go." Then I was pivoting and walking straight for the door to the warehouse.

I had to get out of here.

Out and away from Boo-Boo. She deserved something far better from me. I was blocks away before I slowed, and while I hadn't been running, I swore sweat dripped from my face and hair. It was so hard to get a breath in. It was like someone was squeezing my chest.

Knife out of my pocket, I flicked it open and then closed. I needed a hit. Or something.

No. I didn't.

I was clean. I liked being clean. I should call one of the guys.

Tell them what? I freaked out because Boo-Boo hugged me? I snapped the blade closed, then out again.

No, maybe I could just score a single tab—something to take the edge off. I swiped a hand over my face, then turned in a circle. Where the fuck was I?

The panting made it hard to focus, and I was so hot. I stared at the blade. If I sliced it over my arm, the pain would help focus me, right?

It had worked before.

A scuff of a shoe jerked me around like someone had sent a thousand volts through my system. Bodhi stared at me from the doorway.

The doorway to—I was in a shipping container. I'd come down to the port.

Fuck.

Bile burned in the back of my throat.

"What do you want?"

"Nothing," he said. "Just checking on you. PPG was worried."

I scared Boo-Boo. Fuck. I fell back against the metal wall and banged my head against it. The blows were light, and they didn't do a damn thing for me. I stared down at my trembling right hand and the blade in it.

Slice the palms. One quick cut. The blood would well up…

"I want a hit," I admitted. "I need it. But I don't."

"Okay."

"I'm freaking out, and all you say is okay?" I stared at him.

"What do you want me to say?"

My mouth opened then snapped closed again. Despite being backlit by the gray day, I could almost make out Bodhi's expression. It was—neutral. Not smiling, not scowling—nothing.

"How would you kill me?" That would be something to know.

"I wouldn't," he told me. "I like you."

Oh.

"You know I don't swing that way."

He snorted. "Don't flatter yourself. I don't like you that much."

The absolute blandness in that statement gave it such normalcy I had to laugh. He didn't block the opening but didn't come inside either.

"How would you kill someone who hurt someone you loved?"

"We talking erasure or really fucked up pain and suffering?"

I sucked in a noisy breath and then looked at Bodhi as I snapped the blade closed.

"Really fucked up."

Bodhi's chilling grin would probably frighten anyone else, but it buoyed me.

He'd know exactly how to do it.

CHAPTER 13

JASPER

I'd just left the latest set of logbooks in the office when Freddie exited the clubhouse and shot across the warehouse to the exterior door.

"Hey," I called, but he didn't even slow down before hitting the crash bar on the external door and was out, nearly bowling over JD on his way. The rat shot a look after him and then back inside toward me. I started after him when the door to the clubhouse opened.

Emersyn appeared with bare legs, bare feet, and a tank top. One wolf whistle split the air and then cut off on a choke when I spun to glare. That sent the rats scurrying as I dragged off my jacket and diverted toward her.

Freddie's new friend was a half-step behind her. "Hey, PPG, I'll go."

She pivoted to face him then back to me when I got there. "What happened?" I asked as I draped the coat around her. "And where are your shoes?"

"Freddie got upset about—"

"I got it." The guy didn't wait for a response and just strolled across the warehouse like he owned it then out the door that Freddie vanished through. Yeah, I wasn't sure what the hell I thought of Bodhi.

Freddie *liked* him and he didn't like many. More, Freddie seemed to trust him. It was enough to make me give the guy a chance, but still.

"Inside, Swan," I told her. The sharp look she shot me didn't faze me in the slightest. "Inside, or I put you inside. You want to be out here, you put on something warmer. It's too fucking cold to be barefoot."

She glared up at me then rolled her eyes before she retreated, still wearing my coat. Good girl. Funnily enough, I'd missed the heat in her glares and the fire in her wit when she bit back at me.

The internal door to the common room was open once I got her into the antechamber. Bad security, but I didn't scold her for that as I hustled her into the warmer interior and shut the door.

"Can I tell you what happened now?" She pivoted to stare up at me and I gripped the front of my coat where it covered her and tugged her to me. Mutiny flared in her sweet brown eyes.

"Yes."

I swore I could see the argument gathering before she blinked, then blew out a breath. "Really?"

A smile danced over my lips before I sobered. "Really. Tell me what happened."

"I was dancing. When I came out, Freddie and Bodhi were playing darts and talking about Pilgrim Hills."

I did my best to control my expression. Still wasn't a fan of taking on another mental facility, but Emersyn wanted her mother out of that place. I could appreciate that. "Okay."

"That seemed to be fine, but he was a little—jumpy." She chewed her lower lip. "He was also kicking Bodhi's ass at darts."

Another smile escaped me. "He's damn good at darts."

"They told me to play, and Freddie was showing me how to throw the darts, and then…" Her frown tugged at me. She was worried. "He was standing right behind me and being careful about touch. I thought I was too."

Her wince worried me. "How was he showing you?"

When she turned around, she beckoned me to her, so I moved up behind her and she stepped into me until we were almost touching. There was no mistaking she was right there. Awareness of her swept through me.

Touching or not, there was no mistaking how close we were. The scent of her tickled my nose, and the warmth of her teased me. The urge to put my arms around her was right there.

"I made the shot, and it was a good one, so I got excited and turned around to kiss him on the cheek." She spun to face me and her whole expression fell. "Then he just—left."

Fuck.

"It's okay, Swan." I rubbed her biceps. "I'll go find him." Freddie, when he retreated, had a handful of bolt holes. He really shouldn't be out there alone. While Bodhi went after him, the guy wasn't one of us. "Stay here?"

"I want to go…"

"I know you do," I assured her. "But one, it's safer here for you. And two," I pressed on because this was important. "Sometimes Freddie needs a minute. I promise I'll look after him and make sure he gets back."

This was a promise I had every intention of keeping.

"But I need you to be in here and safe. Vaughn and Kel should be back soon."

"You want me to go up to the suite?"

"Do you mind?" I didn't like keeping her caged, but there was already a rat who needed his jaw broken. Better to keep her out of sight for the moment.

"Yes," she said, folding her arms and retreating a step. "But I'll stay—and I'll go up because Freddie is more important right now. Will you text me or call me as soon as you find him?"

"I will." I followed her and pressed a kiss to her lips. "Thank you. I'll bring him back…"

"Jasper," she called before I made it a couple of steps. Turning, I barely caught my jacket as it hit my chest. Sobriety tempered the light in her eyes. "You'll need that."

"Keep that gorgeous ass in here…"

"I will. Now go." She made a shooing motion before heading for the stairs.

Good girl.

Closing the door to the antechamber, I gave it a beat and pulled out my phone. I fired off a series of messages because I absolutely had to go after Freddie, but she did *not* need to be here alone.

Kel made sure she was armed and knew how to use it. We'd also shown her where the weapons stashes were. Didn't make the trip any easier. I double-checked the clubhouse lock before I turned around.

JD was in sight, so were Tug and Ratchet. As tempted as I was to go and crack a couple of jaws, I would deal with them later. Freddie first.

Lifting his chin, JD said, "All good, Hawk?"

My phone buzzed and I stared at the screen. "All good. Finish up the off-loading and the sort. Then lock up the trucks. Raptor's on his way."

I didn't imagine it, they all started moving faster. With that, I left them to it. Milo was five minutes away. No one except for us could get into the clubhouse, and I trusted Emersyn to stay in.

She'd given her word so I headed out and after Freddie. It had been a while since I had to roust him from a bolthole. He'd been clean for weeks right now. Weeks that had become months. It was one of his longest clean streaks ever.

If he slipped, he slipped. But he wasn't going down on his own. The fact he adored Emersyn pushed him to take bigger chances with her. I would give anything for him to find some real joy with her, but the last thing I wanted was for him to hurt himself on the way.

Outside, I turned the car toward the docks. Despite everything that happened in the stack of old storage containers, Freddie still vanished into that warren of hidey holes when he needed to vanish.

I got it. It terrified him, so he made himself face it. Didn't mean I had to like it. My phone rang before I'd even gone a block.

"Doc," I said when I answered. "He's not hurt as far as I know."

"Good," Doc answered. "I've got my bag ready, and I've got someone to cover here if you need me."

Surprise speared me. Then again... "Thanks, Doc. I'll let you know. That guy Bodhi is with him, or at least he followed him. I'm hoping this is more that he needed a minute to catch his breath and get out of his head and not that he needed to shut off everything in his head."

"I hear you," Doc assured me. "I'm ready. You got the kit in your car?"

"Yeah." Doc had suggested it a couple of weeks earlier and I'd thought it conveyed we didn't trust him. Although Doc said it was more about the idea with Freddie staying clean, he was more likely to OD if he went after a harder drug. The

Naloxone was a nasal spray, and it would buy us time to get him to a hospital or to Doc.

Kel liked it and we had enough addicts in the area that having it on hand wasn't a bad idea. It also wasn't showing a lack of faith in Freddie. As much as I might not like having it there, I liked having Freddie around more.

When I reached the port, I parked near the busted fences and headed in to find him. There were three storage containers he preferred. He wasn't in the first one, but I heard voices when I got to the second.

"...thinking you start with little needles, insert them under the fingernail beds, get them in good and deep. Then you charge them up and start the electroshock. After he's buzzed, you yank the fingernails out and move to putting the needles under his toenails..."

"I thought we'd do it to his penis." The comment from Freddie was far more alert and vicious than I'd been expecting. "You know, fry his dick."

"We get there," Bodhi said. "But you wanted to really fuck him up, so you start small, and you just keep ramping up the pain. So not only is he hurting from the number of injuries, you just keep making it worse and you don't stay in any one area for too long."

"'Cause, you can get numb if you keep hurting yourself the same way." Freddie sounded thoughtful. "Okay, continue..."

"We got company," Bodhi told him as I came around the storage container and met the other man's gaze. He stood outside of the storage container, though he wasn't blocking the door.

Freddie appeared in the doorway and grimaced. "Fuck, hey, Jas."

"Freddie, you good?"

"Hell, no," he answered with a familiar smirk. "I'm pretty fucking terrible most of the time."

I chuckled.

"But yeah, we were just—you know, talking torture techniques." He almost seemed sheepish as he raked a hand through his hair. Despite Swan's description, Freddie looked —mostly okay. Calmer as his eyes and his hands were steady, and he didn't look sweaty.

"So I heard." I pulled out my cigarettes and lit one. "Mind if I hang out?"

"I'll leave you two to talk," Bodhi said. "Gonna go find food and booze. Maybe get laid." He pointed a finger at Freddie. "Don't get dead."

"Not planning on it," Freddie told him. "Thanks, man—and if you need to come back to crash, just text me, and I'll get you in."

"Yep." The guy gave me a look. "PPG, okay?" At the question, Freddie shot me a look.

"He means Boo-Boo."

"Oh, I know who he means." And I'd pretty much figured out what it stood for. The only reason I hadn't broken his jaw was cause' he had gone after Freddie and brought good information. "Not a fan of the nickname."

"Good thing it's not yours then," he said with a smirk that promised he'd never not use it now. Fucking great.

Just what we needed.

"She's fine."

"Cool. See ya." Then Bodhi strolled away, leaving Freddie and me alone.

I sighed, exhaling a stream of smoke as I watched the man disappear as he turned past another storage container. He could be a problem.

"Is Boo-Boo really okay?" Freddie asked.

I nodded. "She's fine. Worried about you."

129

"Fuck." Freddie sat down in the opening and scrubbed his hands over his face. "I freaked out on her."

"You need to talk about it?"

He opened his mouth as if to answer even as he shook his head, then paused. "I—" The hesitation wasn't an immediate denial or rejection. "I don't know."

"Okay." I could accept that as an answer. "I'm going to send her a message to let her know I found you, you're fine and we're gonna hang for a bit. That work for you?"

A sheepish look crept over his expression and he glanced down at his hands. "Yeah, I didn't mean to worry her. I should have just gone back, but—"

"There's no should. She worries because she cares." And she thought *she* had been the one to freak him out, but I kept that part to myself for now. It wasn't something he needed to be burdened with and she wouldn't blame him any more than I did.

"Yeah, that would be good. Thanks…"

I pulled out my phone while I scanned the area, then sent a message to her, Doc, and the guys. That Freddie was fine. We were together and probably gonna hang out for a bit. We'd be back later.

Answers buzzed back on the screen, but I closed it and shoved it in my pocket. For the next hour, I smoked and Freddie brooded. He needed time and I gave it to him. We could talk when he was ready.

"Jas," he said. "What if I can't ever be what Boo-Boo wants?"

I considered how to tackle that question. "You want the kind answer or the truth?"

Surprise stamped across his face. "Are they different?"

"In the long run? No. In the short-term, though?" I lifted my shoulders.

"The truth then."

"Don't decide what she wants for her," I said. "It's not fair to you or to her. One thing about Swan, she is just as majestic as she is fierce. Only don't tell her what she does or doesn't want. Also—she has a mean right hook when she gets going."

All of which was true.

"She's one of us, Freddie," I reminded him. "She's seen us at our best and at our worst." Seen him. Seen me. "She's not running."

"But I am?"

"So?" I shrugged. "Day isn't over. You can always run back."

He blinked.

"Tomorrow is another chance. Day after is one too. Don't discount her. She's tougher than Raptor." Then because it was Freddie, I added, "But don't tell him I said that."

He laughed. It was what I wanted.

"Not sure I'm ready to go back yet."

"Okay," I told him as I lit another cigarette. "We got time. Though, I'm going to insist we get food in a bit."

"Okay."

The hope that kindled in me at that easy acceptance was hard to ignore. Freddie had his demons, but he wasn't running from them or trying to pretend they weren't there. He was asking for time.

I would damn well make sure he got it.

CHAPTER 14

EMERSYN

Two days. Two days and Freddie hadn't come back to the clubhouse. Instead, he'd gone to Mickey's. Jasper promised he was all right, but he needed a minute. I was torn between going to Mickey's to see Freddie and giving him space.

As it was, I didn't want to crowd him. If Freddie didn't want to be here, then I shouldn't force the issue. That wasn't who we were, except worry for him was like a rash under my skin. I kept replaying the moment over and over.

I shouldn't have turned around and kissed him. He was sensitive to touch. We both were, yet he was right there, holding me, and I thought—

Groaning, I fell back on the bed and stared up at the ceiling. Vaughn had admonished me not to worry before he'd left to work. Kellan was doing something out in the warehouse with Milo, and I was sitting in here feeling sorry for myself.

I'd just rolled over to reach for my phone when there was a knock at the door.

"Come in."

The handle turned and Rome peeked inside. He'd been absent more than present lately. Working on a project was all he'd said when I asked.

"Hey," I greeted him as I sat up. There was a spritz of green paint on his dark shirt, right near the collar. But I had a feeling that was an old stain because his skin was clean. The smile hovering on his lips deepened as he met my gaze. "You're back."

"Yes. Liam is here."

He was?

"We want to take you out."

I scooted to the end of the bed and then glanced at Liam as he appeared in the doorway behind Rome. Side by side, they were so alike, and at the same time couldn't be more different. It wasn't just a matter of haircuts, but how they moved, spoke, and right now?

Not to mention how they both looked at me? Warmth raced through me as I stared up at them. "Freddie isn't back yet."

"I know, Hellspawn. Jas has him so does Doc. We can take you over there to see him if you want."

The offer was wildly sweet and so tempting. "If he was ready to see me, I think he would have come back." Jasper said it wasn't me, but I had misstepped. I knew better, maybe more than any of them.

"Starling," Rome said as he came forward, and when he held out his hand, I took it and let him pull me up. "If you need to see him, we will go. You don't have to talk to him or make him talk to you."

"Have you guys seen him?" I glanced back and forth between them.

"I have," Rome said, even as Liam shook his head. "He's struggling, but he didn't fall."

Closing my eyes, I let out a breath I hadn't realized I'd been holding since Freddie bolted.

"I talked to Jasper," Liam admitted as Rome hugged me. "Freddie's just trying to figure out some things in his head. But, Hellspawn, he wouldn't want you beating yourself up."

I made a face. "I just feel like I pushed him too hard."

"Did you?" Rome asked. He held my hands as steadily as he held my gaze. "Push him?"

"Maybe?" That was the question. On the one hand, he'd asked me to push; on the other, I hadn't thought it was too much. I'd also been distracted by Bodhi's talk about Pilgrim Hills.

"Yeah, I'm looking right at her," Kellan said, and it tugged my attention from Rome to where Kellan stood just beyond Liam, who had twisted to look at him. He had his phone to his ear. "Yep, hang on."

Liam shifted deeper into my room to let Kellan in. He held up the phone and the speaker was on.

"She can hear you. We all can," Kel advised him.

"Boo-Boo, you aren't supposed to be worrying about me."

Relief swarmed through me. It was so damn good to hear him.

"Seriously, I'm good. I'm even doing work for Doc. Like, actual honest shit work. And by honest, I mean he's paying me and by shit work, I mean shit work." There was a hint of a smile in his voice. "I'm cleaning the clinic and doing some odd jobs here. But I'm good. Go out with the big bros and have fun."

I glanced up to find Kellan watching me.

"Are you sure?" I considered all the ways I could ask the question. "I know I pushed—"

"You didn't," Freddie told me. "You really didn't. I was the one hovering over you, and I was already freaking out a little. But it's good, Boo-Boo. I promise. Go on your date with the guys. I'll be back soon."

"Okay." I believed him and at the same time… "Next time —it's your turn to hug."

He was quiet for a moment before a huff of laughter escaped. "Deal."

"Be good to yourself?" It was more of a question than an admonishment.

"Cross my heart, Boo-Boo. You guys take care of her."

"We will," Liam said. "Call us if you need *anything*." *That* was most assuredly an order.

After Kellan ended the call, he held out his hand. "C'mere, Sparrow."

Rome let me go as I crossed to Kellan. Curling one arm around me, he tilted his head so he could hold my gaze. "Freddie is good. He asked for help. He's getting help. He knows you're here for him. He knows we're all here. Go out with the twins, stick with them, have some fun and then come home."

I bit my lip, still a little worried but also a little amused. "Are you sending me out on a date?"

"Do you not want to go?" The question held no judgment or hint of suggestion, just a verification.

"Yes, I want to go, but—"

He pressed a finger to my lips. "No buts, Sparrow. Just a yes or no. You do not have to carry everything for any of us. We split the load, carrying each other." He trailed his finger down my nose then to my chin, and finally to my chest, where the Vandals tattoo was visible just below the neckline of my shirt.

"I don't want him to be hurt."

"None of us do, Hellspawn." The absolute patience in Liam's voice had me tilting my head back. "And we can wait

—as much as I'd rather not, we can wait for him to be back here if that will be better for you."

That wasn't really fair to them. At the same time… "Doc is looking after Freddie," I said, checking with Kellan. "Jas was there yesterday."

He nodded. "And I'll go later today and check on him myself. If I think that there is something you need to know, I will call you guys."

Blowing out a breath, I nodded slowly before glimpsing at Rome then Liam and back again. "Is that okay with you guys?"

"Yes," Rome said without hesitation and Liam nodded.

"Thank you, Kel," I murmured as I pushed up on my tiptoes. He gave me a light kiss.

"Of course, now, have fun and be a good girl." Then he fixed the guys with an entirely different look. "Take care of her."

He didn't linger as I turned to face the guys. "What should I wear?"

"Nothing at all would be fine with me," Liam said with a slow smile, but then we'd never get out of here.

While I was still worried about Freddie, hearing him had helped. I could take a deeper breath. Fifteen minutes later, I climbed into the backseat of Liam's SUV.

I was in comfy clothes, a jacket and boots. I also had on a brand new holster that Kellan had gotten for me so I could tuck a pistol into it at the small of my back under the jacket.

Rome had also grabbed my overnight bag and put it in the back. Scooting to the middle, I put on my seatbelt and leaned forward to see them both. Liam glanced over his shoulder at me.

"Do I get to ask where we're going?"

"No," Rome answered before Liam did. "We're going back to the fairgrounds."

I blinked. "Where…"

"Yes," Liam said. "It's secure. I have a company doing work for me there, and you're both going to be safe. Trust me?"

"As long as you're going to be safe, too," I told him. The corners of his mouth tilted up.

"You really want to test whether or not I'll spank that ass of yours, don't you?"

That shouldn't send such a delicious shiver through me, but it did. So, I went with it. "Maybe," I teased him. "But remember, we protect each other."

The whole concept of sharing the burden, of protecting each other, of the loyalty they had for each other—it all burned inside of me.

"Yes," Rome said, glancing at me. "I'll remind him. You're okay to go?"

"I'm a little nervous," I admitted. "We barely got there last time before—"

"I know," he said, holding his hand back to me and I gripped it. "They will not be a problem."

"You're also armed," Liam reminded me. "So are we. And there's security." He stressed the last part. That was important so I slid my free hand up to rest on his shoulder.

"Then I'm ready for my date." Excitement skittered through me. I'd gone out with the guys before—Jasper had taken me to the resort, Rome had taken me painting, I'd gone to the movies with Jasper and Freddie… Liam even took me shopping.

I hadn't gotten to go out as much with Kel or Vaughn. I needed to fix that. Mickey too. However, I was still uncertain about him. We needed to talk more.

There always seemed like there was more we needed to do and not enough time.

"Relax," Liam said as we left the warehouse. "I can *feel* you worrying."

"You cannot," I retorted, but I squeezed his shoulder and Rome's hand before I leaned back in the seat. "It's hard to relax sometimes. I keep thinking of all the things we need to do—that I need to do."

"That's why we're a *we*, Hellspawn," Liam reminded me. "We help each other. Freddie's in good hands. Everything else is moving along. We have a few minutes to breathe. We're going to take advantage of it."

"The date is important to him," Rome told me, and Liam snorted before he gave Rome a light punch.

"Like it's not important to you."

"It's important because it's Starling, not because it's a date."

I had to hide a smile as Liam rolled his eyes, yet the smile on his face just grew. When I caught his gaze in the rearview mirror, he winked at me.

The drive didn't take that long, and then we were at the fairgrounds. It was still daylight, and like the first time we'd come, there was cracked pavement in the parking lot. It felt isolated from the highway and empty. Only, we didn't stay in the parking lot and there was a new fence up around the property and a gate that opened when Liam touched a button.

There were also men standing near the gate who nodded and lifted a hand as we drove through. I twisted in the seat to glance back at them. While I'd seen two when we came in, there were more.

"About a dozen on site right now," Liam told me before I could ask as he drove slowly through the old fairgrounds. It was kind of sad, in a way. The place that time had moved past, leaving abandoned wooden buildings where games were once played, and there likely stuffed animals to win.

Usually, you didn't drive through the fairgrounds. It was a completely different feeling passing the neglected buildings with a history I could almost smell and hear. There would be music and voices. Buttered popcorn and sugary funnel cakes with their whiffs of cinnamon.

Liam pulled up to a large building that looked like it had once been a theater—or maybe an amphitheater. A permanent big top with its round shape and spires still holding some elements of its former glory in the faded red colors.

Even as Liam opened my door, I found myself straining to see where the flags might have been fluttering in the sky. As it was, I did a slow circuit. The whole place just—felt like it was holding its breath.

"It's almost sad," I said softly.

"What is?" Liam lifted his arm, and I slid next to him, tucking myself against his side.

"That this place is just—abandoned."

"Don't judge a book by its cover," he whispered as he locked the door and then guided me over to the door Rome was unlocking with a key code.

The lock was brand new, and so was the door. Power hummed inside, the clang of lights coming on rippling out like a wave as we moved through what had to be a stage entrance toward the center. While there was still stadium seating all around on three sides, the center was dedicated to one thing—hanging silks and a padded floor.

My mouth fell open as I stared upward at all of it; then, I did a slow pivot. Rome had already stripped off his jacket, as had Liam.

"You set up a silk stage?"

"Something like that," Liam murmured, before he reached for my jacket. "Trust us?"

That really wasn't even a question.

CHAPTER 15

EMERSYN

*T*he air in the open venue wasn't heated, but it also wasn't damp inside. There were hints of sawdust in the air. It was kind of funny, it seemed like every venue I ever performed in always had a woodsy element to their air quality. Maybe it was the staging or the building and deconstruction of sets.

It didn't matter. Closing my eyes and taking a deep breath transported me to the space I'd always been the most comfortable in. The stage. The performance. Becoming someone else.

Warm hands settled on my hips and I leaned back against Liam. He pressed his lips to the back of my head. "This is okay, right?"

"Already doubting yourself?" I glanced up at him.

He shook his head. "No, but it occurs to me that we were assuming you would want to do this and I don't know how you feel about performing anymore."

It wasn't an unfair question. Like me, Liam had stripped out of his shoes and jacket. He wore a tank top and loose sweats. None of us were dressed up. Comfortable clothes were the name of the game. I'd already noticed the bucket of chalk off to the side.

"I was talking to Vaughn about it the other day," I admitted. "Before—it was always about running away, staying away. There was a freedom up there that I never experienced anywhere else."

Rome walked toward us across the mats. He'd lost his shirt along with his shoes. Spatters of paint decorated him. Little droplets, like he'd forgotten to scrub them all off. Or maybe he'd been painting before they came to get me.

It was all possible.

"I told him I was thinking about what it would be like to tour again—when… you know when it's safe. Then wondering if I was being selfish."

"If you want to tour, Hellspawn. Say the word. I'll hire the crew and we'll put it together." It was practically word for word what Vaughn had said.

"I'll go with you," Rome said. "If you want. One of us should." He looked up over my head. "Maybe two of us."

Liam chuckled. "Thanks for inviting me."

"You're welcome." The deadpan delivery pulled a giggle out of me.

"I haven't decided yet. There's a lot to deal with before then, anyway." Like my mother.

My uncle.

I shivered, and Liam tightened his grip around me. "We can make plans, figure out what you'd want to do. It would take time to build and put all the people together."

"And see if I can even still do it." The soft admission slipped out of me.

"You can," Rome said, his faith absolute and shining from his eyes.

I lifted my hands so I could study the scars on the inside of my forearms. Even with all the physical therapy, they were still not what they had been. *I* wasn't who I had been.

"You can," Liam echoed his brother. Wrapping his hands around my wrists, he stroked the ends of the scars with his thumbs. The soft circles sent another shiver through me. "Do you remember what it was like the first time you went up in the silks?"

"Yes." I didn't even have to strain for that memory. It had been terrifying and exhilarating. It took concentration and confidence. Muscle control.

Discipline and faith.

I had to trust myself.

"Can you show me?" Liam asked, his voice a husky whisper at my ear. "Show *us*?"

He lifted my wrists to kiss each one before letting me go.

"We won't let you fall."

"Sometimes you have to fall," I said as I gazed up at the silks.

"Sometimes," Rome agreed. "Trust?"

I raised my brows. "Yes, I trust you."

"Then fall." He motioned for me to turn and fall toward him.

A dozen questions formed and dissipated without me ever giving them voice. He asked for my trust. I trusted him. I trusted them both.

Pivoting, I fell backward and he caught me with a hand on my shoulder, balancing my weight. With a light roll, he pushed me back to my feet. I met Liam's gaze as I went rigid and continued the fall forward.

My stomach bottomed out, but elation flooded me when he

caught me easily, balancing me with one hand and then rolling me up and around. Laughter escaped me when I rocked back and forth between them, spinning like a top, as they controlled the motion and I let my center of gravity balance us all.

Sliding his hand along my arm, Rome changed the game and I fell to the side, except I never touched the ground as he gripped my hand. With my gaze fixed on Liam, I smiled as Rome pulled me up and then cupped my nape as he dipped me back.

His whole body moved, dipping with me even as I held fast. When he pulled me upright and forward, catching my hand, I let myself spin as he twirled me around, stepping over me like I was the silk. The torque and pull on my arm pinched a little, the stretch warming my forearms up and then I was on my feet and facing Rome again.

"Trust," he repeated. It was a single word. One syllable. It held so much meaning. I was facing Rome and just behind him were the silks.

Trust him to get me up there. Trust them to help me fly.

My pulse raced briefly, even as my breathing deepened. I nodded and lifted a foot. Rome bent one knee slightly and I stepped up onto it then lifted my other foot to his shoulder as he stood.

He was the perfect partner. Steady, balanced and he didn't shift as I stepped up beyond straightening as I balanced on one foot and then settled the other on his free shoulder.

My pulse steadied out again as he braced one hand on each ankle. He'd studied every single one of my performances. I stared up at the silks. The lights didn't change. The air didn't shift. And at the same time, everything seemed to balloon, swelling with a greater meaning.

Trust them.

Trust myself.

I reached for the first silk, wound it around my arm, and

then the second. Rome kept sturdy and when I glanced down, I found him smiling up at me.

The question in his eyes asked me if I was ready?

When I gave him a slight nod, he pushed my legs up and then out as I stretched them and then let go as I balanced. The music started, filtering in from somewhere. The notes as familiar to me as my own heartbeat. It was one of the first songs I'd ever choreographed a silk routine to.

The trembling in my arms steadied as I rolled upward, weaving the silk around my torso so I could do a drop. It was —muscle memory and instinct. I angled upward and then began to move with the music. Awareness rippled over me as I glanced down and locked gazes with Liam a moment before I dropped then angled back up.

My heart seemed to fist-bump my ribs when a drop of uncertainty dribbled through me. Would my arms hold? Did I have the form? And then I lifted my chin and spread my arms to fly.

I spiraled up then down again. The routine was familiar enough for me to go through most of it before I let out a gasping laugh, spinning the final bit into an arched pose for the last frame.

A pair of hands began to applaud, and I grinned at both Liam and Rome.

"Now," Rome said as he strode toward me. "Together."

Together?

Of all the things I'd been thinking he would do, leaping to catch one of the silks and pull himself up as he wrapped it around his forearm as I had the other around mine, wasn't it.

"You first," Liam said. "Then me."

Then…

The music started again, and Rome extended his free hand toward mine. It took strength to get us going. Strength and momentum. We started circling, and then he gave me a push as he let me go and we were doing spirals together. There had been one routine where Eric and I had…

I hooked one of my legs around his where he extended them to me, and we spun together, sliding apart and back together. Then, I had my legs around Rome as I tied us up into the silks.

Trust shone in his eyes as he let go, and we flew.

It seemed to last a lifetime and no time at all as we were then standing below the silks again. Liam wasted no time wrapping one of the silks around his forearm and curling his free arm around me.

Laughter vibrated through me as he lifted us upward into a twirl. His was a little more gymnastic and it definitely made me laugh, but after all our grappling, I could grip him and trust his body to keep me aloft as I entrusted his strength.

For more than an hour, we danced in the silks. The guys didn't stay up with me for every single one, but eventually I had to come down. I shook all over as my muscles quaked, and I had spaghetti legs when I tried to stand.

Liam scooped me up and curled me to him. "I got you, Hellspawn.

Yes, he did. They both did. Twisting in his arms, I wrapped mine around his neck and didn't fight any impulse. Fusing my lips to his, I tasted the coffee he'd had earlier and a hint of caramel, like he'd been sucking on one. Then all I was tasting was Liam as his tongue swept in and teased mine.

A hot hand pressed against my back and Liam groaned as I lifted my head to glance over at Rome. Instead of protesting though, Rome just fisted my hair as I leaned in toward him. Kissing him was like filling myself with fresh air.

The freedom I'd found in the silks. The freedom and the joy. It was right there, an effervescence bubbling in my system that I hadn't felt in a long time. Too long.

Liam pressed his lips to my throat and sucked a little bite as I kissed Rome and my whole body shuddered. They were both holding me up, my arms and legs were quivering, and I had no doubt that I was going to hurt later, but I was half drunk on kissing them.

Then they were both pressing kisses along my jaw until it was Liam claiming my mouth. Air grew more precious as I twisted between them.

"Fuck," Liam said on an exhale, finally lifting his head and staring up at the ceiling. Rome's erection pressed against my hip even as Liam's rubbed against the inside of my thigh.

"Right now?" I mean, I wasn't opposed. Heat was rolling off of them and I was so damn hot that the cooler air felt good.

"Not here," Liam growled.

Rome sucked another bite against my throat before lifting his head to look at Liam. A wordless pulse of communication passed between them. I swore they could convey so much with just looks.

"As much as I hate to say it," Liam said, his gaze burning into me. "Get dressed, Hellspawn. We're taking our field trip back. Dinner will be later."

Dinner? Oh, they planned more for here. "I don't want you to have to change your plans…"

Yeah, I didn't get to finish that sentiment. Liam slapped my ass with his open hand. The heat of it burned through my pants and made me gasp. I gaped at him for a moment as both pain and pleasure twisted through me. He massaged the spot he'd slapped as he studied me.

"Yeah, you liked that, didn't you?"

I swallowed as he continued to spread the heat out with his gentle massage.

"Words, Hellspawn."

"Wait," Rome said, though he, like Liam, stared at me intently.

"I—maybe?" It had been unexpected and at the same time.

"You want a second one to be sure?" Liam asked, and when I glanced at Rome, he seemed almost as curious as I'd been. Even with all the adrenaline in my system from the silks, this was… different.

"Yes?"

I didn't have to ask Liam twice. He slapped his hand against my other ass cheek and I swore the burn was more intense than the first one. But soon, he was spreading it out with a gentle massage.

A shudder rolled through me and I clamped my thighs tighter against his hips.

"I think I do," I admitted, more startled at myself than anything else.

"Good to know." Liam gave me a hard, biting kiss that was more teeth than tongue before he set me on my feet.

I wasn't proud to admit how unsteady I was, but Rome balanced me and Liam looked ready to catch me. Sucking in a deep breath, I worked to move toward my boots. We all got dressed without much conversation, but it wasn't until Liam helped me put my holster back on that I looked up at him and Rome, who was standing just to the right of him.

"Thank you. I needed this." I didn't have to explain. Rome just nodded, but Liam smiled. "And I want both of you."

That gave Liam a moment's pause, and he split a look with his brother before he focused on me again. "You sure?"

I grinned and slapped his ass for all I was worth. It stung my hand, and he gave a little jerk, his eyebrows rising as I leaned into him and massaged his ass.

"Yes," Rome said. "She is."

CHAPTER 16

I almost hated leaving the fairgrounds. Almost. As it was, the hum in my system made me wish we could go a little faster. Currently, I was tucked into the backseat with the guys up front again. Rome had started to follow me in, but Liam blocked him and just said no.

"Awww," I complained but Liam gave me a look.

"If I have to wait, Hellspawn, then *both* of you have to wait too." The roughness edging every syllable quieted my urge to tease him a little more.

"Hurry then?" It was a compromise. He leaned in and gave me a hard kiss before he closed the door and sent Rome around to the passenger seat.

It wasn't until we were on the road and away from the fairgrounds that Rome said, "I could have driven, then you could be in the backseat with Starling."

"*Now*, you offer that?" Was that disbelief twining with exasperation in Liam's voice?

149

"You didn't ask," Rome told him.

I had to clap a hand against my mouth to try and keep the laughter in. Not that I was terribly successful. Liam's gaze snagged mine in the rearview mirror. Despite his huff, there was a definite twinkle in his eyes before he winked.

"I'll remember that next time."

"Me too," Rome said, and when he sent me a smile, I couldn't keep the laughter in. I was exhausted, elated, turned-on, and just—

"Enjoying yourself, Hellspawn?" The indulgence in Liam's tone beckoned me to play, and I let my grin out.

"Yes. Although I could be enjoying myself more…you know, if I got to enjoy you."

"Oh, you will," he promised. The shiver of excitement colliding with anticipation had me squirming in my seat. The faint feeling of the sting from where he'd slapped my ass was still there. I clenched my thighs together, and my muscles trembled with fatigue.

None of that could quite touch the wildness in my blood. Each comment and gesture reminded me of our destination and *why* we'd cut short the evening at the fairgrounds…

"I can't believe you guys set that up for me," I said, almost more to myself than to them. "Then again, I shouldn't be remotely surprised. You're all amazing, and you think of almost everything."

"Almost?" Challenge populated the word as Liam flicked a look at me in the rearview.

"Almost," I said. "It's practically perfect. You're amazing, even when you're trying to drive me crazy. Maybe especially then."

"Practically perfect…" It was like he had to turn those words over. "Not sure I want to be your Mary Poppins."

That wasn't what I meant at all, yet giggles escaped me at the most absurd image of Liam in an umbrella as he floated primly through the sky. I almost wept from the laughter when we returned to the parking garage.

Liam's smile when he opened my car door was both indulgent and amused. For a moment, just a moment, I forgot about how vigilant we needed to be. They didn't. Their watchfulness as they scanned the garage before tucking me between them was right there.

Always watching.

Always protecting.

Something deep inside me unclenched. A breath I'd held all of my life? Fists I'd clenched, with my nails digging into my palms until they bled? The gag cutting into my face that kept me silent? It was all of those things and none of them.

Home.

This was what home felt like. Pressing against Liam's back, I hugged him from behind as we slid into the vestibule and then around the corner to the elevator.

"Hey," he murmured, turning to lift his arm and wrap it around me. The hug let me press my ear to his chest, where the thump of his heartbeat steadied me. "What's wrong?"

The question made me smile, the softness of his shirt teasing my cheek. "Nothing." Absolutely nothing.

At the ding of the elevator, Liam guided us in and when I reached out a hand, Rome slid his fingers through mine. This was almost perfect. On the ride up, Liam pulled his phone out of his pocket with one hand and tabbed through the screens. This close, I couldn't miss the sudden camera views of his apartment.

"You have surveillance cameras?" Surprise filtered through me.

"Yep," Liam said, the corner of his mouth curving upward.

How did I—

"Wait," I said slowly as he paused on the sofa on his screen and the elevator doors dinged open.

"Hold that thought, Hellspawn." He lowered the phone and blocked me from exiting with one arm while Rome tugged me to him.

I hated that they had to be so cautious about everything, and at the same time, I utterly appreciated the choice to be safe for them even more than for me. So I kept my questions to myself until we were inside the apartment.

Rome slid my jacket off for me as Liam locked the door behind us and I pivoted to face him, then scanned the room looking for the cameras.

"There," Rome told me, pointing to a smoke detector.

"And the clock," Liam said as he reached for the clip of my holster and freed it. "There's another tucked between the books on the shelf."

He had full coverage of the living room. "So when Vaughn and I…"

"Hmm-hmm," Liam said with a soft laugh.

And the chair with Jasper—

Liam hooked his fingers into the hem of my shirt and tugged it upwards. Rome followed it with my sports bra and the cooler air brushed over my skin.

"I didn't know," I said slowly, turning the idea over in my head.

"He didn't tell you," Rome murmured, then kissed my bare shoulder as Liam skated his hands over my sides, barely brushing my breasts to hook his fingers into the waistband of my leggings. "There are no cameras in my room."

Oh. It was hard to keep track as Rome slid his hands to cup my breasts, and Liam tugged my pants down.

"There are in mine," Liam said with a grin.

Shock and lust twined through me at the heated look in Liam's eyes as he stripped the last of my clothes down. He didn't wait for me to pull off my boots, just tugged them off and tossed them.

On a knee in front of me, he gripped my hips. With his thumbs caressing a line down to where my thighs met, he chuckled before pressing a kiss to my tummy. "You still with us, Hellspawn?"

The calluses on Rome's fingers added to the sensations as he massaged my breasts and rolled my nipples. His sweats did nothing to hide the erection pressing against my ass. "I'm—"

The words barely formed in my brain and stuttered out before they reached my tongue when Liam lifted my right leg and nudged it over his shoulder. Then pushed it higher.

Oh, he wanted my right leg straight up. It was like a reverse-standing monkey pose. I pointed my toes as I flattened my left foot. The stretch burned through my quads and my ass and along my hamstrings.

After the silks, the pose was almost glorious in the pleasure and pain it released. I could maintain my balance, but Rome braced me even as Liam stroked his hand up the inside of my left leg to cup my cunt.

"Fuck me," Liam whispered. "I forget how fucking flexible you are and how much I like it."

"I don't," Rome said, before he bit my earlobe, teasing it with his tongue. "Forget how flexible you are or how much I like it."

"Bite me," Liam muttered, but there was so much warmth in his voice that I had to laugh.

"No," Rome countered. "Want to bite Starling." Then to prove his point, he scraped his teeth over my earlobe and then down my throat in a series of biting kisses that sent shivers racing over my skin.

My nipples peaked as he began to massage slow circles over them, then he twisted and pinched. Hips thrusting forward, I leaned more firmly into Rome, and then Liam's tongue glided over my cunt.

Stance shifting, Rome moved to wrap an arm around my upraised leg as if he wanted to brace it for me. With his other hand, he continued to massage my breast and then Liam's fingers eased into me as he wrapped his lips around my clit.

The world became one great haze of caresses, strokes, bites, sucking kisses, and pleasure. I couldn't focus on any one touch because they were everywhere. A sound left my throat that wasn't quite human and then Rome was kissing along my jaw. A moment later, his mouth fused to mine as my hips began to buck.

Or I wanted to buck. Maybe. Muscle control failed me. My left leg buckled except I didn't stumble, not with Liam bracing me. He alternated between tongue and teeth to pull another sound from me.

His fingers curved inside me, pulling another wave of pure liquid heat that had me shuddering. His mouth left my cunt, but then he bit the inside of my thigh and the orgasm that had already been stirring just seemed to erupt. It rushed upward, spiraling out as I cried.

Trembling violently, I grasped at Rome's arm and reached for Liam. He caught my fingers as he nuzzled another kiss to my cunt. It was almost too much, and the world just whited out for a moment.

Pretty sure my soul left my body, then came back to the soft pets and stroking hands as Liam lifted me.

"There she is…" he murmured. His lips and cheeks glistened, the light dancing over his face as he carried me from the living room. Oh right, we hadn't even left his living room.

"Wow." That was a word for it. I was floating, absolutely floating and I hadn't gotten to do more than just kiss them. "Where's…"

"Here," Rome answered before I could fully form the question. Oh, he was ahead of us and my gaze snared on his as we came into Liam's bedroom. He'd also shed the rest of his clothes and I got to just enjoy the sight of him.

"Subtle," Liam said with a snort, and I gave him a pat that barely qualified as that, much less a swat.

"Leave him alone. I like it." Not that I needed to defend Rome. The twins loved each other so much, and they tied me up in that emotion, tangling me right between them.

Liam surrendered me as soon as Rome reached for me, and then my skin was on his and it was glorious. He was so warm. Wrapping my arms around him, I nuzzled a kiss as Rome shifted to sit on the bed with me in his lap.

His erection nestled against my ass at this angle and there was a single slight internal tremor at the feeling.

"Ease up," Liam said, his hand coming to rest against my back.

Rome grunted a half-formed sound before lifting his head. "I like kissing Starling."

"I like kissing her too, but there are a couple of things we have to talk about." Firmness underscored each word. Oh, he wasn't playing now. I tried to get my limbs to work so I could sit up, even as Rome grumbled.

Despite his protests, there was no heat in his disagreement. He even helped me sit up better, which pressed his very pretty dick more firmly along the crevice of my ass. The little timbre of alarm faded into the hum buzzing under my skin.

This was Rome and Liam. Fear didn't belong in here.

Pushing my now messy hair out of my eyes, I met Liam's sober gaze and then reached out to cup his face. "Hi."

He smiled slowly, covering my hand on his cheek with his and then kissing my palm. Unlike Rome and me, however, Liam was very not naked.

"Hellspawn," he murmured, half in warning, and half in

exasperated affection. Oh, I loved that tone in his voice. "Focus on me for a moment."

"You're not naked," I informed him.

"I'm aware," he exhaled the admonishment with a roll of his eyes. "Focus."

I made a face and tried to sit up, but that only worked to remind me of Rome's erection. He let out a breath and I had to fight the urge to roll my hips.

There was something just so damn deeply comforting about being here with them, even if the beep of alarm was there, in the distance. A reminder of things—I was not going to think about him right now so I slammed that door.

"With us?" Liam asked again as I lifted my chin. The blur left by the sensation of drunken pleasure faded. It gave me greater clarity and a better view of the concern in Liam's eyes.

"Yes," I promised.

"Good." Still holding my hand, he flicked one look past me to Rome. "You said both of us."

"I did." I frowned as I nodded. "I remember what I said."

His smile was gentle. "I remember what you said too, Hellspawn. The point is I want to clarify what that means. You don't like having your ass played with…"

It brought *him* up but I kept that door barred and shuttered. "I've been working on that," I said. "Vaughn and Kel have been helping me."

"Okay. How far is too far? What do you want? Can you use your words to tell me how you want us?"

All at once, my apprehension was erased at the request. It was both sweet—and so fucking sexy at the same time. "How specific should I be?" Because I had ideas. Rome and Vaughn had been adventurous at times, and fuck knew lately Kel and Vaughn could be creative.

"As specific as you can, because the very last thing either of us is going to do is something that scares or hurts you."

I launched forward, wrapping my arms around Liam. He caught me easily, lifting me from Rome's lap.

"No fear for you," Rome echoed his words. "You like the kissing…and sex."

I did like those. I pressed my face against Liam's throat. Hiding? Maybe. But this was different. This was—safer. Everything was okay here. The guys weren't asking me for more than guidance and assurance.

"Kellan plays with my ass," I told him. "He's used his fingers mostly, and it's—amazing. It was terrifying at first." I could admit that. "It made me think about *him.*" If I had to discuss it, I wasn't mentioning his fucking name. "But then they would retreat, and Vaughn would drive me mad—eating me out or fucking me with his dick, and Kellan would start again."

Heat swept over my face and I lifted my head to look from Liam to Rome and back. Not an ounce of judgment or anger was reflected in their expressions.

"It's okay to talk about that kind of specific?"

"Yes," Liam said. "I'd prefer it. Has Kellan or Vaughn used their dick on your ass yet?"

A shiver raced up my spine. Pain flashed in my memory. Pain. Grunts…

"Right here, Hellspawn." The whip-crack of command in Liam's voice anchored me, and I blinked past those memories then shook my head.

"No," I pushed the word out. "Not yet. Though the last time…it was amazing what he was doing with his fingers. I thought it would be pain always, but…" It hadn't been.

Drawing a slow circle against the base of my spine with his thumb, Liam looked thoughtful. "How much experimenting do you want to do right now? Or would you rather

157

let us pass you back and forth, fucking you until you can't see straight? I still owe you that spanking too."

My breath caught in the back of my throat and I twisted a little so I could see Rome too. Like Liam, he only watched me with concern and interest.

"I want…" The words weren't easy. Then again, life never had been. "I want you. I want Rome. I want—I want all of it, and I don't want to be afraid or worried or think about him at all. Not here and not now."

"Okay." Rome studied me. "Are you afraid?"

I wanted to say no. I really, really wanted to say no. But I didn't dismiss the question or try to rush the answer.

"I'm not afraid of you guys," I said, testing each word slowly. "Not at all."

"Good." That came from both of them, and when I reached a hand to Rome, as he clasped it to him.

"I trust you both…" Also true. No hesitations. "Kel and Vaughn have shown me it can feel good but…I'm afraid I might panic and I don't want to ruin this for you guys."

"You won't ruin anything," Liam said. "If you want to try, trust me, Hellspawn, I'm all in. I've had a thing for your ass from the beginning."

That admission made my face heat more than it should and at the same time, a genuine delight unfolded inside me. "Really?"

"Oh yeah. You're flexible as fuck, and that ass…" He made a little hmmm sound in the back of his throat. "But I want you to want it, Hellspawn. Not to do it just because you think I want it—which I do, only that's not the only reason to do it."

Liam was so good with words and to hear him half-stumble on that sentence helped more than I could have imagined. When I glanced at Rome, he shrugged.

"I like your pussy," Rome said. "I'm sure your ass is fine. But Liam wants it more."

There was a beat, just a perfect pause as he said that with a perfect deadpan. It was just Rome and he was perfect.

Tears filled my eyes at the unabashed acceptance there. That acceptance they had for each other was all focused on me.

"I want to try," I said, then glanced at Liam. "I want to do this all the way—both of you, at the same time."

"Anything you want, Hellspawn." Liam wrapped a hand around my nape and dragged me in for a kiss. It was all demanding passion and commitment, devotion and strength. Releasing me, he blew out a breath. "Now play with Rome and let him relax you again while I get stuff ready for us."

"Liam," I said as he released me back to Rome.

"I know," he whispered, touching my cheek with his finger. "I know."

The hell of it was, I was pretty sure he really did.

CHAPTER 17

EMERSYN

Kissing Rome was one of my favorite things. When our mouths moved together, he seemed to take it as permission to add to every caress of his tongue with a stroke of his fingers. It also gave me equal opportunity to explore him. The way his muscles shivered and moved when I trailed my fingers over them.

The roughness of his fingers in places gave way to the smoother calluses from using cans of spray paint. A groan escaped me as he kissed a path from my mouth to my throat. Inexperienced or not, Rome loved to explore *me*.

More, I loved it when he explored. The different ways he would kiss and taste my skin. How he would massage my muscles. It brought relief to the aching muscles in my back and legs. Too much work too soon without enough prep.

Dangerous.

At the same time, exhilarating because I'd *done* it. I could still fly. The scrape of his teeth over my pulse point. The heat of his skin teasing my breasts. It could all be sensory over-load and yet, I just wanted more.

I moved to rest a knee on either side of him on the bed as I traced my fingers over his chest. The lines of his tattoos beckoned to be explored. The warmth of his palm cupping over the tattoo on my chest had me leaning back.

He glanced down at the Vandals tat, and I grinned slowly. He hadn't really seen it since it had healed. It was smaller than the one on my stomach and I'd gotten to enjoy this one far more.

"I like this," he murmured, tracing a finger along the border of it.

"Me too. Right over my heart. Where all of you belong." In my heart.

Rome lifted his gaze up to study mine. "You've always been there."

"In yours," I said slowly, and it wasn't a question. He nodded.

"Always."

"I wish I'd known you then." I pressed my forehead to his, and stretched my fingers out over his heart. "Wish I'd known all of you."

"You know us now," Rome said, and he was right. I did know them now. He kissed my lips as he stroked his hands down my sides. "What do you need?"

"I have everything I need." I really did. I had all of them. "But I want you."

He fisted his cock, drawing my attention to it. It strained upwards, red-tipped and damp with pre-cum. I loved the art he'd added to his dick. Who wouldn't love seeing themselves inked onto such precious skin in such fine detail?

"My mouth?" I asked him because as much as I was enjoying this, I had already had a couple of orgasms.

"Later," Rome said as he slid his hand over my hip. "Liam wants to spank you now."

Exhaling an explosive breath, Liam let out a laugh. "I was going to say something."

Glancing over my shoulder, I savored the sight of Liam standing there in only his sweatpants. "You still have on too many clothes."

At the challenge in my tone, he raised his brows. "You really want this spanking."

"If I'm going to get it," I teased. "I might as well earn it."

"Hellspawn," he said with a shake of his head as he chuckled. "Tell me the truth. Is this okay?"

He stroked his hand over my ass. At this angle, I was still hovering over Rome and he balanced me but was also sitting up so we were chest to chest.

"I want to know," I said after a moment, giving the question some genuine thought. "I trust you."

"Then the word I want from you is 'stop' if at any point you want us to stop. For any reason, and I don't need you to try and explain. If you need me to stop…"

"…or me…" Rome volunteered.

"Say stop."

"That doesn't seem particularly fair to you," I pointed out. Then Liam's hand landed against my ass with the sharpest of stinging slaps that lit my whole body up. Tears burned in my eyes because it genuinely hurt, though as he massaged the spot it spread the heat out, and some of the tension in my muscles leaked away.

"I didn't ask about what's fair to me," Liam informed me. "Right now, we're doing something that has the potential to scare the fuck out of you. You're trusting us to take care of you."

"Yes," I told him. "And I do trust you."

"I know, Hellspawn," he said, his soft tone soothing. "But

we're trusting you to let us know if it's too much. We have to work together."

I held Rome's gaze then glanced back at Liam's. Where his fingers rubbed against my ass cheek, the heat had begun to just sink into my whole body.

"Can you do that? If it's too much, we can stop right now and I'll happily trade out with Rome."

No, that wasn't what I wanted. I honestly did want them both. I wanted to claw back that piece for me. For us.

"I can do that. If I want you to stop—no matter the reason —I say stop."

His smile softened his whole expression, and some of the earlier elation ballooned through me. "That's my Hellspawn. Now—fuck my brother because he's patient as hell, and he's right—it's time for your spanking."

The thrill that went through me at those words was both intoxicating and a little terrifying. But then, the fear just slid away when I looked at Rome. Liam was behind me while Rome was in front of me.

I was in the safest place in the world. Cupping my hand against the back of Rome's head, I dropped my free hand down to caress his cock. It was still hard as a stone, silky soft and so hot against my palm. Rome's eyes dipped closed at my caress.

"Yes?" I asked him and his smile unraveled more of the tension until I was free-falling.

"Please, Starling."

Two sweet words and I angled myself over him even as I teased the head of his cock along my cunt. Back and forth more to torment both of us, but not long. Anticipation clenched in my stomach, I sank down on him as he sprawled back on the bed. The position had my ass angling up and even waiting for it, the second smack against an ass cheek sent a shockwave through me.

Although it wasn't pain so much as heat, I let out a shout of startled surprise. Rome filled me and I flexed my inner walls around him as he brought his hands to my hips to help balance me.

"Can you handle three more, Hellspawn?" Liam's voice was rough as he massaged my ass. The heat penetrated deeper and when I rolled my hips to rock against Rome's cock it held just an edge from the sting where Liam's hand had impacted.

"I can," I promised, shifting my hands to Rome's shoulders. "But I need to move too." Because I could feel Rome with every pulse of my cunt, and I wanted to move.

"Hold that thought," Liam told me, and I grinned at Rome as he braced me. The three strikes came in rapid succession, yet only one of them actually stung. I clenched around Rome with each slap and he let out a breath.

"I like that," he told me and I laughed. There was something else inside of me that was unlocking as the heat sprawled out in my system.

"Me too," I told him.

"Good to know," Liam said as he kept massaging my ass. "More later. Now for a test, Hellspawn. Distract yourselves…"

He might have said something more, but Rome tugged me down for a kiss, and I sank into it as he pushed up. The thrust, combined with his tongue mirroring the movement, was intoxicating. So was the vibrant warmth that seemed to glow from my ass.

The idea of my ass glowing just added an element of humor to the desire and I laughed. Totally chuckled into Rome's kiss. Fucking could be intense. It could be physical. It was often breathtaking and mind-blowing. Sometimes it could be downright painful, though.

However, there was a joy in this that I had trouble coping

with. Even as I laughed, tears slid down my cheeks. Liam's fingers teased at my anus, the pre-warmed lube he'd dribbled was easing his strokes.

Rome cupped my face as he settled me back and tears splashed from my cheeks onto his. "Stop?" The question threatened to break me.

The concern in his eyes. The concern and the love. The brush of Liam's lips against my shoulder as his hand stilled, his fingers right there.

I shook my head slowly. "Please don't stop," I whispered. "I need you."

"We won't," Rome promised as Liam pressed a finger passed the ring of muscle. Apprehension gave way to amazement as he added a second finger and then a third.

All those times when panic had begun to claw through me faded away. I pushed back against his fingers then down onto Rome. This was almost too slow. I needed *more.*

"Yes?" Liam whispered against my ear as a low sound left me.

Had I said that aloud? "Yes," I told him. "Don't stop."

"Hold her still," Liam ordered.

Rome arched up to nip at my breast, and when he began to suck at the nipple, it almost distracted me from Liam telling him to keep me there. I wanted to move. Needed it.

I squirmed but a light slap against my ass stilled me.

"I don't want to hurt you," Liam growled. "Let me do this for you."

Shuddering at the warring sensations competing with the riot of my own emotions, I tilted my head back. "Sorry…" I slid my hand through Rome's hair as he nuzzled my breast.

"Nothing to be sorry about, Hellspawn," Liam gripped my chin, and I turned to meet his possessive kiss, opening to his demand as he dribbled more lube against my ass.

Excitement began to bubble up through me as he moved,

the heat of him against my back even as Rome gave a little push to remind me he was there. When Liam released my lips, Rome claimed them. Then there was so much pressure against my anus, I froze.

The thud of my heart was so loud and seemed to vibrate against my ribs. His cock was so much bigger than his fingers.

"Easy, Hellspawn," Liam murmured. "Relax. It's me. We're going to go as slow as you need." He stroked my back as Rome pulled back to gaze up at me. Locking my eyes on him, I clenched against the invasion. Even knowing it was Liam, hearing him, and feeling him… I expected pain.

"It burns," I whispered.

"Bad?" Liam had gone utterly still.

I shook my head slowly. "It's—hard to describe. There's—so much pressure." A tear slid down my cheek, and Rome lifted a hand to cup my face, swiping away the moisture with his thumb. "Keep going."

Liam brushed his lips against my shoulder again and pressed forward at my urging. Then, he was just—there. And I was so full, his cock in my ass and Rome's in my cunt. Like the sting from the spanking, the burn just edged the pleasure, and I shuddered.

Poised, we held still. Or I did as they both ran their hands over me. Liam stroked my back as Rome ran his hands up and down my arms. We probably made such a sight… for once, I wished there were mirrors in here…

"Liam?" I sounded almost hoarse and Rome had begun to tremble. Or maybe it was Liam. Hell, it could be me. I was so damn full.

"What do you need, Hellspawn?"

"Are there cameras in here?"

Silence greeted that question, and if I hadn't been staring right at Rome, I would have missed the hint of a smile.

"Yes?" Liam answered, his tone guarded. "No one can see but me. Well, and Rome 'cause he has the codes."

Triumph fountained up through me. "I want to see."

That earned me another pause and then a low, dark chuckle. "Oh, Hellspawn. I will show you anything you want to see."

When his teeth scraped my shoulder, I let out a groan and it was the last words we spoke as Liam eased back and I pushed down against Rome. Then Rome pushed my hips up so I could roll back onto Liam.

It took us a moment to find that rhythm, sweat dribbling along my arms and down my chest. If I thought I'd been flying before, it had nothing on this. I writhed between them, trading kisses and caresses. I hooked my hand up behind me to hold onto Liam as I clasped Rome to me.

We rocked forever, slow and steady, and then the urgency began to build. The glide of their skin against mine was erotic.

The pressure would build up and there was a moment where a flash of pain intruded, but then Liam would kiss me or Rome would murmur, and the dreadful memory would fade.

Banished.

When the trembling increased, Liam said, "Rome, tease her clit a little."

He barely brushed his fingers against me and I detonated. I clenched around them both as my orgasm dragged theirs from them and then we were just clinging together, soaked in sweat and tears, and… elation.

Even as I shook, I laughed. The feeling so intoxicating, I clung to them. Worry flickered in Rome's eyes, but then his face relaxed into a smile, and Liam huffed a laugh against my back. His chuckle broke something else loose inside me and then we were all laughing, even Rome.

I don't even know how long we laughed before Liam eased off of me and they rolled me over, easing Rome out and then we were just lying there side by side on the bed.

"How are we doing?" Liam asked even though there were still little giggles escaping. "For real."

I tried to sober up to answer the question, except it was hard when all I wanted to do was smile. "I feel like we just won… like I won."

"Yeah?" He raised his brows and the intensity in his eyes couldn't be ignored.

"Oh yeah." I licked my lips. "Course, I also feel hot, sweaty, and sticky—but…like, can we try that again?"

His laughter was the sweetest sound. Even better was how wide his grin was. Rome nuzzled a kiss to my cheek and then said, "That means yes."

CHAPTER 18

DOC

"*B*lanka," I told the young woman who'd been translating for her grandmother. "Can you please tell her that she has to take her pills? Every day, no exceptions. She takes one in the morning when she gets up, thirty minutes before her morning tea."

"I will tell her Doctor James, but she doesn't like to wait on her tea. It's what she does when she gets to the kitchen. She puts food out for the cats, and she makes her tea. Then she starts the baking. But the tea has to come first. If she doesn't have her tea, her whole morning is off." Blanka looked so apologetic and I smiled.

"Maybe she can take a glass of water and put it beside her bed. Then she can just take that first pill when she gets up before getting dressed. From everything you've said, it will be almost thirty minutes by the time she makes it to the kitchen and prepares her tea."

Blanka translated rapidly. The old woman understood

English, I was almost positive, but she didn't speak to people outside of her family. When I'd first opened the clinic, she refused to even come inside. We'd made progress.

Mrs. Albescu considered her granddaughter then me. Her blood pressure had improved, but at eighty-seven, there was no reason we couldn't ensure she had the best chance.

When she responded, Mrs. Albescu pointed a finger at me. The rapid-fire words might be indecipherable to me, yet I recognized that tone. She'd do it, but she didn't like it.

"Thank you, Doctor James. I know she is stubborn, but she likes her routines."

"I understand. Unless something comes up, we'll revisit this in a few weeks at her next appointment. Don't hesitate to call me."

Blanka and her grandmother were off and I took the bread she'd baked for me into the office. Freddie glanced up from where he was reading in the corner. "Need me to clean that room?"

"Sure," I told him, and he was out before I could finish. There were no narcotics that he could get to quickly, and while that used to be a concern, I wasn't as worried about it right now. Putting the loaves aside, I updated Mrs. Albescu's chart, then went through the other dozen patients I'd seen today.

Freddie had been crashing at my apartment and hanging out at the clinic for the last week. What appeared to be a slip had turned into something else. I was good with him taking the time he needed for him. At the same time, I worried about him hiding here.

It didn't take him long. We'd mostly just talked in the exam room, and Freddie had taken to cleaning everything. Generally, my volunteer or I did—or the nurse. But for the last week, Freddie had asked to do it.

"There are no more patients out there."

"There usually isn't on Thursdays," I told him. "Bingo down at the Knights of Columbus hall."

"Oh." Freddie shook his head. "I didn't even know that was a thing."

I grinned at him. "Houlihan's has an all-you-can-eat buffet. Jamison's has lady's night. So—the social calendars are pretty booked."

"Anyone ever tell you it's weird how much you know about people?"

"A few," I said, leaning back in my chair. It was after five. I didn't close the clinic until six, so we had some time. "I wasn't planning on cooking tonight. Usually order pizza or tacos."

"That sounds good," Freddie said, folding his arms as he leaned in the doorway. From where he stood, he had an easy view of the lobby and the front door.

Jasper and Vaughn had been dividing their time to come over and hang out with Freddie in the evenings, especially if I had to work late. One of them had been sacking out on my couch while Freddie was in the guest room.

"You ready to talk to me yet?" I'd been good about not pushing, but a week was plenty of time. Freddie was treading water and not getting anywhere fast.

"I don't know," he admitted. It was a lot more than a simple "no" before he walked away. Raking a hand through his hair, he stared into the distance. "Doc—you ever look back at your choices and wonder what else you could have done? Like, you know you had to do something, and you thought you did the best, but then…"

He tapped his head against the door frame and rather than jump in, I waited him out. Freddie was hiding with me for a reason. He just hadn't told me what it was he needed yet.

But he'd also been clean for longer than I'd seen him manage since I came back. That came with its own baggage.

"I mean…I know I had to do something. I couldn't sleep. I couldn't eat. There were nights that the nightmares would freak me out until I puked. I had to take the edge off. But a little turned into a lot, and now the nightmares also have teeth that haunt me during the day." He released a humorless laugh. "Now I'm a colossal fuckup and freaking out because Boo-Boo kissed my cheek."

Freddie extended an arm. The tremors, while faint, were present. "I'm here, scrubbing floors, toilets, and walls, so I don't go and score something. Because as much as this dark little part of me says it will help, I know it won't."

Lowering his hand, he slid his fingers into the pockets of his jeans like he had to do something with them. Anything to keep still, and even then, he was restless.

"So do you ever look back at your choices and go, yep, that's where I fucked up? I should have zigged, instead I zagged."

"Every day," I told him. "Sometimes a dozen times in a day. But thinking like that will choke you, mire you, and keep you from moving. It sucks…we can't change the past, Freddie. We can learn from it, though. Sometimes we can even try to make up for it. But most of the time, we just have to accept that it happened and forgive ourselves."

"You make it sound easy," Freddie said with a sigh.

"Maybe, the words and the platitudes are easy. Living isn't."

"You can say that again." He turned, putting his back to the doorjamb and staring down the hall. "Did I fuck up my whole future with all the drugs I put in my system? Am I always just gonna be one crisis away from wanting to get loaded?"

"I can't answer that for you," I told him, considering every word. "No one can. Addiction isn't a problem that goes away because you wish for it, too. It's like…" I glanced down at my left arm. "Burn scars. A burn heals, eventually. Sometimes the nerves come back. They can even do skin grafts, only the thing about a burn is that flesh is permanently damaged. It's never going to be the same.

"I can ink it, decorate it, do therapy to help the muscles beneath it, and work every day to keep it strong and to keep going—but the scars? They're still there."

He let another humorless scoff. "You're not really comforting, Doc."

"Well, I could lie to you—but I won't. You don't deserve lies, Freddie. Life has cut you a shit deal at times. It kicked you in the teeth when you were down and put you in a corner where you didn't think you had many choices."

No sound of disagreement came from him, and if anything, his gaze went further away. "I just…want to be normal."

Leaning forward, I rested my arms on the desk. "Freddie, there is no such thing as 'normal.' What was normal for me before I went into the army would seem alien now. Because I'm not that guy anymore. I had to find my new normal, and that's what you need to do. Don't try to be someone else— just be you."

Grimacing, he straightened and glared at me. "I suck. I'm a fucking drug addict and screwup."

"You're a Vandal, a good friend, an even better brother, and you'd bleed for the guys, which you have."

"So?"

"You also went into that facility without a single bit of hesitation to get Little Bit out."

Bringing her up might not have been the right call, and I wouldn't—except he'd mentioned her first.

"You're the absolute best, Freddie. Who you are, it's not

175

just being an addict. It's not that kid growing up in the group home. It's not even the smart-ass little shit who cuts as easily with his tongue as he does with his knife."

There was a hint of a smile, almost pride on his face at that. "Damn, Doc. Didn't know you cared."

"There you go, deflect, evade, push away the compliments. Freddie, you aren't just *one* thing. You're the sum of all your experiences, good and bad." That was what it came down to. "Right now, you're teetering 'cause you want to shut up the demons. Two months ago? You'd have just gone to get something and not had a second thought about it."

He made a face, but he didn't contradict me.

"Not going to lie, when Jasper brought you by the other day, I didn't expect you to be sober. But you were—and you are—choosing to stay sober. It's hard, and I'm acknowledging that. It may always be a fight, but there are groups—"

"Oh hell no, I had my fill of groups at Pinetree."

I didn't laugh 'cause it wasn't funny even if he tried to play it off that way. "These are different kinds of groups. But whether you talk to a group or a therapist—or Jasper or me. We're here. We'll listen. If you want someone to go with you, to have your back? We can do that too."

Freddie had never liked strangers. He hated being cooped up with them. I got it.

"I've done my own share of group therapy sessions. They aren't great, but sometimes, they can help when nothing else does."

"You?" He frowned and shook his head. "You barely drink, and I know you don't do drugs."

"No, not anymore. I had to do a lot of oxy while I was recovering. That was its own problem." One that didn't necessarily impact me as much. But I'd also been violently aware of the narcotic properties and the desire to finish my degree and come back. But I had to get on my feet too.

"There was physical therapy," I told him, not cutting him off if he needed to hear that. "There were also survivor groups—groups with other veterans. Talking to people who get it, who were there... that's what some of the recovering addict groups can give you. Understanding. A place where you don't get judged, because they genuinely know."

"Do you still go?"

"Not as often," I admitted. "Sometimes, I just throw myself into the work here, helping you kids out, helping Little Bit...it makes up for the rest."

"But we don't...if it helps, why not keep doing it?"

"Good question," I said. "One I don't have a good answer for. Perhaps I do need to go back to one, but right now, I feel okay. I have focus. I have...my work." And I had... "How is Little Bit doing?" It had been a few days since I last saw her.

He almost smirked. "If you want to know, Doc, you should go see her."

"Nice," I told him. "Maybe you should take your own advice."

Freddie blew out a breath. "I do miss her...I just—I want to be normal for her."

Yeah. I got that. "Tell you what, why don't you just try being Freddie for her? From what I can see, she really likes Freddie."

"What if I slip?" The little boy inside the damaged young man stared at me. "What if I'm there and I slip? What does that do to her?"

"In my experience, if you slip—she's going to try and catch you. So is Jasper and Vaughn and Kellan and everyone else. They're all going to catch you and her. They'll help her help you up." Then because he needed to hear it, I said, "So will I. When Jasper was wounded, he had to lean on you and Little Bit. When she came back from Pinetree, she was hurting."

There was no mistaking that hurt. Just the thought of the exam when they brought her back was enough to apply flame to tinder on my temper, but I kept it all in check for right now.

"If you slip, Freddie, we'll catch you. Maybe we don't get you before you land in that hole, but we'll damn well be there to help you climb back out."

"You make it sound easy."

The clock neared the six mark, and I rose, picking up my keys. "I wish it were that easy, but that's the thing—if it were easy, no one would want it badly enough. You want to know something else?"

He groaned. "I have a feeling you're going to tell me."

"See, you're learning already. The only person you're hurting when you run away—is you. I'm glad that running this time brought you back to us, and you can stay with me as long as you like, but when you're ready to go home? I'll drive you. None of us want you to hurt or be alone. You make the call."

"Just like that?"

I nodded. "Just like that. Now...we have a bigger problem?"

"We do?"

He walked out of my office ahead of me as I shut off the lights and followed. First, I had to lock the doors and drop the cage. Then we'd go out the back.

"Yep, are we having pizza or tacos tonight?"

CHAPTER 19

EMERSYN

*N*ot going to Mickey's or the clinic had been an exercise. Talking to Freddie on the phone had helped. The three days I spent with the twins at Liam's had helped. Coming back to the clubhouse to find Jasper and Milo laughing together had helped.

The guys helped, but I couldn't entirely suppress the thread of excitement inside of me as Kellan drove me to the clinic. "Rome will be picking you up later, probably with Vaughn."

I twisted a little in the seat to study him as we drove. He cast a look at me, and I grinned.

"See something you like, Sparrow?"

"Yep."

He chuckled and held out a hand for me to take. "Are you listening or just admiring me?"

"I can do both," I promised. "Rome and Vaughn are going to be the ones picking me up later. I know Jasper and Milo

179

are doing a run. You are going to the shop—" I gave him a look. "*Alone*, which is against the rules."

He exhaled. "Not alone, alone. Ripper's behind us with a couple of the new guys. I'm going to give them some basics to do at the garage."

"They don't count. Rats aren't Vandals."

"That's why I have you here to protect me," he said. While his tone was teasing, there was a thread of sobriety to it.

"And you're picking up Freddie." I'd kind of guessed when we didn't have one of the others coming with us.

"Yes, Sparrow, I'm picking up Freddie. He is going to be there for you to see and he asked to talk to me. Is that going to be a problem for you?" He squeezed my hand as though offering comfort for the straightforward question.

With that in mind, I gave it the serious thought it deserved. "No," I said slowly. "Am I disappointed he won't be there for my time? A little. But...I know he's doing what he needs to do for him right now too. I want to support that."

"Even if you miss him," Kellan said softly and I traced a finger over his palm.

"Yes. I never want to hurt him or make him do anything he isn't ready for...." Yes, he had asked me to push him the way I'd been asking Kellan and Vaughn to push me. He also retreated and asked for space. So I'd give it to him. "Just... take care of him?"

Lifting my hand to his lips, Kel pressed a kiss to my knuckles. "I will. We all will."

The fact I knew that before he said anything didn't change the relief I experienced. "Can you do me another favor? I know I'm asking for a lot."

I'd been thinking about this for a while, but I noticed that Kel didn't play as much as he could. He carried so much weight for everyone. In some ways, it had all been Milo's burden initially. When Milo went to prison—I still hated that happened to him—then it had become Jasper's task.

"Name it, Sparrow. If I can, I will." Simple, direct, and not offering me a single promise he couldn't, well, in this case, wouldn't keep.

"Can I take you out on a date?" I hadn't done much dating. However, Jasper has given me some ideas, as had Liam and Rome. Kellan spent all his time looking after all of us, and I wanted to take the time to look after him.

Surprise flickered across his expression. Frowning, he pulled into the lot behind the clinic before he shifted in the seat to face me. "You want to take me out?"

"Yep. Someone has been teaching me to drive, and if you let me borrow your car, I can drive us too."

"Now might not be…" He began slowly.

"I'd take precautions," I told him. "I promise. I've also ensured we had backup because I know you don't want me going anywhere without at least two of you…and maybe we have to wait. I get that—I won't even sulk. Much."

The corners of his mouth deepened into a smile.

"But I want to take you out. I want—to take you on a real date. You and me. And our security will probably be a couple of the guys so we can work all of that out. Say yes? Please?"

"Sparrow…" he said on a sigh. "What am I going to do with you?"

I grinned. "Whatever you want. I'm flexible." Yes, I meant it exactly as it sounded and he laughed.

"Yes, you are." Pressing his hand gently against my chest right over the spot where the tattoo was, he brushed a kiss to my lips. "Let's get through the next few weeks… then yes, you can borrow my car and take me anywhere you want."

Grinning, I kissed him again. "Thank you."

He chuckled, shaking his head as the door to the clinic

opened, and Mickey stood there. "Go on, behave yourself," he told me. "And stay…"

"With Mickey or Rome, but only inside the clinic. Stay armed. Don't leave without company and check-in." I met his gaze. "I have zero intentions of disappearing on you without a fight." That was a promise.

"We have zero intentions of letting anyone get that close," he reminded me. "Now go before I spank you.

I slid out of the car but ducked back in to tell him, "Turns out I like spanking." Then I winked and shut the door. His expression was worth it and because I was feeling a little triumphant, I added a bit of a sway to my step as I headed toward the clinic.

Mickey watched me with a mixture of curiosity and amusement. He glanced from me to the car, then turned to the door as he pushed it inward. Freddie came walking out, and, fuck, he was a sight for sore eyes.

Some of the tension I'd been trying to pretend wasn't there eased as I locked gazes with him.

"Hey, Boo-Boo," he said. "Looking pretty damn good."

It was like he was making a peace offering I didn't need. I'd been the one to misstep… even so I wouldn't leave him dangling out there. "At least I'm pretty, right?"

That got me a genuine grin and a laugh. Instead of bypassing me, he opened his arms.

"You sure?" I asked, and he curled his fingers.

"Get over here, Boo-Boo. Give me a squeeze. Kellan's gonna make me do grunt work, and you probably smell a lot nicer than he does."

I crashed right into him, wrapping my arms around him and squeezing him tight when he returned the ferocity of the hug. Lifting my eyes, I locked gazes with Mickey. He dipped his chin while giving me a small smile.

"Missed you," Freddie whispered next to my ear, and I

pulled back, determined to keep this light and upbeat for him.

"Then we need to work on your aim," I suggested. It was an old joke, though it got me another smile.

"I promise." He raised two fingers. "Scout's honor."

"Freddie..." Mickey began.

"Don't say it, Doc," Freddie declared as he pulled away and tapped those two fingers against his chest before he pointed them at Mickey. "Didn't say what kind of scout."

I waited for Freddie to slide into the passenger seat, then blew them both a kiss. Kel nodded, then gave the building behind me a pointed look.

Maybe it was the time with the twins or the new tattoo, or the fact that Kel said yes to the date *and* I got to see and hug Freddie, but I smirked as I saluted and he held up a single finger.

It just made me laugh.

"C'mon, Little Bit," Mickey said from behind me, his tone amused and a little aggrieved. "Inside, before you start a riot."

"Who says that's not exactly what I want to do?" I dared him. Inside, I glanced around the back of the clinic as he closed up and locked the door.

"Well, I would say you could probably get what you want without trying too hard."

To be honest, I wasn't sure if that was exasperation or admiration in his voice. It seemed awfully quiet. I checked the time.

"Am I early?"

"A little," he said, motioning to the stairs. "Come on upstairs. I started coffee about fifteen minutes ago." Based on the fresh scent, I could tell, so I shrugged out of my coat, leaving the light jacket on.

Upstairs, I hung the coat on the wall pegs then glanced around the room. The walls with their posters from movies and shows. The colorful carpets. The comfortable sofas and tables with chairs. Mickey had made a place where the community kids could come and hang out.

"Is it still okay with you for me to volunteer?" I followed him into the kitchen, where there were three huge platters in addition to the coffee, two with sandwiches and a third with cookies.

"Of course it is," he told me and motioned to the food. "Help yourself. Steph dropped those trays by this morning. She likes to check on me periodically without looking like she's checking on me."

I frowned. "What is she worried about?"

"Well, as hard as it may be for you to believe, Little Bit. I was a bit of a hellraiser back in my day."

"In your day," I said, almost snorting. "Five years ago?"

He laughed. "I wish, Little Bit. The point is, I was one. Doesn't matter how old I am, Steph is still my big sister. She still checks on me."

I made a face. "Is that your way of telling me that Milo will always be overprotective?" I skipped the sandwiches and eyed the cookies. Before Kellan drove me over, I'd spent time in my studio. The itch to get back in there more often was a living thing inside me.

Dancing more, meant more calories. I needed more proteins. I'd been healing and we still had physical therapy, but not like before. Liam also said I was going to get more self-defense training. Pretty sure he just wanted another reason to grab my ass.

I pulled out one of the peanut butter chunk cookies and took a deep breath, inhaling the scent as I glanced over to find Mickey watching me with a little smile on his lips.

"Milo is always going to want to protect you, Little Bit. We all are. And yes, you're always going to be his baby sister. We younger siblings just have to suck that up."

"Uh-huh," I said as I took a bite while he poured the coffee.

"You look good," he said slowly, still watching me. "You're feeling good too."

Leaning back against the counter, I looked at my cookie and then over at him. "I am… I've told everyone." Oh, saying that felt weird. At his sudden sharp look, I winced and shook my head. "Not Milo, not yet. It took everything I had to tell you guys, and…it helped a lot to verbalize it, as insane as that sounds."

Coffee mugs in hand, he crossed over to me and set one down next to me. Instead of backing off, though, he touched a finger under my chin.

"Doesn't sound insane at all. You suffered in silence for far too long, and that silence was every bit a part of your prison as the house on the hill or Pinetree."

There was no escaping the knowing in his eyes, and for the first time, I didn't feel the need to run away from it. Yes, Mickey knew. They all did. They knew that my uncle had raped me as a child and continued to rape me throughout my adolescence.

They knew, and they were still here. He didn't get to take them away too. The cookie was almost too dry on my tongue as I tried to swallow it. He let me go as I picked up the coffee and attempted to wash it down with a sip.

The minute I realized I was looking away, I lifted my gaze to meet his again.

"That's my girl," he murmured. "You keep right on fighting, Little Bit. You're a hell of a lot tougher than you look, and you've been tough as old boots."

I made a face at that description, then took another sip of the coffee. "Thank you—I think."

"You're welcome. And don't knock old boots. They are always there for you and keep you dry and warm. They also take a beating, whether walking through hundred-and-forty-degree weather in the summer or twenty below in the winter. Old boots are reliable, comfortable, and valuable."

Well, when he put it that way...

When I offered him my cookie, he took a bite slowly, his gaze on mine. I watched him chew it before taking a bite of my own. In a near-comfortable silence, he split my cookie with me. After it was gone, I cradled the coffee cup like I needed something to keep there for defense.

"Yes, it's definitely all right for you to still be here," he said, finally answering my earlier question. One I'd almost forgotten I asked. "The kids are going to be excited. You up for showing them some dance steps?"

"Yes."

"Good."

Then the silence stretched out a little more strained, and he sighed.

"I know I have a lot to make up for, Little Bit." That snapped my attention back to him. "I plan on doing everything it takes. So put me through my paces... Make me earn it."

"Make you earn it?" I raised my brows. We'd been making peace, but there was still an element of discomfort. That betrayal and rejection, no matter how well-intentioned, still stung.

"Yep," he said as a bell rang, indicating someone had come in downstairs. Leaning close, he murmured, "Make me earn it." Then he brushed a kiss to the corner of my mouth. A shiver raced through me before he walked out of the kitchen. "Do your worst, Little Bit," he said over his shoulder. "Your absolute worst."

A laugh escaped me as I followed his progress. "Maybe I will!"

Maybe I would.

CHAPTER 20

LIAM

I'd spent the day at the office, working. I made sure I was seen there, at the store, and at the former Blue Diamond. It was set to reopen soon with a new name and a whole new look.

Head on a swivel, I kept watch for who was watching me. I made calls, I delivered mild threats, and I waited. I'd done everything the king asked of me—save one item.

That was coming due.

Instead of going to the clubhouse or stealing Hellspawn away to come with me, I'd returned to the apartment alone. I worked out, showered, had dinner, and waited.

It was hard not to let my thoughts drift back to earlier when Hellspawn told me a story that she did not want to tell me, and yet she did. She found the courage to let me into the darkest corner of her life.

The hardest part of listening to that story was not being

able to erase all the bad things that had ever happened to her. I knew from the first moment I laid eyes on her at the clubhouse that she was not that fragile, delicate flower that they were all treating her like with kid gloves. I heard about the bruises and saw evidence of him watching her sit there bleeding without a care in the world, or so it seemed—honestly, I'd been kind of a dick.

What else was I supposed to do? She was incredible. Fierce, fiery, and so fucking full of vinegar. I'd never found myself so damn attracted to the idea of being burned before. She wasn't a flower, she was a flame.

Then there was Rome.

Rome, who worshiped the ground she walked on, but he wasn't treating her like spun glass. If I were honest with myself, I'd say Rome saw her better than any of us. Or maybe he just let himself see…

* * *

"The day you called me princess in that alley and I punched you." The softness in her voice gloved the core of steel beneath it.

"You told me to never call you that," I said as I studied her carefully. "You nearly broke my nose, so I took it pretty seriously."

It had been one hell of a punch too. It actually sparked tears in my eyes. The strike had been almost perfect. I'd felt that. I wanted her to do it. Not so much to hurt me, but more to improve her form and strike. She could throw a punch and fuck if I didn't want to ensure that every punch she threw would land.

She laughed. "I'm not going to apologize."

Pure flame. My hellspawn is a firebrand.

"I don't want an apology," I said, even as I chuckled. "It was fucking glorious. Pretty sure if I called you a name you didn't like right now, you could break my nose."

She grimaced, and I almost regretted making it a joke, but at the same time... No fucking way was I going to hide anything from her. She'd earned that respect. She also earned it with her work and with her determination to learn.

"I don't want to break your nose now," she said slowly, her dark eyes flicking away from me as though she needed to look elsewhere for this part. I didn't like that. I wanted her gaze on me. I wanted her to know she wasn't alone. Even if I could reach over and cup her chin to force her to look at me, I wanted it to be her choice.

Always her choice.

"Not asking for an apology, Hellspawn. You never need to apologize to me. I literally just want to see you."

At that, she turned her head, focusing on me again. It was a gift when she let me see her, when she didn't hide behind the shadows in her eyes. Her gaze locked onto mine that tiny smile hovering at the corners of her lips.

"How do you do that?" she asked with a slow shake of her head. "How do you take something that should be dark and painful and filled with regrets, and make it almost entertaining?"

I shrugged. "Better to laugh than cry. Better to inflict harm on the ones who doled it out to you." I'd make no apologies for who I was, either. "I've made choices in my life, Hellspawn. Some I had no choice but to make, and others I just wanted. Somewhere along the way, I made peace with what I could control."

Running my hand over my jaw, I studied her. She was tearing herself open for me. I could do nothing less.

"I wanted a better life for my brother. For the Vandals. Everything I've ever done, except for one choice, has always been about them."

Her gaze zeroed in on me, and I knew I had her full attention.

"I told you my parents would've welcomed Rome with open arms, and they wanted to. Mom—she tried more than once with him, but Rome didn't want this life. I did."

I wouldn't dress it up and put a neat little bow on it. I wanted the money. I wanted the power. I wanted what I saw in their eyes when they came to see us at the home. I wanted that confidence. I wanted an opportunity. I wanted the fuck out of that neighborhood...

Except leaving him meant leaving the other half of myself. For as long as I could remember, we had always been a we. An us. Our biological parents were a mystery. I had the money and the time to look them up—but they hadn't wanted us, so fuck them.

Rome?

He was the other half of my soul.

"This wasn't the life he wanted. He didn't want to leave the guys. He's never wanted much."

Understanding kindled in her eyes.

"Exactly," I told her. "You are the one thing that he wanted and the one thing I refused to take. Didn't matter how much I wanted you too."

"I'm very glad that we got through to you then," she said, and I had to laugh. "I don't know if you've noticed, but I can be relatively stubborn too."

"No shit." Then we were both laughing, but the humor in her eyes died almost as quickly as it ignited, and I sighed. "Rip the Band-Aid off, Hellspawn. Tell me what you need me to know. You can tell me anything, abso-fucking-lutely anything."

She could show up at my door covered in some guy's blood that she just killed and bludgeoned to death. I'd be okay with that, except for the fact that she had to do it on her own. Kind of like seeing the brain matter that we found on the stapler. Picking up the little bits and pieces that she and Freddie let slip about the doctor at the Pinetree told me a lot.

My firebird could kill. Had killed. Likely would again.

And I would do what I had to to clean it up for her if I didn't kill them first. There was so much I would do if I could go back in time. So many I would cut down, tear apart, and clear from her path. They would never have touched her.

"You know, I don't remember the group home or Milo—when I

was a baby. I didn't know a life before the one I have," she said slowly, as if needing a moment to gather together the story she wanted to tell me. "Mom and Dad—they were my parents. They were always there. They cared about me. I mean, Mom cared. I think Daddy did. I remember him caring."

To be perfectly blunt, I couldn't tell if she was telling me or asking me. It's much as I wanted to press on that point, so I waited.

In the middle of a fight, no matter how well you might know an opponent, sometimes the only thing you could do was wait them out. Let them make their choices and be ready to counter.

Hellspawn was in this fight, wrapped in barbed wire, surrounded by landmines and tripwires. If we knew just what darkness lurked in the upper echelons, it would be me.

I just wish it had never touched her.

Her expression turned thoughtful. "Although the more I think about it, I don't know how much Daddy was there. I feel like he was." But try as she might, even with the look of strain on her face, she didn't seem all that certain.

Yeah, I might have to wait for my opening, but I wasn't going to let her wade into this alone. Holding out my hand, I let her slide her icy fingers into mine and I wrapped an arm around her and settled her against me.

She could tell me the story as slowly or as fast as she needed. It didn't matter how much the itch between my shoulder blades increased — when this was done, I'd have the target. And I'd know what I needed to know to inflict the damage that needed to be inflicted.

"For as long as I can remember," she said, leaning her head against my shoulder and digging her fingers into my arm, "My uncle has always called me Princess. His princess. My darling sweet princess."

Another sigh escaped her.

"I don't think he ever called me Emersyn. Not so I would

remember it. I was his princess. The perfect princess. His—"
She shuddered. Her chin came up.

The story spilled out of her, every dark, depraved thing. Each time I thought she would stop, she didn't. I wanted to tell her to stop gutting herself for me, but at the same time... No, I wanted to scrape all of that out and burn it.

She'd lived through it. I could fucking listen to her.

Princess was what her rapist uncle called her.

Dressing her up in fancy clothes and showing her off—her reaction to me getting her all those things made so much more sense.

C'mon, Hellspawn, show me the path through the landmines. We'll destroy them together.

* * *

At ten on the dot, the phone rang. I'd been expecting his call all day. Though I'd wondered if he would reach out earlier, he hadn't. He'd waited until our appointed time. Staring at the phone, I took a breath and settled more into my skin before I picked it up.

"O'Connell."

"You're going to make me order it," the king said without preamble. "Aren't you?"

"Your majesty, I told you, she is not involved." Not that it would matter to him. "Nor do I want to involve her any further."

"This isn't about what you want," he said, his voice cool and distant. We might as well have been negotiating a stock price or a sale. "The club you procured will be reopening soon?"

"Yes. I would send you an invitation, but you're not usually a fan of public events." Or any events that I was aware of.

"Bring Emersyn Sharpe to meet me. I'll text you the location in three days." That wasn't a request or a negotiation. "If you fail to appear, I will accept that as your battleline and will dissolve your position *and* you. Then I will acquire Miss Sharpe for myself."

Excuse the fuck out of me?

"You don't want me to take her. Bring her to meet me." Then he chuckled. "It's about time we had a face-to-face anyway… and Bishop?"

"Your majesty?" That I managed to respond at all without gritting my teeth or spitting the words was due to years of practice.

"She better be worth it."

Then the call ended.

I stared at the phone and then toward the windows overlooking the city. Bring her to meet the devil, the devil *I* hadn't even put a face to in all these years, or he'd come for her anyway.

A headache formed behind my eyes. She wanted to be my partner in this, to protect me even as I wanted her nowhere near it. How many battles had she already fought in her life? How many had she already survived?

She did not need to wade into this.

Yet…because I wanted her and the king's damn enemies took her thinking Rome was me, she was now in this.

All I'd done was entice the son of a bitch by keeping her away. Goddammit, when I told her I'd only ever chosen one thing for myself… I hadn't considered what this life and power could take from me.

No, it didn't get to take her. I hadn't spent the last decade learning every part of the Royals and shielding Milo only to sacrifice her on the altar.

The king was right, it was time we met face to face.

I pressed Kellan's contact info before putting the phone to my ear. As soon as he answered, I said, "We have three days.

Then he'll send me the place to bring her. He wants to meet or he's coming to get her himself."

"Then we need a plan," Kellan said.

I had a plan.

Face to face, I could kill him.

CHAPTER 21

KELLAN

"We can't send her," Milo said. Before I could correct him, he scowled and added, "We *shouldn't* send her."

"Don't misunderstand me," I told him as I washed my hands in the sink. So far, Vaughn and Jasper had been keeping their thoughts to themselves. Freddie leaned against the wall, arms folded. Frankly, I didn't want him to feel the pressure of the conversation, but I also wasn't cutting him out.

I'd spent half the day tearing apart an old engine and rebuilding it. The work was painstaking, but I'd needed it. Wanting to get rid of the grime, I worked the soap around my nail beds and between my fingers.

"I don't want to send her and I want very much to find an alternative, but I'm not seeing one that allows Liam to stay in place." I'd had this conversation with Liam, and I'd allowed him the chance to try and sway the king.

The man wasn't budging.

Milo groaned, rubbing a hand over his face. Despite his frequent absences—or maybe because of them—he'd lost some of the jagged edges left by his incarceration. Or perhaps he'd been working them off with a certain heiress who had also been absent.

He seemed more inclined to listen and work with us. Anger flashed across his eyes. "What does Liam say?"

"I say, I can leave the Royals. The whole point was to learn their operation and get close to the guy gunning for Milo," Liam announced as he entered the kitchen with Rome and Doc right behind him.

"Where is Boo-Boo?" Freddie asked, straightening.

"She's going upstairs," Doc said as I shut off the water and reached for a towel, "to shower and change."

I nodded. "We're not keeping this from her, but I want everyone's unedited thoughts before we have her join the conversation."

There was what we wanted and what we should do. Then there was what we needed to do.

"As I was saying," Liam continued, heading to the coffee machine. "I could just leave, abandon it and move on with my life, except…"

"This king asshole isn't likely to let you walk away," Jasper said. "Not based on everything you've said." There was just a hint of bite to those words. We'd all been left out of this initial planning.

The grinder firing up cut off conversation for a few seconds. Doc checked his watch before setting himself up in the doorway. Rome just opened the fridge and pulled out a bottle of water.

"No," Liam said as he slotted the portafilter into place to pull the shots. "He won't. You only leave the Royals feet first.

That part bothers me less than abandoning Ezra." He cut a glance at Milo. "Or Adam."

Not an unfair call. I leaned back against the counter. "Then we need another plan."

"I have a plan," Liam said. "I'll go to the meeting and kill him. That ends his threat to Milo and Hellspawn."

"And if he decides to not show up?" I asked, because while his plan sounded great on the surface, there were numerous opportunities for it to go awry.

Pinching the bridge of his nose, Milo said, "I hate myself for saying this... but Kel is right."

That statement landed like a stink bomb. Jasper's expression tightened, and Vaughn looked more fierce than resigned. I kept an eye on Freddie, who seemed to be holding it together, and then Rome, who stared at his brother with an enigmatic look.

It was Doc who said, "If she goes in, then we need a solid extraction plan. A way to track her and Liam, and backup for what happens when it all goes fucking sideways."

"Thanks for the show of faith," Liam muttered, but shook his head and waved off Doc's raised eyebrow.

"We're all on edge," I reminded them. "This isn't easy for anyone. We're not making these decisions lightly or alone. The point here is to make the best call that keeps us safe and our enemies either in check or eliminated."

At the moment, I favored the latter far more than the former. But I would take the former if it brought Liam and Sparrow back in one piece.

"Why the fuck does he want to meet her?" Freddie asked. "Has anyone actually addressed that?"

Rome carried the milk over from the fridge as Liam continued with the coffee prep. I recognized self-soothing behavior when I saw it. Ms. Stephanie told me once that was why I worked on cars.

It let me take apart and put things back together again. I could make it stronger, better, or at the very least more reliable.

"Because she's his girlfriend," Jasper said. "That part I actually get."

"It's leverage," Milo said, and I nodded. Liam's expression tightened but he didn't deny any of it.

"It's because he threatened him." Rome's response was also valid and earned a snort from Liam. "Because they took us."

Still not a denial.

"Break up with her," Freddie said. "Why reveal more business to someone you're not seeing? That doesn't seem rational, right? And from everything you guys have said—this dude is just a businessman."

Liam cut a look at me. It wouldn't work. He didn't even try to refute it. Although, there was more to it than that.

"We don't know what he is," Milo commented in an exhausted tone. "We know he recruits from the upper echelons. He looks for wealthy, disenfranchised youth who are in it more for the adrenaline than the profit. It's not like Reed or Graham need the money."

After handing a coffee to his brother, Liam used the grinder to start another coffee. "Breaking up with her sounds like it would take the target off her, Freddie. However, if I thought it would work—I'd have already played that card."

But it wouldn't.

"No, it would just remove any 'resistance' from Liam about eliminating her." It was a cold series of words from Vaughn, of all people, but he got it. "None of us want her in this fight, Freddie."

"She's always been in it," Liam said. "As much as we want to keep her out of it—she has been in it. This is her world—our world. From Ezra to Adam to Lainey. There's a chance she would have been up to her eyeballs in it already if she hadn't been on the road."

Even if only as collateral. Not that her being on the road had kept her wholly safe. That brought up another avenue of conversation, but not here and not now. Not in front of Milo.

We had to contain these threats so we could go after the bigger ones.

"Then sending her is our only choice?" Freddie sounded more like he was testing the words. The sentiment. I wasn't the only one observing him. The last week had been a challenge for him.

The rapidly growing closeness between him and Sparrow pushed him in new ways. He'd teetered, but he hadn't fallen. Maybe because his friend Bodhi—there was another problem —had gone after him, maybe because Freddie was developing the tools for confronting his own issues or maybe it was because he was trusting us more.

Or maybe because we'd gotten flat-fucking lucky. I'd take any and all of the above.

Liam handed two more coffees to Rome, who delivered them to Jasper and Vaughn. Instead of going back to his brother, he stopped in front of Freddie. "They won't be alone."

"But it puts her in front…"

"No," Liam said, as he held out a coffee to Freddie. "It puts her beside me, with all of you backing me up."

Next to me, Milo stiffened as he lifted his chin. I wasn't the only one who noticed. Doc shifted his weight and Liam had to be aware of the sudden glare Milo favored him with. I didn't think Milo would ever be exceptionally reasonable where his sister was concerned.

"Before you lose your shit," Liam continued without a single look in Milo's direction as he resumed making the coffee. "I've been thinking about this since he gave me the first order to bring her."

The air in the room seemed to balloon with the tension. Vaughn switched his gaze from Liam to Milo, and Jasper rose to lean against the table. It put him within arm's reach of Freddie.

Yeah, this had all the potential to go south.

"Hellspawn isn't as fragile as she appears. Do I want to protect her? Absolutely. If I had an easy way to keep her fifty miles from this scenario? Clearly. The thing is, we don't have a way to get her out of this that wouldn't be putting her in a cage, even if we abandoned friends who have more than earned our trust, if not our loyalty."

He finished another coffee and slid it to the side. Rome took it and handed it over to Doc.

"The king is—unpredictable, but at the same time, he's most often proved pragmatic. Rome is absolutely off-limits and has been from the beginning. If he tries to leverage Rome, he knows I will burn them all down. They'd be better off putting a bullet in my head."

"Let's put a pin in that option," Doc warned, and I flicked a look at the clock. Yeah, she would be down any minute.

"Not volunteering for it," Liam said. "The point is, he knows I won't tolerate Rome being targeted."

"Ivy is a new weakness for you," Milo said abruptly. "A new point of pressure to leverage."

"Exactly. He doesn't want to hurt her. Or maybe he does, but he won't. This is about control." Liam's steady, rhythmic motions to make coffee belied his internal turmoil. It didn't matter how fucking calm he looked, or maybe it was because he was so calm…it hid the boiling point of the man below.

Jasper wore his temper like armor. Liam kept his in check for the same reason. It would be a mistake to ever believe he wasn't capable of incredible violence.

"He wants to bring me to heel, put me in my place, and the more I've refused to bring her…" He sighed. "The more it's elevated her worth. So no, I don't want to take her, but I also know damn well and good this is him testing the waters and proving to me what power he has. He needs to learn that I'm a very bitter pill to swallow."

"I don't think so," Sparrow said as she stepped into the kitchen. Her timing couldn't have been more perfect. The comment landed in a moment of perfect silence as the frother turned off.

Doc's lips quirked as Freddie snickered. Even Jasper looked amused, but it was Milo who groaned. "I swear to fuck, you've all corrupted her."

"I hate to break this to you, big brother," she said, a lightness to her manner that called to me. "I've been pretty bankrupt in that department for a long time. I think it might be *me* corrupting *them*."

Not missing a beat, Rome took the latest coffee Liam had prepared and handed it to her with a smile. "Thank you," he said, and she grinned as she rose up on her tiptoes to give him a kiss.

"Thank you."

"I'm the one who made it," Liam grumbled, and instead of being chastised, she just let her smile grow.

"I'll thank you later and confirm the bitter diagnosis for you."

Laughter rippled through the room, puncturing the tension as Milo groaned again. "You're killing me, Ivy."

"Nah," she said, eyeing him. "Unless you're the bitter pill… maybe I should ask Lainey…"

If I hadn't been standing there, I would never have thought it was possible in a million years, but Milo's neck went red and it wasn't from anger.

"I'd appreciate it if you didn't," he choked out, and she

saluted him with her coffee.

"Good, 'cause I really don't want to know."

Then he chuckled and her smile softened.

"I know you're all worried," she said, turning slowly before returning to face me. "I am too. But I won't let anything happen to Liam and I can follow the rules."

Yes, she could. She also brought her own talents to the table. Her own abilities and observations. Charm. Acerbic wit.

"Then let's talk logistics," I said, because the decision had been made. It had been made before we came in here, to be honest. I'd been turning this over in my head since it came up in the first place.

We couldn't cage her. We wouldn't.

We'd armed her, and we prepared her. We'd fucking die to keep her safe, and we'd kill anyone who tried to hurt her… Speaking of which, we had other issues as soon as this king business was dealt with.

"Then we need to discuss Pilgrim Hills and your mother." The hope that flared in her eyes was hard to deny. That woman better be worth it. "And Sparrow?"

"Yes?"

"I want your word, if any of us calls this—*any* of us. You get out. You follow the plan, and you let us cover your exit. Clear?"

While we didn't have the whole plan yet, I had a partial one, and I wasn't bending on this one.

Lips compressing, she nodded slowly. "I give you my word."

That was my girl. Holding out a hand, I beckoned her to me and she came, letting me wrap her up and I rested my chin against her head for a moment. "Thank you," I said in a soft voice. Then lifted my gaze to the others.

"Let's start with *where* this is happening…"

CHAPTER 22

EMERSYN

We had a plan, though it wasn't ideal. If I looked too closely at any of them as we broke it down, there was no mistaking the dislike. Liam didn't want to take me, but he wasn't cutting me out. Rome didn't want either of us to go, but he would follow.

Jasper and Vaughn would be our backup. The king had given Liam a date for when we would be meeting, so they would stay in position to track us the whole day. Milo objected, and that led to a fight because he wanted to go.

For once, I was the one asking him for patience. If he'd been this king's target the whole time, the very *last* place he needed to be was there.

"Then why are you going?" To be fair, that was a good question. My only answer was that the king had me tied to Liam, not Milo. I was the girlfriend, not the sister. While both titles gave me a thrill, I wouldn't want to be the one sitting and waiting while Milo went in.

Round and round, they all went until Mickey ended it. "Milo, take a breath. None of us like the plan, but it's the best we have for the moment. You need to be here with Kel and me… because if things change…"

Other than asking a couple of hard questions, Freddie had said very little. When the argument moved to the common room, I'd leaned against the wall next to him.

We didn't talk, but he hooked his pinkie around mine, and the tightness in my chest since he'd left, relaxed. We were going to be okay. Though, that relief didn't spare me the headache the guys arguing brought on.

Rubbing the back of my neck, I followed Kellan into his room. He waited until I was inside to close the door, then locked it. When I glanced over my shoulder, he shook his head. "I just want a few minutes and no accidental intrusions."

"It's fine," I said. "Just, are you okay?"

He stripped his shirt up and off even as he toed off one shoe then the other. The stained clothes declared where he'd been most of the day, as did the smell of motor oil and fuel.

The combination burned at my nostrils. "I'll be fine, Sparrow," he said. "I need to shower, so can you hang out here for a bit?"

"I can hang out in there if you want to keep talking." I'd showered when we returned and put on comfy clothes and fuzzy socks. The time at the clinic had been fun, especially talking to the kids who liked dance. We'd made it an impromptu dance party with no form or structure. "I have some stuff to talk to you about too—but it's not as important as all of this."

His expression gentled as he blew out a breath. "Sparrow…" When he held out his hand, I went to him and wrapped my arms around him. Kellan, like the others, was a big guy. They all did it because he could pick me right up off the floor, but he chose not to and said he needed this hug.

Curling around him, I stroked my fingers through his hair as he pressed his forehead to my shoulder. This was him seeking comfort and I could offer that.

"Tell me," he said in a quiet voice. "Tell me you're okay to do this and we're not asking too much."

"You're not asking me at all," I told him in a soft voice. "I'm volunteering. I want to help."

Raising his head, Kellan studied my face, searching for something he must have found because he nodded. "You promise you will follow all the rules and instructions, take off if Liam says go?"

I hated that part. But they needed this from me. If it came down to a real fight, then Liam wanted me out of it. I'd be more of a distraction than a help. "Yes, I still promise."

Brushing his knuckles up and down my cheek, Kellan let out a breath then nodded. "Thank you for being a good girl. You're not a runner, not when you want to protect us." The last sentence killed any argument in me. "So thank you for that."

"I don't have to like it to do it," I admitted as I spread my fingers over his chest. The ivy tattoo spiraling around the cross on his abdomen held my attention. "But I also don't like the idea of being leveraged or used as a distraction."

"I know." He kissed my forehead and lingered there a moment with his lips to my skin. I flattened my right hand over his heart as we held there for a moment. "Thank you for being you, Sparrow."

I grinned. "Right back at ya, Kestrel."

He chuckled as some of the tension drained out of him. With some show of reluctance, he let me go and headed into the bathroom. I hoisted myself up onto the counter as he got the water going.

"You comfortable?"

"Best seat in the house," I quipped lightly as he reached for his jeans, and his expression seemed torn between laughing at me and scolding. It was kind of comical.

"Keep it up, Sparrow. We still haven't finished our discussion on swats."

"True," I said with no meekness at all. "But I did discover that a little spanking is not a bad thing." Watching his muscles move and shift as he got naked wasn't a bad thing, either. While I could ogle him, I didn't. As beautiful as they all were in their own ways, I could appreciate them without just staring fixedly at their dicks or their asses.

Admittedly, it was a very nice ass.

"Really?" Surprise filled his tone, but the wary caution in his eyes arrested all of my play.

The new shower had a transparent door and two showerheads. I had to admit, they'd upgraded all the showers and it was one of my favorite features. There was plenty of room inside them for two or more—not that we'd spent any real time testing that.

Yet.

"Yes," I said slowly. "Liam helped me test that theory."

Kellan searched my face again. "And it was good? No bad moments?"

"It was good…we pushed in…other areas. He and Rome helped me as you and Vaughn have been."

Standing there, Kellan raised his brows, and I could almost hear the unspoken command. Don't dance around what he wanted to know.

"It was a little scary, and there was a burn," I admitted. "But it was Liam—like when it was you and your fingers. I liked it. Maybe not all the time yet, but—"

I didn't get to finish the sentence as Kellan crossed the three short steps from the shower to the counter, where he cupped my face and kissed me. The slow, deliberate posses-sion of my lips had me wrapping my legs around his waist.

Steam rose from the shower, but heat poured off of Kellan. The tease and stroke of his tongue as he pressed his invasion made me groan. With one hand, he drifted his touch to my throat and gripped it gently. The pressure of his thumb urged me to tilt my head back, breaking the kiss.

"You have any idea how fucking proud of you I am?" From anyone else, that might sound patronizing, but the wealth of emotion in his voice sparked tears in my eyes. "You are so goddamn brave, Sparrow."

"I'm lucky," I pointed out. "Lucky to have all of you. That all of you are willing to help me, to push when I need to be pushed and back off when I need that too."

The last few days…

"I'm happy," I said. "Even with everything that's going on, and I know there's danger, and there are more things we need to worry about…but I don't ever remember feeling this happy or this free, except when Lainey and I ran away for a weekend at Disney World."

A treasured memory and moment. I'd been growing that collection so much here.

"Good," he said and pressed another kiss to my lips. "This is still okay?" He flexed his hand around my throat, and I smiled.

The pressure turned me softer inside, relaxing me even as it turned me on. "Very okay. Would you like to see how much I like it?"

I spread my legs and he dipped his gaze once before focusing on my eyes again. "Not right this second, my feisty brat, but you're definitely getting one for that."

It sent a delicious shiver up my spine when he issued the warning.

"Although before we go any further along that path, you and I will be discussing terms. Yes?"

I licked my lips. "Terms?"

"Hmm-hmm. Nothing happens without consent, Sparrow. You're going to know what I want to do and how, and you'll tell me what is okay and what is not." He drew a circle against my pulse point. "There is a lot I want to do with you, but we're going to take it slow and deliberate. Erasing any touch on your skin you never wanted there and replacing all the dark memories with better ones."

That elicited an entirely different kind of shudder. Because those flashes still came, maybe not as much as they did...but I also didn't need to hide them the way I had in the past.

"Your water is gonna get cold," I murmured, licking my lips.

He chuckled, giving me the out before dropping a lighter kiss on me and then climbing into the shower. Blowing out a breath, I stretched my legs out before scooting back to lean against the mirror and watch him.

He almost seemed posed with one hand on the wall as the water spilled over him. "I have some hard questions for you, Sparrow."

"Because everything else has been softballs so far."

He chuckled.

Pulling my knee up, I hugged it to my chest. "Ask, I don't know if I can answer all of them, but I'll try."

"You don't have to answer all of them. Some you may need to think about. Even so, I still need to ask them."

That was fair. "Okay. I have a question for you too, when we're done."

He paused to glance at me. "Do you want to go first?"

I smiled. "No, I'm fine to wait. Mine isn't urgent or critical to what we have going on right now."

"First question," he said as he poured shampoo into his hand. Turning, he let me see his side and the way the muscle on his abdomen tapered into his waist. "We still don't know why the king wants to meet you precisely beyond a power play. We also don't know who he is. There was a theory—that it could be your uncle."

That concept spilled ice into my veins.

"That wasn't his voice on the call." I'd heard him when he called Liam. I didn't know that man's voice.

He spared me a look and a gentle smile. "I know, Sparrow. Liam said as much, but the maneuvering has been going on for years. Before, about five years ago, we didn't have the influence we have now. The targeting of Milo, now demanding that you be there. It makes me wary. It also makes me wary of what he may ask for or do when you're there. Are you prepared for the king to possibly push things when you meet him?"

I grimaced. "I'd prefer no one touched me that I don't know." His look agreed with me, but I lifted my shoulders. "I'll do what I need to do to protect Liam and you...but I don't think Liam will let him touch me either."

Kellan chuckled. "No, probably not. But I don't want you ambushed by anything."

"Thank you."

"Second question," he continued, head tilting back to rinse the shampoo. "What do you want to do with your mother when we get her out?"

I blew out a breath. We had to get her, beyond that... "I haven't really thought beyond get her safe, make sure she's okay."

"I need you to spend some time thinking about that. Getting her out is a priority. We're working on a plan, but she can't stay here, Sparrow."

He added the last few words with care, like I needed to understand the why.

"I know," I told him. "I wouldn't ask for that. You don't know her and you don't have a reason to trust her. The clubhouse has to be a safe space."

"For all of us," he stressed and I chewed my lower lip. "She's your mother. You want her out. We'll do that. We can set up a place for her… but Sparrow…"

A sigh escaped me. "We don't know if we can trust her." It was a thought that had been haunting me. "I don't think she ever knew…and I never tried to tell her. I wanted to once… but by then, Uncle Bradley had already made one of my nannies leave because of me telling her. She wasn't the first disappearance, but I think she was the first one that truly resonated. I remember being at dinner…Dad, Mom, and Uncle Bradley. We were at Uncle Bradley's house because Mom and Dad had an event in the city."

Bringing it up was like going back there, but the ice didn't trap me so much as numb the scrabble of panic inside.

"I was going to be spending the week with Uncle Bradley, and I didn't want to…I tried everything I could think of to convince them to take me with them, and I remember sobbing when they left."

Mom had hugged me so tight and whispered in my ear that it would be okay, they would be back before I knew it and then they were gone.

"I wanted to tell her then. It wasn't until they were gone that Uncle Bradley picked me up and carried me upstairs. He cleaned me up and ran a bath…" I shuddered. "Then told me what a good girl I was for the performance. But that I should be better about telling Mommy goodbye, because what if it was the last time I saw her."

A fist hit the wall and I jerked back to the present to see

Kellan flexing his hand. There was a spot of red on the tile that washed away and broken skin over his knuckles.

"I never told her." I didn't want him to make her disappear.

It seemed to take Kellan a long moment to get his temper wrestled away. I took the time to get my heart back under control. Those memories were always cold and slick with grief and pain. They haunted me, but that was back when it hadn't been so bad.

The bad came later.

Shutting the water off, Kellan slid the door open. An apology lurked amongst the anger in his eyes and I gave him a small smile.

"I'm okay. You had one more question?"

"I do and you don't have to answer it." Even his voice seemed to vibrate with an anger he was ruthlessly suppressing.

"Can we curl up in bed after you ask it?"

"We can do whatever you want, Sparrow."

Clasping my hands over my knee, I nodded. "Then ask."

"When are you telling Milo?"

CHAPTER 23

LIAM

"How do I look?" Emersyn did a little pirouette in the middle of my living room while I was working on my tie. She'd chosen a cowl-necked sweater sheath of a dress in soft gray. The outfit clung to her, accentuating her curves. The knee-length black boots completed the effect. Long sleeves on the sweater covered her arms.

"In a word," I told her. "You look stunning." We'd discussed options for meeting the king. As yet, I hadn't heard from him. Whether it was an underground fight, a restaurant, or a back alley, we had to be ready for anything.

The boots were good because they had no heels and they would protect her feet. She'd also put on a clingy little body suit under the dress so if she had to climb, run, or fight—preferably, she would not need to do any of the above—then she could.

"You're not going to be able to wear a gun in that."

"No," she agreed, hands on her hips as she glanced down

at the boots. We'd picked out the outfit together *after* discussing what we would need.

As much as I would love to shower her with gifts and clothes, she'd told me why she didn't like them. Maybe we could work our way to that.

Once I had the tie done, I smoothed it and then pulled on the shoulder holster. I'd prefer something bigger. Or more obvious, but this was a standard weapon. Appearances—

"Liam." Her soft voice pulled me around and I sighed. She was stunning with her dark hair falling in gentle waves. I'd gotten somewhat used to her pulling it up in a ponytail or braiding it. But today, she'd done something different with it after we showered.

Well, after she showered, I pulled her back in the shower with me. If we didn't have to go to this stupid meeting, I could have her naked and in bed…

"It's going to be all right," she said and I exhaled a long breath.

"I should be telling you that." Fuck, I was being such an asshole.

"You can tell me later. Right now, it's my turn." Pushing away from the sofa, she crossed to where I stood and lifted my hand. It took me a minute to realize she was putting my cufflinks on.

"You don't have to do that."

"Lots of things I don't have to do," she reminded me, her smile all sass and her dark eyes so full of secrets. Secrets she didn't hide from me anymore. Secrets she trusted me with. "I want to take care of you."

"Would you be all right with me buying you jewelry?" The question just spilled out of me. She didn't want clothes or other items, and I got it. She didn't want to be a princess, and that was fine too.

She was a fucking queen. However, I wanted…

"Want to spoil me?" The question was a dare and a tease, yet I kept careful watch on her eyes.

"I want everything with you," I said. "I probably want things that aren't legal or moral or even acceptable in some circles."

That got me raised eyebrows.

"So, yes," I told her as she finished fixing the first cufflink then reached for the second. "I want to spoil you. I never see you wearing any jewelry."

A little shrug. "I danced and performed. I was always on the road so taking jewelry with me wasn't practical."

"And that son of a bitch was the only one who gave you jewelry." It wasn't a question, and I grimaced the minute I said the words. "Sorry—"

"No, it's fine. I don't really focus on the things he would dress me up in. It was all for show; he would attach chains to chokers like a leash. Earrings to show off his wealth, the same with bracelets. Sometimes…"

"Hellspawn," I said, cupping her chin gently when she finished the second cufflink. "We don't have to…"

"It's okay." I swear she was soothing me as she pressed her hand to my chest right over my heart. "I've had a lot of time to think about things the last few weeks, particularly the last few days. I hated—telling you, and at the same time, it was freeing."

Understanding flickered in me at that. No longer was she keeping his secret. More, she trusted us with her secrets. Trusted us to know what happened and I hoped like fuck she'd trust us to deal out the retribution for her.

I hadn't gotten a piece of the scumbag partner. But I knew he suffered, and that was enough for me.

"Anyway, I've been thinking about my mom. About a trip to Hong Kong we took when I was younger. She just came and got me and we went and spent all kinds of crazy time together shopping, picking out pretty things, some junk, some expensive… it was *fun*."

The tiniest of Vs formed at her brows, tightening as she looked thoughtful.

"I think it was probably one of the best times we spent together. Just us. No Dad or Uncle Bradley." She didn't discuss her father much at all. Then again, considering what an absolute bastard her uncle was, I wasn't really holding out much hope for the prick who adopted her.

"Anyway," she continued with a little shake of her head. "I was circling to a point and wandered off."

"Totally fine, Hellspawn."

"You were asking me about jewelry. The stuff my mother and I got when we were in Hong Kong was great. I had it for a while, but I think my uncle got rid of it on one of my visits at home." A shrug. "He didn't like me wearing other people's stuff."

Oh. Good to know. Fucker.

"But I'd wear something if you gave it to me." She made a face. "I probably could have gotten to that answer a lot sooner."

Chuckling, I dipped my head to press a light kiss to her lips. I wanted so much more than just a little kiss. But I would settle with this for now. "Do you have a favorite—"

The doorbell rang and I twisted to the door even as she gave a little startle. No one was authorized to come up to this floor except for Rome and the guys. Anyone else would need to be cleared by the doorman and security.

I motioned her back from being in direct line with the door and thankfully, my stubborn little hellspawn listened to me without argument, withdrawing to the hall. I checked my phone.

No missed calls or messages. Tension coiled around the base of my spine. I switched the view to the cameras in the hall. Considering the lack of warning, I'd rather not get my head blown off when I checked the peephole.

It wasn't one person at my door, but two.

"Oh shit." What the hell were they doing here?

"Liam?"

Fuck. I peered back at her. "It's fine. Just—it's fine." I shoved the phone into my pocket and swept up my suit jacket to put it on and cover the gun before I opened the door.

"I told you we should have—there he is!" Dad and Mom stood there looking very pleased with themselves. They were also dressed casual, like they'd been traveling.

"Hey," I said, gripping Dad's hand as soon as he offered it, even as I got an armful of Mom. "What are you guys doing here?" We'd talked what? Last week?

"Surprise," Mom said with a wide, open grin. They'd both been getting some sun and had that healthy, warm tan probably from playing golf. "Oh, you're all dressed up."

"And he has company, Mary," Dad said with a quick look of apology at me. I glanced back to find Hellspawn had come out of the hall. Curiosity reflected in her eyes, but there was more of a question there too.

"Should I…"

"No, Hellspawn," I told her. "Come here…and you two come in."

"Hellspawn?" My mother stared at me, all trace of laughter evaporating from her face. "You're calling your girlfriend Hellspawn?"

"Trust me," I said as soberly as I could muster. "She earned the nickname." Then Hellspawn was there, sliding her hand into mine.

"He's not wrong," she said. "And it's lovely to meet you both."

"Jonathon," my father said as I let them in, holding out his hand to her. She shook it gently then glanced at my mother. "This is my wife, Mary. Give her a moment. Liam's never introduced us to one of his girlfriends before. She's going to be going into shock…"

Dad wasn't wrong, she'd transferred that stare from me to Hellspawn and her eyes were teary. With a rapid blink, she came out of it and smacked Dad. "I am not going into shock and I am not calling this beautiful young lady 'Hellspawn.'"

"I'm Emersyn," Hellspawn said with an open laugh and some relief filtered through me. I had a dozen questions. "It's really lovely to meet you. Liam's told me a lot about you."

"Has he?" Mom said, giving me a look. "He's said nothing to us about you."

"Because I like keeping my private life, private," I told her without missing a beat. "Hellspawn's absolutely worth waiting for." With the door closed, I glanced from her to Dad. "And as great as it is to see you both—what are you doing here?"

"Should we offer them a drink?" Hellspawn glanced at me, and I sighed. Yeah, we were expecting a call from the king at any minute and the last two people on the planet who should be here were here.

"Actually, yes and no," I said. "Bear with me a minute…"

"No, you don't have to say anything," Dad said. "You two are clearly on your way out and have plans."

"I would love to say you're wrong," I told him with an apologetic look at Mom. "Except we are, and if I'd known you were coming, we could have made alternative ones." Like talking them out of it.

"We didn't get to spend the holidays with you and you've been too busy to come down to us. So, when Jonathon said we had to meet with the lawyers for the tax year, I wanted to surprise you." Mom let out a little sigh. "I know you like to keep everything neat and orderly—I just missed my boy."

I sighed, dropping my chin. "Mom…"

"No," she told me as she patted my chest. "You look wonderful, and I'm sure you're a wonderful girl." The last she said to Hellspawn, thankfully. "And Jonathon said we should call you. I was rather hoping we would surprise Rome too."

"Ahh," I said, summoning a teasing smile. "Your nefarious plan."

Dad chuckled as he looked at Hellspawn. "Mary loves to spoil both boys, although Rome tends to make himself scarce because he's not always fond of the attention."

"He's very sweet," Mary said. "I just wish I could get him to warm up to us more."

"I think he likes you," Hellspawn said, and that got all of our attention. "He likes you for Liam. He just doesn't see it as something he needs for himself."

Which described my mirror to a T. It settled something very primitive inside me that she understood him so well. If I wasn't already fucking obsessed with her, I would be now.

"Where are you guys staying? Do you need me to get you a suite?" I would need to arrange some security too, but I kept all of that internalized. "And did you get a car?" Better to set them up with a driver.

I might need Rome to keep an eye on them tonight.

"We're at the Hightower over on Fifth, I got the penthouse," Dad said. "Don't worry about us. However, I would like to invite both of you to brunch on Sunday. That way your mother can get to know your girlfriend and I will have a happy wife on the way home."

Mom glared at him, but I chuckled as he clapped me on the shoulder. "I think we can arrange something. I'll have Hellspawn ask Rome to come too."

"I can absolutely do that."

Mom brightened right up at the invitation. "All right," she

said. "We'll go. It was very lovely to meet you, Emersyn, and I'm definitely looking forward to brunch."

"Me too." Hellspawn even made it sound like she meant it. "Are you going to walk them down?" She knew me well too.

"Stay up here? Door locked?" Voice low, I pressed my lips to her cheek and used the opportunity to speak privately. "Gun in the kitchen, get it, and keep it until I'm back up here."

"Yes, sir," she said, then grinned as I straightened. Fuck, she was perfect.

"All right," I said, offering Mom my arm. "Let's get you on the way, shall we?"

As it turned out, Dad had hired a driver. When we got downstairs, the driver was waiting. Yeah, he knew me well enough to know I really didn't like surprises even though I loved seeing them. It had been quite a while since I'd been able to visit.

"She's the reason," Mom said as we stepped out to the car and the driver held the door open. "Why you've been so busy and preoccupied?"

"She's certainly part of it," I told her. "She's important to me."

Mom's smile grew. "Well, then we shall be on our best behavior on Sunday, won't we, Jonathon?"

Dad gave her a patient, if not indulgent, look. "Absolutely. Go ahead and get in. I'm just gonna have a quick word."

I gave Mom a kiss on the cheek and then withdrew with Dad a few steps. "Everything good?"

"It's fine, I'm sorry about the surprise. I did try to talk her out of coming straight over this evening."

"But she's been worried," I said, not needing him to explain. "Because I've been distant."

"Now that we've met Emersyn, she understands why, but in the future..." Dad gave me a firm look and I chuckled.

"I'll make sure I call more often and not disappear on her."

"All I'm asking, Liam. All I'm asking. Now get back up there to that beautiful young lady, and we'll see you Sunday."

I gave them a minute to get in the car before I called the security company. The vehicle and the driver were one of ours, but I wanted additional security for them while they were in the city.

In the elevator, I checked the cameras and smiled. My girl was standing right there in the kitchen, gun in hand and her gaze on the door.

Hmm... fucking king. I just wanted to go up there and toss her on a bed. She was hot as fuck with a gun and she'd charmed my parents without even trying.

I got to enjoy the whole mental image all the way to the door when the message from the king arrived.

He was ready to see us.

CHAPTER 24

EMERSYN

*J*onathon and Mary O'Connell were absolutely delightful. I'd gone to the kitchen as soon as Liam took his parents down and pulled the gun from the cupboard safe by the fridge. He had them stashed everywhere. It was kind of funny—well, it would be if it weren't so sad—how many weapons he had secured and in what places.

At any point, no matter where we were in the apartment, we could arm ourselves. While Kellan had been teaching me with one gun, they all made sure I understood the differences in the various weapons. Fortunately, Glocks seemed to be the favored weapon, and that one I knew how to use.

I kept track of the time while I watched the door. It was weird, the gun felt almost—comfortable in my hand, and I would never in a million years have thought that was possible. Yet here I stood… at the sound of the lock, I shifted my weight.

"It's me," Liam said before pushing the door fully inward. Relief surged upward and I went to put the gun back up, but he shook his head. "Wait…I have an idea."

Setting it on the counter, I nodded as he secured the door. "Are your parents off to their hotel?"

"Yes," he said with an aggrieved sigh. "Sorry about that."

"I liked meeting them."

A smile flashed across his face. "They liked meeting you." For a long moment, he scanned my face. "I'm not going to convince you to stay behind, am I?"

"You wouldn't like me half as much if you could." It was a tease, but I meant it. I loved that he challenged and pushed me. That he didn't treat me as less. He never had. On some level, he had to want the same from me.

"Okay, I love this sweater, and it's chilly enough to warrant a coat. I'm putting a gun on you because they are likely going to search me."

"And you don't think they'll search me?" I tipped my head to the side. "Because I'm smaller and fragile?"

The corner of his mouth kicked a little higher. "Sexism working in our favor."

Being dismissed was a familiar feeling. I was smaller, weighed less, and hadn't always had the skills or tools I had now.

"He texted, didn't he?" I asked as he worked a new belt onto my waist. The gun would be tucked against the small of my back. The leather crisscrossed in the front of the sweater dress like it was supposed to be there. The faint bagging of the dress at the top added to the coverage, as did the coat he held up.

"In the interest of full disclosure," he said. "The leather coat was from that first order at the store."

The one I hadn't wanted. All the clothes he had sent because he wanted to give me options, and I couldn't separate from what my uncle had done. I ran my fingers over the supple, buttery soft leather.

"I know I said I didn't want them," I said slowly. "Is there a price if I change my mind?"

Instead of dismissing it out of hand, he gave me a faint smile, one that teased and invited me to play. "For three kisses, I'll consider the price paid, unless you just want to buy it with cash." There was just the barest hint of tension to his jaw as he said that.

"How much did that cost you to offer?" I kept my voice as soft as he had, touching two fingers to his jaw and caressing the smooth skin there. He'd shaved for the meeting tonight.

"I like the idea of buying you things," he admitted. "I like being able to spoil you and to make your life easier. One of the things I wanted in this life was the ability to take care of my family, of my brother...now you. That's about me, but I get what you need too."

"Go in half on it for me?" The offer slipped out, and it chased some of the tension from him. "I might need a little loan... I have the cash Lainey got for me, but the rest of my accounts are a little frozen."

One corner of his mouth kicked a little higher. "Done. We're also going to use my discount, fair?"

"Absolutely." Especially because he didn't just decide and was trying hard for me. "I suppose we need to address my accounts at some point?"

"We will," he said as I turned, and he held up the jacket to help me into it. "It's on our list." Then he settled his hands on my shoulder. "If marriage is a requirement to get around some legalities, decide what you want for a wedding present."

Laughter burst out of me and I shot a look over my shoulder. "You're serious."

"Oh yeah. If you have to get married to get your hands on what is owed to you, we'll wrap you up in my names."

Names. Plural.

"Cleary and O'Connell?"

"Well, you're dating at least three of us. That gives us the edge."

Disbelief vied with affection, because he meant it. There wasn't an ounce of bullshit in his tone or his gaze. "I'll think about it."

"Good. All right, tonight… you're my girlfriend. As much as I hate to ask, can you do empty-headed simp?"

Lips pursed, I was hard-pressed not to laugh again. "More camouflage?"

"I really don't want him to see you as the threat you undoubtedly are."

Warmth bloomed in my chest at the words and the depth of meaning underneath them. "Compliments, Mr. O'Connell? That just might earn you a different kind of reward."

"Well, in that case…" He cupped my face, the affection sobering to concern. "We do this together. Oh, and before we go…" He glided his hand down my arm to my wrist, where he affixed a bracelet. It was dull-metal gray, blending in against my sweater and would probably disappear under the cuff.

He turned it over, and there was an actual lock on it, though it looked more decorative than practical. "It's synced to our phones. It's a panic button. Not super fancy, but it will transmit your GPS. You have to push-slide the lock. It takes a little effort, but…"

His exhale said everything.

"You found a way to LoJack me."

"Yes, I did. We can activate it too, but we still need to be in a radius. It's not perfect, but it will do for now."

I wrapped my arms around him. "We've got this, Liam," I whispered. "Now, no more delays. I assume he has us on a clock."

Dislike flickered across his expression as he pulled out his phone and sent a message. "Ready, Hellspawn?"

"To meet the devil?" I lifted my shoulders. "Probably good to bring a hellspawn along for that."

His groaning chuckle was totally worth burying any nerves I might have. Very good thing I had some practice with managing stage fright. As worried as I might be, I was also exhilarated to do this…together.

* * *

HONESTLY, I WASN'T SURE WHAT I EXPECTED FOR MEETING THE king, but a standard corporate building in the heart of downtown Braxton Harbor wasn't it. The distance from Liam's apartment couldn't have been more than ten blocks.

It was early evening, and most of the traffic was heading away from the corporate center. Liam's tension level had ramped up throughout the drive and I swore his expression had gone positively stony as we pulled into the parking garage.

"Left side," he told me when I climbed out of the car. He wanted me on his left so he could get to his gun. "We'll be on camera from here on."

It was something he'd warned me about the previous day, so I nodded. "I'm getting used to being on camera," I said, and maybe it wasn't the most appropriate time for teasing, but his eyes actually lightened for a moment.

He used a keycard to open the door to the elevator vestibule. With a hand at my lower back, he guided me toward the elevator. It had just dinged when the entrance to the garage opened again and he almost pushed me into the elevator to cover me when he let out a half-sigh.

"I come in peace," Ezra said, and I debated whether I

should smile at Ezra or not when he appeared in the doorway. "Hey, this the girlfriend?"

His smirk as he raked his gaze over me was so utterly not the Ezra I'd met previously that I wasn't entirely sure how to react.

"She is," Liam said.

"You going to introduce us?" Ezra slid into the elevator with us and gave me a flirty smile.

"Nope," Liam responded.

"Damn." Shaking his head, Ezra folded his arms as he leaned against the wall. "You need to be less greedy."

"I'll remind you of that the next time you bring your girlfriend," Liam snarked. "Oh wait, you can't find a woman to put up with you."

"Asshole."

It was Liam smirking now, and I eased a little closer to him. I suppose all the leering should make me uncomfortable. As it was, I kind of wanted to flick Ezra on the nose. I'd seen him be a dick before but it was weird to be on the receiving end of it.

"Hey, you're lucky I'm here at all," Ezra said. "I just got a message thirty minutes ago."

Rather than respond, Liam shrugged like he didn't care. The elevator took us almost to the top floors and it required a keycard and a code to open the doors.

Whatever I expected when we arrived, an entire wide-open corporate office with a half-dozen men in suits waiting for us was not it. As much as I said I could handle this, it still left me chilled.

"Gentlemen," the guy in the front said. "Please step out. Miss, please stay there."

Ezra strolled out first. "Well, now, if I'd known this was going to be a party, I would have dressed up." He didn't seem bothered by the man patting him down or the pair of guns he removed from him. "You know, if you want to feel me up, you should improve your ball-stroking technique."

The man frisking him didn't seem impressed. "He's clean."

"Shows what you know. Also, I better get both of those back when I'm ready to leave and don't try to swap them for something different. I know what I carry." What had Lainey said once? Ezra could irritate stone.

"Let's go," the guy in the front said to Liam. He exited the elevator and held his hands out to his sides. Honestly, a part of me held my breath as they scanned over him. They removed three guns from Liam. I hadn't even noticed the ankle holster or the fact he had a smaller gun also tucked into a holster at the small of his back.

Beyond those, they also removed knives. Then they had him take off his belt when the buckle proved to be a garrote. Ezra let out a snort. "Goddamn, man. What kind of date were you planning to take your girl on?"

Heat swept up my face at that comment.

"And does she like to double?"

"Keep talking, Ezra," Liam encouraged him. "I haven't had a good fight in a while. You and your glass jaw wouldn't take much."

"Miss," the guy in the front said as they passed Liam out. "Remove your jacket, please."

I slid it off, and the pat down I received was careful as if the man who did it was very aware of the death glare Liam had on him. They removed the small gun that Liam had tucked into the holster at the small of my back.

"Would you like us to keep your jacket?"

"No," I told him. "I'm a little cold." Not a lie, the fact I'd had to endure the other man's hands, professional and impersonal or not, had left me chilled.

He nodded and Liam took the jacket, holding it up to help

HEATHER LONG

me put it on. The weight of the gun tucked into the inner pocket was solid.

They'd take the one they could see and dismiss everything else because I was tiny and a woman.

"Fantastic," Ezra said, leading the way. "Because you guys are boring as fuck." He used a keycard and a code to open the doors. None of the guards followed us.

Inside the second lobby, there was no one at the reception desk. The sign on the wall read Bay Ridge Global. That made sense, I guess. Liam gently took my arm with his left hand, but it kept me a half-step behind him while Ezra went ahead of us.

Even with the guards on the other side of the locked doors, there was no relaxing their vigilance. If anything, the apprehension in Liam seemed to climb higher. The muscle ticking in his cheek worried me.

For now, though, I did exactly what I said I'd do. I stayed with him. There was another set of doors that opened to another set of elevators.

Almost to the top floor.

Ezra pressed the up button and I caught him watching me in the mirrored doors. Since we weren't supposed to know each other, I eased a little closer to Liam. He didn't waste any time putting me on the other side of him.

When the doors opened, Ezra swept out a hand to let us enter first and then he followed. Despite the dark looks they were shooting each other, the pair were working together. I wished I could thank Ezra, 'cause I was rather grateful that he was here.

The ride wasn't a long one and the elevator opened into another reception area, though this one was far more opulent than the one downstairs. The art on the wall was a Degas, if I wasn't mistaken.

At least, I thought it was. It was definitely something I'd

230

seen in art history classes I'd taken online. A gentleman waited for us, a tall, lean figure wearing a five-thousand-dollar suit and a genial smile.

He reminded me of Brixton. That was unsettling enough. "Mr. Graham, Mr. O'Connell, you're on time. Excellent. His Majesty does appreciate promptness."

They really did call him by that title? I wanted to swallow, but I coughed instead because all the moisture had fled my mouth.

Ezra and Liam just stared at the man, but it was Ezra who said, "Yeah, you're not the king."

"I would never presume so," the man replied in the most unctuous of tones. Then he looked past them both to me. "Miss Sharpe, His Majesty is most eager to make your acquaintance. If you'll go on in, he's expecting you."

We started forward, but the gentleman raised his hand. "Only Miss Sharpe."

My stomach plummeted as Liam's expression went foreboding.

"I'm afraid the pair of you will have to wait. Miss Sharpe?"

CHAPTER 25

LIAM

*N*o fucking way in hell. No fucking way was I letting her go through those doors without me. It had been bad enough watching the asshole pat her down. Even knowing it would happen didn't make it any easier to endure.

Hellspawn, however, never wavered. Her poise was perfection. The lack of discomfort in her demeanor and the fact I *watched* where that fucker put his hands were the only things that kept me from breaking his face.

Right then.

I might still do it on the way out. Smoothing down my jacket, I focused on the string bean in front of me. He was all culture and refinement. Nothing about him suggested a threat. So either he was chum dangled here for us to deal with, or a trap.

Probably both.

"I actually don't know him," Hellspawn said, her tone

more puzzled than afraid. "Why would he want to see me first?" She spared me a look. "Liam, you said we were going to have fun. So far… this isn't very fun."

Ezra chortled like this was all some great big joke. Of all the times for him to play the clown, I had to admire his choice of this one. It was distracting as hell and precisely what we wanted.

Between them, they let me get my shit together. We all had a part to play. "I know, Emersyn-baby," I soothed, rubbing her arm. Even the *name* tasted wrong to say. "He wanted to meet her, not have a meeting with her." Sending her in alone was not my idea of a good time.

My phone buzzed and so did Ezra's. It didn't surprise me, but I still hated pulling it out to check the message on the screen.

Send her in, Bishop.

I cut a look to her. One word from her and I'd get us out of here. One word.

"For real?" She rolled her eyes, every bit the put-upon, pampered, and overwrought heiress. "Fine." She shrugged out of her coat and thrust it at me. "But dinner had better be worth this."

She lifted her hands to tuck her hair back behind her ears. It also gave me a good look at her bracelet.

"Am I free to go in now?" she addressed our host, and he inclined his head. Rather than moving to open the doors for her, though, he stayed with Ezra and me.

I hung her jacket over my arm tucking my free hand under where I could grip the gun. A part of me wished she had it with her, but she was also trusting me to come and get her.

"Five minutes," I said as she opened the door, aware that the words would carry. "Five minutes, then I'm following her."

Consider yourself warned, *Your Majesty.*

My hellspawn didn't miss a beat as she strolled inside. It served to remind me that she had been raised in this world. The Sharpes were old money, cobbled together from investments, corporate expansions, and in a few places, takeovers.

She might be playing a part, but it was one she at least understood. Even if we both disliked it. For now, with the grip of the gun in my palm, I kept my focus on the man blocking our way.

Secretary. Assistant. General lapdog.

Didn't care what his title was. I could drop him in a hole as easily as the next guy. Ezra made a show of checking his watch, then yawned as he did a sweep of the executive waiting room. This whole area was one large, opulent setting fit for a king.

At the five-minute mark, I started forward and the string bean stepped into my path. "Move," I told him. "Or I'll move you." If he was still there in two steps…

Whatever he saw on my face must have convinced him because he pivoted on his heel and led the way toward the double doors to the office proper. Pushing them open, he said, "Mr. O'Connell and Mr. Graham to see you, Your Majesty."

Ezra moved with me. To be honest, I half-expected this whole time that the king would be another call on a video screen. All the way up until he had Hellspawn see him alone.

Intimidation didn't deliver well over a video call. It just didn't. It worked better when we were younger, when shadows could still offer hidden menace. Inside the office, a man stood with his back to us, hands clasped behind. A ring stood out on his finger, but at this distance all I could tell was that it *was* a ring.

Hellspawn stood away from him, on the far side of a sofa, with her arms folded and her expression more puzzled than worried. I shifted directions to head for her while Ezra paused.

"Oh look, open bar. Drink?" He clearly relished his role of playing the fool. "Want something, Liam?"

She gave me a small smile when I got to her. She didn't even look particularly mussed, so whatever had happened in the last five minutes hadn't upset her.

"You might want to ask His Majesty," I suggested, keeping myself between her and the man at the windows. While he hadn't turned, I didn't make the mistake of thinking he wasn't aware of everything behind him.

He had dark blond hair, an expensive suit, and looked to be about my height with a solid build. He wasn't a string bean.

"If that's him, the last time I checked we haven't ever had the privilege of meeting the king in the last ten years," Ezra dragged the words out as he poured himself a drink. "What about you—what did Liam call you? Emersyn-baby?"

"You really do want me to kick your ass," I warned him even as Hellspawn pressed her hand against my back. I still had her coat and the gun.

The man at the windows turned to look at us, and for the first time in a decade, I was face to face with a man who—in theory anyway—was the king. The voice behind so many calls. The face on the other side of the text.

The man before us was the one who had ordered everything from corporate espionage to blackmail to actual deaths, the way some people ordered takeout. He'd wanted Adam dead, and as far as he knew, I'd done that job and taken his place.

Pouring the amber liquid into the glass, Ezra glanced over at the man. "If you're the king," he said as if he didn't have a care in the world. "Prove it."

"Well, you're feeling brave," the man spoke in a low,

almost casual tone. "Arrogance and condescension are not your strong suits, Graham."

"Those are my specialties," Ezra retorted. "His Majesty would be aware of that."

The man's soft chuckle had all the hair on my body standing up. I recognized *that* sound. "You're right, being a royal pain in the ass is your specialty. Not putting up with your shit is mine."

"Your Majesty," I said slowly, disliking the address even more now that I was facing the man in person. He was both everything I expected and nothing at all like I imagined.

Like the fact that a faint, cruel smile crossed his lips as though he were amused by something. This was the kind of guy who probably enjoyed pulling the wings off flies when he was a kid. Or ordering someone to do it.

"With my top bishops, I think we can afford to be a little more casual. Call me Julius."

Julius? "Like Caesar?" Ezra asked, his expression doubtful. "Now, who is dealing in arrogance?"

Everything Ezra did demanded the man pay attention to him, distracting him from me and from Hellspawn. The effort was wasted though, because the king—*Julius*—barely spared him a look.

"Ezra, there's already someone here who can replace you, and if I told him to choose between the two of you, who do you think Liam would shoot?" The almost casual question held a savage kind of barbarism to it. "He didn't even hesitate when it came to Reed."

The stiffening of Ezra's posture was more of his act. At least in this, we'd already warned him of what happened, and more, he knew Adam was alive.

Pivoting, Ezra eyed the king, drink in hand and shrugged. "Then shoot me. But I'm not kissing your ass after you had them damn near body cavity search us. You either trust us, or you don't."

Take his place...

"Sit down, Graham, before your mouth invites you into more trouble than you can handle, and be glad I still find you useful."

With that, Julius left the windows and approached Hellspawn and myself.

"Miss Sharpe, I apologize for their behavior—" He paused to consider me for a moment. "Or at least for Graham's behavior. Liam here seems to be on his best manners." He locked gazes with me and I stared into the dark, assessing eyes.

Not more than three feet apart and I had no fucking clue who this guy was. I knew the movers and shakers in our circle, and he was—a ghost. Or might as well be one.

"I don't blame him for being upset," Hellspawn said, her tone not bored so much as curious. "This hasn't exactly been a *warm* introduction."

"You'll learn that to survive in this world, you can't let sentiment and feeling control you. Let's have a seat, we'll be having a meal delivered shortly, and there are things to discuss."

Things? I narrowed my eyes and then focused on the king. "Forgive me, Your Majesty," I said, choosing each word carefully. The man liked having his ego pandered to whether he recognized it as pandering or not. "I don't think she needs to be here for this part. I can call a car to pick her up."

The guys wouldn't be that far away, and if we were going to be discussing *business* of any kind, I didn't want her in the middle of it.

Julius chuckled. "Liam, my boy, you need to stop thinking with your dick. Consider this a lesson in strategy."

I could just shoot him. The only person out there was the

string bean. His guards were down a level. A bullet through his skull would take out the back half—problem resolved.

The presence of cameras, however, suggested it wouldn't be that easy. This was a man who, to my knowledge, didn't exist or get his hands dirty. The smart move would be to get all the information from him *then* kill him.

"My dick and I aren't confused about anything," I told him coolly. "Emersyn Sharpe isn't part of this."

"She became a part of it when you involved her... oh wait, when my new enemy involved her. She's a target. She's also a weakness for you. One clearly used for leverage already... now take a seat." The whipcrack of command laced every syllable. "We will discuss how we are going to handle that and other matters."

His gaze went past me to Hellspawn, his expression unreadable. At least I didn't know enough of his tells to read it anyway.

"Why?" Her question filled the room, and Ezra stared a hole through the king as though he, too, waged the same internal debate I was. How bad would things be if we just killed the son of the bitch?

"Because, Miss Sharpe—may I call you Emersyn? I think as friends we should be able to address each other by name."

"I didn't know we were friends," she said, a dare edged her words.

"Emersyn-*baby*," I warned. Now might not be the time to bait him. Not when we were still trying to figure out the next move.

Instead of being offended, the king began to chuckle. "So, you are more than just a meek, spoiled little princess from a powerful family."

Her fingers dug into my back at the description. Goddammit.

"Julius, what?" she said, keeping her head, even though

the dare had been replaced by something much cooler. "You know my full name and theirs. If we're to be *friends*, then what is yours?"

Everything in her tone defied the idea that we were going to be friends. Julius' amusement faded some as he regarded her.

"King," he said with a slow, cold smile. "Julius King."

The name meant even less. Son of a bitch.

"Names are cheap, Emersyn. They are dumped on us by parents and can be changed as easily as picking out new underwear. Now, please, take a seat."

The please he directed was at her and I caught Ezra's eye. What the hell was the game here? He shook his head slightly. He had no idea. Trusting Ezra to watch my back, I glanced over my shoulder.

"If you want to go," I told her. "I'll make it happen."

The silence in the room dragged on for a moment, but Hellspawn lifted her chin. Anger glittered in those eyes. Anger and determination.

Goddammit.

She wasn't going anywhere.

CHAPTER 26

EMERSYN

*J*ulius King was… unnerving. It was the only word that seemed applicable. He hadn't been kidding about all of us taking a seat or sharing a dinner. Instead of the sofas next to the unlit fireplace, we moved to an executive dining room with a classic Queen Anne table, wall sconces with crystal covers, and Mr. Măcelar, the sycophantic guy who'd greeted us out front acting as footman, to deliver the meal to the table.

King, himself, took the head of the table. He gestured to the seat to his right, and yeah, I skipped that. I took the seat on the right, the farthest from him while Liam took the seat next to me and closer to King.

Ezra smirked as he eyed the chair at the other end of the table, but rather than pull it out, he took the seat at King's left hand. The message needed no translating for any of us. When Uncle Bradley sat at the head of the table, I always had to sit on his right. That seat was always reserved for me.

Bile burned in the back of my throat, but I worked to keep my expression bland as possible. This world and its displays of wealth and power were all too familiar. I was never safe in this world, so I never pretended it was all right. Liam asked for an air-headed simp.

That, I could do.

"Give me updated reports," Julius said as his man made a point of opening a bottle of wine and providing him with a small amount to sample.

Ezra and Liam exchanged a look then glanced back at him. While neither looked at me, I understood their reticence. The only reason to not fear speaking in front of me was because the king had no intention of letting me leave, or he had another way to ensure my silence.

While I'd never betray Liam, or Ezra for that matter, fuck Julius King. He wasn't my uncle. No, he didn't send fear to crawl through me. Yet, he possessed the same dark focus, uneasy energy, and air of corruption that polluted the world with every breath Uncle Bradley took.

"All my tasks are complete," Ezra said. "Save for the most recent assignment. That, however, is on schedule. In this case, I don't have anything really new to report."

He shrugged as the first round of dishes were set on the table, the silver domes being whisked away to reveal crab cakes with a side of lemon and bits of parsley sprinkled over them to add to the attractiveness.

The smell was rich, decadent, and my stomach clenched. I wasn't starving by any means, but it did smell good. The king finally lifted his glass of wine to sample as he glanced at Liam.

"We already spoke about my current projects." In other words, Liam wasn't playing.

At the king's nod, the footman moved to pour wine for the rest of us. I hadn't touched anything yet, since this was too much like being seated in Hell. Persephone made the mistake of eating the pomegranate seeds. I wanted to be able to leave when it was time.

"Do you not care for crab?" the king asked, and the silence from the guys alerted me to the fact he was probably asking me.

"I wasn't really planning on dinner," I told him, making myself pick up the glass of water. That had been poured from the same bottle and the king had already had a drink of his before the wine. "Liam promised to take me out for fun."

"And this isn't fun?" The man canted his head to the side as though weighing my response, even as his cold eyes seemed to search me.

"Not really," I said, and it wasn't even a stretch to keep my tone bland. None of this was fun.

Liam settled his hand on my thigh, warm strength in his grip like a promise. The coat was no longer in his lap, but I had no idea if he still had the gun. Instead of hanging it up or surrendering it, he'd draped it over the back of my chair.

It was almost insultingly middle-class, or at least that was what my uncle would have said, and I kind of appreciated the gesture. A polite fuck you without actually saying the words. Despite what I was wearing, this wasn't really proper *dinner* attire.

So, the king could suck up all the fuck yous, 'cause he deserved them. Taking another sip of water, I swallowed back the need to scowl.

"Hmm... well, let's try our second course of appetizers. Maybe they will offer you more fun."

Ezra glanced at the crab cakes then at me. With a sigh, he picked up his fork and raced through the eating of them. He actually managed to finish before the footman arrived with another tray of silver dome-topped plates.

He set down a silver-covered plate in front of each of us,

removed the cover and put it over the crab cake plates before sweeping those away. It was efficient.

Our second course?

Oysters.

"Oven roasted," Julius said with the first real sign of amusement since we'd taken a seat at the table. "With mushrooms and watercress. A delicacy," he continued. "One I couldn't quite appreciate the first time I had them, but they must be experienced."

How Ezra managed to roll his eyes without quite rolling them, I couldn't fathom, but he did. Liam flexed his hand against my thigh before he reached for the wine glass. The king was already on his second, and apparently, we were going through with this dinner.

While Liam appeared to take a drink, his throat didn't move. I could do that, I supposed. I'd managed over the years, especially when I was too nauseated to eat.

"I'm afraid that even if I try them, I won't be able to eat very many." The explanation was more to protect the boys than to protect me. "I'm in training, so I tend to be very particular about what I eat."

The king said nothing, just picked up an oyster, then glanced at Ezra. "Tell me about the Hamptons."

"The framework and setup are complete. Once you make your final decisions, I'll move forward. I have a few leads that should satisfy your requirements." They could have been discussing the weather or houses. It could be a code, or it could be exactly what it sounded like.

"And the Blue Diamond?" the king washed down his oyster with a deep drink of the wine that finished his glass before he reached for another.

"On schedule to reopen, but I already planned to rename it."

"Don't like the name?"

That was news. I'd almost forgotten about the Blue Diamond. Well, not forgotten, but it had been months since the shooting and it had kind of slid to the back of my mind. Ria still worked for Liam, I thought. He'd indicated that he'd made provisions for all of them during the reconstruction. While "Jasmine," her stage name, might be on a break, I hope she was getting to enjoy it too.

"It wasn't a name I picked out. It was fine before the refurbishment, but now I think it needs a new identity. A new place in the world."

"What did you have in mind?"

I only half-listened as Liam detailed his plans. I split my attention between watching Ezra watching the king and the king watching all of us. More than once, all the hair on my body stood up as he focused his attention on me.

Liam lifted one of the oysters and ate it with care, sliding the whole thing off its half-shell and into his mouth. Curiosity pricked me as he sampled it. Finally, he nodded with a half-smile. "Not bad."

The encouragement let me finally cave to eating an oyster, because I got the impression they weren't moving the food until I did. It proved a little too salty and the texture wasn't terrible, but the combination of mushrooms and watercress made it unusual.

At least to me.

I ended up having two and I washed them down with water. Drinking the wine, especially on a mostly empty stomach, was a recipe for disaster.

The next course brought another discussion. This one seemed far more in code than the first couple. The soup course was a mushroom bisque. A little heavy, but I went ahead and ate it.

It wasn't until the main entree—steaks with humongous

baked potatoes and grilled vegetables—arrived that the king refocused on me.

"My understanding is you're a performer. Will you be working at the new club?"

Liam's knuckles went white, but his expression didn't remotely shift. "No, she does far more high-end art. The club is great but far below her pay grade."

It was complimentary and dismissive. I clung to the first and ignored the second. The game we were all playing was just amping up the unpleasantness of the evening.

"So you tour? You haven't for the last year," the king said. "Then there was that business about your disappearance. I saw your uncle welcoming you home."

Ice slid up my spine. Mustering indifference might be an impossibility.

"The press speculated that you were being questioned by the authorities. How did that go?" There was no avoiding the comment or just letting that one go. Liam balanced his steak knife like he hadn't just been cutting into the meat.

"I never spoke to the authorities," I said, choosing the path of least resistance with honesty. "I'm sure the lawyers took care of it for us."

Us. Yeah, aligning myself with Uncle Bradley. What a nauseating thought.

"Good, with the influence that Sharpe International wields, along with its subsidiaries, the government would do well to look the other way. Unless..." He paused to take a bite. It worked to snare everyone's attention. The man understood how to control a room.

That was not a comforting thought.

"Unless," he continued. "They were looking to leverage you for insider information or more on the company. Granted, your uncle is the primary CEO and your father the

CFO, it used to be the other way around. I think your father is more figurehead than an actual power player."

The king paused as the footman refilled his wine and poured more water for Liam and me. Ezra waved him off. He'd also halted eating as he studied the king. "This going somewhere? Cause the Sharpes are a bunch of stuffed shirt pricks. No offense, Hellspawn."

Liam sent Ezra a killing look, and it took everything I had to not laugh. It might have been hysterical laughter, but it was right there.

"None taken," I managed in a semi-choked tone before I took a drink.

"I'm speaking to the girl now," the king told Ezra. "Until I ask for your opinion, be silent."

And the friendliness of the night fled. Not that it had been especially friendly. Liam still had his steak knife, and he kept his gaze pinned on the king.

"Can you tell me what the dynamic is on their board?"

"No," I told him, relying on honesty. "I've never paid attention to it. I don't even go to board meetings or share-holder ones." Even when I'd been forced to go to his office, I'd been left there like a pet while he went to the meetings. "I'm afraid you seem to know more about them than I do."

"Interesting."

"Not really," I said, folding my napkin and putting it aside as I leaned back in the chair. What appetite I'd possessed had fled. "I don't particularly care about the business either."

"You should. As the only heir, that means you will come into some considerable wealth. You'll be a power player in your own right."

I shrugged. "Not a game I want to play. I prefer my performances." All true. "Probably why I've been touring from such a young age."

"Hmm." The king studied me a moment. "Your uncle has a reputation."

"Does he?" The ice slicking my spine deepened, but I didn't give into it. There were no secrets from Liam at this table. Ezra hated my family on principle. Frankly, I didn't give a shit what this man who wanted to be a puppeteer thought. "Again, I'm afraid you would know more than me. My uncle and I are not friends."

"But you're close," he said, pressing the issue. "He's brought you up in the past…"

Liam's lips compressed.

"Always with such great fondness. He's very proud of you."

"He's also skilled at small talk at parties. Discussing me is a topic he can control without betraying anything." I'd seen him do it. The man he was in public was not the man he was behind closed doors.

I'd been up close and personal with both. They were just different types of Mr. Hyde. I couldn't get lucky enough that at least one would have been a Dr. Jekyll.

"Simply put, I'm of no use to you—Mr. King."

"Julius." The correction carried the weight of an order.

"I think I shall stick to Mr. King. I prefer more formalities if you wish to interrogate me about my family."

The silence at the table stretched out. The king stared at me, his expression neutral, and yet, at the same time it *felt* like he glared at me. With a soft laugh, he leaned back in his seat and reclaimed his wine. "I like you, Emersyn. More than I expected. You and I could have some fun together."

Ugh. No thank you.

It wasn't until he glanced away from me that I could take a deep breath and some of the tension bled out of Liam. "I have big plans for you boys. Big plans. Tonight is just the beginning. Our court is growing and…we have new players in the game."

The people who had Adam, who'd taken Rome and me. If I were to guess, that had to be who he meant.

"Old ones too." The king spared a look at Liam. "It's time to clear the board, one square at a time." He paused as the footman returned to remove our plates, before he poured coffee for each of us and added a dessert to the table.

It was all so lovely, and I wanted none of it.

Only when he was gone did the king lean forward.

"With that in mind, Emersyn, I have a question for you."

Again?

"Tell me," he said as he raised his coffee cup. "Do you have a preference between my bishops here?"

Oh, that was a trap.

CHAPTER 27

EMERSYN

*D*id I have a preference? Yes, I did. I had a preference for not continuing the conversation. As it was, Liam stepped right into the middle of that verbal grenade.

"Of course, she has a preference," he stated. "She came here with me. She'll be leaving with me. She's *staying* with me."

"Are you certain, Bishop?" The challenge in the king's voice couldn't be mistaken for anything else.

"Deathly certain," Liam warned him, though, to be honest, I didn't think it was a warning.

It resonated far more like a promise.

The meal dragged on after that. Every comment seemed to have two or three possible meanings. My nerves were screaming by the time we finished. Somehow, I think the only one who enjoyed the whole thing *was* the king.

What a prick.

Then why wouldn't he? This was all his idea. When the last dish had been cleared away and he rose, I could have cried from the relief. Were we finally getting out of here? None of our plans included being in here for hours.

Hopefully, Liam got word to the guys who'd been shadowing us, but I wasn't even sure how to ask him. Neither of us left the table though Ezra had excused himself once to go to the restroom.

"Mr. Măcelar will see you out," the king said as he rose. "Welcome to the Bay Ridge Royals, Emersyn. While you may only be a pawn at the moment, I expect you will move up quickly."

Wait… what?

"Excuse me?" Liam damn near growled the words as he stood, taking a step toward the king so they were face to face.

If he was at all worried about our reaction, it didn't appear on Julius King's face. If anything, he seemed amused by the anger threading through every molecule of Liam's being. I swore the air around him vibrated with a very real sense of rage.

"I didn't stutter, Bishop," Julius told him, his bland expression not even betraying a ripple of unease. "She's either a Bay Ridge Royal or she's dead." The careless ease with which he delivered that proclamation sent ice through me. "She is the reason you executed Reed."

"What?" The exclamation slipped out of me. While I was gripping Liam's arm, he was the one keeping me from head-on confronting the king now. "Why would you have him killed because of *me*?"

Ezra eyed the king with a far less friendly expression than the belligerent one he'd sported throughout the meal. Adam was his best friend. While he'd not responded to the earlier dig at Liam, Ezra couldn't miss this one.

The chuckle the king released was both humorless and

almost cruel. "Because he attempted to make an unsanctioned move, Emersyn. He brought you into this game when he asked you to marry him."

Everything inside of me stilled.

"My people do not make moves without my authorization. Curry power? I expect it. Foster alliances? I demand it. Make a choice that brings a new player to the board?"

He focused on me, and the chill from earlier was back. I had to dig my fingers into Liam's arm in an attempt to keep him still.

The tension threading Liam's muscles was a living, breathing thing that threatened the oxygen around us. "You had me kill him because he wanted to marry my girlfriend?"

"You should be thanking me," the king told him. "After all, he went after her before you—or maybe because of you—" He offered a shrug like the why of it all mattered little to him. "Not his first mistake, but definitely a costly one. Why else try to acquire the Sharpe fortune through its only heir for his own?"

His offer had nothing to do with my fortunes. Well, fine, maybe it had something to do with it, but that wasn't the main reason. Adam had tried to help me, and it nearly got him killed. Anger struck a match inside of me.

"Do you know my uncle?"

"Personally?" The king paused, his cold gaze closing in on me. My mouth went dry at the possibilities behind that question. "No," he answered himself. "We've met in passing, at events, the occasional charity, theatre opening…"

"You don't know him, but you are acquainted."

"Bradley Sharpe likes to be well-acquainted. His hunger for power is well-documented. We'll discuss him more in the future."

I'd pass.

"For now, be a good pawn and do as you're told." He

flicked a look toward Ezra then Liam. "Be glad I'm allowing Liam the preference you have since I have plans for Ezra elsewhere. Good evening, gentlemen. I'll be in touch."

Mr. Măcelar stepped forward as the king turned away from us. A muscle ticked in Liam's jaw as he watched the king stroll away. Julius King owned this room and, in his opinion, he owned everyone in it—including me.

Liam made no attempt to follow, but I didn't doubt for one instant it had anything to do with lack of desire. He wasn't leaving me. I hadn't been brought here for leverage—or maybe I had been, but it wasn't just leverage for Liam.

"If you'll head back to the entrance," Mr. Măcelar said. "You will be allowed to collect your weapons and shown out. His Majesty will be in touch soon."

"Then the evening is done?" Ezra asked as though clarifying.

"Quite finished," the footman, butler—whatever Măcelar was to the king—stated in a firm tone. "Your presence is no longer required."

"Great." Ezra cut a look toward me. "Emersyn-baby…" he held out his hand, blithely ignoring Liam's growl. "It's been a real pleasure getting to meet you."

Liam's arm flexed beneath my fingertips. The movement was almost imperceptible but it wasn't resistance. He wanted me to play along. Shifting a step, I reached out to take Ezra's offered hand.

I was missing *Hellspawn* so much right now.

He closed his fingers around mine in a light, if firm grip and gave the barest tug. It pulled me toward him by a couple of steps before he kissed my hand. "My apologies," he murmured in a low voice.

Before I could ask him what the apology was for, he pushed me away from both of them before he launched into

Liam. His fist collided with Liam's face in a meaty, crunchy blow that made me flinch.

At first, I didn't think Liam would fight back, but the second blow was all the room he gave Ezra before he slammed a fist into his stomach and doubled him over. The extreme gagging exhale was so pained that I thought he would vomit.

"Gentlemen," our escort attempted to intervene, but I cut him off and glared at him.

"Stay out of it," I ordered him, and he blinked down at me like he'd forgotten I was there. "Mr. King," I spit out his name, refusing to use that ridiculous title, "set this up by reminding Ezra not once but twice that Adam is dead and trying to blame Liam for it. Let *them* settle this."

I'd never been more grateful to know about a ruse in my life. If this was how I'd learned of Adam's "death," I didn't know if I could have continued to play along. As it was, Liam and Ezra exchanged a flurry of blows, but poor Ezra really was no match for Liam.

When he dropped Ezra with his arm in a locked hold, I stepped toward them. "Don't hurt him…" I had to give them a way out of this. "Please."

Liam cut a look at me. The chill in his eyes didn't match the air of manic rage billowing around him. "He—"

"He's grieving," I whispered, not finding it hard to reach for the sadness that all of us were tied up in this. "It's not his fault, and it's not yours."

It was mine.

Releasing Ezra abruptly, Liam snagged me with an arm and dragged me to him. I curled into him as much to protect him as to take the shelter he offered.

"It's not your fault either, Emersyn-baby. Reed knew he was playing with fire." Rough comfort or not, I didn't think Liam was wrong. Adam had made a choice, but that choice had been to help me, and that asshole they worked for decided to eliminate him for it.

If I hadn't already despised this man for seemingly wanting to kill my brother, I'd have every reason to hate him now. He'd hurt Ezra. He continued to hurt Liam. He used his power to elicit fear, and when that didn't work—he used brutality.

He and my uncle probably had a lot in common. That thought was not comfortable at all, and a chill wrapped around my spine.

"Come at me again," Liam said, his attention on Ezra. "You won't walk away. Thank Emersyn that I'm letting you go for now."

Spitting the blood from his mouth on the opulent rug, Ezra smirked. "Don't do us any favors. Trust me, next time? You aren't going to see me coming."

He did *not* have to sound like he enjoyed it. Liam took a step forward, but I wrapped my arms tighter around him. Yes, this was a play, a ruse, a misdirection—but no more.

Liam cut his gaze down to meet mine as I shook my head. "Please?" Could we go? Could we get out of here? Could we just stop?

I didn't ask all of those things, I just said the single-syllable plea and he nodded once. Grabbing my coat, he pulled me to him. "Keep him here while we leave," he said without looking to either man. "I'll be in touch."

With that, we were moving. I had to hurry to keep up with Liam's long strides, but he didn't loosen his grip on me. There was no stumbling. The one moment I thought I might, he curled his arm tighter around me and lifted me off my feet and he didn't set me down until we were at the elevator.

Inside it, I glanced at him, but he shook his head once. Head pressed against him, I waited. We exited to the lobby where Liam collected his weapons—and mine—then we were in another elevator and descending to the annex where the car had been parked.

We didn't say a word while he'd gone over to the SUV and checked something on his phone. I said nothing when he opened the passenger door and urged me inside. Head on a swivel, he scanned around us as he buckled me in. I was capable of doing it myself, but the barely contained fury surging around Liam wasn't an act.

He was beyond angry. Once he was behind the wheel, he took my hand, and then we were pulling out. Ezra stepped into the path of the vehicle, and if not for Liam's lightning-fast reflexes, I was pretty sure we would have hit him.

They glared at each other. Their expressions were almost unreadable to me. It was like the most uncomfortable game of chicken that neither gave on until Liam took his foot off the brake, and Ezra jerked himself out of the way at the last second.

Tires squealing on the pavement, Liam accelerated out of the garage and onto the road. I gritted my teeth as he didn't even hesitate to pull out onto the busy street. There were horns blaring and more than one shriek of brakes, but he didn't slow or look back.

Instead, we raced through the city like someone was pursuing us, and it wasn't until we were almost to the highway that he glanced at me.

"You okay?"

I had no idea where we were going and I wasn't going to bother him with questions. Instead, I just let out a shaky little laugh and blew out a breath. The laugh had nothing to do with any of this being funny.

"No," I said slowly. "I'm not. How are you?"

"Pissed."

Yeah, that was about right. "He wanted to rub Ezra's face in the idea that you killed Adam."

A single nod. "He doesn't want us to be allies. It was why he decided to test me by offering you to him." The words came out harsh as Liam ground them out between his teeth.

"My preference." I made a face.

"Yeah," he said on an exhale. Then the phone rang. I scowled at the display but then Jasper's name appeared. I hit answer without Liam telling me I had to. "Jas," he said as I exhaled a sigh, "hey."

"You two good?"

"No," I said, this time with a real smile. "According to some very good sources, I've been asking to get spanked."

Dead silence greeted that comment, then Jasper said, "Huh."

Liam cut a look at me and his smile, a real one this time, transformed his whole expression. "That's five right there, Hellspawn."

Hearing him say Hellspawn again improved my mood a thousand percent. I grinned at him, tightening my hand on his. "Are you supposed to threaten me with a good time?"

Jasper's laughter came through the open line, and I closed my eyes to savor the sound of it mixing with Liam's huffed chuckles.

"Oh, Hellspawn, are you sure you're ready for me?" There was just a hint of a warning to lick along those words, but it didn't stop the anticipation from curling in my stomach.

"I can handle you," I told him.

"Goddamn," Jasper said. "Do not make me horny listening to this…"

"Unless?" Liam prompted.

Unless?

"Unless I'm invited." The smirk in Jasper's words was adorable.

Liam slid a look at me. "We're not going back to the apartment."

We weren't.

"Yeah, I got that. Vaughn's got Graham, he's watching his back. I've got you two. Where we going?"

I raised my brows as Liam drummed two fingers against the steering wheel. "Old house," he said finally. "Let Kel know we're not gonna be back until tomorrow." Then he let go of my hand and ended the call.

"We're not?" I said, rolling my head to meet his gaze. The agitation around him scraped against my own.

"No," he said. "And if you really aren't ready for all of this tonight, Hellspawn, that's fine…"

"I said I can handle you," I told him, putting my hand on his again. "Tonight was…"

"Fucked up," he said. "We'll talk about it…but not right now. Right now, I want you at the house with us, and then I want to do whatever I want to you."

"Whatever?" I teased even as I shuddered. Maybe all of this should scare me. Liam could be a scary guy.

But the idea of Liam *and* Jasper?

"Whatever," he agreed. "You ready for that?"

CHAPTER 28

EMERSYN

*W*hen Liam said the house, he meant an actual mansion located outside of Braxton Harbor in the Bay Ridge hills. A wrought iron gate boasting three separate security cameras opened when he entered a code then let us down a long tree-lined driveway.

The house waiting at the end of the drive was not visible from the road, had a circular drive out front and what had probably been a lovely water feature, though it was empty and motionless at the moment.

Liam didn't pause there, swinging around to the garage and pressing a button to open the doors. He turned the car around and backed into it, a move Jasper followed, backing right into the slot next to his.

Not waiting for the doors to close, Jasper was out of his car and had my door open. The heated look in his eyes as he swept his gaze over me warmed me to my core, but it wasn't just passion. There was a measuring look in those gray eyes that made me shiver.

"I'm okay," I promised him. Our evening with Julius King had been like being trapped in a bottle where time elongated to impossible lengths. Now that we were free? I wasn't sure what made me more dizzy... the fact we survived or Liam's rather blunt plans.

Both?

"She's better than okay," Liam said as he pushed out of the car and glanced through at both of us. "She's fucking amazing."

Jasper frowned briefly, then straightened as he cupped my face. His palm was warm, the calluses on his fingers so familiar. The slow caress eased the sudden pound of my heart.

Or maybe not so suddenly, but all at once, I was violently reminded of my racing pulse as it seemed to beat out a rapid tattoo against my ribs. Pretending everything was all right wasn't new to me, but being able to let go of that pretense? To slide back inside my own skin? I savored the safety they wrapped around me. I leaned into Jasper's touch, aware that they were looking at each other over the car.

"What about you?" Jasper was asking about Liam; concern edging every word flooded my eyes with tears. Absent the animosity between them that so often seemed to crackle and burn with their every interaction, the promise of their friendship, brotherhood, and the trust between them bound me up in an embrace I never wanted to leave.

For all their mutual gruffness, I'd learned a lot about Jasper's colossal heart and Liam's fierce determination. They both loved with everything they had and they were violent in their need to protect it.

That they'd ever been put at odds broke my heart.

"I'll live," Liam said on a harsh exhale. "I know you want to know what happened."

"You're both here, in one piece, and…" Jasper leaned back to glance down at me, a smile softening his lips. "You're both where I can protect you."

The soft snort from Liam made me grin, but then I didn't think he could make out the twinkle in Jasper's eyes. I could. Running my hand down over Jasper's abdomen, I skated my fingers against his belt buckle even as I raised my brows.

"We'll tell you," I promised Jasper. "Later." Liam didn't need to relive that meeting right now.

Catching my fingers in his, Jasper took a step back and helped me out of the SUV. I could easily slip out on my own, but I craved his touch. I craved them both.

The whole meeting had been unsettling as hell. Worse, I didn't understand the game the king seemed intent on playing, only that I was now tied into it and that infuriated Liam on every level. As much as I disliked the king, I loathed him for what he was doing to Liam, to Ezra, and to Adam.

As I stood, I turned to where Liam waited. The red mark on his cheekbone was going to turn into a bruise. Blood flecked the corner of his mouth, and another soon-to-be bruise was marring his jaw. Ezra had definitely gotten a few shots in.

Even under the low illumination of the garage's lighting, his blue-green eyes warmed away the chill. "You still up for this, Hellspawn?" The fact he kept putting me first, seeking confirmation and assurance, despite the wants and needs he'd already expressed, just added another delightful layer to his sometimes prickly personality.

I leaned backward, trusting Jasper to keep me from falling. His legs tensed as he slid an arm around my middle and let me tuck up against him. I could answer him with reassurance. I could tell him yes. I could dig out all the pretty words I possessed and offer them up.

"Where and how do you want me?" Those were all great ideas, but all I wanted to offer to him, to any of them, was me.

Jasper's exhale carried the edge of need, and there was an intensity that snapped into Liam's expression that sent heat to lick its way through my system. I didn't need him to tell me he had ideas. They were burning in his eyes.

"Inside," he said, flicking a look at Jasper. "You in or just watching?"

Arm tightening around my middle, Jasper dipped his head to press his lips behind my ear. "Am I in, Swan?"

"Would you really just watch?" I was certain of his answer, but maybe like Liam, I wanted to make sure too.

"If that was what you needed," Jas said, his voice as soft as his lips where he pressed kisses along my throat and his beard where it tickled me.

"Hmm... I'll make you both a deal," I said, locking my gaze on Liam's.

"We're listening, Hellspawn."

Jasper hummed an agreement as he settled his hands on my hips. A moment later, he moved them to my belt. The gun and holster were off. The whole action was so smooth it just made me giggle. I liked that they trusted me to wear the weapons and to use them. I was equally fine with the ease with which they were removed.

"Tell me what you want," I said. "If you want something I can't do or can't handle, I'll tell you to stop."

It was the deal I had with Kellan. It was the same deal we'd used before.

"But what I want right now, is you." I held Liam's gaze until he nodded then I shifted my attention to Jasper. "And you."

He squeezed my hips.

"But are you two okay with sharing?"

"Have to see if the pretty boy can keep up," Jasper teased and Liam snorted.

"Keep up? Those are fighting words." Not that he sounded at all opposed.

"Side wager?" Jasper said and I blinked. Wait, a wager? What?

"I could be persuaded." Liam circled the vehicle then held out a hand to me. "C'mon, Hellspawn, inside. Then I want you naked."

My whole body clenched at those words. Jasper's teeth scraped over my pulse point, but he let me go and one moment, I was facing Liam and the next I was over his shoulder and staring at his ass as he headed for the door. His hand smoothed over my ass.

"You earned five," Liam said in a tone that was as darkly seductive as it was enticing. He didn't wait for confirmation before dropping a slap across my asscheeks. Even through the sweater dress, the fire blazed across my ass and I let out a strangled sound.

"Fuck," Jasper said on a harsh exhale. He was right behind us. "Make that sound again."

"Agreed," Liam said and his hand landed on my ass again. This time, he spanked out the next four in rapid succession. I gripped Liam's belt as he massaged the heat, spreading it down to my thighs.

My cunt went soft and if I'd thought I was wet before, it had nothing on this. I didn't get a glance at the house as Liam carried me through and then upstairs. There was a warmth to it, a scent of coffee and spice with hints of other pleasant aromas overlaying the dust that I couldn't identify. The house might look unused from the outside, but it didn't feel that way in here.

Not that I wanted to. If he wasn't dressed, I'd bite Liam's ass right now. As it was, I could imagine the muscle rippling beneath his clothes as he moved. Upstairs, a door pushed inward and I'd have known it was Liam's without a single look around.

It smelled like him. Like his body wash, his aftershave, and the way his sheets smelled after he'd slept in them. My ass was still on fire as I landed on my back on the bed. There were two equally tall, equally fierce, and wildly hot men staring down at me with wild eyes.

"Side wager?" Liam asked as he reached for his belt.

Jasper rubbed at his beard as he watched me. "Liam told you to get naked, Swan."

He had told me that. I reached for the first boot and hauled it off. Then the second. I started to scoot forward, but Jasper reached down and slid his hands up my legs and under the skirt.

"Keep score in orgasms," Jasper said. "Whoever gets the most out of her, gets one full turn while the other has to watch."

I shivered as his warm fingers grazed along my thighs to my panties.

"That makes Hellspawn the scorekeeper." It wasn't a question.

"Yes," Jasper said as he peeled my panties down. Once he had them, he nudged my thighs to the side until I butterflied and gave them both an open view of my cunt.

Belt sliding free from his pants, Liam studied me. "The rest of the outfit, Hellspawn."

But Jasper kept a hand on my right thigh, keeping me bare to them. Clothes off, but don't move. I arched my hips then pulled the sweater dress up as Jasper began to smile slowly.

"Addendum to the wager," Liam said as he shed his

weapons. The door behind him was closed. But the guns weren't locked away. He just set them on one side of the bed.

Only when he returned, did Jasper move to take off his own weapons. Anticipation licked over me as I wiggled the dress up and over. It was gonna mess up my hair, but I really didn't give a shit about that.

Hot hands covered my breasts before I got the dress clear and I found Liam waiting for me to see him before he began to roll my nipples between his thumbs and forefingers. The fabric provided a barrier to some of the contact, but the pressure had my back arching.

"Name it," Jasper said, pulling my attention to him where he stood bare-chested in a pair of jeans that were already undone.

Liam twisted one nipple with a little more force. It was just at the point of pain and I arched my hips. Fuck, I wanted more. My breath came in sharp little pants. I kind of wanted to beg, but I didn't want to interrupt this moment between the two of them.

"Whoever blows their load last gets to tell Hellspawn what to do to the other…and the person who blew first has to deal with the edging."

Shock and delight curved through me as Liam released my nipple then leaned down to suck it against his teeth, fabric and all. A moan vibrated out of me and Jasper chuckled.

"You think you can handle her doing whatever she wants to you?"

"Whatever we want her to do?" Liam said, his voice dipping. "Oh, I can handle it."

They were both looking at me.

"I can handle anything, but one of you better have a dick inside of me soon, or I'm going to orgasm just from you talking and I'm giving myself a point for that."

Eyebrows raised, Liam grinned. "You want a cock, Hellspawn?"

A cock? No.

"I want your cock," I told him as I rolled to sit up and put a hand behind me to release my bra. "I want Jasper's cock. I want very specific cocks." As serious as we'd been, that last line pulled a laugh from me even as I said it.

"We established you have preferences," Liam teased, some of the darkness pulling back to let him out again.

"We have."

"Good to know," Jasper said before he put out a fist and looked at Liam.

"You're a dick." Liam's retort wasn't remotely annoyed despite the comment. He put his fist out and they were both doing rock, paper, scissors.

Laughter bubbled up through me as they did the same one over and over again until it was finally scissors from Jasper and paper from Liam.

"Fuck," Liam swore and Jasper just chuckled.

"I intend to—go see if Swan will suck your cock, since she's so excited about getting it." He glanced at me, and his gray eyes were positively glowing like there was a sun shining behind them. "Legs spread, Swan…I haven't eaten today, and I'm starving."

Oh.

Fuck.

Me.

CHAPTER 29

JASPER

*F*rom the moment I locked gazes with Liam, his rage communicated itself. It was a living, breathing entity surging around him like some ghost monster in a movie. Whatever the fuck happened during that meeting had pushed him to the point of being homicidal.

A place I'd only ever seen him go twice before. On one of those occasions, I'd been standing right next to him as we rained all that rage down on the man who'd assaulted Freddie. We'd torn him apart. Killing the son of a bitch hadn't eradicated the anger. It sure as fuck hadn't made any of us feel better, least of all Freddie.

What it had done, though, was unite us. It fueled our unity and fed the fire driving all of us. No one would ever hurt one of us like that again.

Ever.

When he flicked his gaze down to the car, I understood all that rage. Maybe it had everything to do with the meeting.

Or maybe the meeting had only ripped open the scar tissue on that old wound. One of us had been hurt.

She'd been hurt badly and for a long time.

Emersyn had told him. I nodded slowly. While he'd invited me to join them, everything that happened next was up to her. We weren't pushing.

Swan, however, didn't try to coddle us or make us feel better. Instead, she just threw down a challenge. When she said she could handle us, she damn well meant it.

Fifteen minutes and a game of rock, paper, scissors later, with her sprawled naked on the bed in front of me and her pussy bare for my inspection… I went to my knees without a second's thought.

"Fuck," Liam swore and I just chuckled.

"I intend to—go see if Swan will suck your cock, since she's so excited about getting it."

I couldn't get enough of her, just stroking my hands over her thighs and drinking in the picture she made. So fucking gorgeous. The playfulness that danced in between the shadows sliding around in her gaze beckoned to me. If she were a siren, I'd have already beaten myself bloody against the rocks to get to her.

"Legs spread, Swan…I haven't eaten today and I'm starving." Fuck, if that wasn't the truth. Her pretty pussy glistened with dampness and heat. I loved how bare she kept it, no secrets hidden from me. The way her vagina seemed to flex at my nearness. Or maybe it was how turned on she was.

The bed shifted and I glanced up in time to see Liam feeding her his cock, just like I suggested. Fuck, that was hot. I trailed a finger down the seam of her cunt, spreading the lips a little wider so I could savor every reaction.

She curled a leg over my shoulder. Another chuckle escaped me as she nudged me forward with her foot flattening against my back. The angle tilted her hips upward, an entreaty, an invitation—fuck, a seduction.

"I guess I'm not the only one who is feeling greedy," I teased. A hum of sound escaped her and Liam groaned. Grinning, I buried my face against her cunt, lapping up the musky sweetness even as I pressed two fingers into her. No time to adjust, she clamped down on my fingers as I sucked her clit against my teeth.

The speed at which she detonated surprised me and caught even Liam off-guard. She hadn't been kidding about how much she wanted. He let out a shout and I had to pause as she swallowed and then he pulled back and ended up splashing her chest with cum.

"Well, that was an easy bet to win," I said slowly as they both gasped for air. I curved my fingers where they pressed into her and she gave a shudder.

"Fucking worth it," Liam said in a raw voice before he leaned in to kiss her. The trembling in her limbs made me grin.

"Definitely," I agreed. "And we're at one-zero." I thrust my fingers and then went after her clit again as she gasped. The sound of her moaning into Liam's kiss was almost as hot as when she moaned into my mouth.

Need throbbed through me, and my dick ached, but I wanted to wring another couple of orgasms out of her before I took my first one. The night was young, after all.

Between us, Liam and I had her thrashing again in minutes. Sobbing sounds came from her throat as he sucked her nipples and I teased her clit. Even as she began to spasm and twist, we kept her in place.

"You can take it, Hellspawn," Liam told her. "Can't you?"

"Fuck…" She groaned the word with her whole body as her hips thrust up toward me. She'd soaked my beard and it was fucking wonderful. There was no restraint in her reactions as she let out another cry.

Speaking of restraint—mine was shredding. I dragged my fingers out of her, and kissed her cunt once more as I unzipped my jeans and peeled out of them.

Rising, I hugged her legs to my chest, before I seated my cock inside her with one furious thrust. The spasming of her walls fluttering around me teased me, but I was not going to be a two-pump chump, especially when she let out another of those ragged cries.

Liam lifted his head, clearing the way for me to see her and he moved next to her. Her pupils were totally blown as she arched and twisted to meet my thrusts. I wanted to roll her over and fuck her from behind.

Later, I promised myself as she flexed and pulled against me. I only released her legs to surge forward into her arms when my balls began to drag upward. Emersyn's mouth opened to mine, a litany of unrecognizable syllables spilling out of her until I silenced her with a kiss.

The dig of her fingers against my back urged me on. It took only one brush of my fingers between us to set her off, and I happily followed her orgasm with my own. Liquid heat spilled out of me and shot into her.

For a moment, I imagined her flat tummy rounded and heavy with a child. Fuck, I'd never wanted to get anyone pregnant before. Didn't matter that it wasn't happening right now. The sudden need the image aroused seemed to make me come even harder.

I was still kissing her, though it turned slower, lingering, and deeper as I drifted back into my body. My dick seemed to tremble inside of her, or maybe it was her trembling.

Ice water dripped down my back and I dragged my head up to glare Liam. But he held out the ice-cold bottle of water to me almost as a peace gesture.

Fine. Fuck it. I rolled us over so I could sit up some while Swan sprawled against me. Her eyes were half-closed. I downed about half the bottle before I helped Liam coax her into drinking.

"We're not done with you yet, Hellspawn," Liam told her, and that had her eyes fluttering open.

"Four orgasms," she whispered. "I'm winning."

I laughed at the delighted note in her pleasure-drenched voice.

"Yeah, you are," he told her. "Drink some more."

I balanced the bottle for her and she began to drain it. When she finished, Liam walked away and then came back with a washcloth.

"Hold her," he ordered and I had no problems with that command. She writhed as he wiped her down. The sweat on me would be itchy soon, but I could rinse off in the shower.

Huh, that explained why Liam's hair was damp. He'd already done that.

"Too much," she whispered, an aching note in her voice as Liam cleaned along her cunt. He slowed his hand, easing up on the pressure. "Better."

"Good girl," he soothed. Flicking a look at me, Liam raised his brows.

"Bring it," I told him. "I'm already in the lead."

He laughed.

"Roll over, Hellspawn, and get that ass in the air."

The command was enough to make me pause for a moment, yet there was nothing in her dazed expression except pleasure. No unease. No hesitation. No fear.

She rolled over so obediently it sent another pulse to my dick. I eased up as Liam moved behind her with a bottle of lube.

Oh, fuck yeah.

Twenty-five minutes later, I kicked back on the bed while

Liam eased into her ass. She was on her hands and knees, chin up and gaze on me. Her mouth formed an "o" as he pressed into her. Her eyes half-closed and a low whine escaped her.

Fisting her hair with care, I tilted her head back. "Open those beautiful eyes for me, Swan. Tell me how that feels…"

"Are you for fucking real?" Liam asked on a huff of laughter.

"Yeah, I am. I want to know how it feels to have your cock in her ass. I want to know she's enjoying it." I raised my eyes and locked gazes with him. "I need to know."

He nodded, running a hand over her back. "Answer him, Hellspawn."

The trembling of her lower lip increased, and her face went pink and flushed. Eyes open again, she stared at me. "Yes, it feels so good," she muttered, the words pushed out like she couldn't believe she had to tell us. "He feels so good…it burns, but—oh…" A grunt escaped her as Liam moved. "It feels good, Jas. I promise."

"Long as you like it," I hurried to soothe her. After everything she'd said, I had to know she wanted this. Wanted *us* like this. Fucking her cunt was everything. I adored her mouth. However that ass—I wouldn't lie—it held appeal but only in as much as I wanted every part of her.

"Love it," she whispered, and when she reached out to me, I held her hand. "Love you…"

They began to move then and it was like watching her fly in her silks. Her whole body moved with his thrusts. Her nipples strained, her muscles rippled, and fuck, I didn't know where to watch her.

The tattoo between her breasts declared her ours to the whole fucking world. Mine. Ours. Fucking always. When she dragged my finger to her mouth and sucked on it, I chuckled.

"Need more cock, Swan?"

"Always," she said on a moan, and then reached for mine. I was already stirring, but it might take me a minute. Not that I had a single problem with her wrapping that sweet hand around my dick and beginning to stroke.

Fuck no.

No complaints at all.

The hours bled past, the evening giving way to night and it was dawn when I pressed the vibe against her clit while I fucked her from behind. She was splayed out for Liam to watch her where he sat in the chair. Her cunt was a hot fist, taking every inch of my cock and trying to hold onto it as I thrust.

The vibe, though, ramped up quickly from a gentle stroke to a mad little suck and her scream was like music to my ears. "Tell Liam how you want him to stroke his cock, Swan..."

This was a little torturous for all of us, but Liam having to just sit there and watch as I took our girl apart just seemed to give my pleasure that little bit of extra.

"Tighter," she ordered, her voice wrecked. "Stroke in time with—fuck—with Jasper."

Yeah, I wasn't being easy on her at all. If anything, we'd gentled out some around two in the morning, paused to eat and shower, then she climbed on Liam's cock and kept him warm in her pussy while he fed her.

After that, all bets were off and we fucked her on the table. We'd only brought her upstairs for this round because Liam had toys here and I wanted her to come until she couldn't.

Even as she orgasmed around me, I kept up the pressure until her screams became sobs. Liam came all over his own hand and I blew my load inside of her as I dragged the vibe off.

Our beautiful girl all but collapsed after that. It took some effort, but between Liam and me, we got her cleaned up and eased between the sheets. Her ass was sore, red, and flushed from a second spanking. Her cunt was definitely going to be sore, so we used cooler cloths on it to pet her sensually abused pussy.

Fuck, what a night. Liam vanished, only to come back with more water. I showered, cleaned up, and dragged on my pants before I took the second chair in the bedroom. We sat there in silence, staring at her sleep in the middle of the bed.

We should probably climb in there with her, but the peacefulness on her expression chased away my weariness. That right there was the reason we had done fucking everything. That was what was under threat.

"I need a cigarette," I said after a minute. Coffee and a couple of cigarettes, maybe.

"I need to tell you what happened," Liam said, anger bleeding into his tone. "Should have said earlier but..."

"You needed her and she clearly needed us."

"C'mon," Liam said. "I don't want to wake her up."

"Yep," I said as I rose and followed him into the hall. "Liam... whatever it is... we'll deal with it."

And if that meant murder and mayhem? Well, sign me the fuck up. I was always down to kill for my family.

CHAPTER 30

EMERSYN

A knock on my open bedroom door pulled my attention from the book Jasper had pressed into my hands before he left. He was reading this series and wanted to know what I thought.

Milo leaned against the doorjamb, his deep brown eyes focused on me. From his damp hair, I guessed he'd just showered. "Hey," he said. "You busy?"

"Nope, just reading." I snagged the receipt on the nightstand from—oh, it was from when we stopped to get ice cream on the way back—tucked it between the pages before I focused on him. "Need me?"

He chuckled. "Always going to need you, Ives. Come on." He nodded to the sitting room. "Hungry?"

"I could eat." I eased off the bed with care. Despite sleeping on and off for most of the day after my night with Liam and Jasper, I was still a bit sore. Liam had drawn me a bath while Jasper went to cook. It had been sweetly domestic in a way.

A part of me had wanted to go exploring in the house, especially when I found out it was where Liam had grown up after he'd been adopted. It was outside the city, which meant he'd had to get transport in regularly to see Rome.

As many questions as the house had answered, it had also offered up new questions. I hungered to know everything about them, but I was also willing to wait for when they wanted to share.

"Grab your jacket, let's go out. I want to take you to one of my favorite spots."

Going out with just one of us was against the rules Kellan had set up. "Let me text Kel real quick." And get my gun.

Milo's expression tightened briefly, then he let out a laugh and shook his head.

"I just wanted—"

Raising a hand, Milo said, "Ignore me, Ivy. You're doing the right thing. Kel set the rules for a reason. I respect it."

"But you don't like it?" Getting to know Milo took effort on both our parts. It was infinitely worth the effort, but this uncomfortable space between us was still filled with all the years I didn't know him and littered with the rubble of the life he'd always imagined for me.

"I don't have to like it." The deflection almost made me smile. It was a lot like what I would do if I didn't want to answer a question.

"That's not what I asked."

His lips compressed, even as his gaze darkened as he glared at me. Eyebrows raised, I waited. To be fair, Milo absolutely terrified me in the beginning. He was huge, loud, and chaotic energy seemed to surround him. I'd stood up to him to protect Jasper, to protect the guys... didn't change how much he scared me or how much I'd hated him trying to push me out of their lives.

"Ivy," he practically growled my name. I was more familiar with that tone because they all got that tone when they were annoyed by me in some way but planning to let me have my way.

Arms folded, I waited. This was important. "Your feelings matter to me."

Whatever he thought I was going to say, that was clearly not it. His mouth opened then closed abruptly. Straightening, he raked a hand through his hair. "I spent... a lot of years being the one who made the calls. I was the one with the plan. I could see all the angles. I—"

Blowing out a breath, he lifted his shoulders as if he lacked the words to explain.

"It's hard when I remember I'm not that guy anymore," he said finally. "Send a message to Kel. I talked to him earlier and said I was going to take you out to lunch."

Olive branch offered.

"Thank you." Olive branch accepted. "And I think you're still that guy."

I picked up the phone and sent the text.

"I wish I was," Milo said in a soft voice. "But I'm not the same guy who went inside and it took me a while to see it."

Kellan answered almost immediately. The bracelet that Liam had given me was still clipped to my wrist. The guys could all track me as needed.

"He said to let him know if we leave the territory." I still wasn't sure how much of Braxton Harbor counted as their territory. My lips pursed.

"Problem?"

It was my turn to huff. "I don't know what is defined as our territory."

A grin softened the more rigid lines around his mouth. "I do…grab your jacket and your gun."

"Hey, you managed to say that without a grimace."

He rolled his eyes at the teasing even as I sent Kel a thumbs-up and a kiss-blowing emoji. He sent back a clap and I laughed. Did that mean I just earned one?

At Milo's inquiring look, I shook my head. He was doing great. Some things we were not going to be discussing… like ever.

Ten minutes later, I was in the passenger seat of his car, and we were pulling out of the warehouse. Freddie was still at Mickey's but not just to stay there. He was working at the clinic *and* liking it.

ME:

Heading out with Milo for lunch. Be back later.

I didn't want to push him, but I also needed him to know he was wanted.

FREDDIE:

Check in when you're back?

ME:

Promise.

"Question," Milo said, glancing at me. "Feel free to tell me to fuck off."

"Okay, I think I can manage that." I tucked my phone into my pocket with a little smile. He'd hearted the promise. "But thank you for the permission."

Milo chuckled. An honest-to-god real chuckle. "You are such a little shit sometimes."

"Thank you."

His chuckle deepened into laughter as he shook his head. "I'm trying to be serious, and you have jokes."

"Milo, I hate to be the one to break this to you, but you don't have to try to be serious." I kept my tone solemn as I enjoyed the battle he was fighting against laughter. "You were born for the scowl and the growl."

Silence greeted my statement and he blinked as he transferred his attention from the road to me. I wasn't sure if he was shocked at first or more amused. His eyes narrowed. "You think you're funny."

"Yep," I told him, absolutely unrepentant on this front. "And so do you." Teasing him was *fun*. I didn't get to do it often.

His snort didn't dissuade me at all. "*Anyway*," he said, stressing the word like "moving on." "This thing with the Royals. Are you really okay playing this game?"

In spite of my teasing, I didn't dismiss his question out of hand. "Yes," I said slowly, "and no." Jasper and Liam discussed some of the meeting with me, but from their tone and word choice, they'd already done it while I'd slept. They were too calm. Eerily so.

Below the surface, however, they were both so unimaginably raw—angry seemed far too tame a word for them. The emotion flowing through their eyes seemed almost primal. While I worried about them, their closeness was damn near tangible. Even when they snarked and picked on each other, they weren't trying to draw blood anymore.

After we briefed the guys, Liam seemed even more aggravated, if that were possible. We'd gone to brunch with his parents and Rome came too. The time with his family only emphasized how surreal the idea of normalcy was, even to me. My normal, mainly where family was concerned, was not this.

His parents were coming back for his birthday, and I

couldn't wait for that. I liked them. I liked how they loved him and Rome both. We were going to have to do something special for their birthday…

"Ivy?" Milo's verbal prompt reminded me not to zone out mid-conversation.

"Sorry, it just reminded me of the argument you all had when we came back and filled you in." The fact I'd been "co-opted" into the Royals was not ideal. Far from it. I couldn't really wrap my mind around that. It felt like some kind of *game,* but one with rules I didn't understand and no one had explained.

"I don't know if I'm okay playing it because it's upsetting to all of you, and that was *not* what we had planned. Liam's been—"

"I know," Milo said gently, not needing me to explain. "He's blaming himself. He's in this mess because of me."

"Don't do that," I said, shaking my head. "Did he let himself get recruited and then pursue them to get more information? Yes. Did he do it to protect you? Also, yes. But you didn't force him and wouldn't have had to, regardless. Liam protects the people he loves."

That included all of them.

"With us for just a little over a year, and you know us so well?" No judgment lived in that question. Or maybe it was a comment and not a question.

Either way, I loved that he said *us.* "I want to know all of you. I love getting to learn little things and big things. But the loyalty? The devotion? I've seen that from the beginning." I hadn't forgotten how torn up Jasper had been while he and Milo were at odds. Neither of them wanted to back down. "I wanted to be worthy of that kind of loyalty. I had—have Lainey. She's worth her weight in gold, but I'm not so proud I can't admit that I want what you guys have too."

"You have their loyalty, Ivy," Milo said, all the gruffness abandoning his tone.

"I know I do," I said. "But I'm talking about before… also, this isn't about me."

"The hell it isn't," Milo countered, then he lifted his chin toward a building we were approaching. The neon sign on the side read Mad Meatballs. "Before you say anything, try them first, and then tell me what you think."

"This place is your favorite?"

"Yep, Mom used to bring me here when I was little. It's a hole in the wall, and they had a fire a few years ago. Rebuilt with the insurance money, but the guy who owns it? He's still here, he still makes the most amazing meatballs. The day after I got out of prison… came here to eat. Made myself sick."

Pulling into a parking slot, he stared at the building but it didn't feel like he was here with me. Or maybe he was, but he was also in the past.

"Mom…she was a mess. Looking back at what I know now, she'd always been strung out on something. The only time I can remember her being clean was when she was pregnant with you." He sighed, then rubbed at his eyes as if chasing the images away. "She really wanted you. Talked about you all the time. Talked to you…"

The laugh he released ended on a cough, like he had to clear his throat.

"I talked to you too. You would always settle down kicking if I talked to you. Mom said I had the magic touch."

Guilt raked its claws through me. "That's a lot of pressure to put on a kid."

"I didn't care. For a little while, it was kind of perfect. Mom was clean, you were coming, and she was really invested. She let me help her decorate the nursery. We shared a bathroom, your crib in your room, my bed in mine. I always left the bathroom doors open so I could hear you."

His sigh pulled me to sit sideways in the passenger seat, though neither of us made an attempt to get out.

"My point," he said in a thick voice. "You were wanted, by me and by Mom. We wanted you. You had her loyalty and when she went back to the drugs… well, you still had mine."

Tears burned in my eyes.

"If we'd been a little older, maybe we could have made it work to keep you with us…" He tapped his fist against the steering wheel. "All I wanted for you was the best."

"I have it now," I told him, reaching over to put my hand over his fist. I didn't want him to beat it against anything. "I have you—best brother ever. Liam might argue, but I'll fight him."

That pulled a real, if not wet, laugh out of him.

"Though Rome is pretty awesome."

"You're not too bad, if we're comparing siblings," he informed me, and it was my turn to snort.

"But I'm a little shit."

"Yes," he said with a grin. "You are. Turns out, I need a little shit in my life."

That sounded so wrong and so funny. We were both laughing now. "Well, good… cause you're kind of stuck with me. If we circle back to what you were asking me in the first place… then yes, I'm okay with doing this because I want to help protect all of you."

His smile faded and he sighed. "I wish…I wish sometimes I'd left a few years ago. I'd left and taken the target on me away from them."

"I don't want to judge," I told him as I squeezed his hand. "But that's pretty stupid."

He frowned.

"I'm just saying, you went to prison for them. Didn't take

the target off of them or you. You could be miles away, and the target wouldn't go away because they are going to want to protect you, just like I do, and how you guys have been protecting me… even when I didn't know you were there."

"Didn't do as good a job about that."

"Did what you could about what you knew. Not your fault I'm a very good actress." I had a lot of practice.

"You ever going to tell me what happened?"

That question seemed to suck all the oxygen out, extinguishing the humor and the tears with it. "Maybe. Someday," I said, exhaling each word individually. "Right now, I want to hear about you and our mother…about what you want to do. You said you wanted law school before. What about now?"

"I don't know, Ives," he said, turning his hand over to clasp mine. "The Vandals don't need me anymore and you're doing all right. Not really sure what there is for me to do."

"Wow, did you bring all the stupid with you today?" I asked, sniffing. I hated crying, it always made my nose run. "If you just want me to stroke your ego, I can totally do that, but of course, we need you. I'm just getting to know you, and I had no idea how much I've needed you all my life. I may not be able to kick your ass, but I'm pretty sure Liam can and would if I asked. So don't be such a drama queen… now take me inside and buy me food."

The last came out a demand the corners of his lips kicked up. "If you asked, huh?"

I shrugged. "He might like me a little."

His snort was downright delightful. "Just a little."

I grinned. "What can I say—I'm a little shit."

My stomach picked that moment to growl. Milo shook his head again, this time turning off the car. "C'mon, bratling, I owe you food."

"Yay!" I clapped my hands playfully, but I also waited for

him to circle the car and open my door for me. "And I meant what I said..." I locked eyes with him. "I need you."

He dragged me into a quick hug, before pressing a kiss to the top of my head. "Okay," he said, tucking me under his arm and locking the car. "Meatballs and stories."

That sounded perfect.

"Milo," I asked as we headed up the walk.

"Hmmm?"

"Do you know any fun, embarrassing ones about the guys?"

"Maybe," he teased. "You'll have to ask them."

However, he was smiling and he was here. No more talk about not being needed or leaving to protect us. If I had to, I'd talk to all of them about it. They needed Milo, he might not see it, but I did.

CHAPTER 31

ROME

he new work was almost done. I'd spent every free moment of the past few weeks on it. The idea wouldn't leave me alone. I could see it in my sleep. Thought about it while eating. Worked on the details while in the shower. The only time it didn't chase me was when I was with Starling.

I couldn't be with her all the time, even if I wanted. She needed time to herself. Time with the others. Time was the one thing we had. We set the schedules. We made the rules. For Starling? Anything was possible.

The dark paint on my fingers had begun to stain around the nails. I didn't care. It would wash away eventually. But it took time and effort... like the work itself.

I packed the gear into the vehicle I'd promised to use rather than make my way on foot or by bike. I preferred be under my own power. Walking cleared my head, and biking gave me ideas, but I took the car to make Kellan happy and Liam worry less.

They wanted someone to go with me, but I didn't. So I just picked times to leave when no one was looking. I took care and I was armed. Time and space. I scanned the area once before climbing into the car.

A few more days... Then I would bring them.

For now, I started the car before pulling out my phone to check the messages. Starling had sent me three different tattoo ideas. One of them included a paintbrush. There were a few more messages.

VAUGHN:

Dove's got some tattoo ideas. I think we can incorporate them all.

I looked at her pictures again. I'd have to think about it.

MILO:

If I asked you to paint Ivy, like something I could frame, could you do it?

Could I? Yes. Would I? Probably. So I sent him a thumbs up.

There were two messages from Jasper in the group chat about scheduling at the clubhouse. They were planning more runs soon, and he wanted everything covered with Starling.

LIAM:

Freddie wants to talk to us later. You free?

I sent him a thumbs-up and a question mark. He might have already picked out a time.

KELLAN:

Come back. Freddie's friend is here. It's time to move.

Time to get Starling's mother. I sent a thumb's up. I would be back in under thirty minutes. He'd only sent it in the last ten minutes. Good timing.

There was a message from Liam's mother. She always sent them after seeing us. I didn't open it right now. That could wait.

The warehouse was full. The presence of everyone's cars, including Doc's, made me the last to arrive. I backed mine into place as the outer door closed. Liam waited for me, leaning against his car. He straightened only once I turned off the engine.

His expression was tight, his eyes cooler than usual and his mouth a thin line. "What happened?"

"The king has a job for Hellspawn." Those were the last words any of us wanted to hear.

"Does she know?"

"Not yet." His tone said he had no intention of telling her.

Locking gazes, I raised my brows. Telling her would be a bad idea. Not telling her would be a worse one. The king had been tolerant of Liam's delaying tactics, but he didn't think that would last.

My mirror's mind hadn't changed on that. But he didn't want to involve her in the first place. I got that. We didn't get to decide that for her.

He glared. I shrugged.

She trusted us. We needed to be worthy of that trust.

"I fucking hate when you're right," Liam muttered, then bumped me on the shoulder. "C'mon, let's get this over with. That Cavendish dick is back."

"He brought the news."

"Yeah. Don't remind me." Liam was not happy. He wasn't in a hurry to get inside.

"He helped Starling."

"Cavendishes don't do anything for free. I don't want her owing him."

Pausing, I looked at my other half. "She won't owe him. We will."

The Vandals would owe him, as a whole. If he did us a favor, we would owe him one. While Starling was a Vandal, we would take the burden and pay the price.

"Don't try to soothe me with your logic," Liam grumbled, even as some of the dark clouds around him dissipated. "I'm also putting *terms* on what we owe."

I nodded. I didn't really care. Starling wanted her mother out of that place. We'd get her out, with or without the problem that was Cavendish.

"Rome…" Liam sighed.

"Freddie likes him." I knew this, he didn't have to tell me. "He trusts him."

"Mostly," Liam admitted. "He wants to trust him, but he's doubting himself."

We'd all seen that. "He can trust us." We'd get him through. Just like we would Starling.

Liam chuckled. "Sometimes, brother, I wish I had your faith."

I shrugged. "I have enough for both of us."

Inside, we found everyone in the downstairs living room. Starling perched on the arm of Kellan's chair. Her eyes lit up, and she smiled as we came in, but Kellan's hand on her thigh kept her in place.

That was fine. I went to her. She tilted her head up and met my kiss as I dipped my head. I searched her face as I traced a finger down her cheek. The smile in her eyes matched the one on her lips. Worry was there too, but not fear.

Good.

Another kiss, then I surrendered my spot to Liam, who

picked her right up off the arm of the chair as she wrapped her arms around his neck. Kellan sighed, but Milo clapped a hand over his face.

The fact he'd been grinning told me he'd done it more to pull the attention off Starling. Jasper said something to him, and Milo elbowed him even as Vaughn laughed. Instead of giving her back, Liam just carried her over to the chair near Kellan's and settled with Starling in his lap.

Some of her humor vanished as she leaned into Liam, her attention on him and not the rest of the room. Good. He needed her right now. I headed into the kitchen to grab us beers. Doc was leaving it with a pair of beers as well.

"I got Little Bit's," he told me and I nodded.

Doc had taken a station up near Kellan and Liam, which put him in easy distance of Starling. I grabbed the arm of the sofa nearest them. That put Freddie between Jasper and me. Vaughn was on Jasper's other side. Milo had moved to lean against a wall, and that left Bodhi seated by himself on the other couch.

"Now that we're all here," Kellan said as I handed Liam his beer, "we're talking step one to getting Moira Sharpe out of Pilgrim Hills. Doc has researched the facility, as have I. The security there is more like a prison than a hospital. High-end or not, getting in won't be easy. We need to identify where she is in the facility itself, then get her out as quietly and safely as possible."

"Freddie went in last time… to get me." Starling glanced toward me then past to Freddie. "It might need to be—"

"Not a chance in hell," Milo said even as Jasper shook his head and Liam all but growled, "Fuck no."

Kellan cleared his throat. "Sparrow," he said, focusing on her. "Sending you in needs to be an absolute last resort. To be honest, we'll just burn the place down and grab her with the evacuees before…"

"I'll go," Bodhi said. "I mean, the women are kept in a different wing, but I like the therapy. I can even start the fire."

Silence greeted his pronouncement. Freddie leaned forward. "Won't they know you? I mean, you were already there."

Bodhi shrugged. "They'll probably put me in lockdown for a week, solitary, and then put me through some intensive psycho-chemistry. Be fine."

"You sound certain you can get out of there," Milo said, his tone both dismissive and skeptical.

"Well, I did get out once," Bodhi said. "Not hard to sound certain. Everything burns. Every door has a lock that requires a key. You just need to figure out the key." He tapped the side of his head.

"Bodhi," Starling said, as she leaned forward. "I can't ask you to do this."

"You're not asking, PPG. Besides, your little *ménage à— quatre, cinq, six or sept*—or whatever, they're not going to go for it. Besides, it'll be fun…"

"Why are you helping?" Milo asked, just cutting right to the chase. "I get that you helped them before…and I am grateful that you helped Freddie and my sister. But this is— this is above and beyond what you do for a stranger."

"PPG's not a stranger," Bodhi told him. "I like Freddie. I like PPG. I know O'Connell too—don't like him, but I know him."

"Feeling is mutual, Cavendish," Liam all but growled. Then Starling pressed a hand to his chest and looked at him. It took no more than a scant moment before he huffed out a sigh. "I didn't say I wouldn't work with him."

"What do we need?" Getting Bodhi would not be difficult. The confidence wasn't feigned. So what else did we need?

"Backup would be nice," Doc said slowly. "The problem is

that if we just send him in, we're leaving the whole burden of getting us in and her out. My friends can back a play once we're ready to rip down the doors, but they're the nuclear option."

"What does it cost us to bust it down and just go in?" Jasper asked. "Real cost, physical resources, actual manpower." He flicked a look at Starling.

"They have armed security," Kellan said, his tone not dismissing the idea out of hand. "Patrols on the perimeter, security fencing, one primary road access that requires passing through a manned gate." He ticked off the items on his list.

"The male and female residence wings are separate, at least from what we can tell. Each requires a card key access, and I'm willing to bet that with the high-end they have running there, it will be different keys for different areas. The medical facility is located between them," Bodhi said, drawing it out on a sheet of paper.

Steepling his fingers together, Kellan frowned as we all studied the diagram.

"A raid on a place like that is either going to need to be surgical," Doc said with a slow shake of his head. "Or we're going to need a lot of bodies and guns. There's no way to go through security that heavy without casualties."

He wasn't the only one who looked at Starling.

"One man can do what an army can't," Bodhi said with a shrug. "Besides, nobody likes me, so it's not really a loss if I don't get out."

"Bodhi," Freddie snapped his name and shook his head. "That's not helping."

"Hey, PPG wants her mom. You guys don't want PPG going in there. None of you want to go in. I don't mind so much. Could be fun."

"No one is going in until we have a solid plan to get you

out," Kellan said, but there was a problem with any of us going in.

Any of us, *not* Starling.

"If the women are kept separate, Bodhi," Starling asked. "How do you get to her?"

"Same way I got into the doc's office at Pinetree. Same way I got in and out of my room. Secure facilities breed lazy orderlies and nurses." Bodhi seemed confident and it didn't come across as a lie or like he didn't know how.

"To be fair," Freddie said. "I got out at night the same way… everything has a workaround."

"But you're saying Pilgrim Hills is tighter than Pinetree," Vaughn stated. "That makes it harder…"

"Unless," Liam said slowly. "We get you keys before you go in."

"How do you plan to do that?" Kellan said.

"Anything can be bought," Liam countered. "We know people with influence…" And he didn't like it, mainly because the king had a job for Starling.

Everyone was giving her lessons; from Kellan teaching her to drive, Milo and Kellan teaching her to shoot, Liam's self-defense, and Vaughn helping her with strength training. She'd been dancing more.

The night we took her to the fairgrounds had helped, a lot. We needed to take her again. I liked flying with her. That didn't mean whatever job they had for her would be something she'd want to do.

"We'll discuss it," Kellan said. "I'm not sold on any of this. Sorry, Sparrow. We're not giving up, but the risks outweigh the rewards now."

"I can go in to get my mother," she said, her voice steady and her eyes fierce. The fact none of us wanted to go wasn't lost on her.

"Too much risk," Kellan told her. "We don't know if it was

your uncle who put her there, and if he finds out you're there?"

She shuddered, and Liam turned a baleful look on Kellan, but he didn't say anything. "Kellan is right," I said. "You going is too much risk for you. I don't want to lose you." It wasn't so hard to admit. "I don't want you hurt again. We will find a way."

Her expression changed. "You don't fight fair."

"I'm not fighting." I wouldn't.

"I'll fight," Liam stated.

"Me too," Jasper said.

"Sorry, Boo-Boo," Freddie said. "I'm going to fight you on that too."

"She's not going," Kellan said in a firm voice. "Enough about the fighting. Bodhi, thank you for the offer. We'll think on it. Now if you'll excuse us, we have other business to discuss…"

We needed to get in, get her mother, and get out. There had to be a way.

There was always a way.

CHAPTER 32

EMERSYN

The door to my dressing room slammed open, and I jerked around to see Eric standing there. His expression was thunderous. The rest of the company was out there too, so I wasn't as worried about his mood, but his mercurial temperament had been worsening.

"I'm not ready yet," I told him in a far steadier voice than I was feeling. Since returning from "vacation," I'd been avoiding Eric. I'd pretty much avoided all of them. Every part of my body was sore, but practice had helped.

Performing would help.

Losing myself in the music and the movement would undoubtedly help. The door shut with a decisive thump, and I barely managed to contain my flinch. The heat of him coming to stand at my back would have been difficult to ignore, even if I hadn't been doing my cosmetics in the mirror.

Eric loomed over me, he was easily six foot plus, while I

was most definitely not. With hands that trembled, I concentrated on getting the glitter right. Not that my face needed to be perfect. The beauty of the silk dancing was in the lines of my body, not my face.

A vise closed around my chest as he gripped my nape. The pressure of his fingers pulled me up onto my toes as he glared at me.

No.

Not at me. At the hickey on my breast. Terror spilled into my blood with every harsh pump of my heart.

"Who the fuck is he…"

Bile surged up from my stomach. I couldn't answer that. Even if telling him would get him killed. Even if I wanted…

No. I couldn't want that. The pressure on my neck increased, and the cosmetic brush fell from my fingers as pain shot down my arms. I barely had time to even catch my breath before he slammed me back against a wall and crowded into my space.

"Who. Is. He."

Pain vied with terror as Eric's face pressed into mine and his hand went to the front of my leotard. It was going to rip. Eyes closed, I tried to be somewhere else. He was angry and his grip on my arm, then on my breast was so painful. I just— had to relax. I tried to slow my breathing. Once he was done…once he was done… it would be be—

"Sparrow."

No, that voice didn't belong here. I lo—

"Sparrow!" The command could not be ignored and I jerked my eyes open to find Kellan holding my forearms in his gentle grip. His hands were warm shackles, grounding me even as he helped me sit up.

Concern etched the lines of his face not hidden in shadows. Light spilled into the room from the single light in the bathroom. It was a blue night light that turned white when motion was detected. I didn't like the dark. Most of us didn't.

I wasn't there.

Eric wasn't here.

The rapid race of my pulse echoed beneath the sharp pants of my breathing as I tried to drag in oxygen.

"You're safe, Sparrow," Kellan said in a soft voice as he slid his hands up my arms. The calluses on his fingers and palms were rough on my skin. Another reminder of where I was and who I was with.

When he cupped my face, I wasn't ready for his thumbs to wipe away the tears on my cheeks. The panic didn't want to subside. If anything, it seemed to burn in my stomach like bad hot sauce.

"I'm here," he continued in that low, soothing voice. "Right here. You. Me. The guys are out there. You're safe. No one is getting to you."

The words buffered the sick crawl inside I hated so much. I swore I could still smell Eric…he'd been dead for months and it was like he'd just been there.

"Sparrow." The sharpness in Kellan's voice snapped my gaze up to him. "Eyes on me." He took one of my hands and flattened it against his bare chest. "Feel me?"

Not entirely trusting my voice yet, I nodded.

"You know where you are?" He seemed to be searching my eyes. When I swallowed and glanced around the bedroom, his sigh scraped over my raw nerves.

"Yes," I managed to say. It came out squeakier than I meant it to. "Sorry."

"You have nothing to be sorry about," he told me firmly. "Do you need to tell me what happened?"

"Bad dream," I told him. It had been a while since my last one. I'd gotten somewhat used to not having them. One, sometimes two, of them always slept with me, or I slept with them. That usually kept the dreams away.

Kellan didn't say anything, just rubbed my arms slowly, then pulled me to him. Neither of us had any clothes on. The heat spilling off of him seemed to wrap around me even more firmly than his arms.

I curled my arms around him, pressing my face into his throat. The prickles of stubble on his jaw were scraped against my forehead. I rubbed against them slowly, almost craving that bite of pain.

"Talk to me, Sparrow." He rubbed his hand in a slow circle against my back even as his dick stiffened under my ass.

Dicks did that.

A little laugh escaped me. It might be a watery chuckle, but it helped to dislodge the boulder of the past threatening to crush me. "Bad dream," I repeated, then sniffled. "I was…I was getting ready for a show, and I'd just gotten back from seeing my uncle."

My mouth went dry as that memory crawled out of the pit. I'd had more bruises than just that hickey. He'd been—

"Don't think about *him*," Kellan ordered, his tone fierce, but his eyes were gentle as he lifted my chin to look at him. "You stay here with me."

I opened my mouth to apologize again, then swallowed it. Not thinking about Uncle Bradley when it felt like I'd just been there in my dressing room again, right down to the soreness and the bruising, was hard.

Even Eric's growing cruelty and violence, as much as I hadn't wanted it, was preferable to my uncle's. How fucking twisted was that?

"I'd come back, and I'd avoided Eric." I tried to lick my lips, but everything was so dry and tasted like ash. "I was…in the dressing room—getting ready. We had a show. I'd cut it close with my arrival."

"You wanted to limit interaction."

I nodded. "I was sore and…" I closed my eyes, sucking in a deep breath. It was like all the rot stunk everywhere. It was on me. In me. I was the— "He left marks…Uncle Bradley." Maybe he didn't need the clarification, but I did. "Bruises. He always did, only sometimes he was careful. He hadn't been this time, and there was a hickey that I'd not covered up. I'd gotten the others even though there was one, and I thought the leotard would hide it."

Forcing my head up and my eyes open, I met the grave look on Kellan's face. My next breath was shaky, because the burn of bile was in my throat again.

"Eric charged into my dressing room. He was already furious. I hadn't returned his calls or come to see him. Then he saw the hickey…and I think he lost his mind. He grabbed me…"

I grimaced as Kellan's eyes flattened.

"You don't want to hear this," I told him.

"No," he said. "I don't, but you went through it, so I can damn well listen to it. Get it out of you, Sparrow. Lance the wound and get it out. If I could dig his sorry ass up again and bring him back to life, I'd kill him a lot slower for you."

My smile wobbled but it was there. "I like that he's dead."

It wasn't the first time the thought crossed my mind.

"I like that you guys tortured him too." And based on what I'd seen? They'd put him through hell. There wasn't an ounce of sympathy inside me for his fate.

"We were happy to kill him—except that I would love to kill him again."

That pulled another smile from me. "You know…I might help this time." I grimaced at the idea of even seeing him. "Maybe."

"Anything you want, Sparrow." He shifted us on the bed until I was curled in his lap and he leaned against the headboard. They'd put a cushioned one on my bed so I could sit there to read or watch a movie. I didn't spend a lot of time in this bed sitting.

I had no idea what time it was as we sat there. My racing heart had begun to calm finally. His slow even strokes up and down my arm helped. The steady beat of his heart helped.

"It wasn't the first time," I admitted. "Eric had been getting rougher. Meaner too. The first time I told him no because I was sore, I couldn't tell him why and it made him mad."

That just led to a pattern of it.

"Most of the time, I could coax him out of the moods. And I'd only ever had sex with him because I wanted something for me. Something fun…that didn't hurt." I made a face. "That didn't really work out."

"He was a dick," Kellan said flatly. "His choices aren't yours. You wanting to share your body with who you choose is your prerogative. Just because you fuck someone once doesn't mean you have to again. Sparrow…who you fuck and how often you fuck them is your call. You don't owe anyone *shit*. If he was too insecure about himself to see your pain—then he deserved even worse than we gave him."

Tilting my head back, I looked up at him. "How do you always know the right thing to say?"

"I don't," he told me without apology. "If I did, I'd have convinced you to trust me with all of this long before now."

"Well, I think you're better at it than you think. I'm just stubborn."

His soft chuckle rumbled in his chest, then grew as I grinned.

"Maybe just a little," he said, the amusement softening all the harsh little points. "A smidge."

I had to bite my lip to keep from laughing. He traced a finger over my shoulder.

"Do you feel better?" So much emotion underscored that question.

"A little," I said after a moment. I genuinely needed to consider it. And at the same time… "I don't really want to go back to sleep, though."

"It's fine. I have to get up in about four hours anyway." The hint of a lazy smile under those words pierced the gloom draping over everything.

"Early is on time."

"On time is late," he teased.

"And late means we just stay in bed."

His laughter soothed more of those broken, jagged bits the dream unsettled. "Sparrow, you can keep me in bed anytime you want."

"Anytime?" It wasn't a test so much as a tease.

"Anytime," he promised, brushing his knuckles down my cheek. The touch was so light and gentle, barely there, and yet I felt it all the way to my soul. "Can you do something for me?"

"Anything."

"Anything?" He raised his brows, but how his lips twitched made me smile.

"Anything I can," I promised. "I'm learning that there are more things I can do than I realized." I'd learned there were more ways to give and receive pleasure. Kel had helped me to take that back, and fuck if Liam hadn't taken it the rest of the way.

A little shudder raced through me at the memory.

"The day in the dressing room," Kellan continued, his voice still soft and his tone soothing. "Where did he hurt you?"

"There was...you want me to tell you?" I was trying to pack that memory away.

"Hmm," Kellan hummed, tracing his fingers to my jaw and then rubbing his thumb against my lower lip. "Hiding from it gives it power over you. I don't want anything to have power over you."

I caught his thumb in my teeth, not quite biting it. He didn't pull away, only shifted me forward a little until I was sitting right on his erection and it tucked up against my pussy.

Letting go of his thumb, I smoothed my palms over his shoulders. "Like with anal."

"In a way," Kellan said. "Something triggered the dream. A bad memory, the conversation we had about your mother..."

While he wasn't fishing, I still found myself looking down. "A part of me thinks she's in there because of me."

"I can see that," he said, touching a finger under my chin to lift my face so I'd look at him. "What about the rest of you?"

"If my uncle put her there to lure me back—that would be because of me. But what if something has always been wrong and...she's there because she needs to be? What if this has nothing to do with me...or my uncle?"

I hated even questioning it.

"We won't know until we get her." His resolute attitude told me we would. It didn't matter how the planning had gone, we would get her. "Now, tell me where he hurt you."

I wrapped my hand around his nape. "He grabbed me here..."

Kel's eyes flattened.

With care and not really squeezing, I flexed my fingers against his nape. "He squeezed, then he dragged me backward and slammed me into the wall..."

Even describing it, just those few words had my heart

starting to race. Kellan wrapped his hand around my throat. Like me, he didn't squeeze. The warmth of his hand settling there like a necklace helped the mad rabbiting of my pulse.

"I want you to remember something, Sparrow," Kellan told me in a firm voice. "You're here, with me. That prick is dead. The other prick will be soon. They are no one. They don't get to have you or leave a mark on you."

I swallowed. "We're taking it back."

He nodded slowly. "We're taking it all back."

Closing my eyes, I took a deep breath and pulled in Kellan's scent. It was right there, warm and a little musky. I could smell hints of coconut from the soap he used to clean his hands.

"He wanted to know who gave me the hickey," I said, meeting Kellan's gaze. "It was here." I touch a spot just to the right of my new Vandals tattoo. "There were more, but he couldn't see them because of the leotard until he tore it…"

The blue light playing over Kel's features gave him an almost peaceful countenance, but that was just a mask for the fierce man beneath it. While every word tasted like chalk and ass, I kept going, buoyed by the strength he was sharing and by the fact that Eric was already a memory.

CHAPTER 33

DOC

Freddie grinned from where he leaned against the wall scanning the street below. Vaughn had Emersyn up on his shoulders as she pinned lights. The whole upstairs of the clinic was coming together. Jasper brought in a banner, but the piece on the wall that Rome had finished that morning was just…fucking brilliant.

It was Steph, but from when they were kids. She was a little younger, but her half-smile and gentle eyes just seemed to radiate kindness. She was also surrounded by kids. It was —a perfect mural for her. We were never changing it.

"I see her car," Freddie called.

"How much time do we need?" Kellan asked as he checked his watch.

"The food is set up, Milo got the cake, Liam brought the beer and this is the last string of lights." Vaughn turned as she curled the toes on her right foot.

It was kind of adorable.

"She's going to kill you all," I informed them. Steph's wrath would be amazing. She positively loathed surprises, and a surprise party was just going to set her off. But she'd also be floored by the loving care they were all taking.

It was Milo's first time at home for her birthday in a few years. It was Little Bit's first birthday with her. Liam being back in the fold helped too.

"Nah," Jasper said as he clapped me on the shoulder, a shit-eating grin on his face. "She's gonna kill you 'cause you let us do it."

Little Bit burst out laughing and I shook my head. Well, he wasn't wrong.

"See if you can get us five minutes?" Liam said from the kitchen. "The chili is ready and so are the cheese fries, though we're waiting on the garlic bread."

The whole place smelled amazing.

"On it." Kellan jogged downstairs.

"I'll help," Freddie said, following.

"Oh shit," Jasper laughed. "You're gonna end up with twenty minutes."

"Should I go down to help?" Little Bit asked as she lifted one leg to glide it over Vaughn's head, then slid down. He caught her easily and set her on the ground.

"Nah." I shook my head. "Freddie's been working hard, and he hasn't gotten to fill her in on working here. And he deserves the accolades."

It would make Steph's day too. Especially with how many days clean he'd been. That would make her whole damn year. He even brought up support groups earlier today, so maybe he was ready.

Finally.

You couldn't make a person get clean and sober. You couldn't solve their problems. You could only support them. They had to want it.

They had to want it, had to work for it, and had to keep on working and wanting it. Little Bit laughed at something Vaughn said as Rome brought her a beer. Milo rolled his eyes, but there was a hint of an indulgent smile on his face.

Liam stuck his head out of the kitchen. "Chili, cheese fries, bread is almost ready… anything else?"

"Nope," I said, shaking my head as I diverted into the kitchen. We'd debated on where to throw the party. The community room at the clinic was perfect. She wasn't going to expect it, and it wasn't that unusual for me to *want* to take her out for dinner on her birthday or for me to work late.

She'd worked late herself. Then she'd messaged. There'd been a tough one today. I could always tell by the word choice she used. The more formal her words were, the more complicated her day had been.

The worst days were when she had to remove the kids. No matter how necessary for their safety and their health, it always tore her up inside.

"You good?" Liam asked and I scrubbed a hand over my face before turning to the sink to wash them.

"Yep," I told him and shook off those darker thoughts. We all had enough pain and suffering, we didn't need to go borrowing it.

"They're in," Jasper said from where he stood at the door. "And coming up."

We didn't turn off the lights or scatter to jump out at her. Surprise parties were one thing. Scaring the shit out of her was entirely another.

"So, I told Doc, if you want to pay me to scrub toilets, I'm totally down. But I needed hazard pay for the rooms. And I wasn't going near his office." Freddie's words carried up the stairs along with Steph's chuckle.

"Well, I'm very proud of—"

Freddie was through the door first and he cut to the side to let her see all of us waiting.

"Surprise!" The shout came from all of us, and Little Bit even blew a party horn as she tossed confetti. It was ridiculous and sweet.

Not to mention funny as hell.

Dumbfounded didn't begin to cover Steph's expression.

"Happy birthday, Ms. Stephanie." The quiet greeting from Rome pulled her whole attention, and she smiled at him. The tears in her eyes were gonna get me killed later.

But I could handle it.

"Thank you, Rome."

"Happy birthday, Ms. Stephanie," Vaughn said, pressing a kiss to her cheek.

"Happy birthday," Jasper tagged in and gave her a one-armed hug. Then Liam stepped up and gave her a full-on hug.

The misty eyes were getting worse as one by one, they all wished her a happy birthday and gave her a kiss or a hug. Kellan showed them all up as he pulled a rose out of the inside of his jacket to give to her.

"Happy birthday," he told her.

"Oh, you wretched children," she muttered with a sniff as she blinked rapidly. She was losing that battle against emotion and when Milo stepped up to give her a hug, he also pressed a tissue into her hand.

Good man.

She sniffed, then gave me a death glare. "You are in so much trouble."

I spread my hands. "I was out-voted."

"You voted *against* giving me a party?" The mock outrage pulled real laughter from the whole room. "The things I put up with from—"

It was clear the moment she saw the mural. Her smile

faltered and her eyes grew damp again as she put a hand to her lips.

"Rome?" she asked, not that it was an honest question.

"It's you," he told her. "Doing what you do."

The very real tears spilled over onto her cheeks. "And you doing what you do, you beautiful boy. I would love to give you a hug."

He appeared to consider it, which was more than he usually did, and then he said, "Okay."

Shock rippled across her face, more than had appeared when she realized we were all here. He opened his arms and stepped up to her.

Watching Steph hug Rome felt a little personal, so I cut my gaze to Little Bit. Her smile was so wide, and I swore I could feel it in my soul. When she glanced at me, her eyes were dancing.

It was like everyone was holding their breath. The hug wasn't long, but he'd given her one and to my knowledge, he never had.

"Well, I'll be damned," Freddie said with a laugh. "It's a birthday miracle."

It was the right thing to say because fresh laughter rippled through the group, and as Rome stepped away, Steph headed straight for me, with wet eyes and all. I braced for it and laughed when she crashed into me for a hug.

"After I have a healthy cry about all of this, I am so kicking your ass," she muttered in a voice wet with tears.

Leaning back, I bought her a little time to get herself together. "I love you too, sis."

She huffed. "You are such a little shit."

Little Bit cracked up and leaned into Milo, who just wrapped an arm around her and chuckled. I'd have to find out what that joke was all about.

Finally, Steph turned to face them, and their expressions

made every bit of her embarrassment worth it. I'd bet on it. "It's a good thing that I love all of you."

"We're awesome," Freddie told her. "We know."

That set off a fresh round of laughter.

"I'm glad I can smell food," Steph said, still chuckling.

"I did promise you dinner," I teased. "I just didn't tell you where."

"Hmm." She narrowed her eyes. "You think you're clever."

"I think there's chili and cheese fries."

"Michael James," she sputtered. "That's terrible for my diet."

"Which is why it's a special meal, just for you," Liam said as he nodded to the kitchen. "It's all ready for you to get the first helping. Then we're eating at the table family-style."

The last two words quelled any further objections.

"I heard calories don't count on birthdays," Little Bit offered up. "I'm thinking the good and bad things don't either."

Steph eyed her, lips pursed for a moment. "You know, I think I've heard that myself."

"Then it can't hurt," Milo said, offering her his arm. "Ms. Stephanie."

"Oh, stop it," she said with a genuine laugh and roll of her eyes as she swatted him. "Let's go, all of you, to the table. There's food and garlic bread, and I'm starving."

"Ms. Stephanie," Freddie said as he moved to stand next to Little Bit. "Are you hangry? Do you need a candy bar?"

I groaned, but she laughed and Freddie grinned. Little Bit elbowed him gently, and then he slung an arm around her shoulders. She leaned into him and he smirked down at her.

Something uneasy in my gut settled and I wasn't the only one who relaxed. Freddie putting himself first to figure things out was critical, but there had been no mistaking the fact Little Bit missed him and he missed her.

"Michael," Steph said in a firm tone and I glanced at her. The smirk on her face was adorable. Yes, I hated being called by my full name. No, she didn't give a damn. I ambushed her with a party, so my name was my punishment.

I could live with it.

"Ma'am?" I retorted, and she did the perfectly mature thing by sticking her tongue out at me, much to the raucous laughter from the guys.

It took a moment to sort everyone out. Milo took one end of the table with Steph on his right and Jasper on her other side. I took the seat on Milo's left, across from Steph. Liam claimed the other end of the table with Rome on his left and Kel on his right. Vaughn sat between Kel and Jasper across from Little Bit. Little Bit sat next to Rome with Freddie on her other side.

We should have been a tighter fit on this side with four to their three, but Little Bit barely took up any space. I also had a feeling if we needed to, she'd end up in a lap. That was happening more and more.

"Who wants cheese fries?" Milo said as he started those going around the table. In the meanwhile, we were all passing our bowls to Liam who filled them with chili.

Garlic bread followed. I got back up to get the wine and poured a glass for Steph.

"Only one," she informed me when I dropped a kiss on the top of her head. "I still have to drive."

"No you don't," Kellan said. "Drink and be merry, *if* you want. Jas and I will get you and your car home."

I chuckled. "See, you can drink and be merry."

"Go away. I'm not talking to you yet," she informed me with a grin that took any sting out of her stern smile. "But leave the wine."

Vaughn snorted. "Anyone else need anything? Dove? You want another beer?"

"I should say no," she said, head tipping to one side. "But then, I don't have to drive either."

"Nope," Liam and Vaughn said in the same breath, and I hid another laugh as Milo rolled his eyes.

"Have a drink if you want to Ivy. Plenty of food here to soak up the alcohol." Milo's expression as she made a face at him arrested me. The contentment there had been absent for so long, I'd forgotten what it looked like.

But it was Steph picking up her wine glass and blinking rapidly that I enjoyed almost as much. Little Bit's adoption without Milo had always rubbed her wrong. She'd hated it and had such high hopes at the same time.

And that just drew my mind in a full fucking circle to Bradley Sharpe. Fucker. Mother fucking pedo-rapist. I'd found a photo of him online and stared at it until I had it memorized.

I wanted to make sure I didn't miss that asshole anywhere. There had been discussion on going after him, but we were shoring up everything—

"Hey," Milo said, a faint frown in place. "You good?"

"Yep, just thinking about work."

"Well, stop," Little Bit said, leaning forward to look around Freddie at me. "It's a party. No stern faces, no thinking about work. All happy thoughts. Or at least silly fun ones."

"Silly fun?" Steph asked after she washed down another bite of her food. "Define silly fun."

"Well…" The way Little Bit elongated that word warned me something was coming. "Embarrassing stories about baby brothers could be silly fun."

There it was.

Jasper choked on his swallow of beer and Kellan smirked, but Freddie flat-out fucking laughed.

"You know, you're right. I never thought of asking Ms.

Stephanie for stories about Doc." Freddie looked at her. "He did throw this surprise party for you."

"Et tu, Freddie?" I drawled. "Just gonna back the bus over me?"

"Beep beep," Rome said without missing a beat and more laughter split down the table.

"I know a few stories," Ms. Stephanie said, "about all of my boys."

"Oh shit," Vaughn muttered and Milo snorted. It was my turn to grin.

"Welcome to the underside of the bus, boys," I toasted them. Little Bit's ever-widening smile helped to fill in that cavern of darkness the stories of her uncle had begun to unearth.

A darkness I once thrived in, and if I had to—I'd use it to get the vengeance she richly deserved.

"Where should I start?" Steph asked, and I took another long drink. "Alphabetically or by age?"

"I'll go first," Freddie volunteered. "So youngest to oldest. Cause I know their stories have to be way more embarrassing than mine."

"Birthday girl's choice," I offered. Steph's grin grew as we locked eyes. "You know... when you're talking to me again."

Her very indelicate snort of laughter added another piece to fill in that void in my soul.

"Ascending age it is," Steph said before taking another sip of wine. "When Freddie was six, he decided he didn't want to go to class that day and some of the older boys had smuggled in some illegal firecrackers."

"Oh," Freddie said with a laugh as he leaned back. "This is a good one."

"You blew up the toilet?" Little Bit guessed.

"Toilets," Steph corrected. "On three different floors."

Freddie was right—it was a good one.

EMERSYN

 *M*s. Stephanie's birthday party was a delight—
the woman herself was very nice. I'd thought
that from the day Milo introduced me. She was profoundly
comforting in a way that was hard to describe. While Milo
wanted me to talk to her more, maybe even confide in her...
she would never be to me what she was to him or the guys.

For Jasper, she seemed, if not a surrogate mother, then a
favored and treasured aunt. For Mickey, she was his beloved
sister. For Liam, Kel, and Vaughn, she almost came across as
part godmother, part friend.

I couldn't really put my finger on her relationship with
Rome, but the hug earlier had meant the world to her and he
hadn't seemed like he minded. That made her pretty damn
special. Freddie? Freddie craved her approval and wanted to
make her laugh. He *valued* her.

And Milo?

He just loved her. There was a faith and a devotion to her

that had to have been nurtured over the years. If I were to label it, I would call it a friendship even though it went past that and past family. Maybe because she'd been the one reliable thing in his life after our mother died.

The stories she told elicited groans and laughter, but they also gave me a magical window into the lives of my brother and his closest friends when they were growing up. Stories that made them light up with humor as she reminded them of another time and place.

I loved the whole shared experience. Even Mickey's… His road diverged from theirs, but the more I saw them all together, the more I realized how their paths converged. None of the stories reflected the shadowy parts of their routes, just the more colorful aspects.

"You stole a car when you were twelve?" I stared at Kellan.

"I didn't steal it—" he said.

"He borrowed it," Liam, Milo, Jasper, and Vaughn chorused.

"Exactly." He grinned, his expression almost smug. "It was a sweet car. They even paid me a hundred-dollar finder's fee."

Ms. Stephanie shook her head. "You could have ended up in juvie."

"You thought fast on your feet," Kellan said, pointing a finger at her. We'd finished dinner, lit the candles on the cake, sang happy birthday, and cut into the sugary monstrosity.

I was going to die a very happy death from chocolate coffee overload. The creamy mousse top layer had been downright intoxicating. As it was, my stomach felt almost too full. I was happy to just lay there on the sofa, my head propped against Vaughn's thigh while he stroked his fingers through my hair.

At this rate though, I was going to pass out. Full tummy. Good company. Everyone was here—even Freddie. When he wrapped his arm around me earlier, it quelled so many fears and worries. I wanted him to get what he needed, but I was selfish too.

I'd missed him.

So many other things were going on, but tonight... tonight everything had paused and taken a breath. It was a breath we all needed. Groaning, I sat up. Vaughn gave me a hand, then rubbed my shoulder.

"You good, Dove?"

"I'm gonna fall asleep if you keep doing that, and I need to walk." Jasper had disappeared into the bathroom so I nodded to the stairs. "I'm gonna go downstairs to pee."

"Stay inside," Vaughn told me and I grinned, giving him a little salute before I drifted out past the little groupings where everyone had paired or tripled off to talk, catch up, or just give each other shit.

Ms. Stephanie and Milo were having an intense conversation that deserved the privacy everyone was giving them. I glanced at Rome's new mural and grinned. He was so talented. Like some of the paintings he'd taken me to see in the "old" neighborhood, it offered me another window into their childhood.

It hadn't been the best, but it also hadn't been the worst. Not for all of them. Freddie's story whispered through the back of my mind. I hated that his childhood had been like that when he was too young to do anything about it.

Or that it had followed him...

Some of my cheer fled as I descended into the darkened area downstairs. Night lights provided plenty of illumination. The bathroom door was open, and the interior light came on with the motion sensor.

The floaty relaxed feeling followed the cheer. I tried to

shake it all off while I washed my hands. This had been a good day with a good night. Apparently, the king wanted me for a job, and he'd sent a phone to Liam for me too.

One Liam "forgot" at his apartment, to be dealt with later. I still didn't quite get why the king decided I worked for him. Or the Royals for that matter.

The Royals. The king. Was that why Adam was always such a bastard to Lainey? And Lainey, we hadn't talked in… a couple of weeks. I'd been so preoccupied the last few months.

Pulling my phone out of my pocket, I scrolled to the app where we still talked. We texted too, but the app that deleted our messages was an old habit neither of us wanted to break.

> ME:
>
> Been a shitty friend. Are you okay? I haven't heard from you.

I stared at the screen like it would make her answer. Switching to texts, I just sent her a blown kiss emoji. That would at least let her know I was thinking of her.

I'd corner Milo tomorrow to see if he'd heard from her. Liam had Ezra's number, and that was my next stop. Opening the door, I nearly ran into Mickey standing right there, hand raised.

"Holy shit," I said, pressing my phone over my heart where it was hammering against my ribs. "Mickey."

"Sorry, Little Bit," he said in a low voice, though the faint twitch to his lips said he wasn't *that* sorry. "Didn't mean to scare you."

"Didn't expect to find anyone lurking outside the door," I scolded.

"Lurking?" He braced his forearm against the doorframe, tilting his head as he looked at me. "Pretty sure I'd stand out a little too much to lurk."

It had been a while since Mickey and I were alone like this. Even on the days I'd come to volunteer, there had been others around. Raising my brows, I made a point of looking him over. "I don't know—you do have a kind of 'shifty' vibe."

"Shifty?" He narrowed his eyes. Pushing away from the door, he crowded into the bathroom with me. "What's shifty about me, Little Bit?"

That question shouldn't send such a delightful shiver through me. I'd been mad at Mickey for a while, and... I'd had good reasons. Then he saved Jasper. And apologized. And told me to do my worst...

"Said it was a vibe," I told him, then made a point of sliding my phone into my pocket as I backed up. Mickey kept prowling forward. "Vibes aren't tangible." I bumped against the wall.

He leaned in toward me, one hand pressing against the wall next to my head. I had to lift my chin to look up at him even as he tilted his head, invading my space, until I swore I could feel the energy coming off him.

"Do you know what vibe I get about you?" He ran his nose up the side of my throat, and I clenched my thighs even as my mouth went dry.

"That I'm sugar and spice... and everything nice?" Where the hell that came from, I had no idea, but laughter sparked in his eyes. Dangling over the precipice, I savored the anticipation of the fall.

"You're far too spicy for that, Little Bit. You're sharp and tart and positively dangerous to my equilibrium and probably my sanity." The door closed abruptly, and it took a moment to register that he'd shut it with his foot.

"So, I'm not—" I didn't even get to finish answering the question before he swooped in to claim my mouth. And there was no mistaking it for the declaration and demand it was. The hand next to my head never moved, but his free hand came to my jaw. His thumb pressed at the corner of my mouth, nudging it wider as he invaded with his tongue.

It was all heat and fire, teeth and tongue. Want exploded in my chest as the length of his body blanketed me, trapping me against the wall. Never had I wanted to spring a trap so badly.

The pressure on my neck as he devoured my lips increased. Between the thrust of his tongue and the low sound he released, I was going to go up in flames. Wrapping my arms around his neck, I pulled myself up, and he clasped a hand under my ass to lift me until our faces were even.

Not once did he let my lips go. Every breath I got to take was only one he allowed before he seemed too determined to eat it from me. The metal from his belt pressed into my stomach, but he kept himself just far enough back I couldn't grind on him.

The scrape of his teeth against my lower lip as he dragged it out had me clenching my cunt. This…was not me doing my worst. Fuck…

My breath came in sharp, hard little pants. "That's what I thought," he breathed the words against my lips before he set me down on my feet. Thankfully, he braced one hand to my hip to steady me.

At least I wasn't the only one affected. "What did you think?" It took a moment to even make the words work, or maybe it was my voice, and still, it came out husky.

"Hmm?" He backed up and reached a hand for the door.

"You said, 'That's what I thought.'" I licked my lips. The full, lethargic feeling from earlier was gone, and I was burning up. "What did you think?"

"You forgot," he said, pulling the door open. "You need to do your worst." Then he winked before he left the bathroom and me.

Staring a little stupidly at where he'd been, I tried to piece that together. That was definitely not my worst. That was me getting kissed rather thoroughly, and it had left an impression. My lips were still tingling and the taste of him lingered on my tongue.

Fuck.

I banged my head back against the wall as I clenched my thighs. Even my nipples had gone tight, and that *need* coiled ever tighter in my stomach.

Kissed the hell out of me? Check.

Left me horny? Double check.

He wanted my worst? Oh, he was going to get it. Thank fuck, one of the guys always slept with me though at this point, I might make do with my hands because I was almost shaking.

From a kiss.

He'd left me almost shaking from a kiss.

Pushing off the wall, I turned to the sink, used cold water on my hands, and then splashed my face. I really did need to cool the fuck off.

If I didn't head upstairs soon, the guys would worry. Maybe I should go make out with Liam or Vaughn while Mickey watched. That didn't really seem fair to them to do that just to make Mickey squirm. Then again, I really didn't need an excuse to make out with them.

A grin pulled at my lips at the thrill skating through me. I necessarily didn't need a reason.

"Hey, Boo-Boo," Freddie said as he hit the last step. "I was just coming to find you."

"Sorry, I had to pee. Took a minute." I spread my hands and kind of winced because it was lame for an excuse.

"It's okay if you pooped too." His bland expression didn't betray a thing. "Everybody poops."

We stared at each other. My lips twitched and he wiggled his eyebrows. Then we were both laughing.

"Thank you for your permission," I giggled. "Never talk to me about my poop again, please."

He grinned. "I bet your shit doesn't stink anywhere near as much as—"

I pressed my hand to his lips. "Nope. Don't do it. Nobody poops. Nothing smells terrible. And we're not having this conversation."

He crossed his eyes and I giggled all over again. Catching my hand, he pressed a kiss to my palm before he tugged it from his mouth. "Fine, I didn't want to talk shit with you anyway."

"Oh my god, Freddie. That's such crap."

Then we were leaning on each other, laughing again. "You're the best, Boo-Boo."

"Right back at you."

"Good enough to take you out on a date? Just you and me, no Jas? I mean—I crashed his date, so he could totally crash ours, but…I want to take you out. Do stupid shit—" He made a face and I laughed. "Stupid stuff. Maybe hit one of the old arcades. They have one up on at Old Willow Park, and they have street vendors too and music. We could just—you know…go out and do what people our age do."

"What do people our age do?" Not that his idea didn't sound amazing, 'cause it did.

"Fuck if I know, boring *shit* would be my bet. But we could have some fun, you know?" He still held my hand, but he fidgeted with his free hand to push some of his hair back.

"I would love to go on a date with you, but—"

His expression fell and I squeezed his fingers.

"Listen to all of it, please?"

He blew a breath out but nodded.

"But I don't want *you* to push yourself. We did that before, and—I can be as patient as you need me to be. I just want to be around you. To be your friend and then…you know…

whatever happens. I've got your back. That said—the date sounds amazing. But I don't know if you and I can go out alone yet."

He stared at me for a moment. "Yeah, I thought of that. We could make it work—if you wanted to."

"I want to, but only if you aren't pushing yourself. I don't want you to hurt."

"Okay."

"Okay?"

He nodded again. "Yeah...Boo-Boo, I want to go to therapy and I want you to go with me..."

"Yes."

"You don't have to do anything, I wouldn't ask you to talk. It's personal..."

"Yes."

"But I think it might be easier if you're there 'cause you know, and you're safe."

"Freddie?"

"Yeah?"

"I'll go. Whenever, wherever. I'm in."

It was the easiest decision I'd ever made. Therapy had always terrified me, but after Pinetree, I got why. I didn't care how scary it was, if Freddie needed me there, then I'd go.

He crushed me to him in a hug and I held him tight. "This okay?" His question just about broke my heart.

"It's always okay," I whispered to him, tightening my hold. "Just tell me if you need me to let go."

"You too."

But we didn't.

Neither of us let go.

CHAPTER 35

JASPER

"*H*eads up," Liam called. I caught the white jacket he tossed me one-handed while I took a drag on the cigarette. "Always figured we would end up wearing the straitjackets, not the actual white coats."

I snorted. Like me, Liam was dressed in white slacks and a white button-down. The jackets were standard medical grade, embroidered with a private hospital name: Harbor View Wellness Collective.

"Is this place for real?"

"As of five hours ago," Liam said as he shrugged on the coat. We'd left the morning after the party, heading straight for Pilgrim Hills. Doc flew behind us, but we came via my rig, and we'd be going back in the rig too.

Doc would ride with us, but it would be a three-day absence for him. Liam and I could split the driving and we were hauling private cargo—Emersyn's adopted mother—

and there was already medical equipment loaded up and ready to go.

It was what we'd spent the morning doing. "Doc will be here in less than an hour. He caught an earlier flight." That was news. I'd take it.

There was a shipping warehouse outside Southside Dale, about an hour north of Pilgrim Hills. The closest airport was Charlotte. The drive was a little over ninety minutes, so Doc got in, rented a car, and headed straight for us.

He was leaving a paper trail of a different sort. Doc was heading to a medical conference taking place *in* Charlotte at a hotel near the airport. Liam had gone dark, Emersyn was under lockdown, and I was on the road.

If we were being watched, and we had no reason to think otherwise, we didn't want anyone to notice anything out of the ordinary. Liam often vanished from the king and from us. His work took him in various directions. My time on the road was well-documented. My name was on the paperwork for the company. Doc may not go to many conferences, but he did get invited.

It worked out that he could "attend" one closer to our destination. I shrugged into the white coat, then went over to the ambulance we'd purchased—well, Liam purchased.

Paperwork for a medical facility, I'd bet it even had land, if not an actual building attached to it. An ambulance that had been painted and customized.

"Anyone ever tell you that you've gotten way too comfortable with all that money," I told him as I opened the back doors and began my own visual inspection. We were going in armed, but we were playing it cool.

I wanted nothing to give us away. It was the stupidest of mistakes that could betray an illusion you were trying to sell. The wrong pair of shoes. An expensive watch. I'd already checked Liam, he wasn't wearing one.

He snorted. "You know, Mom and Dad being wealthy only played a part in why I wanted to go with them."

"I know," I said. I could give him shit, but not on this. "I never thought you were an asshole for wanting a family."

"Only an asshole because I went to the Royals." The smirk behind the words carried, and I shrugged as I checked the gurney, then the cabinets. They were stocked. Not that we actually needed the stuff, but no cracks.

Satisfied with the interior, I stepped down and fished out the cigarettes from my back pocket. "You left our family for that one."

I wouldn't pull the punches on this.

"You betrayed us. Yes, you were doing Milo a solid. Yes, you were investigating them. You were trying to watch his back and ours. I get that *now*." Tapping the cigarette out, I stared at him.

A chill blew between us in the oversized warehouse we'd commandeered. Or maybe Liam had just fucking bought it too. Who knew.

"But not then," Liam said, not flinching from my gaze. "You couldn't even trust me to *believe* I might have something else going on."

"Trust is earned."

"And when did I fail to earn it?"

"The day after Milo took his deal and you walked, for real, on the Vandals." I lit the cigarette as he stared at me. His shuttered expression was hard to decipher, but the surprise that flickered through his eyes wasn't.

We hadn't discussed this. Not once. Yes, he'd come through for us. He'd been doing a job for Milo. Turned out, everything about his "devotion" to the Royals had been a smokescreen all along.

The most effective smokescreen. The one we believed.

329

Rome had never questioned it. At least not in front of us, and we'd never have made him choose.

"The day I took my shit and moved out of the clubhouse," Liam said slowly. "Officially."

I pointed a finger at him. "Bingo. You made a call. You cut ties. There we were at our lowest point. Milo fucking falls on his sword to protect us but doesn't say a damn word to us about *why* he took the deal, and you walked out the fucking door."

The slam of that door had aggravated a wound Milo's incarceration had inflicted.

"I wanted to pull the knife out of my back and put it in yours."

"Yeah," Liam said slowly, rubbing a hand against the back of his neck. "I can see that. Doc was already gone."

"Had been. He walked on us. Then Milo… and finally you."

"You know why Milo took that asinine deal."

Yeah, I did. I also liked that he called it asinine. "I know *now*. Did he share it with you, then? Even when he was having you cut us out because you weren't sure we could play our parts."

Did that last part leave scorch marks? Yeah. There was scar tissue beneath that wound. Had been. Probably always would be. But wounds closed. Bones knitted together. He was back.

That was the important part. At least, that was what I told myself. He and Doc were back and so was Milo. That had to be worth something, especially with Emersyn being right there at the heart of everything for *all* of us.

"It wasn't about trust…"

I waved him off. "No, it absolutely was." I took another long drag and then blew out a stream of smoke. "I'm a hot head. I was in fighting defense mode. Freddie was going off the rails again, two people I thought I could always rely on were suddenly gone, and the only person standing between the outside and the rest of the Vandals was me."

A position I claimed. A position I would never regret. They were my brothers. We'd bleed for each other. Always had. Always would.

"But it hurt," I told him bluntly. "Hurt more than just me. Kel and Vaughn wanted to give you a chance, but even they started side-eyeing after a while, and Freddie?"

I lit another cigarette from the first before crushing the first one out. I needed this edge off. We shouldn't have wandered down this path littered with landmines.

"Freddie is always struggling, and I'm not blaming you but the choices you and Milo made? They didn't help. Not then."

The last few words descended into the chasm between us, dropping like glow sticks and illustrating just how deep it was.

"I could say I'm sorry," Liam said. "But I made a choice. I wanted to do the right thing in the long run, and I had to ignore the short-term."

His response was honest. Didn't have to like it to respect it.

"I am sorry it hurt you," Liam continued. "You're always such a hard ass. I didn't see it."

Shrugging, I spread my arms. "We make no apologies for who we are. You did what you did to protect us. So did I."

"Surprised you could share Hellspawn with me if you're hanging onto this anger."

"Not hanging onto it." I wasn't. "We just haven't talked about it. I'd never let this shit touch Swan if I could help it. What happened between all of us is between us. She's the one thing we all agree on."

Liam snorted.

"Okay fine, Milo doesn't agree, but we're not asking him."

That generated a genuine laugh from him and I chuckled.

"Liam…not holding onto the past. But not going to ignore the shit that happened, either. We all fucked up. We had a lot to lose then…"

"We have more to lose now." The sober expression echoed everything I felt on the subject.

"We do."

We had *everything* to lose now. But we would also fight a thousand times harder. I finished the cig and put it out before collecting both butts to be disposed of later. We didn't need to leave a trail.

"Any way I can make this up to you?" Liam asked.

I shook my head. "Nothing to make up. It's done. I accept why. I respect why. Don't like it, don't have to. Now? Now I know the one thing I wouldn't forgive is the one thing you'll never do."

He'd put Swan first. Just like I would.

Just like we all would. Our calls would be tempered around her safety and her happiness.

"Then we're on the same page." Liam sounded almost surprised and I grinned.

"Had to happen to a slow reader like you someday." I couldn't resist the little jab and his sharp laugh had me grinning.

"Fuck you, Jas." But he was grinning.

We were still grinning when Doc got there. He wore a suit and tie and that gave me pause.

He glared at me. "Shut it," he said with a single finger pointed at me. "You think I look weird, go look at yourself in a mirror."

Thankfully, I wasn't the only one gaping. Liam shook his head. "We look like orderlies. You look like an undertaker."

Doc smirked and flipped us off. "Probably a good look.

We don't want anyone arguing with us. You have the paperwork?"

"Yep. Everything is in order. Facility paperwork is up to date. Website is set up. Privacy orders and a phone line for confirmation."

I twisted to stare at Liam. "A phone line?"

"The only bad plan is the move we didn't plan for. If we get pushback on checking her out to move her to the new facility, they can call and check the orders themselves."

"What if they reach out to her family?" Doc asked. "That's the one variable we can't plan for."

"They won't." He sounded sure. Almost too sure.

"Explain," I said, because while I trusted him, I still wanted to know.

"Think about what Cavendish said concerning these places. The wealthy hide their dirty little secrets behind walls of nondisclosure agreements and doctor-patient confidentiality. Medical records were inherently private. The shield provided cover and security. No one wants to pierce that by involving a family member directly."

"Contacting her family would leave a paper trail." Doc grimaced.

"The wealthy are *fucked* up," I said firmly.

"Yeah," Liam agreed. "But we're fun at parties."

It wasn't funny. Not really. Still didn't stop Doc or me from snorting with laughter.

"Enough fun and games. The sooner we get her checked out and the rest of us on the road, the better I'll feel about this. We didn't tell Little Bit we were leaving…" He checked his watch.

"Kel is telling her today as soon as we're in the clear." That was the plan. We didn't want her hopes up. We also didn't want her to be here. This plan was low-tech, low-fire power, and, in theory, low-risk. Still weren't risking her. She was tough as hell and determined.

"Good," Doc said. "She'll be pissed. But I'd rather have Little Bit mad than in the middle of this."

"Agreed," I said in the same breath as Liam.

"It is going to be hard enough for her to see her mother." Liam had a point. "If we let her see her."

"To be determined," Doc said without argument. And he was right. This was a fight for another day. "You boys ready?"

"You do know we're not kids anymore, right?" Liam asked, his expression pointed.

I smirked. "Yeah, but he's still the old man. Gotta make himself feel better somehow."

Doc rolled his eyes. "Shut up and get in the ambulance and remember when we get there…"

"Yeah, we shut up and be the muscle. You're the doc." Liam clapped him on the shoulder. "Frown a little more, you don't quite look like a dick yet."

"Suck up," I said to Liam cheerfully as I headed for the driver's side of the ambulance. I'd handle that part of the driving. Doc climbed up into a seat inside it as Liam slid into the passenger seat. "You sure about all this?"

"I'm sure," Doc said. "Remember what I said. We talked about the best way to get her and that friend of Freddie's gave me the idea."

Liam grunted. He really didn't like Bodhi, but I ignored that.

"So we pull up with our transfer paperwork, request that she be released into your custody, load her in the ambulance and just drive out." I wasn't reciting it for them so much as for me.

"Hard not to look at that sideways. It sounds too fucking easy." Liam seemed to agree with me.

"Think about all the people it took to get Little Bit into

Pinetree, to keep her there. All the medical professionals involved. Do I think all of them were corrupt? Probably not." There was a hard core of steel under his words. "But in this system, you don't have to be corrupt to serve the bottom line."

"Privacy laws. Physician's practices. Confidentiality." Liam ticked them off. "And money."

"Money is where it usually starts. All you have to do is buy one professional. Once you have a few, it's better not to look too closely." There was a story there, but not one we needed to discuss right now.

I checked my watch. "Two o'clock is the day-to-afternoon shift change. We'll have twice the number of orderlies, doctors, and nurses on site."

"With less than half the attention span," Doc assured me. "Trust me. I've done my rounds. Shift change is the most chaotic unless you're in an ER."

I glanced at Liam. "I'm in. What about you?"

"I'm in," he said.

Opening the external door, I put my foot on the gas. Time to get her mom, and maybe some answers.

CHAPTER 36

EMERSYN

*H*ands on my hips, I glared at Kellan, and he leaned against the bedroom door, arms folded, as not flinching away.

"I thought we were doing this together." Anger licked a path through me. This was supposed to be a group effort. We would talk, we would plan, and we would do it together. "She's *my* mother."

"Yes," Kellan said evenly. "She is. She's your mother. You asked us to get her out and we're doing that. They picked her up an hour ago, and I waited until they were clear of the facility to read you in because we wanted to be sure they could *get* her out."

"You waited to even tell me they were doing it." I pivoted on one foot. The room wasn't big enough to pace. A part of me wanted to just storm away from him, but that was hard to do when he blocked the door. "How is this doing it together?"

"It's not," he admitted without an ounce of apology. "However, we've been running game plans for weeks. The best we'd managed previously was extremely high risk. It also required relying on Cavendish and hoping he had no issues while he was inside."

"Bodhi is the one who brought us the information," I said. "I get that you guys don't want to trust—"

"Sparrow," Kellan said, the command in his voice hard to ignore. "This wasn't about trust. Do I trust this Bodhi Cavendish? No, I can't say I do. I know that you do and that Freddie does—that carries weight. Liam definitely does not. That also carries weight."

I wanted to scream.

"Getting your mother was important. Getting her without getting anyone seriously injured was far more important. Especially with you wanting to volunteer."

"All of you told me all the reasons that would be a bad idea," I countered, trying to fist my temper. "I got it. The thought of running into my uncle or anyone else there was the last thing I wanted."

A shudder crawled up my spine with icy fingers. The pitted feeling in my stomach, combined with the burn in my throat, sparked tears in my eyes.

He let out a soft sigh. "Sparrow…"

"Would you have told me if they weren't successful? Have you made other attempts I don't know about?" I hated this… aggravation surging in my blood. "I've been playing by all the rules. I've done all the things you asked me to do. I don't get mad about having to check every step I take with you. I know I can't go anywhere without at least two of you or a handoff plan in place."

Dammit. The tears started to spill.

"I've been driving and learning to shoot, and Freddie keeps trying to teach me how to use the knife. I really suck at it. Liam and I were going to work on more fighting, but he's been busy, and then… this whole thing with the king and him having Adam killed 'cause Adam asked me to marry him. It wasn't like that and had nothing to do with…"

"Your money and your status? Yes, it did, Sparrow. It was also to protect you. You are not responsible for the king's choices. You're not responsible for our choices either." The corners of his mouth softened from their hard line. "You've been amazing, Sparrow. Determined. Strong. And fierce. Your courage is absolutely not in question."

"Then why keep it from me?"

"Because you would have wanted to go to be there with your mother on the drive back." At my lack of argument, he nodded and said, "And because we didn't know what condition she would be in *if* it worked. I don't doubt you can handle it, can handle her, but I also don't doubt that it would hurt. You didn't need to see or deal with it until we have her here and can get her settled."

A headache pulsed behind my eyes as I sat down on the edge of his bed. It was like someone cut my strings. "I don't want her to be involved."

"I know," Kellan said softly as he knelt right in front of me. When he gathered up my chilly hands in his, another tear splashed down my cheek. "I know you don't. We all know this and none of us want her to be involved, because we hate how it will make you feel."

I dragged my gaze up to meet his. I swore he could see too much with those deep blue eyes of his, and at the same time, I wanted to fall into those eyes and never come out. There was safety in those waters, safety and warmth. There was also a storm that would be unleashed on those that did us harm.

I kind of loved that about him.

"If you were there, your first priority would be to make

sure she is okay. You would risk yourself to protect her. You would risk a lot to do it, even not knowing…"

"She's my mom." How else did I explain it? We didn't have the stereotypical mother-child relationship, but she loved me. We…had our moments.

"Yes, she is." Lifting my hands, he pressed kisses to my knuckles. "Can I pick you up? You're freezing, and you're upset. I don't like it."

"I don't like it either," I admitted, then I was reaching for him. He slid his arms around me and plucked me right up from the bed as I circled his neck with my arms. "But to be clear, I am still mad at you."

"Noted," he murmured against my hair before he pressed a kiss to my forehead. I burrowed into his warmth. "You can feel free to keep yelling at me while I hold you."

"I wasn't yelling." The fact it came out a sulky pout didn't help. "I'm just… I'm frustrated. Lainey hasn't been able to talk in a few days. Ezra is in a mood and trying to cover for me with the king while trying to not look like he's covering. We have no idea where Adam is. Milo won't talk about any of it and he's started disappearing too. You guys all conspire on a plan to get my mother but don't tell me about it and… I'm here, sitting where it's safe while everyone else takes risks."

Balancing me against him, Kellan moved to the oversized armchair he had in the corner of the room. Sinking into it, he settled me on his lap. "What are you angrier about, Sparrow? That you feel helpless where the people you care about are concerned? Or that you're the one who is safe?"

"Yes," I admitted, disliking that he could distill it down like that. "It's not fair…I want to be able to help all of you. Adam got in trouble for trying to help me. Lainey's out there on her own. Ezra's trying to play both ends against the middle, and now Mickey, Liam, and Jasper are out there getting my mom—and don't think I'm not worried that it's the three of them. The three who do not get along."

He chuckled softly. I lifted my head to glare at him. Instead of being remotely chastised, however, his smile grew. "You're worried about the three of them arguing?"

"Jasper put a gun to Mickey's chin," I said.

"Not the worst thing he's ever done," Kellan said with a shrug. Before I could argue, he pressed a finger to my lips. "They're grown men. They can figure their shit out. The issues they had with each other? They date back to long before you joined us. You are a reason for them to get along, not to fight. Besides, I think Doc's trying to get on your good side."

I rolled my eyes and bit his finger. His smile grew.

"Be careful, Sparrow. I bite back."

Despite my best attempts, my lips twitched.

Rather than call me on that, he slid his hands down my arms then to my waist. I'd been dressed for muscle training more than dancing in a tank top and loose sweats. Physical therapy had been helping, but if I really wanted to keep flying, I needed to get myself in better shape.

Tugging at the ties, he loosened them. "I'm sorry the decision has made you unhappy, but I am not sorry we did it the way we did."

Not the words I wanted to hear. The warmth of his fingers slid beneath my tank as he tugged it upward. I had to lift my arms so he could pull it up and over.

"The simple truth is, Sparrow, that we will always put your safety first. If the choice is between you and someone or something else? We're all going to choose you. I hate that it hurt or upset you, and you have every right to be angry with us. But forgive me, Sparrow, we're always going to put you first. Mentally. Emotionally." He trailed a finger down the strap of my sports bra before he pushed his hands under the hem, which was going up only rather than peeling it up over. He tugged it over and then pressed my arms back until it was binding my biceps. "Physically."

"What are you doing?" Not that I was opposed to thrusting my breasts at him, except we were in the middle of an argument. "You're taking my clothes off."

"Hmm," he murmured, brushing a finger down my breast to one nipple before tracing light circles around it. The room was warm, so it was hardly a chill that had my skin pebbling or my nipple tightening.

My thighs clenched as he kept the bra in place, where it was binding me, with one hand. With his free hand, he cupped the breast and bit down on my nipple. It was both sharp and sweet. The drag of his teeth added a spark of pain to the longing he ignited. A slight sound squeaked out of me and he chuckled before he laved his tongue in a slow circle before he kissed a hickey into place.

My hips bucked at the intense sucking feeling as it bruised. "I warned you," he murmured against my skin. "I bite back."

"You did," I agreed in a breathy voice that in no way suggested that my anger was still in place.

With care, he nipped and sucked at the nipple until I was all but squirming in his lap. I wanted to hold his head in place, but he wouldn't give me the increased pressure I wanted. Nor would he linger too long.

"Kellan," I groaned. "We're having a fight."

"Okay," he said, hauling me up and walking me over to the bed. My arms were still pinned, or they were until he slid the bra down and tossed it. He dropped me on the bed before I could reach for him. Then he caught my hand and a fur-lined leather shackle slid around my right wrist.

I stared at it for a moment as he tightened it. Then he

paused to wait for me to lift my gaze to him. "Is this all right?"

"I—" I didn't know.

"What's your word, Sparrow? If you don't want something, what's your word?"

"Stop."

"Good girl," he whispered, reaching past me toward something on the wall. The strap had a clip on it that he, in turn, fastened to one of the rings on the shackle. Once it clicked into place, he glanced at me, eyebrows raised.

"We're still having an argument, right?"

"Absolutely." He smiled. "Anything you want."

Lips pursed, I said nothing as he slid another fur-lined leather shackle over my left wrist. That, was also connected to a strap he pulled out from the headboard.

"I didn't know those were there," I admitted.

"It was a surprise," he said, nudging me to lie down. When he gave my legs a gentle tug, I half expected him to shackle them too, but all he did was peel down my sweats and panties until I was left naked.

Tilting my head, I ran my tongue over my lower lip. Splayed out like this, there was no way to hide how turned on I was. He ran his hand over my stomach, and when I would have reached for him, he pressed a button and the straps pulled wide, trapping my arms.

I blinked.

He gave me a measuring look. All I had to do was say stop. No doubt existed in me at all. If I said that one word, he'd take them off. "So, you're not sorry that you made the call to get her and to keep it from me, or you're just sorry that I'm upset?"

"More or less," he said, lifting my right leg and setting my ankle against his shoulder before he began to massage my thigh. The combination of stretch, the restraints, and the warm dig of his fingers into my tense muscles dragged me off the path.

"I don't like that you did it," I groaned out the last part as he found a particularly tense knot. The liquid heat it released along the back of my leg was heavenly.

"I know."

"I really don't like being kept...*fuck!*" He'd not only freed that knot, he moved to work on the inside of my thigh. The teasing brush of his hand right there next to my cunt and not actually touching anything was heaven and hell.

His soft chuckle drifted over me in a caress all its own. "I intend to, Sparrow. I certainly intend to, but I wanted to let you finish yelling at me."

I forced open eyes that had begun to drift shut to find him staring at me with flame in those eyes. "You'd let me yell at you while I'm all—naked and horny and wet for you?" I mean, I could lie about it, I supposed, but I really didn't want to.

"For as long as you need or want," he agreed, pausing in his massage to trail a finger over to my cunt, then pausing to circle my clit in a slow, measured stroke that was pure torture. I arched my hips, stretching my free leg so that there was nothing to impede his touch.

I was trying to figure out what words to use when he swooped in, and the prickle from his stubble scraped over my thigh as if to bite me all over again before his mouth locked on my clit.

No hesitation, no slow strokes, no easing his way in. No, Kellan feasted on my pussy like it was his favorite meal, and my thoughts splintered apart as he licked, nipped, and even *bit* me to ecstasy.

The first orgasm crashed through me in an unexpected tide. The fact he kept lapping at the moisture escaping me just sent another thrill racing through my system and then my vision whited-out when he pressed two fingers inside and hooked them.

At the sound of fabric falling, I dragged my eyes open to find Kellan watching me with the most indulgent smile as he stroked his cock. Oh, I wanted to be doing that. I licked my lips.

"Kellan?"

"Yes, Sparrow?"

"Can we table the argument for now?"

He didn't laugh, just smiled. "We absolutely can."

"I reserve the right to bring this up again later."

"Understood."

I was panting and already straining, but the straps kept my arms in a t-shape. I couldn't move.

"Anything else you want to say to me, Sparrow?" A devilish twinkle entered his eyes.

"Fuck me," I whispered. "Please."

"My pleasure," he said, lifting my hips and lining himself up. There were no more words as he slammed home and I wrapped my legs around his hips. No words.

But fuck if he didn't bite me again.

We could fight later.

A lot later.

Maybe.

CHAPTER 37

VAUGHN

*R*ome leaned over his sketchbook. We'd only turned on a light in the hall so that the woman who was supposed to have raised and protected Dove wasn't disturbed. Moira Sharpe looked nothing like I'd expected.

The woman pictured in the news and all the websites was glamorous beauty, cold maybe, but immaculate and impeccable. She never had a hair out of place and the perfect cosmetics. Where Dove tended to be pale, Moira seemed to tan regularly, or she had…

Pale, gaunt, and looking almost as bad as Dove had when we got her back from Pinetree, Moira Sharpe had the appearance of a woman who had been through hell. Doc set her up with an IV and pulled blood to run. The four days on the road hadn't flushed her system thoroughly yet.

Occasionally, her eyelids flickered and she looked like she would be waking up, only she never did. At least not entirely. Jasper and Liam said she'd been the same on the road.

"This one," Rome said, and I peered over to see the sketchpad. When I held out my hand, he passed it to me. He'd done the sketches in heavy pencil. The striations could be different color grades.

He'd sketched out a pair of long feathers, a primary and a tail from the looks of them. The tail seemed a little more "damaged," but where the more ragged bits of the feather showed their injuries, they became other birds—seven on each.

On the primary, the birds spilled from the side. On the tail feather, they escaped from the end. The tail feather was in better shape. Made sense. You clipped a bird by clipping its primaries.

"I like it," I said slowly. Both told different stories. The longer I looked at it, the more I realized what he'd done. Yes, there were birds escaping from the tail feather, but they weren't fleeing her primary. They were filling it in. Lifting her up.

"Correction," I continued, glancing over at him. "I love it. Full color or black only?"

"Let Starling decide. Both would be beautiful."

He wasn't wrong. We'd been trading ideas back and forth. Dove hated the scars on the inside of her forearms. They were getting smaller, but they would never go away. Finding something that would help transform them from symbols of pain to marks of survival had pushed us both.

"What if we do another version but in flames? Like a phoenix?"

She was a phoenix, rebuilding herself from the ashes. Her fire might have been smothered, but it had never been extinguished. I passed him the sketchbook back and he flipped the page. A sound came from the bed.

Rising, I studied the frail woman. We hadn't intended to bring Dove to see her, not until we had more certainty about her condition. It had already ignited one fight so Kel relented.

The fact it had been hard as hell for Dove to see her hadn't been lost on any of us. Doc filled her in on the drugs they'd been using. He couldn't just cut her off cold turkey, it would do far more harm than it would help.

Instead, he'd set up an IV drip and he'd been stepping her down slowly. They'd started on the ride back and continued here.

We'd rented an entire villa at the summer resort. It was far enough from Braxton Harbor and not directly related to us, unless you knew our history.

And who the fuck was going to pay attention to our summer jobs when we were still in the group home? The rapid eye movement was back, and she muttered something. The word or words were unintelligible.

We'd had her for seven days, three since they returned from picking her up. Doc had inserted a catheter, and I wasn't going anywhere near that. She had fluids and a nutrition bag. If it went on much longer, he indicated she'd need a feeding tube.

This was some seriously fucked up shit. Nothing in the paperwork indicated who signed her into the facility. In fact, the wording had all seemed to indicate that a doctor and not her family had hospitalized her.

Still, why keep her like this?

It disgusted me.

"They're here," Rome said, pulling my attention from the bed. Our relief was coming. We were all getting a crash course in patient care this week. The sketchbook had vanished, and I put a hand on my gun while Rome moved to the door.

The text messages were perfect for letting us know when the others arrived, but we were still taking precautions.

"It's them," Rome confirmed, and I let go of the gun as he opened the door. Liam and Kellan arrived with Dove. She wrapped her arms around Rome, greeting him with a hug and he accepted it readily.

While touch had not been something Rome ever seemed to seek out, with Dove, he was different. We were all different. We all needed her in our own ways, and we all wanted to look after her.

Thank fuck, she needed all of us. I opened my arms as soon as she let go of Rome and she crashed into me. I picked her up, savoring her nearness. She wore the scents of chocolate, vanilla, and more than a little sugar.

"Did you go get ice cream?" I asked softly.

"No," she whispered, leaning her head back to meet my gaze without letting go. "Liam brought me the biggest ice cream sundae you've ever seen. Then I made him eat it with me."

"Suck up," I said with a nod to where Liam stood with his brother.

Liam just flipped me off. We were all trying to make up for the little deception with her. Especially after seeing her mother, I was glad we'd made the call we had.

"How is she?" Dove asked as she patted my arm for me to put her down. While I was more than content to hold her forever, I set her on her feet. Her attention had moved to the bed. Worry filled her eyes.

"Doc said it could be a few more days. He's still detoxing her." There was no gentle way to put it. "He explained it, right?"

"Yeah," she said with a sigh. "Do you guys mind if I have some time with her?"

"No," Kellan answered before any of us could. "We don't, but we'll be in the other room. Stay away from the doors and windows?"

She spared him a smile. "I promise."

I pressed a kiss to her forehead and then moved a chair over so she could sit next to the bed. "We'll be right through there."

"Thank you."

In the doorway, I hesitated, glancing back to where she held her mother's hand now and leaned forward. Dove looked so small, and there was a deep sadness to her that I hated.

"Give her a moment," Kellan said and I grunted before following them into the little kitchenette. The villa was nice, it was a little more secluded and tucked away from the beach. It was designed more for privacy than access and it fit our needs perfectly.

"Yeah." Once I was fully in the kitchenette, though, there was no mistaking the tension in the room. "What the fuck happened now?"

"Emersyn's old troupe has been making news," Liam said, not wasting time. "They have been for a few days, yet she caught a story on the news a couple of hours ago and then went looking."

Okay that wasn't too bad, right?

"There appears to have been a few deaths," Kellan said, pitching his voice low as Liam had. "Accidents happen. But five of them?"

Five?

"Who?"

Liam listed off three names: Marjorie Carter, Christian and Jaime de la Cruz. None of which meant anything to me. Marta Phillipose, however... "Why do I know that name?" I cut a look at Kellan.

"Bitchy chaperone."

Oh, fuck. "Okay, I don't honestly give a fuck that she's dead." That cunt had let the abuse happen to Dove. The handful of times I'd ever seen them interact during the show, she'd been a stone-cold bitch to her.

"Don't care about the woman," Kellan said, giving me a look before he flicked a glance to the other room where Dove was with her mother. "I care about the timing. A couple of those names were people Sparrow cared about."

Fuck.

"What do we know?"

"Not enough," Liam admitted. "The troupe she was with before broke up and went in different directions. Far as I can tell, they had no real contact or any other connections other than the company."

"And Starling." Rome wasn't guessing. He tacked those words on like they were ones Liam had just forgotten to add.

"Pretty much." Kellan's expression was as dark as it was thoughtful.

"What would be the point of killing them off? If that's what is happening… but a pattern of accidents says it's way more than just accidents."

Coincidence only went so far.

I scrubbed a hand over my face.

"Dove," I said, not waiting for them to explain it.

"Telling her he can get to her through the people around her." The flat note in Liam's voice covered the very real anger in his eyes. "Like the fucking pictures of all of us."

Rome glanced at the other room. "What about Lainey?"

"I called Ezra," Liam admitted. "He grabbed her."

"This is me not asking if by grabbed her, you mean he actually grabbed and kidnapped her," I said. "You trust him with her?" Milo would not care for it, and I didn't blame him, but Ezra and Adam had both come through for Dove and for us.

"With Lainey? Yes," Liam said. "He won't let anything happen to her."

I appreciated the confidence. "What are we supposed to do about her troupe?"

"Not much we can do," Kellan said.

"Ask Starling who she liked."

The suggestion from Rome got his twin's attention.

"Protect the ones she cared about and fuck the rest?" It sounded cold when you put it that way.

"Can we protect the others?" Rome asked, and I sighed even as Kellan shook his head.

"I don't even know if we have the resources to cover what we have *now*," Kel said with a frown. "We may need to move her." He nodded toward the other room. "Or make alternative arrangements."

We were stretched thin. "We don't want her anywhere he's already seen."

"No," Liam agreed. "If he did his own dirty work, I'd be more than happy to bait the hook."

But her uncle was far more likely to send goons, bounty hunters or worse. We couldn't afford to leave her exposed, and if it came down to a choice between her or her mother…

No, we couldn't let it be a choice.

"Maybe we move Dove," I said slowly. "The clubhouse is as secure as we can make it, but if we move her and her mother, we could secure a new location." I glanced at Liam.

"I've thought about the house, but there's every chance in the world that the king knows about it too. I want to keep her away from him for as long as possible. We are fighting on too many fronts, even if some are cold wars."

Liam rubbed the back of his neck, and he looked exhausted. It was wearing on all of us.

"Take her back to the clubhouse," Kellan said. "Liam and I will handle this tonight. I'm going to work on alternatives. As much as we don't want her there, we could secure her in one of the old bedrooms or even lock her in the safe room."

Not ideal…

"We'll get the equipment in place," I volunteered. "It would probably make Dove happy to have her right there."

The fact Liam and Kellan wore the exact same look was almost amusing.

Almost.

Rome's expression wasn't far off. "We need to know what she knows."

Yeah. We did.

"I'm gonna call Doc," Kellan said. "Give her another fifteen minutes and then back with her."

We weren't getting out of this without shedding blood. Frankly, I was ready to do it. The manipulation game of shifting pieces around the board grated at me. Give me a target and a straight fight any day of the week.

"Guys," Dove called, and I wasn't the only one moving. "She's awake… Hi, Mom."

CHAPTER 38

EMERSYN

"You have to eat," Mickey said, crouching next to where I'd taken up residence in the room with my mother. After her brief moment of lucidity at the cabin, the guys had decided it would be better to bring her back, even if they didn't precisely want her in the clubhouse. They also didn't want to keep everyone spread thin looking after her.

Yes, I was tired, but the idea of eating held little appeal. Ever since Mom opened her eyes and started to cry when she saw me...I couldn't shake the misery of what those tears might mean.

Even when I told myself to not try and ascribe meanings or motivations to her tears, I couldn't help but imagine the various scenarios. Most of them ranging from bad to worse. In no world did she wake up and tell me something I was going to want to hear—whether she'd been blind to it all or not.

I hadn't realized how much I dreaded the very possibility until—

"Little Bit." Mickey settled a hand on my knee as he held out the sandwich. I could smell the cucumber and...

"Cucumber and cream cheese?" Surprise rippled through me. I hadn't had one of those in a long time.

"Rome reminded us it was one of your favorites."

How had Rome known? No sooner did I ask the question than the answer surfaced. He'd read and watched all of my interviews. It was how he knew my favorite dance shoes, my favorite performances, and even the movies and shows I liked. Information gleaned from a long series of thoughtless and hurried answers I'd given over the years.

Mickey squeezed my knee gently. "I know you're worried, but she's coming down from the drug cocktail they've had her on. We're doing this slowly to try and avoid potentially dangerous withdrawal symptoms."

"I know," I said, accepting the cool porcelain the sandwich rested on. He'd even cut it into triangles. It was kind of cute. "You explained all of it, but..." I glanced at the bed again.

Not saying anything, Mickey kept his hand on my leg and the strength, not to mention the warmth, helped to push back some of the cold shrouding me. I balanced the plate on my leg, then put a hand over Mickey's, where his rested on me.

"When she woke up before..." I took a moment to check. The guys had been taking turns sitting with me, even Freddie, though it was clear from the way he stared at Mom that he had some serious reservations.

"When she woke up," Mickey prompted me. "Finish the statement, then take a bite."

I wrinkled my nose at him, but his expression didn't change, nor did he seem remotely impressed by my determination. The gentle squeeze of his hand on my leg helped to ground me as I studied the shadows in his eyes.

"She cried when she saw me." It was such a small thing. Only she'd cried so hard and her words had been almost unintelligible.

"And you don't know why," he said, the gentleness there adding salt to my wounded pity party.

I shook my head, then picked up a triangle of the sandwich and took a bite. I half-expected it to taste like ash or cardboard. Except it didn't. The cucumbers were crunchy and the cream cheese was smooth and a little sweet. The bread was soft and it even smelled good.

One bite turned into a second and then a third. I finished the first triangle swiftly and reached for a second. My stomach growled as if it had only taken that little bit of food to awaken my hunger.

"We won't know what caused her tears until she wakes up." Mickey pushed up from the floor to take a seat next to me.

The chairs had been pushed together by Freddie so we could play a handheld game together. While he moved his hand, he didn't withdraw his touch entirely.

"The thing is, Little Bit, we don't know how much of her is responding and how much it is the drugs. The pharmaceuticals they put her on—they were powerful anti-psychotics. They are tailored more for people with severe anti-personality issues, psychosis, or schizophrenia. To my knowledge, your mother wasn't experiencing any of those conditions."

I finished a second triangle and shook my head. "No, she's always been...happy may not be the right word, but more like determined in her optimism." It was a facet of her personality that she'd often encouraged in mine. Keep my chin up, look for the positive, and make my own if I can't find it.

"I didn't think so. However, the type of tranquilizers they are can pretty much blunt the whole world until you're in this cotton candy-infused world where nothing touches you and you can't even find the world."

Scarily enough, I was very familiar with that feeling. When I met Mickey's gaze, I read the understanding there. Of course, he knew.

"You saw that on my toxicology reports when you did the bloodwork."

His mouth flattened, and the anger that spared to life there wasn't directed at me. "I did. So I know you know how it feels, how disorienting it is. I wish we could detox her faster, but without knowing how they loaded her up in the first place, we could do significantly more harm than good."

"No, slow is better." I returned my attention to the bed as I ate more of the sandwich. As much as it hadn't appealed to me when he first came in, now I actually wondered if I could get a second one. Probably better to finish the first one and see how I felt when I was done.

"Little Bit, what can I do?" The question pierced the bubble of worry hovering around me. I claimed the last triangle to eat before I set the plate aside.

His attention tracked me as I moved to slide onto his lap. He leaned back in the chair and wrapped an arm around me as I curled into him and tucked my head into his shoulder. They were all so much bigger than me, and right now, I wanted that. I wanted to be surrounded and held.

I wanted to know that it would be okay, no matter what happened when she woke up. "I want her to be okay," I said as I contemplated the last triangle.

Mickey rubbed my arm, the roughness of his palm doing what his hand on my knee had earlier, grounding me to where we were. "I know you do. She'll know it too. We got her out because you wanted her out. She's going to be okay, it's just going to take time."

"I don't want her to have known," I whispered the last part, then licked my suddenly dry lips. "I just...I just want her to be the one good part that Milo wanted for me."

And I needed her to be that good part for *me* as much as for Milo.

Pressing his lips to my temple, Mickey sighed. But he didn't make me any promises. "I want that for you too."

When he nudged my arm up so that I would move the last bit of the sandwich to my lips, I stole a look up at him. "Thank you."

"For trying to bully you into eating?" Amusement colored the words. "I'm always happy to ensure you're safe, warm, and fed."

"For going to get my mom. I know it was a risk for you, for Liam, and for Jasper."

"Still mad at us for leaving you out of it?"

"No," I said with a slow shake of my head. "I was. I think I was a little more hurt and maybe more worried than I was mad, but I'm not any of those things." Not anymore. Kellan had been right. Once I got over the idea they'd kept me out and listened to him when he filled me in, I understood it more.

Would I go as far as to say that I was okay with it? No. I wasn't okay that they'd kept me out. It felt too close to a lie, but they didn't exclude me for anything other than to protect me.

Since I wanted to protect them as much it was hard to fight against that logic. Not that I probably wouldn't fight again, and I'd told Kellan as much.

"Well, I'm glad to hear that," Mickey murmured, pressing another kiss to my forehead. They were barely-there touches, all comfort and kindness. Passion had nothing to do with the way he cradled me.

I ate the last triangle, relieved that it still tasted good. Once I'd finished, I just curled into Mickey and kept my gaze on my mother.

"Are you sure there's nothing else I can do?" He blew out a long sigh. "I hate seeing you unhappy."

"You hate admitting that too." I didn't mean to laugh, but the growl in his voice sent warm shivers of delight through me.

Delight because he cared, and it was so human and tangible when he let that mask of his go. He was always looking after all of us, always being the "doctor," the mentor, the older brother...

I made a face. I was never going to think of Mickey as a brother, and I didn't want to.

"I don't hate admitting it," he grumbled, wrapping an arm around me more firmly. "I hate that I can't fix it."

Sighing, I traced a finger against his shirt. The cotton of his tee was soft but also more fitted than he usually wore. Mickey's clothes tended to be looser and I always assumed it had to do with his scars. Tight clothes may not be as comfortable.

Now? I wasn't so sure, and it probably wasn't the right time to ask.

"I don't think anyone can just *fix* any of this," I said. "At the same time, all of you do help. Even when you push me or tease me." I lifted my head to give him a look. "Or taunt me."

The corner of his mouth kicked a little higher. "Is that a complaint?"

Before I could answer, the door opened to let Milo in. I glanced past Mickey to smile at him. When he circled the chairs, he grunted with a shake of his head before claiming the chair I'd abandoned.

"Do I need to move?" I asked, not because I was going to apologize for the affection but because I didn't want to make Milo uncomfortable.

"No," he said with a shake of his head, though he did shoot Mickey an amused smile. "I'll cope. How is your mother?"

There was always a faint twist to his lips when he said, "your mother." We shared a mother, but I had no memories of her at all, while Milo clearly had a deep affection for her, weaknesses and all. Then there was my adopted mother, the woman who took me into a wealthy life that he'd wanted for me. A life he continued to believe had been better.

Though I didn't think he believed that as much anymore. I didn't want to enlighten him to the idea that it had never been what he imagined for me.

"Still sleeping," I answered. "Mickey hasn't done his after-noon check yet, but he brought me food and was making sure I ate it."

"Good," Milo said. "I'm going to sit with you for a while if you'd like."

"You don't have to, but I would love the company."

"Sounds like I'm being dismissed," Mickey said lightly. Before I could protest, though, he pressed a finger to my lips. "I know you didn't mean it that way, Little Bit. Although it's good for the two of you to talk, and you don't always need an audience, especially since Milo thinks we're all biased."

For his part, Milo snorted. "And I'm right."

I giggled. I couldn't help it. There was such a dry air of unspoken "fuck you" between the two of them that lacked rancor. No, even their silent flip-offs were filled with affec-tion and loyalty. I didn't have to envy it anymore because they'd opened that circle and wrapped it all around me.

"I would apologize," I told Milo. "However, I'm not

stealing your friends. I would never cut you out. I just don't want to let them go."

Mickey gave the faintest of starts beneath me, as though my words registered. I glanced up to find him studying me. Yes, I knew what I'd said. I got that we were still dancing around each other. He'd hurt me. I'd lashed back.

Then he invited me to do my worst. There really hadn't been any time for that. Not like we might need, and there were other conversations that Mickey and I needed to have. Conversations that…

"Emersyn?" Mom's soft voice yanked me off of Mickey's lap like she'd pressed retract on a pulley.

"Mom?" I moved to the side of her bed, careful not to jostle her hand where they had a port in for the IV. Unlike the last time she woke up, she wasn't slurring at all. There was a clarity to her eyes as she blinked slowly.

"Baby, it is you," she whispered, her voice so rough and dry. With each syllable, a cough escaped her, and I reached for the little cup with the straw.

"I can give her water, right?" I glanced at Mickey, who was already rising to circle the bed and checking the equipment running her vitals.

"You can, just a little. I'd like to ask her some questions first," he said, glancing down at Mom.

He gave me a beat while I pressed the straw between her lips. The water wasn't cold, but she drank two or three sips before she let go of the straw.

"Mrs. Sharpe," Mickey continued while I held the water back. "I'm Doctor James. We've moved you from Pilgrim Hills to a private facility at the behest of your daughter."

All of that was true. Mom glanced from Mickey to me. Her eyes grew damper as she stared at me. "You shouldn't have had to help me…"

"Of course I did. I couldn't stand the thought of you being there."

"Mrs. Sharpe," Mickey drew her attention back to him. "I need you to focus for me… can you tell me your full name?"

"Moira," she said slowly. "Moira Emersyn Sharpe." She pressed her free hand to her face as a tear slipped free. "We named our baby after my family…" She glanced up at me.

"I'm right here," I promised her. The tremble in her hands and lower lip, not to mention the tears in her eyes, weren't my vivacious mother with her hurricane personality. "You're going to be okay…"

"That's good, Mrs. Sharpe." Mickey had her attention again. "Do you remember where you are?"

We'd just told her a new facility, but Mickey didn't respond to my frown.

"You said a new place…a private facility. You didn't say the name."

"Good." Mickey smiled at her. "Can you tell me why you were admitted to Pilgrim Hills?"

She swallowed, then stared at me. Panic flickered across her face. "I didn't know," she whispered, and a crack across my heart turned into a fissure. "I swear…baby, I had no idea, and then…" Hot tears slid down her face as she gripped my hand, and then she was trying to sit up as another sob broke out of her. "You must hate me so much, and I'm so sorry…"

I gripped her tighter, holding onto her as she cried. The sound leaving her was so broken it rasped against all my senses. Tears filled my own eyes, and I wanted to cry with her, but her volume increased as she dug her nails into my arms almost frantically.

"Baby, I'm so sorry… You can't ever… forgive me… I am so sorry…"

Her words were growing more unintelligible. Milo was peeling her hands off me, and Mickey was there, using a syringe to press something into her IV port. Mom's tears didn't slow, but the sound diminished as she began to sag. Milo was careful with how he laid her down.

The fissure through my heart gaped wider. She was damn near hysterical, and even with the sedative Mickey was giving her, the wildness in her expression hadn't quieted. I read all the heartbreak in her eyes, reflecting my own self-loathing and misery back at me.

I put a hand to my mouth to try and stifle the tears that wanted to escape. Mickey glanced at me, only it was Milo who wrapped an arm around my shoulders and dragged me back against him.

"We got you, Ivy," he said, his tone walking the border between harsh and gentle. I wanted to close my eyes, partially in relief that she didn't know and in agony because it was killing her. I didn't dare, not until the sedative knocked her out. Then some doubtful part of my soul wanted to know if she was talking about my uncle or not.

Fuck.

We all stood there as her eyes gradually fell shut, and the pain in her expression eased. It was a respite, no matter how brief, it was a respite. Sooner or later, she would wake up again, and we would have to talk…

"Mickey, you have any idea what she was talking about?" Milo asked, and this time I did close my eyes. I couldn't tell him. Not right now.

Maybe not ever.

CHAPTER 39

EMERSYN

"$\mathcal{M}$ilo," Mickey said in a commanding voice. "Let it go."

Mom was asleep, and we were all keeping our voices down, but the concern on Milo's face scraped at me. There was so little left of his illusions. He deserved so much more than the world had ever given him. Maybe I didn't know about him all these years, but I did now.

I survived. That was all that mattered. I was surviving and I was healing. Milo didn't need to know this. No, I didn't want him to know this. It wasn't the same as not needing to know it. My chest ached with the tears I'd been fisting on to tight.

"So you do know," Milo said slowly and while he'd addressed all of his questions to Mickey, he'd kept an arm around me.

"It doesn't matter what I do or don't know," Mickey told him, and his voice firmed up. "Right now, we deal with the problem in front of us. Little Bit is worried about her mother, and I'm sorry Little Bit, but your mother…"

"She's a mess," I said softly, pulling from Milo to comb Mom's hair back from her face with my fingers.

She would hate to see herself like this. Her hair was matted in places from sweat. Frizzy in others from how she'd been lying there. The lack of cosmetics would make her crazy, since she always preferred to only show the world her perfect face. She dictated what they saw and how they saw it.

There was a vulnerability to her like this. A painful vulnerability that made my heart and soul ache for her. Had she discovered what had happened with my uncle? Was that why they'd put her there? Was it Uncle Bradley?

Bile burned in the back of my throat.

Or had it been Dad?

I pressed my hands together as I stared at Mom. I hated that she'd been put through any of this. I hated my uncle.

Hated him. It all went back to him. To his perverted needs and desires. To his manipulations and twisting of the truth. To his ease with killing off the people who found out.

Killing Mom was probably more difficult than I would have believed when I was so young. But he just put her away, setting it up so she would look crazy. It would prevent her accusations from getting any traction.

Where the hell was my father in all of this?

The more I turned this over in my head, the angrier I got.

"Milo," Mickey was saying. "Look at her." The words registered, and I glanced from my mom to where the pair of them stood. Mickey had a grip on Milo's shoulder. Holding him back? Milo had let me go at some point and I hadn't even noticed.

Worry was shining in his dark brown eyes and a frown tightened his forehead. "She's going to be alright, Ivy." The words came out thick and heavy, yet deadly serious. "You've got her, and we've got you."

Turning, I went to him and crashed into his chest. Mickey let Milo go as Milo wrapped his arms around me.

"I don't know what happened exactly," he murmured, squeezing me tight. "You can tell me anything, I promise. I won't judge. But you also don't have to tell me. No matter what happens, we're going to make sure you're both safe."

They didn't owe my mother anything. Although, they would protect her for the same reasons they'd protected me for Milo.

"I'll tell you," I told him slowly. "Just not right now. There's too much going on and…and she needs to be more herself first."

Because we all had questions, I didn't doubt that the boys did. Mickey made no effort to cover his own interest or the fact he had questions to ask. They'd want to know if she was telling the truth.

The horror in her eyes didn't feel remotely manufactured. Having walked down those darkened paths and been chased more than once, I recognized the fear. I'd tasted it, been choked by it, and trapped for so long that fear and I had long since become intimate acquaintances.

I didn't look at Mickey as Milo pulled back to meet my gaze. "Is whatever it is hurting you right now?" The question put me on the spot, but it was also one I could answer.

"Not anymore." Thankfully, it wasn't a lie. "I've been safe for a long time." Safe with all of them. "Took me a while to recognize it, but I'm not going anywhere."

He studied me intently, searching for evidence of a lie? Or for whatever I was holding back? Or maybe he just wanted to know if he could believe what I said?

"Okay," he said slowly. "You can have your secret."

I licked my lips.

"Until you're ready to tell me." Telling him would hurt him so much. "And whatever it is, we'll take care of it. You and me. I might let the knuckleheads help, but I got your back. Believe me?"

That melted so much of my resistance. "Of course, I believe you."

"There is no *of course*, Ivy. Since I got out, I've given you many reasons to mistrust me. I'm working on it. Never going to love that you chose this life, but I also don't hate having you here."

I sniffled. "Don't hold back," I teased him. "Tell me how you really feel."

"I'm trying. I don't trust easily. I confide even less. I should recognize the same signs in you. But I don't care what it is. I care that it could have or be hurting you. So when you're ready, tell me. We'll take care of it."

All the tears clawed their way up my throat, and I hugged him again. "Thank you," I whispered.

"You never have to thank me," he promised, though I could almost feel him looking at Mickey. I hated leaving him wondering, but not right now there was just so much going on.

A soft knock on the door alerted us before Kellan glanced inside. "Hate to interrupt," he said, his gaze roving over me like he was checking for any injury. "Liam's here, and we've got some plans to make."

"Mickey," I said as I glanced at him.

"Go on, I'll stay with her." He caught my hand, then bent to press a kiss to my cheek, shifting at the last minute to capture my lips in a gentle but firm kiss. I tasted the salt of my tears on his lips, but also the warmth of affection and maybe some coffee.

He nipped my lower lip before he lifted his head. This close, I couldn't miss the concern or the promise in his eyes.

"I'm okay," I told him, squeezing his hand. He flicked a look past me to Kel and Milo.

"Look after her," he ordered, and I chuckled softly.

"Not going to tell me to look after them?" It was a dare, but he simply tugged me to him and kissed me again. This time it was more teeth than tongue. I held onto him as he nuzzled my mouth, teasing my lower lip as he scraped his teeth over it again.

"Behave, Little Bit," he said in a low voice. "I know you're going to look after them. I just need to make sure they are looking after you at the same time."

He winked, and I rose up on my tiptoes and kissed him once more, only I bit his lip before laving my tongue over the wound. A hint of laughter chased me as I let him go. He said to bring it and while that was very tame, I didn't want him to think I'd forgotten.

Turning, I found Milo staring at us while shaking his head. "You're determined to drive me mad."

"Don't think it's a long trip," I said, patting him on the chest as I headed to where Kellan wore an almost indulgent soft smirk. Course, after he shackled me to a bed, I was very much interested in indulging him more.

Milo's groan and Mickey's chuckle followed us out as Kellan tucked me under his arm. "All good?" he asked in a soft voice that wouldn't carry as we headed down the stairs to meet the others.

"Yeah," I said. "I think so." I peered up at him. "She woke up for a little except she was really upset." He searched my eyes and then nodded slowly. "*Really* upset... Mickey gave her a sedative. But we'll need to talk to her more later on when she can calm down."

He exhaled a long breath then tightened his arm around me. "We can do that, Sparrow." We could.

"But it has to wait for now."

"Unfortunately," he said. "We have another issue that's come up."

Downstairs, the guys had boxes of pizza opened up and fresh bottles of beer, soda, and even water. Bodhi lifted his drink toward me.

"Hey, PPG. Long time."

I snorted. "It's only been a week."

He grinned. "That's a long time. Especially if you haven't gotten laid."

Jasper turned around at that comment and started to glare, and Liam looked thunderous.

"Must be sad to be you then," I told Bodhi with a wink as I went to wrap my arms around Liam. I couldn't stop Jasper and Liam at the same time, but I had a feeling that Liam was the one who really wanted to do Bodhi damage. "Not a problem I've had."

There was a beat of silence, and then Liam glimpsed down at me. Amusement curled the corners of his mouth. "Are you looking for another spanking, Hellspawn?"

"Maybe," I told him, before I took his beer. "Or maybe I just wanted a drink." I danced back a couple of steps laughing as Liam snorted then shook his head. Vaughn hooked an arm around me and nuzzled a kiss to my throat.

"We couldn't get rid of him," he said. "So no specifics."

I leaned my head back to look up at him. "Okay." I downed some of the beer then moved to where Kellan had taken a seat. This time, I perched on the arm of his chair. If I started in a lap, they'd be passing me around again.

The pizza smelled amazing and Freddie took a seat on the arm of the chair next to ours while holding out two slices of pizza for me.

"Thank you."

"Welcome, Boo-Boo." He gave Bodhi a look that Bodhi ignored as he leaned back in his chair. Nothing seemed to bother Bodhi, ever. I would bump Freddie's hip but I had my hands full and Kellan wrapped a hand around my ankle while everyone else grabbed food and places to sit.

"Gonna be a short meeting," Kellan said. "We have company."

"Ignore me," Bodhi said. "Pretend I'm not even here."

"We could, if you'd just go away," Liam suggested. "In fact, why don't I open the door and make it easy for you."

"Nah," Bodhi retorted with a grin that would probably antagonize Liam in its cheerfulness. "But thanks for the offer."

"For now," Kellan continued before Jasper could jump in. "You are a guest, Mr. Cavendish. When we decide it's time to go, you will go. Clear?"

"You got it, boss." Bodhi shot him a thumbs-up. "But only cause PPG seems to like you best."

I rolled my eyes, but I wasn't the only one. Vaughn, however, had a hand pressed against his mouth like he was trying not to laugh. I didn't think he wanted to laugh at Bodhi so much as Jasper and Liam. When Vaughn caught my eye, he nodded to them. They wore matching expressions of irritation.

I had to bite my lip.

"Whatever works," Kellan said. "Liam has an event this weekend, and we're all invited."

The club opening…

"And I think we should go," Kellan continued even as Milo opened his mouth. "Everyone, hold onto your objections for now. The point is to be seen. The club is going to have a soft opening, no press. We're going to have some movers from the city and others. We'll also have eyes in that crowd measuring us and looking for weaknesses."

Silence filled the room. The last couple of sentences stroked ice up my spine.

"The king may be there," Liam said, glancing from me to Milo. "It's the first time I think he'll be in a public venue where we can all get a good look at him. Hellspawn and I didn't know him. Neither did Ezra. Doesn't mean none of us do, in any case."

And by none of us, he meant Milo. "And Ivy has to be there for that?"

"Unfortunately," Kellan said, raising a hand. "She's a player in this, we knew that before. She won't be there alone." No, it looked like I'd be there with everyone.

"Is it still a titty bar?" The question crashed into the center of the room, jerking all the side conversations to a halt. Milo pressed a hand to his face, but Freddie just started laughing. Vaughn snickered. Then Jasper. Finally, Liam just shook his head.

"Yes, Hellspawn, but we call it a gentleman's club. Upscale. We're expecting a better class of customers, and the dancers will be protected on all fronts. No more dealing in the club and no one running hookers through there."

"That's cool. Some of the strippers were really talented."

"Anyway," Kellan pressed on and when I glanced at him, his eyes promised me a spanking in my future. Cool. I took a bite of the pizza. "The point is, we're going out for the night. We're going to see and be seen."

He flexed his hand around my ankle.

"We're *all* taking precautions. No one goes anywhere alone. Even if you have to pee, Sparrow, one or two of us will be going with you."

"Sex in the club bathroom," Bodhi said speculatively. "Sounds real classy."

Liam let out a growl, but it was Rome who stepped between them. The twins stared at each other, with Rome's expression far calmer than his brother's.

"Not a criticism," Bodhi said. "Just admiring it. Cause a

classy joint is gonna have a clean bathroom. Much better for fucking. Especially if it's PPG. She deserves a classy joint."

Oh, shit. It was Jasper lunging this time and Vaughn barely caught him.

"Bodhi," Freddie said as he stood up. "Dude... for fucking real?"

"What?" Bodhi spread his hands. "I haven't killed anyone lately. A fight sounds fun."

I wasn't the only one groaning this time. "Bodhi?"

"Yes, PPG?"

"Can you please not provoke any of them? I like you. However, I like them more."

Bodhi stared at me for a beat before settling back in his seat, all relaxed. "You got it, no problem. Just forget I'm here."

Yeah, I really didn't think that would be possible. I stole a look at Freddie, and that was probably a mistake because his lips were also twitching. It took everything I had not to laugh.

"Why is he here, exactly?" Milo asked.

Kellan sighed. "Group unity?"

Yeah, I lost it at that and so did Freddie.

Group unity.

I guess if Liam and Jasper both wanted to kill him, then Bodhi was promoting group unity.

CHAPTER 40

LIAM

*M*y phone buzzed with a message from my parents. Mom's message was short and to the point.

MOM:

Dinner on Thursday, with you and Emersyn.
She said she could coax Rome into coming.
If so, I would really like to celebrate your
birthday with all three of you.

I chuckled at the message. She wasn't even trying to be subtle. I appreciated it.

ME:

Looking forward to it. We don't have to do
anything special.

MOM:

It's the first time I get to celebrate your
birthday with both of you, that will make it
special.

Sometimes it was easy to overlook how diligently she had worked to make Rome a part of our family, even when he didn't want to be there. He always had his own room. She bought him gifts. She asked about him. She'd even secured a position for him at an art academy he didn't want. Though I'd give my mirror credit, he'd thanked her for the last one even as he said no.

I'd borrowed Rome's room to get changed. We were all leaving for the club opening together. It was a show of unity, which would be out of place as far as the king was concerned but it was still a show.

The assignment he'd initially given me had been to keep an eye on them. To get him info on Milo and, by extension, the others. I was supposed to be close to the Vandals, regardless. If he got pushy about it, I would point out that I was doing my job. As much as he'd suggested he might be there tonight, I really hoped he wasn't.

A knock on the door had me pivoting to see Hellspawn leaning into the room. My dick went to a full stiff attention when she pushed the door inward, giving me my first view of her dress.

Or what there was of it.

The body-hugging gown covered her from her neck to her calves, but it was pure lace. The black lace was also perfectly see-*through*.

"What the fuck are you wearing?"

I dragged my gaze over her from her head to her toes. Her feet were encased in simple ballet flats, since she really didn't like heels. Her lingerie under the lace outfit was pure black, yet it was apparent we were looking at the swell of her breasts and the line of her abdomen where it dipped to that sweet cunt of hers.

"A dress," she said, her expression and tone bland. One hand on her hip, she met my gaze. "A dress that is having exactly the effect I wanted it to have."

"Turning me the fuck on?" Because right now, all I wanted to do was rip her out of it.

"You aren't the only one," Vaughn said as he appeared behind her. "The view from back here is almost as hot as it is from the front."

All the moisture in my mouth was gone. The only thoughts I had were carnal and intense.

"Distraction," Hellspawn said with a slow grin at me. "We're making a show tonight, that's what Kel said. We're showing off how strong you are. Part of that strength means I could walk through there naked, and no one would lay a finger on me because all of you are there."

"And you'd break the finger off," I said without an ounce of doubt. "You are *not* walking anywhere naked unless it's into my bed."

"Or mine," Jasper volunteered from the other room.

"Or mine," Kellan said. "But let's not focus on this part of it. As much as looking at Sparrow in that dress gives me all kinds of salacious ideas, she's right."

I glared at him. "Milo is going to kill you."

"No," Hellspawn said as she crossed to me. I'd been in the middle of putting my tie on when she took over for me. "He won't. This is all about setting the stage. You want to send a message, and this is how you do it."

She locked her gaze on mine and I hated that she was right.

I hated that we had to do it this way. "We're not using you for your body."

"No," she said, smoothing the tie down. "You're not. I

know how the game is played, even if I never wanted to play it."

How her uncle played the game.

A muscle ticked in my jaw. This was not ideal.

"Hellspawn," I said with a sigh.

"I want to do this." She took a step back and spread her arms then did a little spin. Fuck, Vaughn was right. The view from the back was damn near as good as the one from the front. The lace dress clung to her everywhere. It highlighted her curves, which had begun to come back. "And I feel beautiful in this."

The last six words arrested me as she faced me again. "You are beautiful," I told her. "It has nothing to do with the dress."

"But the dress is pretty too," Rome volunteered as he left the bathroom with damp hair. He'd showered and was partially dressed. He wasn't going to wear a suit, no matter what I suggested.

"Maybe I could even get up and dance for you tonight," she offered in a teasing tone. "You seemed to enjoy it last time."

"I have no problems with you dancing for us, Hellspawn, right after I shut the club down and throw everyone out, including your brother."

"Who is going to be there," Freddie volunteered. "Maybe don't pick on Raptor too much, or just let us do it."

She laughed. "That's fine, I just—I know this is a plan, and I know we're going to make an example, but I want to have some fun too."

Her mother was recovering in a room here. She'd opened up to all of us about her past. The king wanted her involved in his business. We needed to track down her uncle, and I needed more information on the people who took Rome and her in the first place.

"Fine," I said, holding out my hand and when she took it without hesitation, letting me pull her to me, some of the tension in me eased. Her trust in us was a gift that I would not squander. "Let's have some fun, but if anyone, and I mean *anyone* touches you that isn't us, they are going out in a body bag."

Head tilted, she considered me. Funnily enough, she couldn't see the guys' faces behind her or their nods at my statement.

"I can live with that." When she pushed up onto her tiptoes to kiss me, I ducked my head and savored the way her mouth softened under mine. The public displays were growing more frequent and more effortless.

It didn't bother me that she fucked the other guys or that they were there and watching. I didn't even mind sharing her as long as *she* was okay with it. But there were only six other men I would allow to touch her.

We hadn't discussed it, and we didn't need to. We were all on the same page where Hellspawn was concerned. Rome's perfect girl… woman. The perfect woman for all of us, and Raptor's baby sister, was one and the same.

Life had to have its irony.

"Let's go… Hellspawn, you're with me."

"Hey now," Jasper argued. "Who decided you got to have her in the car?"

The question conjured the mental image of fucking her in my car. It was a very attractive image. Yeah, we were going to explore that further… *later*.

"We're not arguing over it. Sparrow with Liam on the way there. Sparrow with me on the way back. Vaughn has already called dibs on her bed for the night. Keep arguing, and I'll make us a chore chart." Kellan sounded dead serious.

"I am not a chore," Hellspawn argued as she led the way out of the suite to where Milo waited in the hall.

"Nope," he said, holding up a hand. "I don't want to know."

She grinned, then pressed a kiss to his cheek. "I'm just going to check on Mom before I go." The guys were heading down the stairs, so I followed her to the room. We'd set her mother up in Jasper's former bedroom since it had the space, and now it had the medical equipment.

Doc drank in the sight of her like a man in the desert suddenly confronted by an oasis of ice water. Yeah, he had it bad. He should be happy that Hellspawn had found her affection for him again. If she'd been at all opposed...

Yeah, I didn't need to worry about that right now. She gave Doc a kiss, slipping away before he could catch her and then sashaying toward me. It was definitely a sashay. Doc's gaze was firmly entranced by the delicious sway of her hips.

Amusement speared me. She'd come for more than just checking on her mother. Doc was being subjected to how good she looked. When she reached me, she grinned, then glanced over her shoulder.

"You said to do my worst." Then she blew him a kiss.

"Hell yes, I did," Doc said with a slow grin. Oh, this could be a fun game. I offered her my arm and lifted my chin at Doc. He eyed her then me. *Watch her back.*

Not even a question. I would watch every inch of her. "See you later."

The guys were waiting for us with the cars. We divvied up, going two to a car. We wanted options, going and returning. The drive from the warehouse to The Inferno wasn't long.

Arriving after dark gave us the best look at the new fiery sign announcing the club. There was also a packed lot, but I had secure parking for us in the back.

"Inferno?" Hellspawn shot me a grin.

"Well, you did burn up the stage in there."

Her laughter was exactly what I was going for. The night she hit that stage had set my blood on fire. It was also the first time I admitted how much I fucking wanted her. Getting shot right after had sucked, though.

Once we parked, she waited while I circled to open the passenger door. The guys were spilling out of their cars. To be honest, we looked pretty damn good. A fresh wave of amusement and pride hit me.

"Everything okay?" Hellspawn asked and I nodded.

"Better than okay," I told her. "We've got our challenges, but… we clean up nice."

"I make the rest of you look good," Freddie said with an open grin. Jas rolled his eyes but winked at Hellspawn as she laughed. Yeah, this was good.

"Let's go make an appearance." If we were lucky, we could be in and out in about an hour. Then we could see who was getting Hellspawn in bed tonight. Vaughn didn't just get to call dibs.

The secure area behind the club included a locked and coded entrance for staff only. I entered the code and pulled the door open for Hellspawn.

"Thank you," she said with a wink as she sauntered inside. There was definitely a playfulness to her that wouldn't be denied. No complaints here.

The back of the club had some additional soundproofing to mute the pounding beats from the music out front. Tommy was supposed to be back here covering the door. I checked the security pad as the guys came in. Freddie and Rome glided up to be on either side of Hellspawn.

No one had come in the last hour. Before I could make a call, though, Tommy appeared at the end of the hall, hustling toward us. "Sorry, Boss," he called. "John had trouble out front and I went to back him."

"What kind of trouble?"

Being pulled away for an incident was an acceptable reason. We needed to add another bouncer, a floater who could move without leaving an area unguarded. Yes, there were cameras on all the doors. I had the place wired for surveillance everywhere, except *inside* the dressing room, though I'd made sure all entrances and exits were covered.

Jasper moved to where I stood, ready to back me, while Vaughn moved to cover Freddie and Hellspawn with Rome. Kel and Milo ranged between us. This right here was the shit I'd missed running with the Royals: the understanding and the backup.

"Just a drunk guy who got too handsy then thought all he had to do was pay us off." Tommy's expression said precisely what he thought of that. "We were just going to help him out, but we had to call him an ambulance."

I snorted. "Put it in the report and ban the fucker for life."

"Done. Your table is ready. Need me to get John to the door to show you guys over? It's pretty packed out there."

I appreciated the offer. "We can handle it. Stay on the door." Tommy also earned points because while he'd given everyone a glance, he'd not lingered on Hellspawn nor eyed her in any way other than professionally.

Which was precisely why I'd hired him and the other bouncers. No fucking the dancers. No asking for blowjobs on breaks. They were to protect the club and the employees.

Phone in hand, I logged in and checked the surveillance, backing it up to the moment Tommy took off, then scanning forward to our arrival.

No one came in or went out.

Lifting my head, I caught Hellspawn watching me. "Take a picture," I teased. "It'll last longer."

Grinning, she strolled over, snagged my phone, then tilted it so she was pressed against my front and took a selfie.

I made a face as she laughed. Then she stuck out her tongue in the next one.

"Come along, children," Kellan said with an indulgent grin. Despite the moment of tension in finding Tommy missing, we were in good shape.

"You got it, *Dad*," I retorted. "Hellspawn?"

She took my proffered arm then caught Kel's hand with her free one. The music washed over us as Jasper pushed ahead and opened the door. Vaughn slid ahead of him, and we were all moving, keeping Hellspawn and Freddie toward the center, with the rest of us ranging around them.

Five stages ranged around the club beyond the main stage. Three had poles. The other two were designed for the girls to lie down if they wanted to or do gymnastics. But as with the main stage, the men weren't allowed to touch them.

At all.

Tommy was right. We had a packed crowd here. Hellspawn's sudden bounce yanked my attention to her and I followed her gaze to the main stage. I'd made a point of learning all the dancers' names and their backgrounds, and that one was… Jasmine. Oh, the dancer she'd made friends with.

"Do you have any twenties?" Hellspawn asked. "I didn't even think to get any cash out." We weren't quite at the booth yet, so I chuckled.

"I have you covered. Let's get everyone seated, then you can go see her."

"Thank you." The shine of happiness was hard to ignore and my heat fisted as she grinned.

"Who are you going to see?" Freddie asked as he fell back to grab her hand, leaving Kel and me to trail after them.

"Everything all right?" Kellan asked and I nodded.

"We're good. Just…" How did I explain it?

"Yeah, my back is itching too," Kel said before he gripped my shoulder. "It's been quiet."

Too quiet. But I nodded. Once we got to the table, I nodded to the waitress who had opened the roped-off area. We could have taken the upstairs, but I wanted to be on the floor tonight.

Table dances were allowed upstairs and down, but there was a private balcony for when I wanted to be seen and conduct business.

Or maybe persuade Hellspawn for a private performance. Her laughter as she bumped Freddie's hip with hers made her shine.

My phone buzzed in my pocket. Mom's name flashed on the screen. She was probably calling about the birthday. I'd call her later. I wouldn't be able to hear in here anyway.

Milo glared past me, and I turned to find a guy who'd been heading toward us deciding he needed to be somewhere else. I didn't laugh, but when Milo only shrugged, I grinned.

As I said, no one was touching her here.

No. One.

"Drinks are coming," she told me, then turned to hold out her hand. "I can totally pay you back for it."

"I know you can," I said, indulging her. "But you really don't have to. It's worth your smile alone."

"Suck. Up." Jasper smirked from where he'd dragged back a chair. The booth was large, but I'd added a table so most of us could use chairs for freedom of movement. We could rotate who was out of the booth.

I handed Hellspawn five crisp twenties and then tilted my head expectantly. She pressed a hand to my chest before pressing her lips to my cheek. "Thank you."

"Go on and stay where we can see you."

"Yes, sir." The combination of her wink and pursed lips

sent a pulse straight to my dick. Yeah, he'd wanted her from the beginning. So had I.

"Hey," Milo said, following after her, and I shifted to enjoy this show. "Where you going?"

"To see Jasmine..." I didn't catch the rest of it as they moved away. The dancer had already seen Hellspawn and her smile was as wide and welcoming as Hellspawn's was happy to see her.

Jasper drifted up next to me. His attention, like mine, was on our girl. "Good?"

"Yep," I said. "You?"

"Yep."

We were both lying. Kel and I weren't the only ones feeling the strain of how quiet it had been. Effective was one thing, but...

"Look at Milo," Jasper said, laughter filling his voice.

I tracked to where Milo was steadfastly *not* looking at the pair of breasts Jasmine flaunted as she slid into a split right in front of them.

Hellspawn and she chatted away all animated as Jasmine danced for her, but she kept her body low so they could hear each other. One of the guys sitting nearby stood up, but one glare from Milo and he sat right the fuck back down.

A snicker escaped me.

Jasper huffed with laughter as Milo folded his arms and turned away from his sister and Jasmine to eye the crowd.

"He's going to cost you business."

Maybe, but I didn't mind.

Only after she'd given her all of the twenties did Hellspawn wander back over to us. The sway of her hips attracted plenty of notice. But Milo's glare kept anyone from approaching.

My phone vibrated again as she slid onto Vaughn's lap

and reached for her drink. "Jasmine is great, and she might come to sit with us for a few after her set."

I nodded as I checked the screen. Mom calling. I sent her a text to ask if it was important because I was at the club.

Keeping it in hand, I focused on the laughter rolling around the table as Freddie watched a new dancer on the stage.

"Boo-Boo? Can you do that?"

"Do not answer that question," Milo said with a groan. "At least not where I can hear you."

She cracked up, and despite his gloomy, glaring demeanor, a smile spread across Milo's lips. He needed more time with his sister. She softened him. So did Lainey Benedict, but that might be borrowing far more trouble than she was worth.

Mom didn't answer the text. With a sigh, I tucked the phone away. She'd scold me later and I'd apologize. Dad was right, she got excited, and I should remember that she did miss me even if I wanted to keep them at arm's length. That hurt them too.

Two hours. We spent two hours enjoying the dancers and the club's ambiance. Hellspawn loved Inferno, and the guys were entertained by how much the dancers fascinated her. Then again, she liked watching how a body moved, it was part of her art.

I liked watching her body move too.

Jasmine joined us for a short bit, and we spread out to let her and Hellspawn talk. The king never made an appearance, only that didn't mean he didn't have someone here. By the time we were calling it a night though, I couldn't shake the itch between my shoulder blades.

"Hey," Vaughn said as we were heading out the door. "Lauren forgot her keys for the shop and didn't open, so I need to go down and lock up."

Kellan made a face. "I need to run to the shop. There was a call on the alarm system, but it's probably a false alarm. The cops already did a drive-by."

"But you're not going to relax if you don't check it out."

He wouldn't.

"I'll go with Vaughn," Rome volunteered.

"I got Kel," Milo said as he motioned Freddie to go with Jasper.

"Well then…" I wrapped an arm around Hellspawn. "Looks like it's you and me."

"Heading back to the clubhouse," Kellan told me pointedly.

"We'll get there," I promised. "Eventually."

She elbowed me but wasn't arguing.

Once we were in the car, I let the others go first before I followed them out. Jasper was off to the side, as he'd slot in right behind me—and there he was.

"Did you have fun, Hellspawn?"

"I did," she said with a sigh. "It was great. Ria and I are going to get together in a couple of weeks for lunch. Probably at the club unless there's somewhere else more secure you'd be comfortable with."

I love that she asked. Before I could say anything, my phone rang again, and it popped up on the screen that it was Mom.

"Fuck, that's the third time she's called. Hellspawn, hang on." I hit answer on the steering wheel. "Mom?"

"I'm afraid that your parents can't come to the phone, Mr. O'Connell." The man spoke with an average voice and a neutral accent. The absolute lack of emotion didn't help.

My whole body went stiff. "Who the fuck is this?" Everything drained out of me. This was about my mom…about Dad. The parents I'd chosen. The ones who'd chosen me. The man on the phone was going to die.

HEATHER LONG

"Let's just say I'm a messenger. You took something valuable that belonged to my employer. So now, he's taking something valuable from each of you. Have a good evening."

Whoever was on the other end of the phone hung up, but it didn't matter. Taking something valuable from each of us...

An explosion ripped through the night, and Hellspawn let out a scream. The flash of fire in the rearview was coming from Jasper's car. I wrenched the steering wheel as headlights filled the front window.

There was a truck bearing right down on us.

CHAPTER 41

KELLAN

"You know," Milo said with a laugh. "The last thing I ever imagined was taking my sister to a titty bar."

"Gentleman's club," I corrected with a half-laugh. Milo just shook his head as he leaned back in the passenger seat. Neither of us had worn ties. In fact, I was pretty sure Liam was the only one sporting a tie, and that was fine.

He was comfortable dressing up for work. That had become his world, not that he didn't fit into ours just fine. He was just a little more polished. Which was good—Sparrow needed a little polish to go with the rough. She deserved it.

I liked my suits. I liked wearing them. I liked having the right occasion to wear them. But ties? Yeah, pass. There were plenty of other things I could tie up, and I wouldn't be using a silk tie, for I preferred silk ropes and leather cuffs.

"And you didn't take her," I said. "We did. You just tagged along."

He snorted. "Semantics. Did you know she knew that dancer?"

"She's mentioned her before. She met her that day Liam got shot right outside the club." A day that had left me cold. Thankfully, Liam had worn a vest, and the assholes shooting at him hadn't gone for a headshot.

"Just seems weird…" He let out a more prolonged sigh at the end of that thought.

"Why?" Over the past year and then some, I'd come to recognize and savor the myriad of unique attributes Sparrow possessed. She was so much not what any of us imagined or could have predicted.

"She fits," Milo said slowly. "She fits with all of you…I hate that she does and, at the same time, I'm fucking grateful for it. You guys deserve the best."

"But she's your baby sister," I offered. I got it. He'd have to get over it, but I did understand. We'd all walked on glass around her in our own ways. It had taken time to bridge the chasm of her mistrust.

It had taken even longer to get her to open up about her pain.

"Yeah. But I mean, back there at the club, she was talking to that girl, and they were just… in sync. Then I see her with Mayhem, and she and Mayhem are like…cut from the same elegant cloth."

"I'm not gonna say a word about you calling your girl *Mayhem*." Nope. I didn't even want to know how he'd come up with it. No doubt there was a story there.

We hit red lights most of the way to the shop, but I wasn't in a hurry, and it had begun to spit rain.

"Liam calls Ivy Hellspawn."

"Yes, he does. She likes it." According to what Doc told me, she'd also punched him in the face, so Hellspawn definitely fit.

Milo chuckled. "You're missing my point. She fits in our world and in that one. I keep wanting to find a reason to send her back."

Controlling my reaction, I flexed my hands on the steering wheel.

"Then I feel like a fucking asshole because I don't want her to go back. I *like* having her here."

Better.

"And then I have to ask myself, am I thinking about what is best for her or best for me?" He scrubbed a hand over his face. "Fuck, I don't know. She's hiding something. Something the Sharpe woman said to her about not knowing and being so damn sorry. Ivy doesn't want to tell me, not right now. I want to respect that..."

"And you want to protect her," I said slowly. This was ground littered with hazardous landmines. Sparrow said she would tell Milo, but she was also avoiding it. I understood *why*, and I wished I could shield them both from ever having that conversation. Except it was a live round that could go off at any moment.

Neither of them deserved that fallout.

"Milo, she's your baby sister. She's the one person you built up in your head, her life, her dreams, her goals—hell, even her personality. You've had this image of her for almost sixteen years. It was what kept you going when shit sucked. She was the dream. But she's more than that. She's also a person."

A person with her own hopes, dreams, terrors, and nightmares. A person I'd rapidly fallen in love with, and I wasn't the only one.

"I say this with love, brother," I told him. "Don't push her away. She'll fight you and so will I."

"All of you would," Milo said with a half-smile. "All of you have. I'm glad for all of you that she fits here. That she wants to be here. Not sure about how you guys are making the rest of it work, but… you know what, I don't know, I don't have to scrub out of my brain."

It was my turn to laugh. "You know, you could change the subject and talk about your girl."

"I don't have a girl," Milo said. I cut a look at him, but he was staring out the window, and I couldn't make out much of his expression.

"You sure about that?"

"Yep. Pretty sure. Told her the same thing when I sent her back to her world."

Fuck my life. "Milo, tell me you didn't use those words?"

"She's safer there," he said and I sighed. "Maybe she needs to be there. She has a little sister too."

Goddammit.

"Being here, being distracted by me, it was taking away from time with her. I get needing to protect your sister above all else. I didn't want her to feel like she had to choose."

So he took the choice out of her hands. If it wasn't so sad, I'd laugh. As it was, I kind of wanted to punch him. "That's why she hasn't been around, and Sparrow hasn't heard from her much."

Yeah, he didn't answer that part.

I swung the car around the corner, cruising through the urban area where the shop resided. Most of the stores were closed and the street was quiet. Most of this area closed up before six.

After pulling into the lot, I slid out of the car. "I'll just be a minute."

"Need backup?"

I shook my head. "Probably not. Just keep watch from out here."

He nodded once.

His car door opened behind me. "Hey, Kel," Milo called when I was halfway to the doors. I glanced back to find him spreading his hands. "I know I sound like an asshole talking about sending her somewhere she doesn't want to go. I am working on that."

"I know you are," I said. "You being an asshole is really not news to me."

He laughed, except the expression on his face froze and then turned to something unrecognizable as the world turned to flames around me, and what felt like the fist of a giant slammed into my back and flung me forward like a rag doll.

The pavement surged up to meet me. Or that was what it felt like. Blood filled my mouth, my ears were ringing, and the world burned.

Then the lights went out.

VAUGHN

THE DRIVE TO THE SHOP TOOK TIME. THERE WAS A LOT OF traffic heading down toward the village and the night spots that had cropped up all over that neighborhood. Rome was quiet in the passenger seat. Not that he was chatty on a regular basis.

He said what he needed to when he needed to, and that was fine. I'd only had one beer while we'd been at the club. Everyone who drove went light. Freddie didn't drink at all, and Dove had two beers. Rome might have had one, but I hadn't really kept count. Not that we were heavy drinkers.

"I have a question," Rome said. "It's about mothers. Would it bother you if I asked?"

"No," I said slowly, even though I could understand why

he asked. "I was pretty damn fond of my mother. Course, that was also a long time ago. This about Dove?"

"No." When he didn't elaborate, I shook my head and waited. He'd ask when he was ready. "Liam's mother wants us to go to dinner for our birthday."

Ah.

"You don't want to go." It wasn't a question.

Rome shrugged. "I don't care."

"About the dinner or your birthday?" To be fair, it could be either or…

"Both."

Or that.

"But it seems important to her. Starling said it was important for me to go to brunch. The food was nice. Starling was there. Liam was too. His parents were…"

I waited.

"They were who they always are. Starling said she wanted me to like her." His faintly puzzled air pulled another smile out of me. "I don't *not* like her."

"Right, I get where this is going. Moms like to feel needed. They want to make things better. Liam's mom keeps trying to get you there because she wants you there for Liam and so she can take care of you too."

"I see Liam."

"Yes, you do. But you don't see her. Or, more appropriately, she doesn't see you see him."

"So, if I go to the dinner, she sees me seeing Liam, and she feels better?"

"Pretty sure she'll want to give you a gift for your birthday too, but yeah, that's about it. Most parents… the good ones? They don't need much. Liam got lucky. He got good ones. The fact that all these years later and she's still trying to adopt you tells me you got lucky too."

"I don't need her." He sighed. "But Liam does." He settled

a little more in the seat, as if he'd relaxed from the puzzle. "Starling says it will make them happy. I can go to dinner. It's not that hard."

"Nope, and you get to have dinner with Dove too."

Rome smiled at that.

Yeah, I knew that feeling. The smell of smoke hit my nostrils as I headed down an alley to circumvent some of the traffic. Was there a fire? Was that why the traffic was so heavy? I pulled out near the shop and froze.

"Call 9-1-1," I told Rome, as I threw the car in park and launched out of it. The gate was down over the entrance and the fire was inside.

Screams were coming from inside too. I stripped my shirt off to use it over my hands. The gating was hot, but I got the key in and started yanking it upwards when a whooshing sound came from above. A window had been thrown open.

Oh shit.

The explosion knocked out all the glass, and I barely got my hands up to cover my head when the heat rushed out and sucked all the air out of my lungs.

Screams. Shattering glass. Sirens.

Silence.

Doc

I checked Moira Sharpe's numbers. She was definitely asleep. I'd kept her levels steadily declining, but the sedative I'd used earlier had knocked her out. That was fine. She was dramatically underweight and looked like hell.

It reminded me way too much of how Little Bit looked when they brought her back from Pinetree. I hadn't asked about sexual assault nor checked for it. I would check on that with her mother *after* she was awake and more herself.

Setting the intercom to open so I could hear if she woke, I

headed downstairs to make coffee. The guys had ordered Chinese the day before. I could probably reheat some egg rolls.

I'd barely gotten the cup started when a knock hit the inner door of the annex. The rats couldn't get inside without one of us anymore, and I was okay with that. Little shits didn't need to be here. The knock turned into pounding even as my phone buzzed with 9-1-1 on the first message popping up on the screen.

Yanking the door open, I stared at the rat—fuck I had no idea what his name was, he was that new—panted. Sweat dotted his face, and the acrid smell of fear rolled off of him.

"You gotta come, Doc. Someone just dumped a body on us."

"What?"

"I dunno. Word is there are some fires downtown, but then a car ripped through, nearly ran down Manny, stopped long enough to shove a body out, and took off. I didn't get the plates, I tried."

He was half-doubled over. He'd run after the car. "Stay," I ordered.

Closing the door, I went for my bag and my gun. Mrs. Sharpe was still asleep and would be fine for a few minutes. At least she wasn't likely to wake up anytime soon.

Manny was waiting for me when I came out. I didn't bother hiding the gun, I'd just pulled on the shoulder holster. I had another in the back of my belt. "Where?"

"Out front," he said, jerking his thumb. "Big Belly and Bulldog are out there with her."

Her.

Great, some fucking john probably dumped a prostitute. I double-timed it. "Nobody touched her?"

"No, man, she's all kinds of bloody, though. But I didn't want to hurt her. Or—get busted."

Yeah, I got it.

Bulldog and Big Belly were out front, someone had turned on the floodlights, and they had blocked the yard off with one of the rigs.

That was smart.

It wasn't hard to identify where the woman was. She was laying on the ground, wrapped in a blanket, or maybe it was trash bags.

Fuck, I hated people. Her labored breathing rasped against the air. I needed to move her, except I also needed to isolate her C-spine, or I could do more harm than good. It took a moment, but I got her on her back and sighed.

Son of a bitch. They really had done a number on her. The bruises on her face were numerous, swollen, and distorting her features. There was blood at both ears and from her nose.

I got out the stethoscope. "We're going to need an ambulance," I told Manny, who stood there waiting for something to do.

"I'll go call one."

Her lungs were filling with fluid. The sucking, gasping noise...no, that wasn't the lung filling, it was the cavity around them filling. One of her lungs had collapsed.

I went for my bag when she touched my arm with a hand that showed signs of torture and abuse. A whimper of sound escaped her.

"Hey, you're safe," I told her. "I'm Dr. James, and I'm going to help you..."

She tried to talk, but she didn't have air.

"I think your lung has collapsed," I told her, going through my bag. I needed to get a chest tube in so I could get the fluid out. It wasn't going to be pretty. "Hang in there for me."

The grip of her battered hand on my arm tightened, and I focused on her again.

"I know you're scared." Her lips were moving, barely, but they were.

I leaned forward, putting my ear to her mouth.

"Mickey…"

A chill slammed into me. Jerking my head up, I looked down at the beaten woman struggling to breathe.

No. No. No.

* * *

The Vandals will return in Reckless Thief.

RECKLESS THIEF

Preorder Now

The mentor.

The doctor.

The Vandal.

I grew up on the streets despite my older sister's best efforts to keep my nose clean. I thought I knew better. I worked hard. and made money. Who cared if what I did was a little illegal?

Then a little boy paid the price for my carelessness. A little boy and his baby sister. It was the wakeup call I needed, even if the cost came too high.

Rough choices made for rough outcomes and when I had the chance to join the military or go to jail to get straight, I went to the military.

I paid for my thoughtless actions by becoming deliberate.

I paid for my greed by offering service.

I paid for my chance at a better life with blood, sweat, and fire.

That service left me scarred but determined. Medical school and training taught me I could continue to serve.

I walked away from the streets, from the blood, the violence, and costs of doing business. Living a life I stole not once, but twice, I focused on helping, on protecting, and on healing.

Until she came back into my life.

I didn't start this current war, but I will damn well end it.

My name is Mickey James. Little Bit is everything. I fought to stay away, and I'll fight to keep. Our enemies are going to learn that my skill at healing broken bodies makes me damn talented at damaging them too. They drew blood, we'll bury them.

Reckless Thief is a full-length mature dark, new adult romance with enemies-to-lovers/love-hate themes. The dark romance aspects of this tale continue. Please be aware some situations may be uncomfortable for readers. Trigger warnings can be found in the foreword should you require them. This is a why choose novel, meaning the main character has more than one love interest. This is book eight in the series.

AFTERWORD

I'm going to bet you need a moment. Maybe a tissue? Some hot tea? A hug?

Right, I'll hush and wait.

Yes, I know.

I do really know.

It happened. You are going back to read and check to see if it still happened that way? Yes, I'll wait.

Sorry, it definitely still happened.

Right, yes, I'll go sit over here and think about what I've done.

xoxo

Heather

Reader group:
facebook.com/groups/heatherspack
Spoiler group:
facebook.com/groups/teammadatheather

ABOUT HEATHER LONG

I *love* books. Not just a little bit, but a lot. Books were my best friends when I was growing up. Books didn't care if I was new to a town or to a class. They were always there, my trustiest of companions. Until they turned on me and said I had to write them.

I can tell you that my own personal happily ever after included writing books. I've always said that an HEA is a work in progress. It's true in my marriage, my friendships, and in my career. I am constantly nurturing my muse as we dive into new tales, new tropes, new characters and more.

After seventeen years in Texas, we relocated to the Pacific Northwest in search of seasons, new experiences, and new geography. I can't wait to discover what life (and my muse) have in store for me.

Maybe writing was always my destiny and romance my fate. After all, my grandmother wasn't a fan of picture books and used to read me her Harlequin Romance novels.

Follow Heather & Sign up for her newsletter:
www.heatherlong.net
TikTok

ALSO BY HEATHER LONG

82nd Street Vandals

Savage Vandal

Vicious Rebel

Ruthless Traitor

Dirty Devil

Brutal Fighter

Dangerous Renegade

Merciless Spy

Reckless Thief

Always a Marine Series

Once Her Man, Always Her Man

Retreat Hell! She Just Got Here

Tell It to the Marine

Proud to Serve Her

Her Marine

No Regrets, No Surrender

The Marine Cowboy

The Two and the Proud

A Marine and a Gentleman

Combat Barbie

Whiskey Tango Foxtrot

What Part of Marine Don't You Understand?

A Marine Affair

Marine Ever After

Marine in the Wind

Marine with Benefits

A Marine of Plenty

A Candle for a Marine

Marine under the Mistletoe

Have Yourself a Marine Christmas

Lest Old Marines Be Forgot

Her Marine Bodyguard

Smoke & Marines

Bravo Team Wolf

When Danger Bites

Bitten Under Fire

Cardinal Sins

Kill Song

First Chorus

High Note

Chance Monroe

Earth Witches Aren't Easy

Plan Witch from Out of Town

Bad Witch Rising

Her Elite Assets

Featuring:

Pure Copper

Target: Tungsten

Asset: Arsenic

Fevered Hearts

Marshal of Hel Dorado

Brave are the Lonely

Micah & Mrs. Miller

A Fistful of Dreams

Raising Kane

Wanted: Fevered or Alive

Wild and Fevered

The Quick & The Fevered

A Man Called Wyatt

Going Royal

Some Like It Royal

Some Like It Scandalous

Some Like It Deadly

Some Like it Secret

Some Like it Easy

Her Marine Prince

Blocked

Heart of the Nebula

Queenmaker

Deal Breaker

Throne Taker

Lone Star Leathernecks

Semper Fi Cowboy

As You Were, Cowboy

Magic & Mayhem
The Witch Singer
Bridget's Witch's Diary
The Witched Away Bride

Mongrels

Mongrels, Mischief & Mayhem

Shackled Souls
Succubus Chained
Succubus Unchained
Succubus Blessed
Shackled Souls (Omnibus)

Space Cowboy
Space Cowboy Survival Guide

Untouchable
Rules and Roses
Changes and Chocolates
Keys and Kisses
Whispers and Wishes
Hangovers and Holidays
Brazen and Breathless
Trials and Tiaras
Graduation and Gifts
Defiance and Dedication
Songs and Sweethearts

Legacy and Lovers

Farewells and Forever

Wolves of Willow Bend

Wolf at Law

Wolf Bite

Caged Wolf

Wolf Claim

Wolf Next Door

Rogue Wolf

Bayou Wolf

Untamed Wolf

Wolf with Benefits

River Wolf

Single Wicked Wolf

Desert Wolf

Snow Wolf

Wolf on Board

Holly Jolly Wolf

Shadow Wolf

His Moonstruck Wolf

Thunder Wolf

Ghost Wolf

Outlaw Wolves

Wolf Unleashed

.

Made in United States
Troutdale, OR
08/01/2024

21687162R00257